NOMAD/Y

THE MOON BASE PROJECT

a novel by Noah Bond

NOMAD/Y

THE MOON BASE PROJECT

A NOVEL BY NOAH BOND

First Edition. Published at Fort Lauderdale, Florida, by Mission Investments, Inc. Cover design by Ilse Birck. Printed by A-1 Printers, Inc., Edina, Minnesota.

Library of Congress Catalog Card Number: 99-75830

ISBN 0-9673551-0-9

Dedication and Expressions of Gratitude

This book is dedicated to my wife Susan, who continues to endure me talking about the characters as if they existed.

I express my gratitude to V. K. Randall for encouraging creativity in all of us who were fortunate enough to study English under her tutelage at the dawn of the Space Race.

I extend my appreciation to the National Aeronautics and Space Administration. Key facts which serve as the foundation for this work of fiction were graciously provided by NASA.

Recognition must be given to Dr. Sergei Korolev, the brilliant Russian scientist and administrator responsible for sending *Sputnik*, Laika and Yuri into orbit, and for sending the first rocket to the Moon. But for him, there would have been no Space Race, no Apollo Program and no story.

Most of all, I thank He who made this book possible.

Life is a series of inspired follies.

--- George Bernard Shaw

Introduction

Just before going inside, he looked into the heavens. It was a ritual. He would scan the clear skies each evening, marveling at the brilliance of the stars overhead. He would thank his Creator for these wonders and the many blessings he had received. Although he often reflected that he had simply exchanged one desert for another, he had come a long way from his inauspicious beginnings. Then he would ask God to watch over his mother and let her know he would not forget her.

Tonight was different. The sky was disturbed. There were new stars flashing above --- hundreds of them, maybe thousands. Were they getting larger? Was that possible?

Larger meant closer. The stars were approaching him. He was awestruck. Then an explosion occurred on the outer wall of the ancient crater. Its significance took a moment to register. "Impact!" he shouted to himself in disbelief.

He scrambled toward the fragile antenna dish, hoping to save it. He had managed to disconnect it and collapse it when the first meteorite struck several meters away from him. He looked up, but the dust cloud raised by the meteorite blinded him. Carrying the antenna, he headed in the direction of shelter. Four strides later he was stumbling down the side of a small new crater. He rolled onto his back to avoid crushing the antenna.

Looking skyward, he saw the glow of his impending doom, but the meteorite passed through his skull before comprehension occurred.

PROLOGUE

October, 1973

Route 60 cuts across the Florida peninsula above the glitter of the Gold Coast and below the Mouse-induced confusion of Orlando. It is straight, narrow and dull. Dr. Jonas MacPherson was driving it in a hurricane-force wind that blew the rain from the West, right into his windshield. His rate of speed had been diminished to about 40 mph to compensate for the onslaught, but it hadn't helped much. He was alone. "It's so very lonely; you're two thousand light years from home," sang Mick Jagger on the radio, underscoring this fact.[1]

He told himself he was taking some time off to sort things out, to obtain perspective on the strange events that were taking place around him. Subconsciously, he knew he was engaged in mindless flight. He hadn't even told his wife he was leaving town.

Hinrichs, Draper and the rest of the old team were gone. No, not gone. They were dead. And that was the problem. They shouldn't be. None had died under suspicious circumstances. A few could be said to have lived longer than expected. There were no unusual accidents. The only thing was the concentration of death within a short time span.

The team of space scientists had worked together at the John F. Kennedy Space Center in the recently ended Apollo days, when men went to the Moon. In addition to his scientific duties, MacPherson had recruited and assembled the team on orders directly from Werner von Braun. They had worked on the Moon landings, along with thousands of others, but had also worked on a secret project connected with the Apollo program. After the final Moon landing, the team had gradually dispersed. Some left NASA. Others went to Houston. A few had simply retired. One had died.

---

[1]

2,000 Light Years from Home written by Mick Jagger and Keith Richards performed by the Rolling Stones on their album *Their Satanic Majesties Request* (Abkco Music & Records).

But until last August, all the others were alive and accounted for. Now he was the only one left alive. And he simply could not believe the deaths were a coincidence. So he was running. But from whom?

He stopped at a gas station/souvenir shop at Yechaw Junction, a depressing settlement which owed its existence solely to the fact that Route 60 intersected U.S. Route 441 at that point. He ran through the downpour into the store, splashing through the puddles that filled the holes in the gravel. By the time he'd arrived inside, one sock was soaked.

The tackiness of his surroundings and his physical discomfort conspired to distract him from seeing two men at his Buick Riviera. Had he looked, he would have seen one inspecting his right front tire and the other open each of the two doors briefly. At least, that's what it would have looked like.

When he resumed driving, he was headed in the direction of Lake Wales. The weather had not changed, but the traffic was light. Then a car appeared behind him. "The fool doesn't even have his lights on," he said to himself. As the vehicle behind grew closer, he saw that it was a full-size pickup truck with its chassis jacked up for off-road travel. It was approaching fast. Too fast. Too close.

Whomp was the sound made as the bumpers touched. The jolt was minor, almost a relief. Then the truck increased its speed, and with it the speed of Dr. MacPherson. The road was too narrow to do anything but try to stay on it. He didn't even try the brakes because the road was so slick. Instead, he used the accelerator to attempt to get away.

The truck stayed with him until he hit 85 mph. Then he got away. The truck was still there, but not so close. He would have to keep speeding to avoid it. As long as the road didn't turn before the rain let up, he might be O.K.

That's what he was thinking when the steering wheel pulled sharply to the right as the right wheel popped from the axle. The car immediately crossed the narrow shoulder and plunged into the canal on the right side of the road. It started to sink.

MacPherson was not seriously injured. The car had planed across the water at first. The water had cushioned the impact. The seat belt had kept him in the car. Now he unfastened it. His chest hurt where he had hit the steering wheel. The adrenalin was making him function, despite his bruises and shock.

He grabbed his door handle --- and it came off in his hand. He looked at it in wonder for a moment, then dove across the seat for the passenger side door. Its handle came off too. He noted that the car was sinking front first from the weight of the engine. He pressed the window button, but soon realized that the electrical system was now short-circuited by the rising canal water.

There was a water hyacinth on the windshield. The thought flicked through his mind that he might see a manatee up close. The car was filling. He was running out of time. He tried to break the windows with his arms, then with his feet, but could not find a position to support him for a decent kick.

The water was around his neck now. He took a deep breath and resumed flailing at the windows in the murk that surrounded him. He ran out of breath and pulled himself into the pocket of air that had formed at the rear window, which he pummeled with both fists to no avail. Then, as his breathing converted the air bubble to carbon dioxide, he stopped struggling. Just breathing was difficult enough.

Despite his efforts to concentrate, he started thinking that he should have kept his old Volkswagen Beetle, which supposedly floated. "The windows would have worked, too," was his final thought. Had he time reflect upon it, he would not have thought it was an unusual thought for a space scientist. After all, men had reached the Moon on sturdy, reliable vehicles.

/////

Dr. Jonas MacPherson was buried in his family plot at a small cemetery in rural Maryland. There was marble headstone that contained the words he had written down for the occasion. His widow didn't understand them all, but she followed his wishes.

Two strange men in dark suits stood nearby, as if waiting for another burial --- but none was in evidence.

PART I: SUSPICION

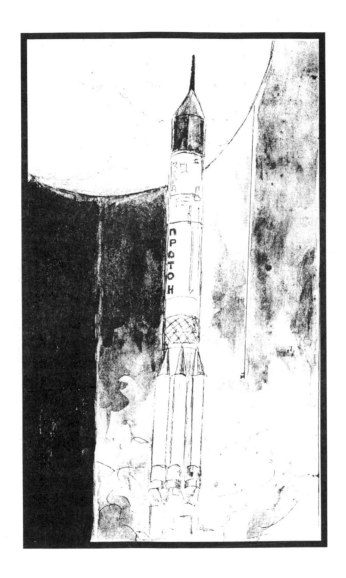

Chapter One
Tuesday, March 31, 1993

"Tits!" she exclaimed. "You all think I got the promotion because I'm a woman. I know it; so don't try to lie to me." Rae Kirkland was in rare form as she stood behind her desk and addressed her former equal --- now subordinate --- Ken Mason. "The real reason you didn't get the job is because you don't have enough drive, enough ambition. It shows, you know. Hell, you didn't even act like you wanted it!" This, of course, infuriated her, too. He was the best auditor in the department, but he didn't seem to care about his career. And now he was her problem.

Mason made a murmuring sound he hoped would pass for a suitable comment, since he had no idea what to say. Then he tried looking out the window of the General Accounting Office at the late winter drizzle of Washington, D.C. The rain had made the large brass letters G A O set in the sidewalk treacherous, as usual. He watched a visitor lose his footing and land on his back. What a miserable climate! If he could, he would move the nation's capital to somewhere dry and warm, maybe Arizona. He agreed with former President Reagan's observation that the East Coast would be a wilderness if the Pilgrims had landed in California.

"You're a daydreamer, too. It's a mystery to me how you ever get anything done."

"Uhm," he murmured again. He had heard this all before from his ex-wife --- before the "ex" became a prefix. Why did people who professed to like him always want him to change?

"So, do you have any questions about my position?"

He studied her for a moment and then said, "Congratulations on your promotion, which I take it you achieved despite some disadvantage inherent in having breasts."

The anger flashed across her face, but then she sighed and said, "Go back to work, you incorrigible bastard."

"It's not that I have anything against breasts, mind you. I remember them fondly (pardon the pun). My ex-wife had some. A pair,

I seem to recall."

"If you want breasts, all you have to do is look at the television."

"Is that where they're kept these days? My ex used to keep hers in a holster strapped to her chest."

"Enough!"

Their relationship was back on a solid footing. He was relieved.

"About my work...," he said, leaving the sentence dangle, incomplete.

"New project for you. Concerns NASA. Stop groaning. As you know, the space program has received our scrutiny in the past, but this time someone wants to know what it really cost for each individual, separate Apollo Mission to the Moon. Without any allocation of NASA general overhead or other excludable amounts. You've worked on the NASA data before; so it should be a piece of cake for you."

"In other words, if Congress decided to do another Moon landing, you want to know what it would cost using the existing facilities," he offered.

"Bare bones," she added. "Only what's necessary. But actual cost then, not today's cost. Then an average cost for all the missions."

"Why would anyone want that now?"

"Who knows? Maybe some Senator is writing a book about the Moon program and is having us do his research. It wouldn't be the first time. I've just been told that the gross figures used for the Apollo program include so many unrelated or unnecessary items that they are useless for determining what any individual mission actually cost the taxpayers, above and beyond what they were paying for NASA to exist and the other NASA projects. Maybe they want to compare notes with the Russians, now that we're talking to each other," she speculated.

"So I'm to draw the line somewhere and try to define which costs were solely attributable to Apollo? What about little matters like Astronaut training?"

"That's a good one. The best approach would be to list it separately, in the Notes to Financial Data section," she said making a reference to their business accounting pasts.

"Keep it lean, but provide related factors and figures?" he asked.

"Exactly."

"Where do I start?"

"Do what you can with the records here. At least get to the point where you have a working draft before you leave."

"Then?"

"Then show it to me; so I have proper justification to send you off to Florida," she said with a smile. "I know you'll work fast here to get away. It's your pace in Florida that has me worried."

"It's brutal in the summer," he said as he left.

Rae turned her attention to the poster on her wall. It urged all who saw it to

DO YOUR PART TO STAMP OUT CRF

It had been there for more than a week; yet no one had inquired what the initials CRF stood for. Rae took this as proof that CRF was epidemic. CRF stood for Cerebral-Rectal Fusion.

/////

The following week he reported that he had combed the applicable GAO records, which were conveniently in the computer data base. More importantly, he had concluded what further information he would need and outlined a plan for its retrieval. The first step was to fly to Orlando.

When his plane rose above the cloud cover over Virginia, he couldn't contain his smile.

Chapter Two
Monday, April 12, 1993

Since the interagency car pool had already distributed all its hulking grey junkers and was saving the decent cars for military officers and other important persons, he was permitted to rent a car. He got a red LeBaron convertible and promptly put the top down.

He smeared on some of the sun block he'd purchased the previous week in Washington, where it was damned hard to find, and left the sprawling Orlando airport in the bright sunshine. It took a little more than an hour on the Bee-Line Highway to reach Cocoa Beach, "America's Gateway to the Moon."

At the Kennedy Space Center, he was given the short tour and shown the hardware that went to the Moon. Then he settled into the vast library. He secured a room for himself; so he could leave his work on the table when he quit, lock it up and find it the same way in the morning. The library was cool and the light was fluorescent. He might as well have been in Washington.

When this had all been done it was 4:00 P.M. and --- he rationalized --- too late to start on a project.

So he left and had stone crab claws (hot with melted butter, although cold with mustard sauce would have served nicely too) on the deck of an oceanfront restaurant. "This is more like it."

/////

Tuesday, April 13, 1993

Mason was generally suspicious of the alleged merits of chronological investigation. "Following the same path produces the same mistakes," being one reason. The other is a belief that most investigations are conducted along such lines simply because no alternative procedure leaps to the mind.

But having just seen the Astronaut training facilities, he decided to begin with the training program. It would be a small project to separate the specific training required for the Apollo Missions from the general training. It would yield him an early accomplishment to be reported. He could tackle the tougher problems later.

By that afternoon, he had concluded that the training program was a statistical yawn, but it was a short yawn. The Apollo training statistics had already been isolated. The Apollo training was costly --- a great deal of overkill. But who could blame them. In the future it should be less expensive, now that the surface of the Moon was a known quantity. He would have to note this in his report.

The other reason the training was expensive was the number of Astronauts who received training. Almost twice as many men (no women --- they were out burning their bras at that time, he recalled) were trained as actually went to the Moon. He would have to figure out what it cost to actually train one man for the job. Averaging the total training cost over the number of men who put it to use would be misleading.

When curiosity led him to investigate why so many had received training, he was surprised to learn that seven Astronauts had left the program after receiving complete Apollo training. Since this made the whole program more costly, he decided to take a closer look. He found a dead end. The reasons for leaving were not given. He only had the names, dates and applicable military reassignments. He stared at the list.

Coughlin, Robert L.	reassigned Navy	13 May 1968
Thomas, Wilbur	reassigned USAF	24 Feb 1969
Balocco, David M.	reassigned USMC	17 Aug 1969
Brown, Demitrius F.	reassigned USMC	17 Aug 1969
Fortney, William T.	reassigned USMC	17 Aug 1969
Xavier, Carlos F.	reassigned USMC	17 Aug 1969
Coe, Henry J.	reassigned N/A	06 May 1972

He figured that Henry J. Coe was a civilian. He wondered idly if Henry J. knew he was named after a compact Kaiser automobile from the '50's.

Then his eyes wandered to the dates. Four Marines had left on the same day. Curious. He could not think of an explanation. It also occurred to him that he had never heard about this mass defection from the program. Although it probably wouldn't affect his figures, he copied the names and dates in case it came up later.

Driving back to the motel that evening, he kept asking himself why anyone would leave the program if his health was still good enough for a Moon mission. The four Marines couldn't all have become unfit at the same time --- unless there was an accident, which would have been reported. It was a puzzle to chew on, along with two Florida lobster tails and some Chardonnay.

He didn't get to be a six-foot-two, 220-lb., out-of-shape auditor by eating Melba toast.

/////

Wednesday, April 14, 1993

The next morning he decided to start with the Moon landing films to get a better feel for the project he was investigating. He resolved to check out the individual cassette tapes for each of the Apollo landings and to review each one, making judicious use of the fast forward if need be. Not willing to hear Neil Armstrong's little speech right off the bat, he started with the following mission. Looking at the missions out of sequence disturbed the Archives Librarian --- which gave Ken a perverse sense of satisfaction. He started with "Apollo XII: Day One."

He had told himself that he was merely acquainting himself with the Apollo program, but he admitted to himself that he was looking for anomalies. He had never completely dismissed the speculation that some of the Moon films were really made on Earth. There would be good reasons, too. The obvious one was to cover up a mission failure. Obviously, this wouldn't have worked if Apollo failed to return at all. It could have successfully concealed equipment failures, like lunar rovers that didn't rove --- or cameras that might not have functioned properly. And the public would need never know if an Astronaut came down with the lunar version of the *turista*. Maybe even a headache. "Does Alka Seltzer fizz at low gravity?" he mused. But if an Astronaut had died, no amount of fake footage would cover it up. His mind turned briefly to the four Marine Astronauts who all quit the program at the same time.

Another reason to fake the footage would be that the Astronauts had too much to do on the Moon to spend their time taking home movies. That would make sense. There were probably secret experiments that were being photographed for viewing in places like Battelle Memorial Institute and Lawrence Livermore Laboratory. Files labeled "BBR" --- Burn Before Reading. Nothing sinister about that. At least not by Washington standards of paranoia.

In the end he concluded that it would be too dangerous to include any bogus footage unless it were absolutely necessary. That didn't keep him from looking.

Late that afternoon, he finally found something that was actually entertaining. It was a scene where an Astronaut approached the camera and, unexpectedly, danced a few Latin steps which Ken tentatively identified as the cha-cha. Then he leapt about three feet. Then the scene changed abruptly on the tape. He knew that this would be the most entertaining point of his investigative day; so he wisely decided to quit on this relative high note.

/////

On his way to his hotel, he passed the Archives Librarian without noticing him. Had he seen him, he would have been curious.

The Archives Librarian was standing at a pay telephone next to a convenience store. He entered the number from memory. A machine answered after the twelfth ring and requested that he leave a message. He identified himself and described Ken Mason, the research he claimed to be doing and added his own subjective observations. Then he hung up.

He had been making these calls for nearly twenty years, but no one had ever called him back. The arrangement had been set up by a single telephone call to him, after which the contact had all been one way. Except that there would be a $700.00 credit to his Visa account on the next statement. It hadn't always been $700.00. It had been $500.00 at first. He sometimes wondered if the amount was indexed to the Consumer Price Index.

The answering machine was monitored by the United States Secret Service.

/////

The *Margarita* was typical: sweet and weak. He could picture Clara Peller from the old Wendy's ads croaking "Where's the tequila?" So he switched to *Carlsberg* beer. After two if them, he felt sufficiently restored to take a short walk down the beach. The night was clear and the Moon had turned silver above the ocean. It was enough to make a fellow dance.

So he did. All by himself. A big, lonely guy waltzing to *The Blue Danube* playing in his head.

Chapter Three
Thursday, April 15, 1993

The following day he established to his own satisfaction that the first mission tapes and films were completely genuine, fulfilling his belief that they would have to be since they would be subjected to tremendous scrutiny. Some of the later tapes appeared to contain redundant material, though. Some may have been filmed on Earth, but --- if so --- they had done a good job. No telephone poles.

While the discovery of any such deception would be exciting, it would bear no relationship to the job which he had to do, other than to remind him that Uncle Sam couldn't be trusted. To pursue it would waste time. To attempt to expose it would cost him his job, his pension, his privacy and possibly his sanity. He would stick to number crunching.

/////

After dinner, he'd lingered in the cocktail lounge watching intercollegiate girls volley ball on the big-screen television, until the commercials robbed it of its interest. He paid his tab and left. His car was several blocks down the beach at his hotel. He liked walking back along the beach.

He had to leave by the front door and walk between buildings to get to the beach. It was as if the sand and the ocean were irrelevant to the restaurant, or something to be avoided. He had noticed that the locals paid little attention to the very things the tourists craved.

"I recently stopped tryin' to find me (*thump! thump!*). The game of chance now rules my destiny (*thump! thump!*). Fortune picks my happiness, my strife (*thump! thump!*). I'm a silver ball on the roulette wheel of life (*thump! thump!*)."[2] The rockabilly sounds came from the bar next to the restaurant.

2

Silver Ball on the Roulette Wheel of Life is a song copyright 1971 by Jon Agee.

"Are they kidding?" he asked himself. "No," he concluded. If the words were intended to be a satire on country music, the joke was lost on the shouting and stomping patrons.

"Hey, mister!" came a shouted whisper from the shadows behind the adjacent building, which housed the rowdy establishment from which the music emanated. He turned and listened, but heard only the country rock music escaping from the bar.

Then she stepped out of the darkness. She was about eighteen, he guessed. About five-foot-six. She had long blonde hair ---halfway down her back. She had on cowboy boots with high heels on them, a fringed skirt and a cowboy hat. Her breasts were covered only by her hands. She wobbled slightly as she approached him.

"Can you help me out?" she asked.

"What are you trying to do?" he responded warily.

"Get home."

"Where's home?"

"Several miles from here. By the Minuteman Causeway. It's not far."

"Do you need money for a cab?"

"No. I have money. I just didn't feel like standing on the highway, topless, trying to catch a cab," she said, reasonably enough. She might be a bit drunk, but she was not foolish.

"That's understandable," he conceded. "My car is parked just down the beach in front of my hotel. I could lend you a shirt."

"I'm not going in your room. You're not a lech, are you?"

"Not in good standing. Couldn't afford the dues."

She giggled. He leaned against the side of the building and removed his shoes and socks.

She fell in step with him as he walked toward the water. The sun was down, but there was a full Moon rising over the water, turning from gold to silver as it got higher. The Atlantic was calm, lapping at the beach as they walked. No one else was about.

"It's hard to walk on sand with your arms on your chest," she observed. "You can't use your arms to keep your balance."

"Those boots can't help any either."

"If I take them off, I'll ruin my pantyhose."

He said "Oh," but he might as well have said "Duh." It had never occurred to him that cowgirls wore pantyhose with their boots. "Had Dale Evans worn pantyhose?" he wondered to himself. "Or stockings --- since there were no pantyhose back then. Did she have on a garter belt under that cowgirl skirt?" The mind boggled.

He was brought back to the present when she stumbled and grabbed his hand to steady herself. She continued to hold onto his hand after she regained her balance. He felt reasonably sure her motivation was solely to avoid falling. She still held one breast in the other hand.

"Is one more important than the other?" he found himself asking.

She laughed and said "Pretty silly to cover one and not the other, isn't it. They're about the same." She let her other hand drop to her side. They strolled down the deserted beach in silence, her nipples becoming hard in the cool night air.

"Why didn't anything like this happen to me twenty years ago?" he wondered to himself. "Timing is everything."

The shirt was the size of a blanket to her, but she put her arms in, rolled up the sleeves, and did some kind of trick involving a knot in front --- leaving a bare midriff. The result was effective, if not neat.

Now that she was clothed, he introduced himself. She was Courtney, it turned out.

"Why are you dressed like a cowgirl, Courtney?"

"My date's a redneck," she offered. "Likes country music and country bars. Not much else to do around here." Then she added, "I guess he's not my date anymore."

"I don't mean to pry, but...."

"We had a disagreement. He wanted me to enter the wet T-shirt contest and I wouldn't. Not because I'm a prude. Because if you want to win you have to take off your shirt, which I wasn't about to do. But a lot of the girls do it. There's a $100.00 prize, see. But I said, what's the point of making a fool of myself, getting all wet and probably losing on top of it all?"

"Uhm," he murmured.

"I mean some of these girls do this for a living. They'll do all sorts of things to win. I even saw one strip naked, but they disqualified her! Anyway 'Prince Charming with a Coors' starts buying me shooters --- you know, tequila in shot glasses --- to try to get me drunk so I'll do it. But when the time came, I wouldn't."

"Here's my car," he said, grateful to change the subject.

"Put the top down?" she asked. And he did. No sooner had they pulled out than she resumed. "So he didn't get pissed off, which surprised me. He said 'Let's take a walk on the beach.' We hadn't got too far, when he started kissing me, and I kissed him back. Well, one thing leads to another and, next thing I know, my halter top is lying on the sand and I'm telling him we have to wait. Then he steps back and looks at me --- my breasts, actually --- and says 'You coulda won.' I realize then he is drunker than I thought. ' Maybe you will now!' he shouts, and picks up my top and runs back into the bar before I can stop him." She quickly adds, "Turn left here."

"You don't live with somebody, do you?" he asks, realizing that bringing her home in his shirt could be awkward.

"Only a biker gang," she replied playfully. "No. I live at home with my mother. I'm going to the community college; so I can't afford to move out. I don't want to leave her all alone anyway."

"What happened to your father?"

"He was killed in a car crash when I was a baby. I don't remember him. He worked at the Cape. He was a scientist."

"I'm doing some work at Kennedy, but I'm an auditor. Not as exciting."

"My father worked on the Apollo program. That's the Moon landings. His name's on a bronze plaque with the other scientists' names. Dr. Jonas MacPherson," she said with evident pride. "They're all dead now. All the scientists he worked with. That was a long time ago."

"Wait a minute! That's not so long ago. I was around then. I remember watching the Astronauts on television live from the Moon."

"Were you a baby?"

"No," he groaned. "I was in college. About your age."

"Oh. You don't look it."

"Thanks. Thanks a lot."

"We're here. It's just past the house with the FOR SALE OR LEASE sign in front."

Her mother came out the door of the house when they pulled into the driveway. 'Mom' turned out to be an attractive woman in her 'forties, with a trim figure --- and a stern look on her face. There was not going to be a quick getaway.

But Courtney jumped from the car saying, "This is Mr. Mason. He rescued me after my date dumped me!"

Mason nodded to her mother, both as an introductory gesture and an acknowledgment of the truth of the statement.

"You must come in, Mr. Mason." It was a command, delivered with a husky voice in a cautiously hospitable manner.

They had coffee, no cake. Courtney returned his shirt with more fanfare than he would have liked. (He'd have preferred to avoid the subject completely.) 'Mom' arched her eyebrows at that point. Courtney casually tossed out a lame story about her missing halter top breaking and being left in her date's car after Mr. Mason had offered her one of his clean shirts. Everybody present wished they'd thought to concoct and rehearse a decent story. Nevertheless, 'mom' apparently concluded that Mason had done no harm --- or indeed was harmless.

So 'mom' became Laura and a small glass of Chardonnay was offered. She inquired "Well, Mr. Mason, what brings you to our little community?"

He gave his usual Aw-shucks-I'm-just-another-bean-counter-from-Washington response. That stopped the conversation for awhile. Courtney topped off everyone's wine glass during the silence, hers being the only one that was empty.

Finally, he asked where Laura was from.

"Virginia. The western part, but not West Virginia. There must be a better way to say that," she observed, "but that's the way I've been doing it all my life."

"Did you come down here with your husband to work for NASA?"

"Yes, we all did. They were going to colonize the Moon, our husbands. We were going to raise the families of these interplanetary explorers and share in the glory." She paused, then added "And that's pretty much what happened --- until it all fell apart."

"You mean the end of the Apollo program?"

"Yes, that. But that wasn't all. I can't tell you how exciting it was in the 'sixties and early 'seventies to be a part of it all. It was amazing. All we did was win! Everything we did was right! God, it was great!"

"Then the program ended?" asked Courtney, who had never heard her mother say an enthusiastic word about the space program before.

"We always knew the program would end. That wasn't a shock. We all thought it would be replaced by the next step. We didn't know NASA would turn its back on the Moon. That was a shock. Everyone was totally disillusioned."

"What do you mean by the next step?"

She looked at him as if he had just walked out of the primordial ooze and had no forehead. "The Moon Base, of course."

"You mean you --- your husband and the other scientists --- actually thought there was going to be a Moon Base?"

"That was his job! That's what he and his team worked on. That was the goal! The Moon Base."

"But I've never read...."

"Think!" she interrupted. "You can remember those times. Weren't you surprised when the Moon was abandoned after the Apollo program?"

He thought. He remembered. Everyone he knew at the time was surprised --- and disappointed. She was right.

"Then my husband and those other disillusioned men, who had participated in this great experiment --- which had been tremendously successful --- were told it was called off just before the final achievement. It ruined their lives. My husband and all the others. They were never the same. Ask the other wives. Some of us still talk. We all say the same thing. It wasn't right! NASA killed our husbands!"

The vitality had left her. She sat back in her chair and gave them a thin little smile.

"Are you O.K., mom?"

"I'm fine. Just got carried away. I keep it inside too much, maybe. Girl Scout cookie, Mr. Mason? The girl across the street hit us up pretty good this year. Got enough to last till Fall. What do you say? Help us out? Courtney, bring in some do-si-do's or whatever they call the peanut butter ones this year."

He had three do-si-do's or whatever they called them this year. They were good. God bless the Girl Scouts; they peddled good cookies.

"That him over there?" he asked, pointing to a photograph on the mantel.

"Him and the rest of his team," she replied. "All gone now."

He went over and studied the photograph. There were seven men standing together, most wearing suits in which they looked uncomfortable and grinning at the camera in the ridiculous way most people do when told to smile. The man in front, whom he hoped was her late husband, somehow managed to look dignified in this assembly.

"Wretched picture, actually," she said. "But it's the only one I have of the whole team. We were close back then."

"I suppose they found new assignments which took them elsewhere," he mused.

"Mr. Mason, you haven't been paying attention," she said with a sigh. "Every man in that photograph is dead."

That stunned him. "But they weren't that old. I mean, statistically, that doesn't make sense. How'd they all die?"

"Accidents mostly. Anderson had a heart attack, but it was known that he had a weak heart. Rheumatic fever as a child, I believe. Two drown --- three, if you count my husband." The she looked at him and asked, "If your car goes off the road and into a canal, is it an automobile accident or a drowning? I've never been sure."

He presumed the question to be rhetorical.

"Anyway, the project was terminated ... and so were the scientists," she continued.

"Mom, you're not saying daddy was killed by someone, are you?" exclaimed Courtney, who had been listening intently.

"No, honey. I'm not. And I certainly wouldn't want Mr. Mason here to get the idea that I'm accusing the government of anything. It's just peculiar, is all. And I've spent too much time thinking about it. Probably should have remarried a long time ago."

"It's not too late," Courtney offered unconvincingly. She believed anyone her mother's age was past such things.

"Well, it's past my bedtime," Mason said, hoping to escape. This was not to happen.

"We are boring Mr. Mason here with our little family discussion," she admonished her daughter. "Show him your frogs."

He started to say "I beg your pardon," but Courtney interrupted. She led him to the Florida room in the back of the house. Her mother followed. There was a large aquarium in the corner, but it wasn't filled with water. Instead, there were some plants and some black frogs with dayglow green markings on them.

"*Dendrobates auratus*," Courtney said with practiced assurance. "They come from an island in the Pacific Ocean off Panamá." The markings were brilliant.

"I've been to a Chatauqua and three county fairs and never seen anything like that," he managed. He was pleased when Laura giggled.

But the pleasure faded when Courtney asked, "What's a Chat-awkward?" How did he get to be this old?

He sighed inwardly and said "A Chatauqua was a sort of fair which was held in the summer in a town called Chatauqua in upstate New York, during the horse racing season at the local track. The idea was to provide entertainment for the race fans when the horses weren't running --- I guess."

"No television, huh?" Thus did today's youth write off all activities of previous generations which did not actually involve fornicating or killing. She was back to the frogs.

"These are poison-dart frogs," she continued. "But they're not poisonous now because they were born in captivity and haven't eaten the ants and other things that make them poisonous in the wild. So you can touch 'em." She picked one up. She didn't look poisoned. She was testing him.

To buy time, he asked her mother "She hasn't been receiving anti-venom shots or anything has she?"

"You don't have to prove anything, Mr. Mason. This is a ritual of manhood she puts her dates through."

The ante had just been upped big time. "Is there any place I shouldn't touch him?" he asked.

"Oh no. You can't hurt him," she teased.

So he stroked the little frog's back twice with his finger. It felt smooth, like tanned leather. The frog didn't seem to object. It looked at him inquisitively with one of its huge eyes.

"Where did you get these?" he asked.

"The biology professor is away this term; so he let me keep them. I helped him take care of them when I took his class."

"Do they ever bite?"

"Only food. They eat lots of things, but mostly I give them fish food. You know, the little flakes that you drop in an aquarium. But biting is not how they poison animals. The poison is secreted onto their skins. If you just touch the back of a wild one --- like you just did, you'll die in minutes."

"Could I have just a little more wine," he requested. Laura led the way back to the living room.

"Did we get too interesting for you, Mr. Mason?" purred Laura. Courtney refilled his glass. He mentally counted to twenty before he picked it up to avoid looking thirsty.

"You live in Washington, right?" Laura asked him.

"Maryland actually. West of the District."

"Do you know a restaurant called the 'Anchor Inn'?"

"Great seafood," he acknowledged. "And just a mile down the road from me."

She hesitated a moment and then plunged ahead. "Mr. Mason, I'm going to ask you to visit my husband's grave, which is not far from there. I'll lend you the map I use to find it. I haven't been up there for years, and don't have any idea when I will be. Please do me --- do us --- this favor and then drop me a line or call me to let me know how it looks. There's no hurry. It'll take ten minutes sometime when you're out that way. We've got nobody left up there and, well, it's a long trip just to visit a grave."

He saw no polite way of refusing; so he assured them that he would. He offered to send them a photograph of it, as well.

As he left the house, Laura MacPherson thanked him for "rescuing" her daughter, for helping with the cookies and for the visit he'd agreed to undertake. But the last thing she'd said was peculiar.

"Take a screwdriver with you."

Chapter Four
Friday, April 16, 1993

The following morning he returned the tapes, but found no one at the desk. Not wishing to leave them without obtaining a receipt, he called out. In a few moments, a man who appeared to be in his late sixties shuffled toward him, saying "Morning. Thought I was the only one around this early."

Sensing that the Archives Librarian was in a good mood, Ken decided to have a chat. "Morning. I'm Ken Mason."

"I'm Will Peterson. I'd have introduced myself earlier, but I never know if someone is going to be around long enough for the effort. What did you think of my collection?"

"Impressive. But the first ones were better than the later ones."

"Everyone says that. It's true, I guess." He paused, then asked "You with the government?"

"General Accounting Office."

"Well, that's close enough," Will said cryptically. "It was all new the first couple of landings. You see, they were like kids on vacation with a new camera, taking pictures of everything. Miles of film --- cinematic miles, not actual miles --- from the first trips. Then later on, coming back with unexposed film. Towards the end, it was all I could do to splice together a decent home movie for them to show their families."

"The Moon doesn't appear to offer a variety of scenery."

"No. Not much nature. No wildlife."

"Not even a cockroach."

"Don't be too sure. We never tried turning off the lights, waiting, and turning them back on. Who knows?"

"I'll try not to think about it," Ken decided aloud.

"Anyway, they must have been doing something else up there during the times set aside for pictures."

"Maybe the golfing was better than it looked."

/////

NASA had quickly become a large agency with far-flung operations. When President Kennedy had announced the race to send a man to the Moon, all the stops had been pulled out. The budget soared. Cost control yielded to urgency. The politicians got into the act, as each one tried to make sure that some NASA money was spent in his district. One spectacular result was that the missions launched from Merritt Island would be run from Houston, thanks to President Johnson and his political cronies in Texas.

It was clear to Mason that there had been over procurement (buying items that weren't needed) and overpricing (paying too much) throughout the agency. He resolved to attempt to separate out these unnecessary costs to the extent feasible in his report.

The cafeteria had chicken salad that day; so he went into the Burger King in town for lunch. As he arrived back at the Kennedy Space Center, he saw a military officer step out of a grey Ford. Not having been in the military, the uniform didn't tell Mason much. "Couldn't be a general if he's driving himself," was as far as he got. He was mulling over his general antipathy toward military types, when he was startled to hear the officer calling out his name. "Mason, is that you?"

Mason put his hand above his eyes to shield them from the bright sun, squinted and identified Clay Marshall --- Major Claiborne Lee Marshall of the United States Marine Corps, to be exact. His former brother-in-law. The Major said "You don't have to salute." Mason self-consciously removed the hand from his forehead and continued squinting.

There was no avoiding him; so Mason gamely asked the only obvious question. "What are you doing down here?"

"National Weather Service reports snow headed for Washington. Thought it was a good time to look after my charges."

"Your charges?"

"Marines in the Astronaut training program. One of the less remarkable duties my department has is to recommend Marines to NASA for Astronaut training. Then we keep track of them until they finish the program. When they finish, NASA takes over. If they don't finish the program, tradition calls for them to be sent to whatever version of Hell we have available at the time. Provides a whale of an incentive. Inter-service rivalry dictates that each service place as many Astronauts as possible." Then he added "They've got civilians now too," as though he didn't think it was a very good idea.

"I thought you were in recruitment."

"I still am. We're responsible for recruiting into the space program too. We like to keep it simple in the military. A recruiter recruits."

By now they had entered the building and Mason had vaguely referred to doing some auditing by way of explaining his presence. The Major insisted they meet for dinner. To his own surprise, Mason readily agreed. He must have been lonelier than he thought.

/////

During the day, the expected excesses appeared. For example, each mission carried supplies of food, water and oxygen far beyond what was needed for the mission. He figured this was simply precautionary, but the increase in payload was significant. He had tried unsuccessfully to imagine a circumstance in which ten days of extra supplies would save a mission which had failed to leave the Moon, or to achieve re-entry. He found this line of thought depressing; so he turned to other matters.

In computing the cost of each mission, he did not include the emergency lunar survival tents for the simple reason that all of these bulky devices still seemed to be in inventory (despite the fact that one was on the manifest of each of the last five missions). Again, this fit with his theory that there was no reason to prolong life a few days in the event of disaster, since rescue from the surface of the Moon was never a possibility. Why was it still on the manifests, though?

The "super-cold Moon Suits" presented a similar puzzle. These high-tech, super-insulated space suits designed for excursions into the dark side on later missions had arrived at the Space Center. Astronauts had trained in them. They had apparently been on the missions, but none were seen in the films. Nor had any returned to Earth. Maybe they were left on the Moon for weight reasons; they each weighed 236 lbs. on Earth But when were they used, and for what?

That evening at dinner, he asked if the Major was aware of four Marines who had quit the space program in 1969? "I never heard of such a thing," was the response. So Mason told him about the entry in the training records. The Major promised to look into it and to "clear the matter up" for him when he got back to Washington the next day, where, he understood, the weather was cold enough to "beeze your fralls off."

Mason gave him his card with the date and names written on the back. He told him it was something he had stumbled across and about which he was curious, but that it was unrelated to his assignment, and unofficial. He also paid for both dinners. Nevertheless, Mason did not expect to hear anything.

/////

Monday, April 19, 1993

"Major Marshall on Line 7 for you, sir," said the assistant librarian just before 2:00 P.M.

"Hello Ken! I'm back in Washington. I thought I'd get back to you before the glacier moves in."

"Chilly?"

"Now don't get smug! At least nobody's getting skin cancer up here. Anyway, I checked on that report about the four Marines, and our records confirm they left the space program after completion of Apollo training, like you said. But, according to our records, we requested them back for some hush-hush mission. They didn't wash out."

"No one said they washed out. It just seemed curious, is all. What happened to them? They never came back to NASA," prompted Mason.

"They went to Nam on this secret mission. Assigned to NOMAD/Y Base, wherever the Hell that is. Couldn't find it on my map of Nam. Might be in Cambodia or Laos, for all I know. Probably not the name of any real place. All kinds of clandestine shit going on over there in those days. Wherever they went, they never came back. We notified their families. None of them had wives or children. They're listed as MIA, which at this point means they're probably dead but still drawing pay. I suspect some accountant is responsible for that."

"Probably right," said Mason. What the Hell! He probably was right. "Well, thanks for satisfying my curiosity. Time for my stroll on the beach."

"I hope a crab bites your ass."

"Anything for a thrill. Take care." The Major hung up.

/////

The evening was uneventful. No crab bites. The hotel had cable, and --- despite himself --- he was watching C-SPAN. There was a panel discussion. At the time, a former Soviet (now Russian) rocket scientist, Dr. Dmitri Shavinsky, was speaking in American English, which was being translated into British English by an unseen gentleman with a French accent.

Mason opened a *Carlsberg*. True to the spirit of *glasnost*, the Russian was saying how easy the Americans made the Moon missions look, with the live television coverage and all. "If you had any idea...," thought Mason.

Then the Russian said something which threw the panel into confusion and made Mason choke on his beer. According to the translation he said "The technological and logistical triumphs of the Moon program overshadowed the unfortunate loss of life in space."

When other (American) members of the panel explained that there had been no such losses, he replied cryptically "There are always losses when there are gains." And life went on more-or-less peacefully for the panel on C-SPAN.

"Mother of Pearl! What is he talking about?" said Mason out loud. The four missing Marines were on his mind again.

The credits at the end of the program advised that Dr. Shavinsky was in America on a visit to the Kennedy Space Center.

"Please don't be a re-run," pleaded Mason to the television. His wish was granted. It had been taped earlier that day for viewing after Congress recessed for the day.

Tuesday, April 20, 1993

He was at the Kennedy Space Center early. When he stopped at the desk for his badge, he remarked that he had seen Dr. Shavinsky on television last night and heard he was going to visit.

"I've been trying to find out how to say 'Welcome' in Russian, but nobody seems to know how," stated the guard. "I suppose no one thought it would come up."

It turned out that Dr. Shavinsky was due next week. No problem to keep working until then.

Later that day, he ran up against the secret experiments. Being secret, there were few numbers to analyze. This bothered him, he knew, solely because he was an auditor. The costs of secret experiments should have no bearing on the costs of sending a rocket to the Moon and bringing it back. The payload figures were available: the size and weight. It was obvious that the secret experiments were large and heavy. "Must have been big secrets."

When he compared the mission reports with the manifests, it appeared that the actual cargos (excluding the Astronauts themselves) carried by the last five missions were several times greater than the cargos anticipated. Was this important --- or was it merely the normal human need to cram as much as could be safely held into the space available?

The telephone call from the office came at 3:10 P.M. It was Rae Kirkland, checking up on his progress. She began by saying, "You can't stay there until Summer."

"Call me back when the snow melts and Washington returns to that heavenly state of 32-degree drizzle we've all come to know and love."

"By the weekend, they say. I didn't realize you appreciated that stuff."

"I'm from Cleveland. I get nostalgic for it."

"How's it going?" she said, getting down to business.

"There are a lot more grey areas than even usual, but I think I'm developing some useful figures. Is the GAO planning to send an auditor to the Moon?"

"No. We'd like to send the House Budget Committee." Rae Kirkland was not really fearless; she just believed that no one cared much what the GAO said. She was right. "Any problems down there that might require my particular talents?"

"Have I been gone that long? I don't recall you having any peculiar talents --- unless it's your uncanny ability to work the daily scrambled word puzzle in your head."

"Once you start, you can't help yourself. If I could do the same with financial statements, I'd be running this place."

"Don't kid yourself. You'd be too valuable to run the place."

"That's some consolation," Kirkland admitted. "Now tell me all the interesting Astronaut secrets you've learned."

"Well, they're like all good Americans. They like to go fast. They overpack. They play golf anywhere. They litter. And they take home movies."

"That's the Japanese."

"*Ah so*. And they have humongous secret experiments and quasi-military terms."

"Like what?"

"What do mean like what? Like 'Commander' and 'mission' and 'NOMAD/Y Base'." This last example slipped out because he perceived that the others were not having any effect. He did not bother to explain that it was supposed to be in Southeast Asia.

"Spell that for me." Rae Kirkland sensed a puzzle.

"That's N O M A D slash Y." He added, "No fair writing it down."

"No need to. I'll run it through the cerebral cortex until it's digested. I think I just mixed a metaphor. Is it important?"

"I hope not," replied Mason. "If it is, mix one for me."

Rae Kirkland called back within ten minutes. Without greeting, she said, "As you know, a nomad is one who wanders about regions we generally think of as deserts. Places which civilized people do not believe can sustain life. They roam about, never settling in one place, because one place can sustain them only for a short while. Does this have anything to do with the Moon?"

"What you just said sounds like it could, but I don't think it does." By now he was sorry he had mentioned NOMAD/Y.

But she continued, "Because NOMAD/Y is an acronym for 'Monday' if you ignore the slash, which I'm inclined to do. And 'Monday' is an ancient corruption of Moon Day, as in Sun Day, Moon Day, Zeus' Day, Wodens' Day, Thor's...well, you get the idea."

Mason frowned. After a pause, he said, "That's very interesting. I'll let you know if it's helpful. Thanks for getting back to me." Then he put his head on the desk and let his mind rearrange all the anomalies he'd uncovered into a new --- albeit incomplete --- scenario. If NOMAD/Y was a reference to the Moon, then where were the Marines sent?

///////

He was surprised he had fallen asleep. "The last of the deep thinkers," he mumbled to himself as he tried to restore circulation to the arm he had placed his head on. It felt like ginger ale. Sore ginger ale.

As he drove the short distance back to the hotel, he kept thinking the unthinkable. What if the extra cargos had been destined for a lunar base? What if all the other stuff that was supposedly just lying around on the Moon --- super-cold suit Moon Suits and lunar rovers --- had actually been left in usable condition for future use.

And what if the four missing Marines had been smuggled to the Moon on these missions?

What had happened to them?

///////

Meeting Dr. Shavinsky presented a challenge. There was no political reason for them to meet. They were not fellow scientists. There was no apparent common ground. How could he even get to the scientist, who was bound to have his own small retinue in addition to the entourage to be provided by NASA? Hell, the FBI or Secret Service might even be there. The more he thought about it, the more unhappy he became.

Or maybe it was the beer. The store had been out of *Carlsberg*. "Can this happen in a civilized country?" he'd asked himself. Distracted, he'd bought an American lager instead. It made him wonder if chilled, carbonated hog drool would taste any better.

"Perhaps a bit of the knitting up the raveled sleeve of care," he speculated. And went to sleep.

Chapter Five

Sunday, April 25, 1993

It was raining hard in the Maryland countryside, but it was still an improvement over Washington in the rain. Mason drove West amid the rolling hills in little traffic. It was Sunday morning and he'd had nothing particular to do; so he'd decided to visit the grave of Jonas MacPherson, Ph.D., Deceased.

He drove the old Corvette like his grandmother would have: carefully. He wasn't a Corvette person. He'd bought it shortly after his wife had divorced him. It had been a gesture, a proclamation to all that he wasn't a dull person. Typically, nobody had noticed. Yet he had defiantly kept it for years, perhaps hoping his image would change to match the car. The opposite had happened. The car had become dull. It needed paint. The windows leaked. The upholstery was torn. The radio hadn't worked in years. Still, it gave him satisfaction. He could no longer see himself owning a real car.

As for romance, he considered himself to be roadkill on the highway of love.

As he spied the turnoff for the cemetery, he thought about the screwdrivers. He'd brought three kinds: Phillips head, flat head and *Absolut.* He figured he could use at least two of them. "Be prepared!" He had been a successful Boy Scout in terms of merit badges; too bad he invariably got lost in the woods.

It didn't take long to find the headstone. It was one of many labeled "MacPherson." He was surrounded in death by his clan. There appeared to be no plot for Mrs. MacPherson. Maybe she would rest alongside her family in Western (not West) Virginia when the time came.

The headstone was polished red granite. It contained the usual carved statistics and the suggestion that the departed Rest in Peace. "What are the alternatives?" Mason wondered just long enough to decide he didn't want to know. The lower portion held a brass plaque, which stated:

IN RECOGNITION OF HIS SERVICE TO HIS COUNTRY
National Aeronautics and Space Administration

It was an unexpected tribute, a nice gesture. Mason was moved when he read it, recalling the dreams that had become reality when men walked on the Moon.

It was also tarnished; so he decided to clean it up a bit --- even if it meant sacrificing some of the vodka and orange juice. The plate was held on by flat head screws with little brass rosette washers to improve their appearance. They came out easily. He got a rag from behind the seat of the car and removed the tarnish methodically. It was a secret he had learned when he'd failed to clean up spilled orange juice many years ago. Then he put ArmorAll on it to retard future corrosion. Before replacing it, he applied the rag to the mossy portion of the headstone which had been covered by the plaque. To his astonishment, there was writing. When cleaned, it said:

FATHER OF THE MONDAY PROJECT.

He stared at it and drank the rest of the screwdriver cocktail from the bottle until it was gone. Fortunately it was both small and weak, for he was barely aware that he was drinking.

Then he got his camera from the car, wondering how long the film had been in it and what else might be on the roll. He took two pictures of the headstone without the plaque and two more after he had replaced it.

Before he left, he took a handful of dirt and rubbed it over the plaque. He wasn't sure why he'd done that. Self-preservation is instinctive.

/////

"We've got to talk. Now."

Rae Kirkland had slept in. He had caught her before her coffee had taken effect. "It's Sunday," she had replied, thinking how lame it sounded.

"I've always admired your sense of place and time, but I need to talk about something else," he responded.

Ignoring the sarcasm, she said "The office is closed today."

"This is too good for the office. I'm coming over."

"I wasn't expecting company. I don't dress on Sunday mornings."

"I'll bring food."

"What kind?"

"Big Macs."

"Never! I won't open the door unless there's brie and French bread."

"Damned yuppie!"

He arrived with the appropriate food just after Noon. The rain had increased steadily. He was soaked from the walk to her apartment. At the door he realized he had never been there alone with her before.

"Well, if it isn't my knight in dripping cotton. Do come in." She was wearing a long sheer bathrobe, which clung to her. Her black hair was straight. She wore no make-up. Her legs were long and slim, her hips just wider than a boy's. She had big shoulders which diminished her adequate breasts. She was no great beauty, but she had this air of smoldering sexuality. She gave him her crooked smile. "To what do I owe this honor?"

"Look. I know I'm probably spoiling your Sunday, but I need to talk to you for a little while. Call Prince Charles and tell him to keep the royal yacht waiting."

"Oooh! Not bad. You're definitely improving. But it's Prince Andrew I want. Not Jug-Ears." She had this irritating way of commenting upon his performance, instead of merely reacting. It was like talking to your high school English teacher. "So, what's going on that couldn't wait?"

He told her everything, omitting only the details of Courtney MacPherson's attire. The account seemed to intrigue her. He was therefore taken aback when she said "So what?" when he finished.

"So what?" he exploded. "So there was probably a secret project to establish a colony on the Moon, and four Astronauts who had been trained for such a project vanished together just before one of the missions, and the equipment that could have been used was evidently taken to the Moon and left there, and everyone who worked on the project is dead! That's what!"

"It is interesting. A little bit out of our usual line of work, but interesting. You really have nothing concrete, though. Just a story from a bitter widow."

"Don't forget the Russian, Dr. Shavinsky!"

"But he didn't really say anything. He just intimated that there had been some loss of life in the U.S. space program, which everyone knows is true."

"No. He was talking specifically about a loss of life in space during the Apollo program."

"Look. He's a Russian. A competitor in space. Why would you believe him anyway?"

"I liked the way he looked. Like George C. Scott as Scrooge." This was unexpected, but probably true. She giggled. He chuckled. Then they sat quietly for a few minutes.

"O.K. You go back down to Florida. Talk to your widow. Look around. Make it look like you're still working on the report. I'll see what I can find out about Shavinsky. Deal?"

"Deal."

"Now get out of here. I need my space." She loosened the tie on her robe and stared him straight in the eyes. "Scat!"

The robe was off before the door closed. She just didn't like wearing clothes when she didn't have to.

Chapter Six
Tuesday, April 27, 1993

"I can't wait to see you again," Laura MacPherson had gushed into the telephone. "I'll chill the champagne."

He hadn't known what to say; so he'd said "So long" and hung up the 'phone. "What the Hell was that all about?" he'd wondered. Women had always been an enigma to him. But it had been a passive role. Now they were lining up for the opportunity to confuse him. Was there an advertisement in the *New York Times* personals with his name inviting all and sundry of the fair sex to join in the mass baffling of a nerdy bean counter?

So his brain turned completely to curly fries when the widow MacPherson stood in her open doorway wearing short shorts and a tight silk tank top --- obviously no brassiere.

After about ninety seconds, he wondered what her daughter would think and managed to croak "Courtney...."

"You can't have Courtney. I've sent her away." Then she kissed him hard on the lips and dragged him into the house.

"Mrs. MacPher...." was all he managed to say before she placed her knee firmly and decisively against his testicles. She swung him to the sofa as he crumpled and climbed on top of him.

"Whisper!" she whispered into his ear. "Pretend you're glad to see me!"

"But I am," he groaned. Understandably, he did not sound convincing. "At least I was."

"I'll bet you didn't expect to see me like this!" she said with a throaty chuckle.

"No, ma'am. And some time --- at your convenience, when you feel like it --- would you please tell me what the Hell's going on here?" he whispered.

She smiled at him and put her lips to his ear. She said "They can hear every word we say. Kiss me!"

He didn't know who "they" were, but after a kiss, he didn't much care. She was a good kisser.

Then she suggested that he take a shower after his long trip, as if he had crossed the Okefenokee Swamp on foot. He agreed only when she promised to make them a snack while he showered. He was standing in the middle of the bathroom floor in his boxer shorts when she flung open the door with her finger to her lips. She reached into the shower and turned on the water. Then she looked at him and began laughing.

"The bathroom door lock never worked," she said, as if that explained everything.

He wished he were Humphrey Bogart, who he was sure would have slapped her hard under the circumstances. For that seemed to be what she needed.

"You poor man," she offered. This did not sound like something she would say if she were going to attack him again; so he took wary comfort from it. He tried to smile, but his lips just got crinkly instead. "We can talk now," she said, pointing to the shower.

"Don't ever do that to a man," was all he could say.

"They do it in the movies all the time. Does it really hurt?"

"People in the movies don't have balls," he stated as though this could be easily verified by reference to any encyclopedia.

"I'm sorry. I really am. I just didn't want you to say anything that didn't fit."

"Fit what?"

"I'm being watched. Someone is keeping track of me. It's been going on since my husband died, but it's been subtle. But since you came by that night, I've got new neighbors who point things at my house. The FOR SALE OR LEASE sign next door is gone. Whoever lives there is not neighborly. More like invisible. There's always a car behind me when I drive. The 'phones are probably bugged. I just don't know what all. But the only way I could think of to handle it is to make it appear that we are romantically involved." She ran her hands over her torso in way he found provocative. "Hence, the hero's welcome."

"I can't stand paranoia," he stated flatly. Then added with a smile "But I sure do like the way you handle it."

"Mr. Mason, I do not believe in halfway measures."

"I guess not. What now?"

"I'll leave. You undress and step under the shower long enough to get wet."

"Just in case they're watching?"

"Exactly. Then we'll go where they can't listen."

He made it a point to wash behind his ears --- in case "they" were watching.

/////

"Did you find the headstone interesting?" she purred as he produced the before and after photographs. They were on a deserted stretch of beach, facing the ocean. The waves were breaking. The wind was brisk. A squall line was approaching. They could barely hear each other. They felt they had foiled any aspiring eavesdroppers.

"What was the part underneath about?"

"FATHER OF THE MONDAY PROJECT?" she asked. "Oh that was what Jonas wanted on his headstone. He evidently thought it would have great meaning by the time he died. Of course, he died sooner than he expected. I always assumed it referred to the Moon Base project, which became a secret instead of a cause for celebration."

"What about the plaque?"

"I don't know where it came from. But since it was placed over the other wording when there was ample blank space for it, I can only assume that its purpose was to conceal the reference to the Monday Project." Then she added, "In the most tasteful way, of course."

On impulse he asked "Have you ever heard of NOMAD/Y?" He spelled it when she failed to respond.

"Never. Sounds military --- or at least government."

"Just a term I came across. Nobody seems to know exactly what it refers to, but it might have been a military base or site in Southeast Asia." This obviously only made her wonder why he'd brought it up, so he continued "There were four Marines who completed Astronaut training and then left NASA --- all on the same day. I have a source in the Marines who told me they were assigned to NOMAD/Y base and never heard from again."

"Had they received Apollo training?"

"Yes."

"I don't believe it! None of the services would ever pull out one Astronaut, let alone four at once! Not while the program was still going forward. When did this supposedly happen?"

"August, 1969. Right after the first landing."

"Impossible! They couldn't have kept it quiet!"

"The NASA records say they left. The Marines confirm reassignment to this NOMAD/Y base, but can't --- or won't --- tell me where it is."

"Mr. Mason, you have stepped into some first-class government bullshit, and it's time to scrape it off your shoes, if we can."

Taken aback by her strong reaction and coarse language, he could only manage "Yes ma'am. Scrape it is." After a moment he said "Try to concentrate on what happened at the time. What exactly did your husband say?" he asked.

"Of course, everything was secret. He'd told me that the closer they came to setting up the Moon Base, the less anyone could talk about it. He especially told me to remember that. And it certainly worked out that way. Towards the end, you'd have thought he was just doing the book work instead of.... Oh. I didn't mean it that way."

"No offense taken," he said, leaving no doubt that offense had been taken. "Please go on."

"Well, he insisted that Courtney and I watch the Apollo XII launch. We hadn't done that for some time, although he was expected at every one. When it disappeared from view, there were tears in his eyes and he was smiling. Then I knew something significant had just happened involving the Moon Base --- and I hugged him."

There were tears at the corners of her eyes now; so he doodled in the wet sand while she composed herself. When his drawing was finished, he asked himself "Mother of Pearl! Did I have to draw a rocket?" But she looked at it and smiled at him.

"Yes, that's pretty much what it looked like --- from a distance, of course. A great distance. Light years, perhaps."

He blushed, but gamely continued. "O.K. Even if they did it on the sly, there must have been something you noticed which might shed some light on it."

"All I know for sure is that Jonas believed that a Moon Base was going to be established and that the Apollo XII Mission was a significant step. I don't have any idea what step it was, but I'm sure it was way past the planning stage."

"What about Apollo XIII?"

She didn't answer at first. She closed her eyes, then shook her head slowly from side to side. "How could I have missed it?" she said softly.

"Missed what?"

"Apollo XIII was the next mission, of course. But they never made it. Fuel problems. They barely made it back. Everyone was upset, but then there was this tremendous relief when they got home safely. But my husband and his team were not as relieved as everyone else. They were still...anxious."

"I'm sure there was a lot of disappointment."

"No. Not disappointment. They were worried. They muttered among themselves at our little get-togethers. They were obviously unhappy. I thought it was a funding cut or something like that. But if...."

"If there were supplies for the Moon Base that Apollo XIII was transporting," he finished.

"Oh my God!"

"Does that fit?"

"It not only fits; it explains so much. My husband was never as confident after Apollo XIII. I thought maybe he was affected by policy changes caused by the near-disaster. I didn't relate it directly to the mission itself."

"He must have known that the Apollo program might be terminated early, leaving the Astronauts stranded at the Moon Base."

"That too. Oh, poor Jonas."

"When you boil it down, all we have so far is a fascinating hypothesis. Do you have any tangible evidence?" he asked, trying not to sound like Edmund Burr as Perry Mason.

She was prepared for this question. She opened her beach bag and withdrew a book, which she handed to him. "You can have this one. I have six more."

He looked at the slim volume. It was entitled *La Fábula del*

Tiburón y las Sardinas.[3] He scanned a few pages. "This looks like Spanish," was the only reaction which presented itself to his deep-fried brain.

"*!Bueno!*" She seemed to enjoy sowing confusion. "*¿Habla usted Español?*"

"I don't even drink *Corona*, lady. Are you going to tell me about this book? 'Cause I sure can't read it."

"Neither could my husband, Mr. Mason. And that's the point."

"It is?" This would take a higher level of thought than his cortex presently had available. Maybe he should add RAM. Another 16 megabytes at least.

Before he could process this last bit of information, she added "Where is the one place a wife never looks?"

He just looked at her, amazed how easily she went from one incomprehensible subject to another. Her eyes told him she was serious. He thought a minute or so, then offered "My ex-wife never touched the deposit slips. Didn't seem to know what they were for."

"Larger than that," she said without apparent amusement.

"Computer? VCR? Under the hood of a car?" he offered.

"You're on the right track. Wrong era. We're talking late '60's."

"Stereo with lots of knobs?" he ventured.

"Does the word 'Halicrafters' mean anything to you?"

"Ham radio!" he shouted, delighted to still be in the game. The fog was lifting, but he still didn't know if he was at the airport or in the harbor. "Was Dr. MacPherson a ham?"

"He claimed to have 'met' some interesting people on the radio. He used to talk about an old blind lady named Kiefer who lived in a place called 'Goose Cove' somewhere on the Gulf Coast of Florida. She had led rescuers to sinking ships and patched conversations from war zones in Central America. He always wanted to meet her."

"Did he use the radio in his work?"

3

This is a real book, quite popular in Latin America in the 1950's. As noted in the text, information about this book is not readily available. The author regrets returning the copy he read to its owner without making notes.

"He was always convinced he could learn things through casual communications which were denied him through official channels. He once told me he had talked to some Russian space scientists on the set. He referred to one of them as 'Dr. Space-insky.' He sat up talking all night, some nights. I don't know if he ever learned any space secrets. I hope he didn't give any away. After he died, I found the books on the shelf behind the ham radio."

"Where did the books come from?" he asked.

"There was a receipt from a bookstore in Miami, which he had used as a bookmark. I guess that's where they came from. I don't know if he bought them, or someone else did, but whoever it was bought twenty copies according to the receipt."

"Twenty copies of a book in a language he didn't speak?"

"Yes. I find that peculiar. Don't you?"

"Peculiar isn't quite strong enough. Do you still have the receipt?" the auditor in him asked.

"It's still where I found it. Since he appeared to be using it as a bookmark, I left it in place."

"That was probably a good idea," he said without knowing why. "Do you know what the book's about?"

"No. The word *tiburón* means shark. I only know that because of all the surfers who come to the local beaches. It could be about a fabulous shark, for all I know. I've been afraid to show the book to anyone or even ask. This is a very small community. You be real careful about who sees that book. We don't know what it signifies. But it is the only thing my husband ever hid from me."

"We should both be careful, I guess. Overabundance of caution is rarely listed as a cause of death, my father used to say."

"Never gobble at a turkey shoot."

"Uhm...right!"

Then she looked directly into his eyes and said "Thank you for helping me with this."

"I thought you were helping me."

PART II: DISCOVERY

Chapter Seven
Wednesday, April 28, 1993

The next morning, Mason returned to the Kennedy Space Center, to review some footage with what he believed to be a revised perspective. It was tedious and he didn't know exactly what he was looking for.

Surprisingly, it turned out to be the scene where an Astronaut approached the camera and, unexpectedly, danced a few cha-cha steps, leaping up at the end. Then the scene changed abruptly on the tape. That was unusual since the cameras were fixed in place and filming continuously. Thinking the Astronaut had done something inappropriate at the end of his dance --- a rude gesture perhaps --- Mason reviewed the scene. He ran the tape back and went through the sequence again, using the slow motion and freeze frame features clumsily --- just as he did on his VCR at home. He did this until his eyes ached and he knew every step of the cha-cha sequence by memory. The Astronaut danced the cha-cha, jumped into the air (or whatever --- he wasn't getting sidetracked on that), and landed. Then the shot abruptly ended.

Nothing! He knew no more than when he started.

He paced the room and silently berated himself for wasting his (actually, the government's) time. The missing footage would have probably been the first "bird" shot from the Moon, anyway. A one-fingered salute for the millions of earthbound viewers. (On the other hand, a Soviet convoy might have passed by at that moment. That would have given old David Brinkley something to wax wry and philosophical about. "Ye gods and little fishes! Back to you, Chet!")

He closed his eyes for a minute to gather his thoughts. It was obvious that this sequence had been edited to show the dance, but cut crudely to eliminate something which followed. Maybe a clue remained. After a moment he realized that his eyes had been drawn to the motion, excluding the details. So, he turned his attention to the cassette again.

It leapt out at him now. Just as the Astronaut landed, his left arm swung around so that part of the name tag could be seen. The tape had been edited before the entire tag came into view. But there on the Moon Suit, just above the left bicep, was this shape:

\
/

Mason quickly reviewed the letters of the alphabet in his mind, realizing all the while that only one letter matched this pattern. The suit belonged to Carlos Xavier, one of the four Marines who had left the program.

And each suit was altered to fit one individual. "FREE ALTERATIONS WHILE U WAIT," came a random message from his overloaded mind. He shoved the thought aside, forcing himself to concentrate. "O.K. So the suit could be altered again for someone else." (He had actually asked about this during his tour -- to the astonishment of his fellow tourists.) "Just because it was Xavier's suit didn't mean he was inside it at the time."

But he just couldn't believe they would alter the Moon Suit and forget to change the name tag.

Come to think of it, Carlos Xavier was probably the only Astronaut who could cha-cha.

/////

Agent Terrance Fox Koestler sat looking at the answering machine...like he wished it would go away. The Archives Librarian at NASA had reported this morning that the GAO snoop Mason was back.

And yesterday he had been with MacPherson's widow most of the day. They appeared to have something going. Was he using his job as an excuse to see her, or was he using her to pry into NASA business? "Might as well flip a coin," he said to himself.

Agent Koestler was an old employee, of the "wet" variety --- a man trusted with operations which might require the loss of blood. Someone else's blood. Of course, the Secret Service was supposed to protect the President and other officials, and their families and visitors. But the rendition of this protection did not always assume a passive role. And the public would have been stunned to learn that the protection went far beyond mere physical security. For more than thirty years "psychological security" had been included. This provided sufficient justification for almost any activity which might prevent the reputation of a President --- present or past, alive or dead --- from being tarnished.

Ken Mason worried Agent Koestler. And he was tired of being passive. It was time for a shot across the bow.

/////

On a hunch --- more like demonic possession, really --- Mason decided to look at the communications between Apollo Astronauts and Earth. He approached Will, the Archives Librarian, casually, simply asking if he was "in charge of that sort of thing, too."

"Houston has all that," had been the reply. "But they may not let you hear them. I don't know if they have transcripts available."

"What about the launches?"

"The launches are recorded in both places, but ours are locked up in a vault as back-up. Only Houston has official records." Then he asked, "Interested in the launches?"

"Not really."

"I thought not," he grunted.

To attempt to appear less the fool, Mason said "I just thought it would be interesting to hear some of the conversations."

"All the good ones were on the T-V news." The old man wasn't giving him any opening.

"Is there a log book showing the time and durations of the communications?"

"That you can access through the computer."

"Thanks. Maybe I will. I'm pretty much finished with my report, but I want to have a firm grasp of the program --- in case anyone asks me."

"That ever happen?"

"Only when I'm not prepared for it."

It took about seven minutes to find a menu on the computer which listed COMMUNICATIONS. He selected it and found another menu:

DIRECTORY: COMMUNICATIONS

PRE-IGNITION
LAUNCH
ORBITAL
RE-ENTRY
POST RE-ENTRY
MOON
OTHER

He didn't know if his activity was being monitored; so he selected LAUNCH. The computer then prompted him to select a mission, which he did. The screen then displayed the date, time, duration and direction of each transmission. (An arrow pointing up indicated a transmission from the Earth; an arrow pointing down indicated a transmission to Earth. Primitive, but effective.)

Since no sirens had gone off yet, he exited and selected MOON, using Apollo XIV, which he felt was safe. The same format appeared, with similar information. He exited Apollo XIV and checked to see if all the Apollo Missions were available. They were. There were no extra missions either. So, he exited MOON and tried to select OTHER.

ACCESS UNAVAILABLE

was the message. It certainly sounded nicer than "access denied," but it meant the same thing.

He intentionally turned from the computer and went on a conspicuous search for a snack. He wanted everyone to know he was not using the computer. He returned to the counter and inquired if Will had anything he hadn't yet seen that might be interesting.

"You've seen more than most can sit still for," was the reply.

"Even I may have reached my limit, though. You wouldn't have any games on that computer, would you?"

The Archives Librarian suddenly assumed a conspiratorial look and leaned toward him. "Ever play chess against a computer?" he asked.

"No. I can't say that I have."

"You do know how to play chess?"

"Yes, but it's been a year or so."

"Then prepare to lose," he said. "You'll have to use my terminal. The public terminals can't access all the programs."

Mason came around the counter, trying to recall how the pieces moved. Did knights move three spaces and have to include a 90° turn?

"You sit here. I'll set you up and then get out of your way. I have another terminal I can use in the back for NASA business."

So Ken selected the INTERMEDIATE level and played chess against the computer, losing the first game quickly. He was startled when a disturbing computer voice informed him "You have failed miserably! Your King is mine! Hahahahahahaha!"

"What ever happened to 'Checkmate'?" he wondered to himself. Then, he mused "Was that Vincent Price?"

Resignedly, he set the competence level to NOVICE and tried again. There was a level below NOVICE, but he was damned if he would set it on DUNCE. Will came by several times to watch and then lost interest. Mason congratulated himself on being a poor chess player. He hadn't realized that it was an asset.

Like most government offices, the computer worked in MS/DOS. "Was it possible that Windows was too complicated for real rocket scientists?" he wondered. When Will was absorbed elsewhere, he went to the DOS prompt and typed DIR COMMUNICATIONS and pressed Enter. He wasn't sure he would get anything, but a list of all the files in the communications directory of the computer appeared. He repeated the process with the subdirectory OTHER, which this time yielded.

He noticed that his pulse rate seemed to have increased. He was presented with a choice of three files: HOUSTON, GROUND and MISC. HOUSTON and GROUND seemed to cover all the known bases;

so he tried to enter MISC, but a password was requested. For lack of anything else, he typed MONDAY, but that failed. Knowing that Will was certain to return soon, he quickly typed NOMAD/Y, but the computer would not accept a password with a slash (/). So he typed and entered NOMADY...and held his breath.

Bingo! He was in. The transmissions occurred regularly for years! This couldn't be a single mission! It couldn't even be several missions, because of the frequency of transmissions from the Moon!

He examined the dates of the last transmissions. He felt his jaw drop but left it; it was taking all his effort to stay in the chair. Not shaking was an accomplishment too. The final date was February 6, 1973. The last flight --- Apollo XVII --- left the surface of the Moon on December 13, 1972. The shuttle wasn't flying until later. "Who in blazes were they talking to?" he asked himself.

Then he noticed that only the down arrow symbols stopped on February 6, 1973. The up arrow symbols continued for another two years. If this was the Moon Base log, the transmissions from the Moon had suddenly stopped, while transmissions originating from Earth continued. What did this mean? Was contact lost? He did not have time to dwell on this prospect.

"Have you managed to win one yet?"

"Just finished another one."

"That mean you won or lost?"

"Lost," he mumbled as he managed to get the chess program back on the screen before Will was in position to see the screen.

"Well, you sure tried hard enough. You always get in a sweat over chess?"

Will was right. Mason's face was covered with perspiration. "You should see me when I play Pac-Man," he responded.

"My doctor won't let me play it anymore," responded Will. "Raises my blood pressure."

"Well, thanks for the use of the game. I need to get one of those myself; so I can improve my game."

"That's the trouble with the world. Two people can't schedule enough free time to play a game of chess," the Archives Director observed.

He went back to his motel and showered. His mind was racing the whole time. The computer screen replayed itself in his cortex. Each time he mentally re-read information about the last transmissions, he would hear "Hahahahahahaha!"

Even though he was unsure of the significance of his findings, he felt he should share them with Laura MacPherson over dinner. Maybe the two of them could sort this out.

However, the prospect of an evening of steak and/or lobster with Laura quickly dissolved into chaos. An ambulance was pulling out of the driveway as he drove down the street. Laura was in the yard talking to two policemen in an agitated manner. He stopped at the curb and jumped out of the LeBaron.

Laura ran to him and threw her arms around him, crying. "It's Courtney! She's unconscious! They took her to the hospital just now. Come on!"

She told the policemen she would contact them later. Then they drove to the hospital, with her giving clear directions amid hysterical outbursts. Strange what you notice under stress.

"The frogs! Those damned frogs!" she repeated.

"What happened?" he shouted as calmly as possible.

"She picked up a frog...." she just stopped there.

"From the aquarium?"

"Of course from the aquarium! Have you seen them running loose in the house?"

"What happened then?"

"She said 'Mom, it's sticky.' I didn't know what she meant at first. She dropped the frog back in the aquarium, took a step toward me and then fell face forward on the floor."

"You think the frog poisoned her? How can that be?"

"I don't know. I just don't know."

"Do you know what kind of frog it is? So you can tell the doctors?"

She nodded. "Courtney had a written description. I gave it to the emergency rescue man."

He accompanied her to the Intensive Care Unit, where they

found Courtney in a coma, attached to monitors and an IV drip. The IV was supplying her with a saline solution and atropine.

The doctor had no idea whether this treatment would work. It was simply the only one available that he felt had a chance. There was no known specific anti-toxin for the frog's secretion. The doctor kept repeating that she was "young and strong" and had survived so far. This apparently was the best hope.

/////

Thursday, April 29, 1993

At 2:37 A.M. Courtney suddenly opened her eyes and mumbled "Cheeseburger." Laura burst into tears and started kissing Courtney. Mason wondered where you could get a cheeseburger in the middle of the night. It sounded like a good idea, though.

Laura had him summon the duty nurse, who summoned the resident. As he watched the room fill up, he decided it might be a good time to call Rae Kirkland.

Rae did not agree, having immediately called into question his ability to interpret the information available from "any clock in the damned universe."

The sarcasm meant she was alert. He complimented her on being one of those fortunate persons who could awaken with a clear head. She expressed the hope that he hadn't called simply to find this out.

"I wanted to call you earlier, but I didn't get the chance. Get comfortable. This may take a while."

She groaned softly.

"I've been...uhm, precocious over at NASA."

"You mean sneaky."

"Perhaps," he conceded. "I found a tape showing Xavier on the Moon."

"Was Abby Lane with him?"

"Not Xavier Cugat! Carlos Xavier...one of the four missing Marines!"

"On the Moon? How can that be?" She certainly was awake

now.

"The name was on his suit. All I could see was part of the name patch, but it began with an 'X.' The only person with a name beginning with an 'X' was Carlos Xavier."

"Doesn't mean he was inside the suit. Could you see his face?"

"No, I couldn't. Maybe someone with the right equipment could, though." He was not going to give up. "But think of it. Each suit has to be custom fitted to the individual Astronaut's physique."

"What?"

"For his individual --- shall we say --- plumbing."

"I get the idea."

"They can re-fit a suit. I asked."

"You asked?"

"When I took the tour."

"Did anyone laugh?"

"No. But there were some strange looks in my direction."

She smiled as she pictured this. Then she apologized for interrupting.

"If they are going to all the trouble to re-fit the suit, do you think they would overlook the name patch? I sure as Hell don't."

"What Astronaut would go to the Moon wearing the wrong name patch even if they did?" she added.

"Good point. I hadn't thought of that...yet. But I get the feeling these guys aren't that humble."

"Well, that's certainly worth waking me up for."

"Oh, that's just the beginning."

"You have been busy," she observed, nearly stifling a long yawn.

"Zealous service to the taxpayers," he quipped. "Anyway, then I got into the communications files on the computer (not one of the terminals available to the public)."

"Are we talking about unauthorized access?"

"Uhm...yes."

"Oh, you have been having fun, haven't you?"

"I guess so," he admitted. "Can I continue?"

"Of course. I'm all ears."

"I found a file called MISC which required a password. Guess what it was?"

"Open sesame?"

"N O M A D Y," he spelled with satisfaction.

She could feel her neurons leaping about in her skull---like they might be trying to get out, but speech was out of the question at that moment.

"You see! There's a link that's not supposed to be there," he pointed out. "Even if the file had contained old weather reports from Omaha, it doesn't matter! NOMAD/Y is not supposed to have anything to do with NASA or the space program. It's supposed to be a military base in Southeast Asia!" With a flourish, he added "A military base where Carlos Xavier was supposed to have gone, instead of the Moon!"

She found her tongue. It had been in her mouth all the time, she noted. Lying on its side like a beached whale. "Dammit, Mason! Are you going to tell me what was in the file or do I have to come to Florida and choke it out of you?!"

"I was just getting to that," he said with forced casualness. He was enjoying this.

"Not old weather reports from Omaha, I'll bet."

"Correct!" He explained the up and down arrow symbols and then told her how the down arrow symbols stopped after about two years, but the up arrow symbols continued after that. "Whoever ground control was talking to stopped calling back. Then the calls stopped altogether, as if contact was lost, and that ground control was trying to re-establish it, but eventually gave up."

"Could the Astronauts have returned?"

"The transmissions continued after the end of the Apollo Missions, but ended before the shuttle missions began."

"Do you mean that nobody was supposed to be in space then?"

"No Americans."

"Good point. Could we have been talking to Russians in space?"

"It's possible. From the file itself, I don't have a clue. They could have been talking to Eskimos for all we know. It could have been a coded log of conversations with someone's girlfriend."

"Or a nomad, wandering the Gobi Desert, whose name starts with 'Y.' Or maybe the 'Y' stands for *yurt*, which is what they call their tents."

"I always knew the crosswords would ruin your mind some

day," remarked Ken.

"You may be right about that. Anyway we should try to ask Dr. Shavinsky if there was communication between NASA and the Russians during that time."

"If we can get to him and get him alone."

"And get him to talk," she added, wondering if she should make the approach. She probably had more chance of getting the old Russian bear alone than Ken did. "Well, I guess I should thank you for letting me sleep until almost three. I'm not going to sleep any more after hearing this."

"Uhm."

"There's more?"

"Only the exciting part."

"You're like one of those plants that only blooms one night a year."

"Thank you. I hear they smell good, too."

"They're fragrant. You're flagrant. Are you going to tell me what happened or not?"

"I was getting to that," he countered. "I had an appointment with Dr. MacPherson's widow."

"A date! You had a date. And please refer to her as Laura. It will save time and not strain credulity."

"O.K. Maybe it was a date," he admitted. "But it didn't happen, anyway. When I arrived, they were taking her daughter to the hospital."

"What happened to her?"

"Uhm. Did I tell you about the frogs?"

"Frogs," she said flatly. "Good Lord, Ken. Will this take long?"

"I told you it would, but I'll try to be brief."

"I'd appreciate that." And she listened to his narrative about the poisonous frogs from Latin America. As soon as she heard that Courtney was apparently going to recover, she surprised him. She said, slowly and evenly "Don't clean the cage. Don't touch anything."

"I wasn't going to pet the frogs."

"I mean it. Don't let anyone near them or the cage. I'll see if I can get an expert in to see what happened." She was insistent.

"What kind of expert?"

"Exotic toxins. As I understand it, those frogs only secrete poison when they eat certain insects. I'd like to know what they've been eating."

"Is that relevant?"

"Look, the frogs obviously ate something that wasn't supposed to be on the menu. Maybe something that can't even be found in this country. Now that would be interesting."

"O.K. I'll keep everyone away from the tank. It's an aquarium, not a cage, by the way. I'm going to take Laura home soon. You can reach me at the motel in the morning. If not, I'll call you before Noon. *Ciao!*"

"Nobody says that anymore," she said as she hung up.

"I do!" he said to the dead line before he replaced the receiver.

//////

At 8:36 A.M. Courtney was discharged from the hospital. Ken drove them back home. After Courtney was put to bed, Laura offered make breakfast for Ken. He never heard her. He was fast asleep on the couch. "Thank Goodness," she said quietly. "I'm not sure I could have done it."

Whereupon, she fell asleep on her bed, fully clothed.

Chapter Eight
Friday, April 30, 1993

Her alarm clock announced that it was 2:30 A.M. Rae Kirkland rolled over and shut it off without opening her eyes. She immediately called Ken at his hotel in Florida. She had programmed the number into speed dialing before retiring.

After 14 rings, he answered "Mason."

"Just thought you'd like to know we have invitations to the reception for Dr. Shavinsky. You can bring your new girlfriend too. And none of your supposedly dead Marines is listed on the Viet Nam War Memorial. *Ciao!*" Then she unplugged her telephone and went back to sleep, smiling. Revenge was so sweet.

"Hello. Hello! Awww, shit." He went to the bathroom. When he returned to bed, his annoyance kept him awake.

/////

Exactly five hours later, Agent Koestler repeated the sentiment after listening to the tape recording of the conversation made automatically by his illegal wiretap.

"These people have to be stopped," he determined. He didn't know what they were after, or what they might find. All he knew was that Mason was probing into sensitive information. Information to which all access had been forbidden by President Nixon's personal staff.

And the widow MacPherson was involved too. What was her role? What had happened after all these years to arouse her interest?

Being 7:34 A.M., Agent Koestler wisely decided he needed caffeine for the further consideration of these questions.

But he already was sure that he didn't want any Russians involved. "Just what we need. Damn Bolsheviks." Then he added, "Asia begins at *Potsdammer Platz.*" This Cold War slur, if uttered in Russian, could have serious health consequences for the speaker.

Rae had intended to arrive at National Airport early, to avoid the morning rush hour traffic. The fact that both rear tires were missing from her Cougar ended that dream. By the time the taxi got her to the airport, she was late. For the first time in memory, the flight had left on time. The next flight to Orlando was sold out. A major event was planned for Disney World, it seemed. It appeared to involve gay rights, of all things. "I always knew Mickey wasn't as pure as he appeared to be. That insight came to me one day when I looked at my Mickey Mouse watch at 6:30," she mused. She refused to even consider the possible significance of "moosh-ka, meesh-ka, Mouse-kateer." In any event, the upcoming festivities had also removed all seats to Tampa from the market. Rather than wait on stand-by, she booked a flight to Miami and raced to the gate.

"Astronauts, frogs, computers, missing wheels and a secret code word. Why not gays and lesbians consorting with Mickey Mouse in the bright sunshine?" she thought as the plane ascended through the cloud cover. The last thought she had before she closed her eyes was of Walt Disney spinning in his grave.

Whhhrrrr!

It is said that there are three kinds of people in Miami: those who speak Spanish, those who will soon learn Spanish and those who will move to Palm Beach.

At Miami International Airport Rae managed to rent *"un carro muy cómodo"* from a hitherto unknown agency for the *"precio barrato"* of only $45.99 per day without the collision damage waiver. (The agent's attempt to sell the CDW had been nothing short of heroic, reinforcing Rae's suspicion that the profit on this item must be 500%.) For her (thankfully, the government's) money, she had obtained the use of a 1993 tan Cadillac Seville with 33,646 miles on the odometer.

She promptly added four more miles driving around the boat yards along the Miami River, searching for the expressway that had been promised by a large overhead road sign as she left the airport. Fortunately, it was a clear day. She finally caught sight of one of the two tollways which serve the airport and managed to find an entrance ramp. Like countless tourists before her, she was so relieved to be on the expressway that she cared little that the signs indicated she was heading toward the Keys. Her patience was eventually rewarded with a sign indicating she could go toward Naples instead by turning North on the Sunshine State Parkway. She did and soon found herself headed in the right direction.

She celebrated by turning on the radio. After scanning through some Spanish language stations, she heard the unmistakable sound of marimba and steel drums. "When in the Tropics, reggae!" she said aloud. With what seemed to her to be an inconsistent accent, the man from the islands sang:

> Know you been through some deeficult times.
> Heart doesn't always heal fast.
> Been through dese things justa few times myself.
> Know they not all in my past.
>
> Doan want to hurt you or chase you a-way.
> Won't ask for your heart or your hand.
> Someting inside me I jus' got to say.
> Want you to please understand.
>
> I love you --- keep reading.
> Didn't want to; so doan ask me why.
> Words in this note will make it easier.
> Won't see the tears in my eye.[4]

"You wimp! You wrote her a note?" She hit the scan button. She was rewarded with Gloria Estefan. She couldn't understand the words, but the music had her moving in her seat.

And she stomped on the pedal.

/////

---

[4]

I Love You...Keep Reading is a song copyright 1973 by Jon Agee.

"She'll be here," Mason said without conviction.

"But when?" Laura responded. They were at his motel. In the lounge, because his room wasn't furnished for entertaining while clothed. They had agreed to meet Rae here because it could be found easily.

Laura was uncharacteristically nervous. She knew it. The only reason she could think of was that she was about to meet a friend and associate of Ken. A female friend. This thought did not give comfort. So when Rae arrived, she surprised both of them by shrieking, "There's a Cadillac!"

"Manatee County plates," he replied. "Aren't we looking for Dade?"

"No. The rental cars used to have special plates identifying them as rentals, but this was considered dangerous. So now they all have Manatee County plates."

He looked at her incredulously. "That worked?"

She smiled and said, "You can fool some of the people all of the time...."

They left the lounge and met Rae at the entrance, where she checked into a room adjoining Ken's...to Laura's consternation.

"Nice to meet you, Laura. We'll talk later. I'll be ready in ten minutes. You drive, Ken."

For eleven minutes, Laura questioned Ken about Rae and their work. Just when Laura was satisfied that the relationship was strictly business, Rae appeared in a sensational business suit that appeared to have a transparent mesh blouse under the jacket. Laura stared. Ken didn't, but it taxed his willpower.

There was a period of silent appraisal between the two women. Ken opened both car doors. Then he shouted, "Come on! We're late!"

Rae insisted on sitting in the back seat, ceding the territorial advantage to Laura. It wasn't a charitable act. She had never successfully forgotten the scene from *The Godfather* where a hoodlum was garroted from the back seat.

/////

The reception was at the Hilton, in one of those large rooms with partitions. Not all the partitions were opened. There were other events in progress. Except for a half dozen Russians (with a like number of Russian security forces blending in as inconspicuously as 8-foot, ill-suited zombies can), the group seemed to be local NASA types. The enthusiasm level of some of the latter reflected the fact that they had been ordered to attend.

They acquired drinks --- Chablis for Ken and Laura; vodka rocks for Rae --- and approached Dr. Shavinsky, who was chiding his hosts for serving Finnish vodka.

"It is like offering Suntory scotch to the British. Or California wine to the French, maybe. It may be good, but it's not...diplomatic!" He relished the word, then laughed.

Attempts by the Americans surrounding him to discuss the space program were politely rebuffed. He was in no mood to confront the fact that NASA was preparing for Mars, while the Russians were simply launching satellites for Western capitalists. "We will talk business tomorrow." The Americans were not prepared for small talk; so a silence ensued.

Rae moved in and introduced herself first, then the others. Dr. Shavinsky seemed pleased. The American scientists began to talk among themselves. Agent Koestler stood nearby, listening.

"I believe you knew my husband, Dr. Jonas MacPherson," offered Laura.

"Knew of him," he replied. "A brilliant man. Sadly, the leaders of our countries had different views in those days; so we never actually met."

"But you spoke with him, did you not?" she insisted quietly.

Dr. Shavinsky continued smiling, but his demeanor changed subtly. He did not reply at first.

Agent Koestler, who had been admitted as a security agent by using false credentials, walked briskly to the lobby and phoned in a bomb threat, allegedly targeting "those Godless Communists."

"I may have spoken with him at one time. I don't remember. It was so long ago."

Ken and Rae looked on in disbelief as Laura continued. "You had an amateur radio, didn't you?"

"Ahh. The amateur radio. They call it the 'pork radio' for some reason, I believe." He was stalling. He knew she had him, but didn't know whether to admit it.

"It's ham radio, not pork," corrected Ken. He was rewarded by stares from all; so he added "Uhm...I thought you'd want to know."

Dr. Shavinsky tried to use this to divert the conversation. "Ham is a different part of the animal, is it not?"

Laura was not being diverted. "He called you 'Dr. Space-insky'." It was a statement. He nodded. It was an admission.

Another Russian approached him rapidly and whispered into his ear. He turned to them and said "I have to go now." He began to walk away. Then he stopped and turned back. "There is a bomb reported. You should leave also."

They all left together. Once outside, Dr. Shavinsky said "They won't let you come with me. It is dangerous for you."

Rae had a flash of brilliance. "Then you come with us."

The unexpectedness of this suggestion stopped him in his tracks. "What do you mean?"

"If someone knows you're here and wants to harm you, then you should leave the hotel," she said calmly.

Dr. Shavinsky looked to his bodyguards for guidance. They obviously agreed with the logic, but had no plan.

"Tell me your idea." he said to Rae.

"Let's go to a restaurant," suggested Ken.

"I would like to try some of these rock crabs."

"I know just the place," Ken offered, wondering whether the Russian was referring to stone crabs or rock lobsters.

/////

It was crowded in the Cadillac. Two American ladies and three burly Russians. Dr. Shavinsky insisted upon driving. He liked to be in charge, even though he had no idea of where he was going. Laura rode in the passenger seat to give directions. Rae sat in back, uncomfortably wedged between two Russian bodyguards, whose hands rested on her legs more often than not. She ignored them, trying to imagine the consequences if the car was involved in a serious accident. Specifically, would they find Russian fingerprints all over her stockings?

Ken was in the following car with a Russian driving and another in back. The one behind him was asking him what was the "most good regional seafoods."

"Uhm. Let's see what they have when we get there."

/////

They ended up at the inevitably named Spaceport Seafood Grill. Dinner was a huge success. Everyone had conch chowder to start, followed by both stone crabs and lobster tails. (Ken had not figured out which Dr. Shavinsky wanted to try.) There were bountiful quantities of what the innkeeper tried to pass off as Chardonnay. (Rae helpfully explained to the Russians that 'Chardonnay' was the Florida word for 'kerosene'.) There was always a hand reaching for another claw or tail. Melted butter was spilt and shells were cracked. Before the table was cleared for dessert ("You must try the Key Lime pie"), it looked like the scene of some crustacean battlefield where both sides had lost.

/////

Agent Koestler watched the scene of gluttony from a barstool in the adjacent lounge, where he was subsisting on soda water and pork rinds. He was not a hateful person. Hate interfered with logical thinking. He allowed himself a break, though. He would hate them all while they ate their Key Lime pie.

After the pie, Agent Koestler was himself once more. Detached and ready to go. So when the after dinner drinks began arriving, he cursed.

"Looks like she's not going to show," observed the bartender, who incorrectly assumed he was waiting for a date.

Koestler stared disgustedly at the bartender and inquired, "Do you have anything to eat besides pork rinds?"

"Got three flavors of beef jerky."

Agent Koestler declined to inquire as to the identity of the three flavors. His stomach overruled his curiosity.

Ken asked "Did the Americans ever communicate directly with Russian spacecraft before the shuttle program?"

"No. It would have been impossible. It was designed to be impossible," lamented Dr. Shavinsky. "Americans could only talk to other Americans."

This eliminated the last reasonable explanation for the MISC communications. Rae looked at Ken in acknowledgment.

Laura MacPherson opened her purse and withdrew a thin book, which she handed to Dr. Shavinsky without speaking.

"*La Fábula del Tiburón y las Sardinas!*" said Dr. Shavinsky in perfect Spanish. "You *Yanquis* aren't supposed to read this sort of literature."

"You speak Spanish?"

"*¡Claro!* Of course!" Then with a grin, he said "Who do you think put the missiles in Cuba?"

"Uhm."

"You did that?" asked Rae.

"A most successful operation it was," he said proudly.

"Uhm. I thought you were stopped," ventured Ken.

"You thought we lost. Because your government told you America won. But it was never about missiles in Cuba. Castro may be a Communist, but we always knew he was crazy."

"Then what was it all about?" asked Rae.

"Missiles in Turkey, of course."

"Missiles in Turkey?" mumbled Ken.

"Look! It is simple. America had ballistic missiles in Turkey aimed at Russian cities. As you might imagine, the Soviet leaders didn't appreciate this situation. When the 'Cuban crisis' was over, the American missiles had vanished from Turkey."

"Uhm."

"So, Mrs. MacPherson, what are you doing with this book?"

"Have you read it?" she asked.

"Yes. It was part of the training for the Cuba mission. It assisted in the acquisition of the Spanish language and, at the same time, exposed me to the most popular anti-American literature."

Everyone simply looked at him; so he continued. "You see, this book is about a *tiburón* --- this word means 'shark' --- and the *sardinas* --- which means 'sardines.' The shark is America and the sardines are the small countries of Central America and the Caribbean."

"Oh." said Laura and Rae in unison.

"Uhm."

"So it is most unusual to find such a book as this in America." He turned to the front and noted that it was printed in México. "Where did you find it?"

"Hidden behind my husband's ham radio."

"Hidden, you say?"

"Dr. Shavinsky, this was the only thing my husband ever hid from me. There were six copies. He apparently bought twenty copies. I don't know what he did with the others. I thought maybe you'd know something about them."

"Your husband spoke Spanish?"

"Couldn't even order a *taco*."

"I see," although it was obvious he didn't. "Can I keep this one?" he asked unexpectedly.

"I'm sure he would have wanted you to have it," she replied enigmatically.

"Do you know anything about these books?" inquired Rae.

"Maybe I will think of something." He put the thin volume in his jacket pocket.

"Dr. Shavinsky, I saw you on television last week," said Ken.

"They assured me that no one watched this show!" Dr. Shavinsky stated in mock outrage.

"Uhm...yes. Well, I couldn't sleep."

"It was a tragic loss for the world that you did not become a diplomat, Mr. Mason," he chided.

Ken forged ahead. "You referred to American losses in the Moon expeditions, but nobody died in space during the Apollo program."

"You are correct, technically," he replied cryptically.

"Uhm. What do you mean by 'technically'?"

"Let's not discuss this now. It is late and I grow sleepy from all the good food you have shown me. Now that the thoughtful Mrs.

MacPherson has provided me with bedtime reading material, I am ready to retire."

Rae sensed that Ken was about to press the matter and cut him off. "I plan to awaken early and go for a walk on the beach, before it gets too hot. Anyone care to join me?"

Laura jumped right in. "I will. How about you gentlemen? We'll be walking right by the Hilton."

"I will look for you."

/////

Agent Koestler stopped on the way home for Rolaids. Then he drove home and into the carport quietly; so as not to disturb his new neighbors, the MacPhersons. He would look in on them before retiring for the evening.

Chapter Nine
Saturday, May 1, 1993

It was 29 degrees Fahrenheit, yet drizzling in the capital. The television weathermen had predicted this. The new leadership no longer required them to predict sunny weather for May Day.

The scientists were seated off to the side of the reviewing platform, watching the rockets being pulled by on their flatbed trailers. Dr. Dmitri Shavinsky was watching them on television from his room. He pitied his colleagues shivering in the Moscow winter morning. It seemed to him that his knees ached briefly from the damp cold displayed on the screen. The broadcast was live; so it was still dark in Florida.

"They should be roaring into space, not being dragged behind a primitive vehicle along a cobblestone square," he grumbled to himself.

But the Soviet space program was gone. The Russian program that replaced it was on hold, not in small part because some crucial facilities were now located in foreign sovereign nations like Kazakhstan and the Ukraine. The Ukrainians weren't bad people. Once they stopped flaunting their independence, they would become reliable neighbors. But the Kazakhs --- they were impossible! And the Baikonur Cosmodrome, home of the Russian manned space flight program, was now a Russian outpost six hundred kilometers inside Kazakhstan.

The space station MIR circled the Earth in a deteriorating orbit, discorporating itself as though attempting to commit suicide before being consumed in flames upon re-entry into the atmosphere. The glory days were over. His position in society was that of the venerable ancestor who had accomplished something fine once --- long ago. He knew this.

Nonetheless, it was driving him crazy.

/////

"Clay Marshall here!" announced the voice on the telephone. It was 7:52 A.M. and how in Hell did the Major know he would be there? "Hello, Ken?"

"Good morning."

"Still enjoying the sun at taxpayer expense?"

"Almost got it wrapped up."

"It's warm in Washington; so you can come home anytime. Cherry blossoms and all that crap." Then he came to the point. "Y'know those Marines you were asking about?"

Ken was instantly alert, but tried not to show it. "Those guys that all went to Viet Nam?"

"Well, I got to thinking about it and decided the information I received --- and passed on to you --- was...unsatisfactory. I ordered someone to look into it."

"Uhm."

"It turns out that these four guys were on some kind of secret mission, but their chopper was shot down over Cambodia. They all died. This was at a time when no American was supposed to be near Cambodia. So it was hushed up for political reasons."

"Bullshit!" thought Ken. But he said, "That's been known to happen, I guess."

"Thought you'd want to know that we really didn't lose track of them." Major Marshall sounded relieved.

"I do appreciate you filling me in --- even though, as I said, it didn't have anything to do with my research. Just something that had me curious."

"Curiosity killed the cat, *amigo*. Take care."

"Thanks. 'Bye." Then to himself he said, "Was that a warning?"

/////

Agent Koestler had not overheard the conversation he had witnessed the previous evening. He was, therefore, not prepared for Dr. Shavinsky's decision to take a walk on the beach. He hid his shoes and socks in a tree, rolled up his pants, unbuttoned the top of his shirt, and tried to look casual as he strolled toward the surf, prepared to sacrifice his new Ralph Lauren slacks if need be to preserve the

American way of life.

/////

Rae wore shorts slit on the sides and a windbreaker unzipped just far enough to suggest that she wore nothing under it.

When Laura arrived, she commented to Ken about Rae's "Anna Mae Wong" shorts and revealing attire. Ken reminded her that Rae was his boss. Besides, the point of the exercise was to talk to Shavinsky. If that's what it took, so be it.

The sun was bright red just above the horizon. There were no clouds. The ocean was dead calm. The beach was deserted.

Rae played with the zipper as they approached Dr. Shavinsky, who was standing in surf in yellow and purple paisley "baggies" he had purchased at a drug store on the way home the evening before. "Do you approve?" he shouted.

"I think they're perfect," said Laura.

"I wanted more colors, but the shop didn't have. Such a drab country is America. Let us walk and exercise our young bodies."

As they headed North along the shore, Laura asked "Did you read the book?"

"Yes. Most interesting."

"More interesting than the first time?" asked Rae.

"Oh yes. Much more."

His responses were not revealing; so Rae said "Doctor, if you don't tell us why it was more interesting, it may be necessary to drown you right now."

"Aha! You come to the point, young lady! Well done."

They waited a moment, while Dr. Shavinsky looked around. When it was clear no one was nearby, he said, surprisingly, "Everyone into the water!"

"Why?" asked Laura, grateful that she had worn a bathing suit with a wrap.

"It is simple," he said. "The salt water ruins the electronic devices. It is instantan...."

"Instantaneous," offered Ken.

"Thank you. So if you want me to talk to you, you can swim or

-70-

take off all your clothes. It is your choice, ladies." He cast an eye at Ken and continued, "Mr. Mason, I'm afraid you have no choice."

Laura was saying, "Well, since you put it that wa...."

She never finished the sentence because Rae had turned her back to them, removed her windbreaker and walked into the surf with her hands across her bare breasts.

Dr. Shavinsky followed Rae into the water without a word or a sideways glance.

Ken looked at Laura and shrugged.

"Wonderful." Laura said as she unsnapped her wrap and flung it away from the sea. As he followed her, Ken was furiously reviewing the space program expenditures to try to keep the blood in his brain.

After making them all dunk thoroughly, Dr. Shavinsky began. "So far as I can tell, the text of the book is the same as the other edition I have read, but that is not the point." He stopped there.

"I could drown you now," offered Rae by way of encouragement.

He simply smiled, reflecting that it was amazing what a topless woman could get away with. "The point is not the text, but rather the position of the text on the page."

"How long do you think he can hold his breath?" Rae asked Laura.

"Think!" he beseeched them. "Why would this matter?"

"Code!" said Ken, surprised at himself.

"Code?" said Laura.

Dr. Shavinsky tried to ignore Rae's breasts, now floating uncovered near the surface, and turned to Laura. His left eye didn't quite make it all the way around to her, imparting a crazed aspect to his features. Yet he spoke confidently. "Yes indeed! I believe this book was used as a code book. Your husband would send someone else with a copy a message such as '54,2,5'. This would mean to seek page 54, to look at the second line and to go to the fifth word."

"Coordinates," said Rae, "for a code."

"Like the Bible. *Romans 8:31*," offered Laura. "If God be for us, who can be against us?"

"She's from Western Virginia," explained Ken. "It's called the Bible Belt."

Laura turned to Ken to rebuke him for what sounded to her like an apology for her upbringing. Before she could speak, Rae added " 'Once you have them by the balls, their hearts and minds will follow.' Richard Milhous Nixon, 1974."

Laura turned back to face Rae, but just then Dr. Shavinsky, who had ignored this exchange, continued. "That may not be exactly how it worked, but that's one way it could have worked. Since Dr. MacPherson did not speak Spanish, it may have worked differently. However, I congratulate him on his selection. This book is anti-American propaganda. It wasn't even printed in the United States. It was very clever. Although it is not my...uh, compartment, I'm certain there were persons in our government who attempted to find out this code. They did not succeed."

Rae was more direct. "Was your husband diabolical, Laura?"

"I never thought so before," she said with some hesitation, as though she might have to revise her opinion in this regard.

"Pardon me, but what is this all about? asked Ken. "Have we just handed over the launch codes to our ICBMs?"

"I don't think so, Mr. Mason, but it is a good question. 'What was this book used for?' At this time, I don't know. But I have a suspicion. And I will test it when I return to Russia."

"Uhm."

"Then I will find a way to tell you. Be sure of that." Then he surprised them by saying, "Mr. Mason, something is troubling you. It concerns the Moon, does it not?"

"Yes." He was unsure how much to disclose.

"Let me help you. I will try to keep it simple."

"That would be refreshing," observed Rae.

Laura repositioned herself between Rae's breasts and Ken's eyes, which had begun to stray despite his efforts to concentrate on the conversation.

"In the 1960's, when America was preparing for the first Moon landing, all the employees of NASA were hard at work on the project, right?"

They all nodded as if they guessed so.

"Wrong! At this time NASA was conducting tests of a thermal generator in The Bahamas. You didn't know this did you?" he asked, pleased with himself. "Ask yourselves, what was NASA doing testing a thermal generator?"

"Just what is a thermal generator?" asked Ken.

"The one they were testing floated in the Atlantic Ocean. It was a long tube. The bottom was in the cool deep water. The top was in the warm sun. The difference in temperature was used to generate electricity. The principles involved are simple. The idea has been around for centuries, but it frequently requires a technological breakthrough to transform a good idea into a working product. There are hundreds of examples."

"One would do." Laura prodded.

"You call this a 'for-instance'. Am I right?"

"Yes sir," said Ken.

"I will try." Dr. Shavinsky thought for about twenty seconds and then said "Your 'Stealth' Bomber. Did you know that shortly after the British invented radar, they began building simple wooden aircraft, called 'Mosquitos,' to avoid the radar that they knew the Germans would eventually have."

"No."

"But the Germans went further. They designed and built a sophisticated high-speed bomber that could not be detected by radar. Unfortunately for Hitler, it was too complicated to fly. It crashed. At the end of the war, American military scientists discovered the German project and also produced such an aircraft. It was called the 'Flying Wing.' It too crashed. Now, however, the same basic design is flying. It is the 'Stealth' bomber. But it doesn't crash because it has what the others did not have: computers to help fly it."

"Why didn't we ever hear about this thermogenerator?" asked Rae.

"America is such a curious country," he replied.

"Why is that?" asked Laura, hoping this would produce a response to the real question.

"If the experiments had failed, you would have heard about it. The evening newspaper would have exposed another waste of your taxpayers' Dollars. But, you see, it worked!"

"So we never heard of it," Laura found herself saying, although she was still grappling with his theory of American journalism.

Looking at the puzzled faces around him, he urged them to "Correlate heat and light."

"Bright is hot and dark is cold?" ventured Rae.

Racing even farther ahead of them in the conversation, Dr. Shavinsky asked them consider why the Americans spent so much time flying over the dark side of the Moon. He might as well have asked them to turn base metal into gold; so he offered an explanation. "The Moon has poles. The region of the Lunar South Pole is never exposed to the rays of the Sun. This is important because the sunlight raises the surface temperature to about 120 degrees."

"Centigrade?" asked Rae.

"Yes. Now what happens at 100 degrees Centigrade?"

"Water boils," Laura responded.

"Correct. So there can be no water where there is sunlight. But there is water near the Lunar South Pole at the Aitken Basin. It is frozen...with pieces of rock."

"Like a glacier?" asked Rae.

"A small glacier, although it isn't moving. We estimate there to be approximately 100,000 cubic meters of water." He wondered whether he was wasting his time, when Ken put it all together.

"The South Pole never heats up?"

Dr. Shavinsky smiled. "Correct. Continue, Mr. Mason."

"Then, if you put a thermogenerator at the edge of the area of permanent darkness, you could have power."

"Reliable water and power supplies --- on the Moon!" marveled Laura.

"Lunar infrastructure," added Rae.

Dr. Shavinsky laughed. "You must do well in Washington. Now you know why NASA was experimenting with thermogeneration. Look for the NASA records on this project and see if anything coincides with the Apollo Project. By the way, these records may be with the National Oceanographic & Atmospheric Agency, which was the agency that supplied the testing facilities in The Bahamas."

"Are you saying that NASA hoped to generate electricity on the Moon using the temperature difference between the dark and light sides?" asked Laura.

"Exactly, Mrs. MacPherson. That is it." Then he added, "They may have actually done it!"

Ken recovered first. He asked "Dr. Shavinsky, what else do you know about the Apollo program that we don't?"

"There was more to the American Moon program than the public was told. Something may have gone terribly wrong. We will talk again after I compare the book with the signals we received."

He abruptly bounded out of the water and began to walk back to his hotel, leaving them too bewildered to speak.

Rae announced she would take a swim and said she would catch up with them further up the beach. This suited Laura just fine. She herded Ken back to the shore.

/////

"Glad to see that you two are becoming such great chums," offered Ken.

"You are merely an exasperating man, Mr. Mason," replied Laura "but she could be the Bitch High Priestess."

"Don't tell her that," he cautioned. "She might be flattered."

"Look, I don't want to talk about her. What do think about what Dr. Shavinsky just told us?"

"Aside from the information overload, it looks like he believes NASA was trying to develop a Moon Base."

"Which is what Jonas said would happen."

"But what went wrong?"

They walked in silence for a moment, thinking about that.

Rae, thankfully restored to clothing, caught up with them before the conversation was resumed. She took charge even before she reached them. With a loud whisper caused by her recent sprint to catch them, she instructed "Ken, you go back to Washington today and get to work on this thermogenerator business. Call David Sinclair at NOAA. Tell him I need the file, but also get him to give you an overview...." She stopped to take some deep breaths, then finished "...in case we can't understand the damn thing."

"Uhm."

"I've got a few calls to make, but let's get something to eat first. It's still too early to call people."

Laura, who only wanted Rae to disappear by then, announced she wasn't hungry.

"Then you can have coffee," Rae replied. When it appeared Laura might refuse, Rae looked squarely into her eyes and added "Maybe you haven't figured it out yet, but you may have just committed treason, Mrs. MacPherson."

Laura was too stunned to say anything but "Please, call me Laura."

"Sure, and call me Mata Hari."

/////

They all walked down the beach to the restaurant where Ken had met Courtney. Naturally, this encounter was not mentioned. But they sat on a deck and watched the ocean while drinking their coffees. A squall line approached. Violent wind and rain passed them just off shore. They kept their thoughts to themselves until Rae spoke up.

"Laura, will the weather be nice this afternoon?"

Surprised, she responded truthfully that "You never know for sure in Florida, but yes --- I think so."

"Good! Then you and I can go to the beach together and have a long talk while I get some much-needed sun on my pale body."

"But, I..."

Rae cut her off. "Laura. You and I need to talk. Now. And not just about the Russian."

Laura looked at Ken, who only looked perplexed.

"I'll drive," said Rae, closing the deal. Then to Ken "Have a nice flight."

"Uhm. I'll call you when I get in." When both of them looked at him, he clarified this by saying to Rae "I'll call you after I've talked to Sinclair."

Both of them smiled so sweetly at him that he couldn't wait to leave.

/////

They drove North in the rented Cadillac. Rae consulted a map briefly.

"Where are we going?" inquired Laura.

"Cape Canaveral National Seashore. Ever been there?"

"I don't go to the beach much. Today was the first time in...at least six years. I guess it doesn't seem so special when you live here."

"Yeah. I haven't been to the Smithsonian since I moved to Washington. But I did go there once with my high school class."

"As in 'the Big Class Trip to the Capitol' everyone is forced to take?"

"Exactly. You, too?"

"A rite of passage in Virginia. So, where do you come from?"

"New Jersey. That suburb between Philadelphia and New York City. I come from the New York side. You know why the Capitol isn't in New York?"

"They wanted a neutral location, the way I remember it."

"They needed a place where nothing was going on; so the politicians could feel important."

"Oh. I take it you're not political."

"You can't live in Washington and not be political, but I try to keep to office politics. For instance, did you know that Ken would be my boss if he could get himself interested in politics?"

"Is that what we're going to discuss?" she asked.

"I wish it were," Rae said with conviction.

Nothing more was said until they arrived at the parking area. They locked their purses in the trunk and headed to the beach with two beach towels, a bottle of 'Hot Body Tanning Oil' and a protesting Styrofoam cooler which they carried between them. It was weighed down by ice, low-fat yoghurt, Evian and four wine coolers.

They made camp near an Australian Pine, a tall, graceful plant that is not a pine at all. In fact, as Laura explained, the Australian Pine was a contender to become the Official Florida Noxious Weed, although the Florida Holly (which was really the Brazilian Pepper) would probably edge it out. It made no more sense to Rae than it did to the natives of Florida. She was happy to be stretched out near it, listening to the breeze make a sighing sound as it passed through the pine needles (or whatever they were). Furthermore, Rae had calculated that the tree would begin to shade them at just about the right time to avoid a sunburn. This was critical because she had removed her windbreaker, exposing her nipples to the sun. "No bathing suit," she said by way of explanation. Laura shrugged. She was simply grateful Ken wasn't along.

Either from skepticism about Rae's calculations in this regard or from an abundance of caution, Laura applied sunblock to her nose, ears, neck and shoulders. Uncapping the 'Hot Body Tanning Oil,' Rae remarked "Florida really is a crazy place. It's like the last frontier in some ways. It wouldn't surprise me if they had showdowns in the streets at high noon."

"It's a bit more subtle," Laura said darkly.

"You're right. It's time to have a serious discussion." Rae took a piece of paper from a side pocket of her discarded windbreaker and handed it to Laura. "Be careful. That's my only copy." The paper was a typewritten note dated yesterday, addressed to Rae. It said:

THIS IS INFORMAL, INCONCLUSIVE AND OFF-THE-RECORD. THE SUBSTANCE I REMOVED FROM THE AMPHIBIAN PERSONALLY LAST WEEK IS EXTREMELY TOXIC, PROBABLY LETHAL TO A PERSON IN LESS THAN PERFECT HEALTH. THE TOXIC COMPONENT IS UNLIKE ANY FOUND IN THE UNITED STATES. ON A MOLECULAR LEVEL, THE AGENT APPEARS TO BE THE SECRETION OF A TYPE OF BEETLE KNOWN TO EXIST ONLY IN CENTRAL AMERICA. THE HYPOTHESIS THEN IS THAT THE FROG INGESTED SUCH A BEETLE. ACCORDING TO MY RESEARCH INTO THESE CREATURES, THIS WOULD NOT HARM THE FROG IN ANY WAY. THE QUESTION REMAINS AS TO HOW THE FROG WOULD HAVE FOUND THIS BEETLE IN FLORIDA.

THE FROG MAY BE FED, BUT DO NOT ALLOW ANYONE TO TOUCH IT. IT IS NOT KNOWN HOW LONG IT MAY SECRETE A TOXIN. I HAVE MADE SOME DISCREET INQUIRIES AMONG COLLEAGUES AND WILL ADVISE YOU OF ANY NEW INFORMATION. SINCE IT IS POSSIBLE THAT THE TOXIC AGENT WAS INTRODUCED INTENTIONALLY (WITH OR WITHOUT KNOWLEDGE OF THE CONSEQUENCES), BE EXTREMELY CAUTIOUS.

"You had someone examine the frog?" was her first confused reaction to the note. Then came the outrage. "Who gave you the right?

Does Ken know about this?" The note trembled in her hands as she spoke.

"Someone tried to hurt you or your daughter, Laura. It could be attempted murder." She let it sink in. "But, because of the way it was done, it was probably intended as a warning. And, no. Ken doesn't know about this."

She found comfort in that, although she wasn't sure why. "None of it?"

"Not the examination. Not the report, either. One of the reasons I sent him away was so I could discuss this with you alone."

"But...."

"I know you don't know me and you trust Ken, but Ken is a man. His reaction will be to protect you and your daughter. Of course, he won't have any idea how to do this; so this report will only make him and those around him miserable."

"You ever been married?"

"Never."

"You should try it. You might be good at it."

Rae smiled.

"Unless, of course, you have a thing against men. I mean...."

"I am not a lesbian, Mrs. MacPherson. I have even resisted the bi-sexual trend which is all the rage in this country according to the magazines at the check-out counters." She sighed and added "The only thing I have against men is that they are intimidated by me."

"That's not surprising," Laura observed.

"I'll take that as a compliment." Then Rae asked Laura about the role her husband had played in the Apollo Project. When she was finished with the story almost forty minutes later, they were in the shade as planned.

"And I have no idea where he was going on the day he died."

Rae opened two wine coolers and handed one to Laura. "Planters Punch," she said, reading the label aloud.

"Tastes like Hawaiian Punch."

"Tastes like crap, but it's cold. Any idea who would want to send you a warning, Laura?"

"No. At least not then. So much has happened since then, though...."

"Maybe we should assume the warning was intended to prevent what has been happening," Rae speculated.

"But if that's so; then the person who tried to warn me must have known what was going on."

"Good point. But how could he have known we would contact Dr. Shavinsky?"

"Well, I guess he couldn't," she admitted, "but he had to know there was something to be uncovered."

"Tell me about your new neighbors."

"Ken told you about that, huh? Well, it's true. I've never seen them. I don't even know if there's more than one person. There's never any lights on the side of the house facing ours, of all things. I keep my drapes and blinds on that side of the house pulled all the time now."

"You've never seen anyone?"

"The FOR SALE sign came down. I called the real estate saleslady, but all she would tell me was that I had new neighbors and she was sure they would be introducing themselves to me --- or why didn't I bake a cake and take it over to them if I wanted to meet them. Then she told me it was against the law for her to tell me their race or religion and hung up!"

Rae couldn't help but chuckle at the account. Laura joined in, saying "I never realized how ridiculous that would sound."

"Maybe you should bake that cake...." She let the thought hang in air.

"If we're going to talk about this, can we make it pie?"

"Key Lime?" Rae asked hopefully.

"If you want, but it won't taste like last night."

"What was wrong with that?"

"Too sweet; not nearly sour enough. They didn't use Key Limes."

"I thought Key Lime pie meant lime pie from the Keys."

"No. They're a distinct type of lime. Real Key Lime pie makes you pucker up. You can't help yourself."

"These coolers could use some Key Limes then," Rae observed as she finished hers without apparent difficulty. "Drink up. Let's take a swim."

Laura drained hers. When she looked back at Rae, she was

removing her shorts. "And you're not a lesbian? That's for sure, now?"

"Yes! Have you seen anybody on this beach in the last half hour?" Rae asked.

"No."

"I don't want to ride back in wet shorts. And, if I were you, I wouldn't want to ride back in a wet bathing suit. But that's your choice. Me? I'm going skinny dipping in the Atlantic Ocean. I've never done that before. Have you?"

"No. Not in the ocean."

"Well, what are you waiting for? You may never get a chance like this again!" With that, she tied her car keys around her neck and ran across the sand, wading into the late afternoon breakers.

"Well shit, Laura," she said to herself. "What are you waiting for?" She scanned the shoreline in both directions. No one was there. She walked into the surf past the sandstone rock formations that looked like so many oversized baked potatoes tossed randomly along the shore. She was naked in the ocean. It felt good.

/////

They stayed in the surf longer than they had intended. They stayed until they saw the only other vehicle in the parking area leave. Agent Koestler was driving it. He didn't smile much as a rule. He was grinning now.

When they returned to the shade of the Australian Pine, everything was gone but the ice chest and the bottles. The top of the ice chest was missing, as well. Had it not been for the ice chest they would have thought they had the wrong tree. That's why he had left it.

Then Rae noticed the shoe prints. "This is not amusing, you bastard!" she shouted in the direction of the trees.

"That's an understatement." Laura sat down on the sand and put her head in her hands, like she might cry. Rae knew she had to act fast.

"Look. This is a bitch. There's no denying it. But there's no one else on the beach...."

"That's what we thought before," Laura observed wryly.

"Well, now we're sure. This is probably a prank. I have the keys to the car. It's still there. Hopefully, our purses are still in the trunk and the tires aren't flat." She almost added "--- or missing."

"Yeah. And we can hide in the ice chest if somebody comes."

"Where did you go to school? Our Lady of Sarcasm?"

"O.K. Let's go, then. Grab the ice chest."

"What do we need that for?"

"We can't leave trash on the beach," she said as though their situation were normal. Rae decided this was a healthy sign and grabbed her end of the handle. By the time they arrived at the Cadillac without incident --- except for ice water sloshing on Laura's legs because Rae's end of the handle was higher since Rae was taller --- they were beginning to believe everything might just turn out all right. Nevertheless, their relief when the trunk opened and revealed their purses was tangible. Neither noticed that the license plate was missing.

With the doors locked, they could shield themselves. Laura's confidence was growing. Rae, on the other hand, screamed "Those bastards! No floor mats! Rental cars always have floor mats!" Then she tried to detach the carpeting in a way that wouldn't trigger a damage claim. "Glued! Do they think we're going to steal them!"

Laura left the protection of the front seat to inspect the trunk. Smiling at her resourcefulness, she emerged with the spare tire cover, which was made of the same carpet.

"All right, Girl Guide!" Then Rae added, "Got any more?"

"No, but there's one of those triangular warning signs. It's metal...."

"But it's available. Beggars can't be choosers. I'll put it up front. Got any hankies or scarves in your purse?"

"No. How about Kleenex?"

"The regular size?"

"Of course not. Extra tiny. Fits under a fingernail."

"Well, let's keep them handy."

"Look, Rae. It's going to be dark in about an hour. Let's stay here awhile. Once it's dark, we'll be fine if we sit low."

"That's easy for you to say. I've got to see over the steering wheel."

"So you cover your breasts with the spare tire cover."

"What will you use?"

"I'll scrunch."

"What a sport! Let me buy you a drink." She reached behind the seat into the Styrofoam ice chest and pulled out a wine cooler. "Is it against the law in Florida to have a drink in the front seat while naked?"

"I hope not," she said as she opened the bottle. Then she added, "I hope you have enough gas to make it to my house."

"Barely."

"I hope that was a joke."

/////

When the sky over the ocean turned from pink to lavender, they finished their coolers. Rae turned to Laura and said, "I usually don't go this far on the first date, y'know."

"Sure. All you Jersey girls say that." Then Laura added, we should probably dump the empty bottles in the trash barrel in case we get stopped."

"Get stopped? Don't say that! Don't even think it!"

Laura insisted they keep the ice chest, though. When pressed for a reason, she offered that she could put it over her head. Rae chose not to pursue that.

By the time the Cadillac entered the highway, a sense of adventure had replaced the initial feeling of dread.

"They waited for darkness," observed Agent Koestler to himself as he pulled his dark blue Oldsmobile onto the road behind them. Then he picked up his cellular telephone to report that someone was shooting firearms from a 1993 tan Cadillac Seville with no license plates that was speeding South on U.S. Highway One just North of Cocoa. He urged caution. There were times when Agent Koestler really loved his job. "God bless the United States of America!"

It took six minutes and thirty-two seconds, by his stopwatch, for the Florida Highway Patrol cruiser to fall in behind the Cadillac. Agent Koestler speculated as to whether the trooper would follow procedure and wait for backup or initiate contact immediately. He was rooting for a lapse of procedure. He'd waited long enough to teach these bitches a lesson. He was rewarded when the top lights and siren suddenly went on.

Rae adjusted the spare tire cover. Laura pulled the emergency sign up and tried various arrangements at concealment. Inexplicably, it disturbed her that the most effective position required that the sign be upside down. She felt this might be a gauge of her inability to cope with events; so she kept this thought to herself.

Rae slowed down and lowered the window. Then she made a waiving gesture to indicate that the trooper could pass her if he wanted to. This confused the trooper inside the FHP car. Agent Koestler laughed. "She's gone into denial!" he gloated.

"I don't think he's going to pass us, Rae," offered Laura with an air of resignation.

"Of course he's not going to pass us!" she shouted back. "Help me find a side road or someplace to turn off the highway!"

The trooper's amplified voice boomed through the night. "Slow down and pull over to the side! This is the Florida Highway Patrol. Pull over carefully, starting now!"

"Sideroad!Sideroad!Sideroad!" screamed Laura.

"Got it!" Amazingly, Rae put the Cadillac through a 90° right turn at forty miles per hour without rolling the car. Then she stopped in the middle of the road and just breathed.

The trooper was unprepared for this maneuver and chose to brake only, skidding past the side road by some thirty-five feet before receiving some external velocity in the form of Agent Koestler's front bumper. It wasn't enough to hurt anybody, but troopers do not gracefully accept multiple indignities inflicted upon them over a short time span. In other words, the trooper was quite upset when he missed the turn. Now he was thoroughly pissed off. And the first person he saw was Terrance Fox Koestler, trying unsuccessfully to formulate a tentative smile.

His training served him well this time. Instead of shooting Agent Koestler, he inquired whether he was injured. Agent Koestler noticed that the blood vessels on the trooper's neck were unusually prominent; so he said "My arms and neck hurt real bad, officer," hoping for sympathy.

"That's because you rammed into the back of my patrol car and interfered with justice. Now get out of your car." So much for sympathy.

As he limped from his car, he decided to try distraction. "That car you were following is still there, officer."

"What? Wait here! Don't move your vehicle!" The trooper ran to the intersection and looked down the side road. The Cadillac sat there, stationary, with the lights on. He drew his revolver. As he approached, a pair of arms appeared at each front window. "Get out of the car slowly, with your hands in the air!" He wished he hadn't forgotten his megaphone.

"Can't you come here, officer?" said a woman's voice in reply.

"You heard me. Everyone out of the car now! Hands in the air!"

Laura made a whimpering sound. Rae said, "Don't worry. I'll take care of this." Whereupon, she adjusted the spare tire cover in front of her and, hugging it for dear life, emerged with as much grace as she could muster with the knowledge that her backside was exposed. She faced the trooper and stared at him.

"Hands in the air!" he insisted again.

"Forget it!" she shouted back, even though they were only about eighteen feet apart by now. "I have nothing on under this. Our clothes were stolen at the beach."

"Why should I believe that, lady?"

"How many women have you personally met who wore spare tire covers?"

"Is that what that is? I wondered." He was beginning to believe her when he remembered the firearms.

"Where are the guns?"

"What guns? There are no guns!"

"How many more in the car?"

"Just my friend, who's really kind of shy...and very naked. Can we go now?"

"Where's your license plate? This your car?"

"Look. I don't know what happened to the damn license plate. It's a rental. I have the papers in the glove box. I'll go back to the car and get them."

"Have your friend bring them here."

"That's it! Enough's enough. I'm going back to the car and hand you the papers out the window. If you want it on your record that you shot a naked woman in the back, it's your call."

"Let not your heart be troubled. Neither let it be afraid. *John 14:27.* For God hath not given us the spirit of fear, but of power, and of love, and of a sound mind. *2nd Timothy 1:17.*"

Catching the last of this, Rae remarked, "Keep it up! Something must be working. I don't feel any bullets in my ass yet." Then it occurred to her that she had continued to hold the spare tire cover in front of her while walking back to the car. "Never mind. I think I know what worked." She made a mental note to eliminate fan dancer from her diminishing list of career choices.

Gun still drawn, the trooper warily approached the window. His left hand held the brightest flashlight in Christendom. Rae sighed deeply. Laura was still furiously reciting verses from the scriptures, the yellow emergency sign virtually embedded in her chest and a small package of Kleenex on her lap. Rae opened the glove box and shoved the rental documents out the window at the trooper, who quickly scanned the interior of the car with the beam before taking them. His demeanor changed as he read.

"Looks like we've all had a bad day. Do you think you can make it home O.K.?"

"Yeah."

"I'd give you an escort, but some bozo rear-ended me when I hit the brakes. Which reminds me, don't ever turn like that again. You could have killed yourself."

"Just trying to pull over, officer."

"That you did, lady. Drive safely."

"You don't happen to have a spare shirt or pants...."

"No. Sorry. But I do have two raincoats. I'll bring them."

The trooper returned with two official Florida Highway Patrol raincoats after a minute. Laura buttoned hers all the way up to the neck before she realized what she had done. Rae had noticed. Laura said defensively, "It felt so good to have something to button, I guess I just couldn't stop."

It took great patience to back the Cadillac slowly down the side road and exit the crash scene slowly. She wanted to floor it. But her patience permitted her to get a good look at the accident involving the patrol car. Rae had noticed a car pull in behind them when they entered the highway from the beach parking area. Since traffic had been light, it could have been this same car. Perhaps the driver had been responsible for their situation.

There was a long, dark-colored Oldsmobile with a smashed grill. The damage appeared to be cosmetic. She couldn't see the driver. He wasn't in the car. There was someone in the back seat of the patrol car, but the light was inadequate for identification.

"I owe you one," said Laura.

"Make it a large one, with lots of ice!"

Chapter Ten
Sunday, May 2, 1993

Courtney breezed into the kitchen at 7:21 A.M. the next morning. "Smells good. What is it?"

"Key Lime pie."

"For breakfast?"

"Of course not! Yoghurt, cereal or eggs for breakfast," she replied. "The pie is for the new neighbor."

"I thought you didn't like the new neighbor."

"Well, maybe I decided it was time to be neighborly."

Sensing a dose of etiquette on the way, Courtney changed the subject. "I'll get myself some cereal and juice." Then she saw the raincoats hanging next to the door. "Where did you get these?"

"From a nice highway patrolman."

"Were you in an accident or something?"

While Laura weighed what to tell her daughter, Rae stepped into the room behind Courtney unnoticed, startling her when she said "We witnessed an accident on the way home from the beach; so the trooper loaned us these to use as cover-ups."

"Rae, meet my daughter, Courtney. She usually doesn't jump quite that high in the morning. She must not have noticed you asleep in the Florida room."

"Hi!"

"Please to meet you, Courtney. I work with Mr. Mason in Washington."

"Have you been telling mom all about him?" she asked, suddenly interested.

"No," she replied, thinking it may not be a bad idea, though. "We didn't get around to that."

"What did you talk about then," said Courtney in disbelief.

"Your mother was teaching me Bible verses."

Whereupon, both women chuckled and Courtney said "O.K., don't tell me. It's none of my business anyway."

Pie in hand, at 9:45 A.M., Rae and Laura rang the neighbor's doorbell. Then they used the knocker. Then they pounded on the door. Then they twisted the doorknob.

After that they peeked in the front windows. Then they knocked at the back door and tried the doorknob there.

"Looks like no one's home. Let's forget it," suggested Laura.

"I'll check the garage for a car," said Rae, walking in that direction. She was looking for an Oldsmobile.

"This is Florida, remember? We have carports."

"Son of a bitch!"

"What?"

"It's a yellow Mustang! Nothing like the car that hit the patrol car last night."

"That means someone's probably home."

"Good point. Let's go."

Watching through the curtain, Agent Koestler congratulated himself on renting the Mustang the previous evening after the accident. He would get the Olds in for repairs today. There was no hurry, since he would have to drive the Mustang as long as he stayed next door to the widow MacPherson. He was unhappy at the prospect of driving such a high-profile vehicle, but he'd wanted it to be obvious to all that this was not the car they had seen the previous evening.

/////

Laura and Rae returned through the back yard, intending to enter the house through the Florida room. "Hold it!" Laura said, stopping cold.

"What is it?"

"See the large fur ball by the screen door?"

"Is that a big cat?"

"No. That's Snooks, our neighborhood raccoon. Anytime I have interesting garbage --- stale bread, turkey carcass, big bones --- I let her recycle them. I don't give her enough to become dependent, just to vary her diet. She probably came earlier, looking for a treat, and fell asleep."

"She's tame?"

"More like tolerant. We're allowed to live here if we make it worth her while. That's probably how she sees the relationship."

"How do you know it's her. Don't they all look alike?"

"They have different markings. And Snooks has a big scar on her right rear paw. But she's the only one that would feel safe enough to nap at our door."

"How many others are there?"

"Hard to say, but she doesn't let any others stick around too long --- unless she's physically attracted to him."

"I hate to sound like a city girl, but what about rabies?"

"Extremely rare for a person to contract rabies from a raccoon. Most people get rabies from bats. Lightning kills more people in Florida than all animals combined."

Just then the raccoon rolled on her back and stretched. The hind legs stuck straight in the air for a few moments, revealing a pink belly with six black nipples; then her hind legs twisted her ninety degrees as gravity brought them both down at once. She regained full unconsciousness immediately. Her pink tongue protruding through the side of her mouth between sharp teeth.

"Now that's the sleep of the innocent," remarked Rae. "You know, people in my part of the country shoot at raccoons because they tip over the trash cans."

"Yes. That's a capital offense in Florida too."

/////

Rae's cellular telephone rang when they returned to Laura's kitchen. It was Ken.

"I spoke with Sinclair at NOAA. Very helpful. Do you hold his marker or something?"

"Voodoo doll. Get on with it."

"He says NOAA did conduct experiments with thermogeneration back about 1969, and that they actually built what he called a 'portable working model' thermogenerator and tested it off Andros Island."

"Did it work?" asked Rae.

"He says it did, but that Congress killed the funding."

"What happened to prototype they built?"

"NOAA was ordered dismantle it and turn it over to a United Nations agency which was supposed to field test it."

"Did they?"

"He doesn't know. He said the records end with a receipt for the equipment in May, 1970. The receipt is from the U.S. Navy, which was transporting it."

Rae thought for a moment, then asked, "Do you know what agency?"

"The *Department des Illuminations Logistiques.*" He mangled the pronunciation, his tongue approaching a square knot halfway through *Illuminations*, but they got the idea. "It's French," he added redundantly. "By the way, the UN never heard of it. I checked."

"Never? Could it have a new name or have been incorporated into another agency?"

"We never heard of it either. At least, there is no reference in the GAO computer files."

"Let me see if I have this straight. We developed and built the world's first working thermogenerator and then killed the project. Then we gave this marvel to a non-existent UN agency and closed the books."

"Uhm. Actually, we turned it over to the Navy for transport to the UN," said Mason.

"That's right! We don't know that it ever reached any UN agency. The UN may not know anything about it."

"Could have had trouble delivering it to a non-existent agency," interjected Laura, who could hear Rae's end of the conversation. "Maybe it's in a Navy warehouse marked UNDELIVERABLE."

"D...I...L.; I...D...L," mumbled Rae. "Other than 'LID' I don't see any words there."

"Don't forget UN," offered Ken. "If the agency name is bogus, why should the UN part be correct?"

Rae scribbled UNLID on a pad with a pen that ran out of ink on the last letter. No one spoke.

"Oh my sweet granny's fanny! Hold onto your knickers, kids."

"What do you mean?" asked Laura.

"It's LUNDI!" Rae announced triumphantly. "And LUNDI means...."

"Monday! In French!" finished Laura.

"Which is equivalent to 'Moon Day' in French," added Rae. "The same devious bastard who coined NOMAD/Y had a hand in this too."

"Speak kindly of the departed," reminded Laura, who realized they might be talking about her husband.

"I meant 'devious bastard' in the most complimentary way."

"Sorry. I never realized it could be a compliment...until now. And you know Jonas once said to me that, no matter what happened, on a good day someone would be able to figure it out."

"On a good day?" she asked. "And did he have any personal preference as to days of the week?"

"He liked the beginning of the week. He used to say that by the end of the week you were merely re-hashing the ideas you had on Monday."

"He may have had a point."

"This has got to be more than just another suspicious coincidence," observed Ken. "By the way, would you like to know where the Navy took the thermogenerator?"

"That'd be good."

She heard papers shuffling as he consulted his notes. "It was put aboard the *USS Commanche* at Andros Island in The Bahamas on May 12, 1970. The next port of call for the *Commanche* was Port Canaveral on May 14th, where it was in port overnight before leaving for Newport News for four months in dry dock." Ken was in his glory. "I thought you might ask."

"Laura, if you don't kiss this man the next time you see him, I may have to."

"Would this fall under the heading of patriotism?" Laura asked coyly.

"Yeah. Either that or treason. That aspect is still a little murky to me."

"Uhm. So now what?"

"I'm going back to the motel. I'll call you later. In the meantime, everybody think hard and keep quiet."

"The plates are from Manatee County," announced Laura.

"What plates?" asked Rae, confused by this unorthodox commencement of a telephone conversation.

"The license plates on the neighbor's car are from Manatee County. Unless you're in Manatee County, that usually means it's a rental car."

"Florida is so full of surprises. Just when you think you're still in the United States, up pops another reminder you're in Disneyland," Rae observed.

"And Courtney says she saw a car pull into the carport once, and it was definitely not a yellow Mustang. She should know. I think she'd sell herself for a Mustang."

"Don't dwell on that thought. Not healthy for a mother. What color was the car she saw?"

"Dark and big... 'an Old Fart's car' as she so colorfully described it."

Rae suddenly remembered that Laura would be calling from the house phone, which could be tapped. "That doesn't prove anything. Don't think about yesterday anymore. It was just a prank some kids pulled on us."

"That's a switch!" retorted Laura.

"I've had time to think. Why don't you meet me for lunch; so I can tell you all of Ken's secrets?"

"Good," said Agent Koestler to himself as he listened to the conversation. "Not perfect, but good. If it's true." He regretted his impulsive behavior of the previous day, following along to watch the fun. Especially following too close, to be exact. He decided the assignment was getting on his nerves. All he knew was that these people were a dangerous combination. Their meeting with the Russian scientist was an ominous event, but it could have been completely innocent for all he knew.

/////

"But I really wanted something sporty. Don't you have a

Camaro or Mustang or something?" Rae inquired of the fifth car rental agency she had called. "You did? Just last night? Oh, don't tell me it was red. That would kill me! Red's my favorite color," she added, hamming it up. "Oh, it wasn't? Did you say 'mustard?' Is that like Dijon?" she asked, putting him on. "No? It's like Plochmann's you say. Well, O.K. Thanks, anyway." As she folded up her cellular phone, she added to herself "Plochmann's?"

Then called Ken, again using her cellular phone and trying not to think about the dreaded roaming charges that would appear on her next bill. She gave him an abbreviated version of the events of the previous afternoon, omitting all references to the loss of their clothing, and adding the part about the rented Mustang. She concluded with "Ken, the three of us are up to our eyeballs in something we don't understand. How did this all start?"

He considered the question, then said "Uhm. I guess it was when I saw that those Marines had all left the program the same day, but that was explained later."

"But you didn't believe the explanation."

"Not exactly. I mean, I didn't think it was a lie at the time. I just never...."

"You didn't buy it?"

"Something like that. Like when you're told something and it fits, you believe it. The explanation just didn't quite fit my image of the way things work."

"So then you met the attractive widow MacPherson?"

"Uhm, yes."

"Any chance this was arranged? Just how did you meet her?"

"It's kind of a long story, but suffice it to say that I met her daughter, Courtney, who needed a ride home from some bar on the beach where her date had deserted her. If that was an arrangement to introduce me to her mother, it was damned devious."

"We've got devious to spare here," she observed wryly.

"No. It just couldn't have been a setup. I was halfway out of the driveway before Laura showed up," he exaggerated.

"And threw herself across the hood?"

"We're getting sidetracked here," Ken protested. "Meeting Courtney and her mother was pure coincidence. Take comfort that we have a known truth here to build upon. At that time I had no thoughts that the Moon program was anything except what I'd been led to believe."

"Then Laura told you about her husband and his plans for a Moon Base?"

"And his accidental death in a place where he wasn't supposed to be, don't forget," he reminded her. "And all the other dead scientists in his department, too. But even all that was just some more things that didn't fit right."

"So?"

"Then you had to come along and tell me NOMAD/Y was an acronym for MONDAY."

"Then you went to the grave and saw the marker with the hidden phrase FATHER OF THE MONDAY PROJECT, which supported Laura's story. But Laura sent you there. She probably knew it was there all the time."

"She told me to take a screwdriver," he recalled. "It was a setup."

"Why would she set you up?"

"I had the feeling she was fed up with not being believed."

"Makes sense. Is that all? I mean this was a pivotal event."

"I think that's all. But, even though I was stunned by that, I didn't have any theory or concept in mind then. I was sort of fumbling in the darkness, I guess."

"What was it that got you involved? The charms of the widow MacPherson?"

"I see what you're driving at, but what got me...focused...was the videotape with the 'X' on the arm patch. And Laura had no part of that."

"Good." Then she added, "When did you reach the Point of No Return, then?"

He hesitated. "I've reached it?"

"We've all reached it."

"I see. Well, it was probably when I accessed the secret Moon transmissions using the password NOMADY."

"That was probably what hooked me," she confessed. "Then I had to come down and meet your widow, to see if she was for real."

"And....."

"She's the genuine article, all right. Right off the bat she walks up to a Russian space scientist and hands him a book she doesn't understand --- and I'm not just referring to the language."

"It got his attention."

"That it did. And somewhere along the line we got someone else's attention. The kind we could probably do without."

"You mean the neighbor?"

"At least the neighbor. Who knows who else. When did this start?"

"He moved in after my first trip down there. But until yesterday, there was nothing definite."

"I wasn't going to tell you, but it's time you knew. The exotic frog wasn't eating its usual diet when it made Courtney sick."

"I thought she was going to die."

"She could have. I had an analysis done...off the record, very discreetly. You can't accurately predict the amount of toxin a person will absorb by touching a frog that has been eating exotic insects. Whoever changed the frog's diet must have known this."

"Which means he didn't care one way or the other," concluded Ken sadly. "You think that's the neighbor?"

"Could be. No proof."

"Hell, we don't even know how many neighbors there are."

"We're the government. We can find out anything," she reminded him.

"By gum, that's right!"

"Don't ever say 'By gum' again. Same goes for 'By cracky.'"

He ignored this. "Be careful. I'll see what I can find out."

/////

Rae and Laura were both eating what passed for *crepes* at the Cocoa Beach Pier. They were drinking French Colombard --- undoubtedly Gallo, but dependable in contrast to diverse and unpredictable nature of the Chardonnay found in abundance these days.

"I have to go back to Washington." Laura looked lonely already.

"I can't just stay here for no apparent reason. And my presence probably draws attention to you from your neighbors. But we're not abandoning you. We have some research to do; some things to look into."

"I understand that. I'll be O.K."

"I know you will. I've got to be honest with you though. I don't know that we'll ever be able to find out what actually happened with your husband or the Moon Base Project. But, we'll keep trying."

"What about Dr. Shavinsky?"

"He's our best hope right now, but who knows what he can tell us. Who knows what he will tell us. If he tries to contact you, let me know. I've written down my cell phone number. Memorize it and destroy it. Burn it. I've been shopping. Here's one for you too. There are several batteries; so you can leave it on all the time. Snap the used battery in the charger; it will recharge in four hours."

Laura took the phone from her. It weighed less than a pound. "It's certainly compact."

"That's so you can keep it hidden. You don't want the neighbor to see it. Hide the charger and spare batteries as well. If he doesn't know about it, he won't be figuring out a way to listen in. So, use it only when you're on the road. Most importantly, use it only to call me or Ken. I have one for him too. I'll have to give you his number later. Use your home telephone for everything else, including casual calls to me or Ken. It's a safe assumption that your home telephone line is tapped. The house is probably bugged too."

"I've been adjusting to that possibility."

"Get used to it fast, Laura. It's better to be safe than sorry."

"Paranoia is healthy?"

"Up to a point."

"I didn't think you brought me here to talk about Ken."

"*Au contraire, madame!* Now we discuss Ken."

Laura flushed. "I didn't mean to sound disappointed...."

"Strictly business." Rae cut her off. "Since we are both avowed non-Lesbians, contact between you and Ken would appear more natural."

Laura's eyes widened, wondering what she was going to propose.

"You can lose that Southern Belle, oh-my-gracious look any time now."

"Sorry. It was instinctive."

"I'm sure it's served you well on many occasions. But I'm not proposing anything scandalous; so don't get your hopes up."

"Sigh."

"That's better." She ordered them each another skimpy glass of wine. "Ken is shy...for lack of a better word. He got married too young and carries around this sense of inadequacy, which may have been there before the marriage. I didn't meet him until he was getting divorced. It wasn't messy. They didn't have any children. Not much else either. Her name was Cindi --- with an 'i.' She attracted a typical Washington type --- lobbyist, I think --- who showed her the high life."

"Highbinder."

"Haven't heard that term for a while, but you've captured the essence. Anyway, she was too young to appreciate dependable. She opted for flashy." Rae shrugged. "He was fool enough to ask why she didn't love him anymore. She told him she was still in love; she just wasn't in like anymore."

"Sounds like a bad country song."

"Doesn't it? Anyway, he was crushed. Happens every day."

"A man is hurt not so much by what happens, as by his opinion of what happens."

"That's a good one. What chapter and verse?"

"It's Montaigne. I studied philosophy in college."

"Then you're not a religious zealot?"

"I hadn't thought of myself as one. Wisdom is where you find it. The Bible brims with it."

"How did you reconcile your religious beliefs with the scientific life you lead?"

"I never saw a conflict. God gave us reason and encouraged us to use it. You need look no further than the Parable of the Talents. Faith was given to us to complement reason, to give us answers unavailable through reasoning alone."

"Faith in God?"

"Faith in anything. Everyone has beliefs which can't be proven. They aren't confined to religion. How many people believe the Great

Pyramid of Cheops was constructed by aliens?"

"You're not saying its as good to believe in UFO's as it is to believe in God, though."

"No, but I reserve the right to change my mind if the aliens come up with something comparable to the Gospel."

"Ah yes, the gospel according to Zrak." The wine arrived and they each took a sip. Then Rae continued "O.K. So reason and faith are not mutually exclusive. I'll have to let that concept sink in. I take it that you don't subscribe to the Theory of Evolution."

"I think Darwin got it right with survival of the fittest, which came to be called Natural Selection. When someone comes up with one good idea, people listen to anything that follows."

"So you're sticking with faith on evolution?"

"Since the Theory of Evolution has never been proven, it is an act of faith to believe in it. 'To believe that the diverse life on this planet was created through Darwin's mechanisms is like believing that a hurricane blowing through a junkyard will build a Boeing 747,' according to Frederick Hoyle, the British Astronomer."

"That might have stopped old Clarence Darrow cold. But let's get back to Ken. I'm less likely to get a headache. In response to the situation with Cindi, he affected this aimlessness...the attitude that nothing can bother him if he doesn't care."

"But you're saying he affects it?"

"I've always thought so. But I've become convinced lately. He's certainly become involved in this matter. At first, I thought it might just be you...."

"Just me.... But?"

"That didn't come out right. It is you. You're a key ingredient, anyway."

"O.K. Understood."

"That's why I'm talking to you. If you want to keep contact with us without arousing suspicion, you'll have to pretend to be romantically involved with Ken. You will have to make it happen. He would never initiate it. Is that too much of a stretch?"

"Have you ever slept with him?"

"Wow! You are full of surprises today. And, no. Definitely and emphatically no!"

"Why emphatically?"

"It just never occurred to me. First of all we work together; so it's strictly *verboten*. Agency rules, as well as my own. But mainly, the chemistry isn't there. Maybe we're too different."

"Maybe you're too much alike."

"Now there's a cheerful thought. I'll have to think about that sometime --- like when I'm on a flaming airplane at 35,000 feet. But the bottom line is still the same. No chemistry."

"And you think there might be chemistry between Ken and me?"

"I don't know about you, but Ken is fairly a-bubble with chemicals when you're around. So be gentle."

"Boil and bubble, toil and trouble."

"MacBeth."

"Welcome to McDonalds, my name is MacBeth, can I take your order?" Laura giggled.

"No thanks, I just stopped in for a McWhiz," Rae rejoined.

"Have it your way."

Chapter Eleven

Tuesday, May 4, 1993

"761 kilograms," said Ken cryptically as he came into Rae's office. That's about 1,674 pounds."

"I knew I shouldn't have eaten all that damn lobster. Did it go to my hips?"

"Uhm. Maybe I should start over."

"Good morning. How are you? Those would be nice," she said with mock wistfulness. "A single white rose. A cappuccino with cinnamon sprinkled delicately across the foam. That would be very nice." She sighed and gazed at him. "But, of course, your affections have been stolen away by the attractive widow MacPherson."

"You are having trouble getting back into the swing of things, aren't you?"

"I just forsook the balmy breezes for this!" They both gazed silently at the rain that had been falling all morning. She motioned him over to the window, standing next to him. "O.K. So what weighs 761 kilograms?" she whispered.

"The thermogenerator," he whispered back.

"The thermogenerator?"

"The one that NOAA built for NASA. It had two main pieces connected by a flexible cable or pipe."

"Don't toy with me. Would it fit on an Apollo spacecraft?"

"Yes."

"Payload?"

"Within the parameters. They wouldn't be able to carry much else but the crew and life support."

"Another piece that fits." By way of explanation, she added "Sometimes I feel like we're trying to assemble a jigsaw puzzle with random pieces we've found here and there."

"Isn't it a little late to have second thoughts? We've already attracted unwanted attention."

"That's a good reason to have second thoughts," she advised. "However, it reinforces my belief that we're on to something. The question is why are we doing this?"

"It's our job to look into government projects."

"But it appears that the government doesn't want us to look into this one."

"Well, I'll concede that someone who is probably working for the government doesn't want us to investigate. I sure would like to know who that is, by the way. But I still maintain that this investigation falls within the purview of my specific assignment to find out the cost of an Apollo Mission. The instructions were to eliminate non-essential costs. If a thermogenerator was taken to the Moon, that's a non-essential cost in my book."

"We've both been in Washington too long."

"You disagree?"

"No. I agree. That's what worries me. It's a classic example of bureaucratic rationalization."

"Thank you."

"It wasn't a compliment. By the way, I asked a friend who's doing research on a telescope to take a good look around the South Lunar Pole. He said he would." She walked back to her desk and said in a normal voice "Enough commiserating about the weather. Are you done with that NASA report yet?" She gave an exaggerated nod so he'd know the answer she wanted.

He took the hint, but added a twist. "It's in the word processor already. I doubt that I'll have to spend the taxpayers' money for another trip...."

"But you're willing to do so if Laura MacPherson encourages you." The trouble with being under surveillance, she reflected, was that you had to be acting all the time, because you never knew what was being heard or recorded.

"I'm hurt!" He feigned despair for a moment.

"The truth hurts. Now get out of here. I want that report on my desk by the end of the week."

/////

What in the world was a copy of *Izvestia* doing in his inter-office communications envelope? He flipped through the pages, looking for a note or an underlined passage. He found neither, but on the sixth page he found a sketch by a person as artistically challenged as he was. It was a scorpion.

No, wait. The claws were too big.

He went straight to Rae's office. "I think we've heard from Dr. Shavinsky," he said, putting the newspaper in front of her.

"This is Cyrillic!"

"The lobster isn't," he noted.

"You think this is from Shavinsky?"

"I've gone through the list of everyone I know in Russia...."

"O.K. Point taken."

"That looks like his name, if you don't count the occasional backward or Greek-looking letter."

"Nice of them to capitalize it."

"Uhm. Yes, that was my second clue --- after the crustacean in the margin."

"Let's see what else we can glean. I'd like to have some idea what it says before I ask someone to translate it. He might have to be shot for treason for talking to us."

"I didn't see any word that looked like *kaput*, if that's any help."

"There's a word that looks like 'México' with a backward 'K' and a date. There are other names, too."

"Doesn't sound like a purge announcement," observed Ken.

"Sounds like a trip. I'll get Natalie to translate it."

"Don't mention my name."

"Why not?"

"If they lock you up, I can bring you doughnuts."

"Thanks!"

/////

"Go on, lover boy. You can do it." Rae goaded him to make the call.

He called on the regular (presumably tapped) telephone. He was sitting on the corner of Rae's desk. Rae was seated behind the desk, listening on the speaker phone. "Uhm. Laura?"

"Yes, Ken."

"Well --- uhm --- I've kind of missed you since I've been back...."

"Why Mr. Mason, if you go on like that, you'll put all sorts of crazy notions in my head," she teased. "How you do carry on!"

Rae's hands flew across her mouth to stifle the laughter. She seemed to be sliding out of her chair. No sir, this wasn't going to be easy, but he plowed ahead.

"If it's all right with you, I thought I might come down for a visit some weekend, since my NASA assignment is over." Hopefully, he added "We could go to the beach, have some lobster, relax."

"Hero's welcome?" she suggested. Rae shot him a questioning look, which he ignored.

"Uhm. Maybe...but without the uhm, uhm.... You know the part about the --- uhm --- generals," he finished in desperation. But it wasn't over.

"Now, I don't want to hear any talk about you leaving your generals in Washington. Two star, aren't they?"

Rae was nearing convulsions. He tried to remain calm, even though clearly not in charge.

"Two. Uhm. Two stars, indeed."

"Do they like lobster?" she asked as innocently as she could.

"They're not big eaters," he said dryly. It was the first thing that popped into his mind. He regretted it instantly.

"You bring them on down here and we'll work them up an appetite."

He gave up. "See you on Friday, then." He hung up and peered over the desk. Rae was sitting on the floor, laughing and wiping tears from her eyes. "Was that good for you, too?" he asked, rhetorically.

"Oh yes! Oh my yes!"

PART III: CONFIRMATION

Chapter Twelve
Saturday, May 8, 1993

Rae drove Ken to BWI airport on the pretext it was more or less on the way to her mother's, whom she was going to visit for Mother's Day. After dropping him off, she drove straight to the Philadelphia airport. She boarded US Air Flight 1607, a non-stop to Cancún. No one knew she was doing this --- she hoped.

Immigration was efficient. Customs turned out to be a matter of pressing a large button and walking right on through when a green light was illuminated. But it took almost a half hour to complete the process of obtaining the rental car, even though she had reserved it in advance. "These reservations they make for you, they don't tell us." She took the full insurance after reading a *New Orleans Times-Picayune* article taped to the counter which told of an American who spent four days in jail before the credit card company convinced the police that his card provided adequate insurance for the accident he had caused.

But soon she had instructions --- maps seemed to be unavailable --- and her Nissan Tsuru complete with a "yak" which she believed to be a reference to the jack. As instructed, she drove South from the *aeropuerto* to the big sign that said CUOTA - MERIDA and turned West. She was on the *autopista*, a four-lane divided highway through the jungle, which the natives can't afford to use --- even the few who have cars. She encountered almost no other vehicles. The first Pemex service plaza she passed was abandoned. Every few miles there would be piles of limestone boulders in the large center median which someone had spray-painted in various shades --- lime, yellow, purple, pink --- for no discernable reason. The word surreal came to mind more than once during her journey. One hour and nearly 200 *Pesos* later she left the toll road at Piste. As she drove East about a mile out of town, she saw the top of a limestone temple rising above the jungle. She had arrived at *Chichen Itzá.*

She had been assured that, although a French scientist might prefer the *Villa Arqueológica* hotel run by Club Med for the Mexican government, any other prominent person would stay at the Mayaland Hotel. That was where she headed.

She and her sparse luggage were taken by an electric cart, the type with the annoying beeps found in airports transporting the lame and halt, to a Mayan-style hut, complete with thatched roof. This was referred to by the staff as a "bungalow." It even had a Mayan name, *Dzibichaltún*, which might be pronounceable after ingesting enough tequila, she reflected. Happily, it differed from the local Mayan huts she had seen on the way in several key respects. It had a bed instead of a hammock. It had air conditioning. It had bottled water. Best of all, it had real plumbing. Maybe. It certainly looked like real plumbing; however, the sign next to the toilet paper roll ominously advised not to put paper or anything else in the *inodoro*, which clearly referred to the toilet. The word itself sounded like an attempt to say "indoors" in Spanish, which made her wonder at its origin. At least she wouldn't forget it.

It was nearly 5:00 P.M. when she emerged from her hut, freshly showered and dressed for the tropics. As she walked down the concrete path toward the main building, she returned the gaze of a large iguana catching the last of the afternoon sun. It was only when she wondered if they tasted like chicken --- as guides always tell tourists, it being a perverse ritual --- that she realized she was hungry. At that time she reached the shady stone patio, where drinks and snacks were being served. She picked a spot where she could see both the front door and the entrance to the dining room. With the help of a smiling waiter named Rosario, she ordered a *Dos Equis Lager*, which was exactly what she needed.

The local Mexicans, who were indeed Mayans, tended to be short. The Americans tended to be slovenly. The few Germans tended to be constantly shouting at each other. The ubiquitous French frequented another hotel altogether. So, spotting the Russian scientists was a simple task. The question was what to do next. Dr. Shavinsky and another gentlemen were heading toward the front door. She quickly produced what she hoped was an adequate amount of colorful *Peso Nuevo* notes, which she left on the table, and fell in behind them.

The front door was actually an arched entrance about twenty

feet high. Framed by it was the ancient round Mayan observatory, the *Caracol*, its limestone now blazing orange in the setting sun. She was not the first person to miss the top step outside the door at that time of day. Fortunately, the steps were wide enough that she did not tumble down all of them. Unfortunately, her skirt was around her neck when she came to rest. Or maybe this was fortunate, because her presence could not be overlooked. Dr. Shavinsky was at her side when she managed to look up. "You move fast for your age," she commented.

"And you move unpredictably," he observed. "First you are in Florida, and now you are here --- turning wagon wheels."

"It's cartwheels. And yes, I'm fine, thank you. I'd love a drink."

Shavinsky was all smiles. "Dr. Ivan Konosov of St. Petersburg, please meet Miss Kirkland of Washington. She will be joining us for dinner."

Dr. Konosov was significantly younger than Dr. Shavinsky. He was also tall and lean. With an accent that sounded more French than Russian, he announced that he was "honored to make your acquaintance, or as they say in México, *¡mucho gusto!*"

"*¡Mucho gusto!* yourself Doctor," she replied amicably as she arranged her skirt and allowed them to help her to her feet. "You speak Spanish?"

Dr. Shavinsky answered. "Do not ask him what languages he speaks. We will starve before he finishes, which reminds me of what we used to say in the old days. 'We were starving in Russia. Soviet!'" He pronounced the last word as "so, vee et" so no one could miss the joke.

"It was a lucky day for the cabaret when my colleague decided to become a scientist," said Dr. Konosov unexpectedly. Rae nodded her solemn agreement, then winked at Shavinsky.

Led by Dr. Konosov, the three of them strolled down the road to a small hotel called the *Hacienda Chichen*. He explained that the Mayaland was indisputably the best hotel in the area, but that the *Hacienda Chichen* was where the first archaeologists who worked at *Chichen Itzá* had lived. It had been a plantation before anyone came to visit *Chichen Itzá*.

"You're an archeologist?"

"Not exactly. I'm a professor of languages."

Rae looked perplexed; so Shavinsky explained. "Dr. Konosov was the first person to translate the Mayan hieroglyphic language. He is too modest. There is a meeting of his colleagues here."

"They come from *Copan, Tikal, Uxmal, Palenque*...like in the old times," observed Dr. Konosov. "And now Russia."

"When the Mayan hieroglyphics were translated, Dr. Konosov was unable to raise the 25,000.00 United States Dollars demanded by a government official for the exit visa; so he missed the party they had to celibate."

"It was a conference," Dr. Konosov corrected. "And the word is celebrate. Celibate means you don't have sex."

"Then I wouldn't have come either," said Dr. Shavinsky, intentionally missing the point. Rae and Ivan exchanged meaningful shrugs. When Dr. Shavinsky bounded up the front steps ahead of them, Dr. Konosov said to her quietly "I have tried to explain to him that intentionally mispronouncing a foreign word as a conversational gambit is linguistic deceit, but...."

"You mean...?"

He raised his first finger to his lips and nodded.

They entered the *Hacienda Chichen* through a room that spread out thirty feet on each side of them and a like amount above, but which was only about twelve feet across. Then they were outside, on a tiled veranda with tables and chairs, fresh flowers on the tables, overlooking a tropical garden. It was elaborate yet simple. A small fountain bubbled. Spot lights illuminated the Royal Palms. Rae immediately felt that she could live there --- provided the *inodoros* worked.

"*¿Bix a bel?*" Dr. Konosov greeted the Mayan waiter, dressed in white pants and white *guayabara*.

"*Malob. ¿Cus tek?*"

"*Malob Xan,*" said the Doctor, completing the exchange. Then he ordered them all *Dos Equis* beers, explaining that "The ice is safe here, but the *Margaritas* are harsh."

"That wasn't Spanish, was it?" she said. It was not a question.

"It was Mayan! That was how he did it!" Dr. Shavinsky was enthusiastic. "The others ignored the Mayan language when they tried to decipher the hieroglyphs. Ivan learned the language and the culture. He learned how they thought!"[5]

Dr. Konosov said to her "I would learn how to swim before I would study fish. It is as simple as that."

"My friend is brilliant!" insisted Dr. Shavinsky. "That is why I brought him with me," he added unexpectedly as the beers arrived.

"This is news. I thought I brought you."

"That is why I too am brilliant, my friend," Shavinsky said with a laugh, which proved contagious. "Take a drink of this fine cold beer, which will soon warm in the jungle, and I will explain. You see, in the old Soviet Union, most professors had a second occupation. Mine was obvious. I soon had no more time for teaching. But you, Miss Kirkland, are a smart biscuit, as they say; so you tell me what a professor of languages might do."

"Translations...for espionage?"

"And...." he prodded.

"And....Codes!"

"Bongo! This is what you say, right?"

"Bingo."

"I have given Dr. Konosov the book which Mrs. MacPherson brought to me. I have also given him a copy --- a most unofficial copy --- of records we have of some mysterious transmissions which originated from the Moon. But first I must ask you, did you inquire about the thermogenerator?"

She looked around. It was early yet. The veranda was empty but for them. She took the plunge. "It exists...or existed. It went to

---

5

There are many aspects of this story which require the acceptance of unusual events. One of these is that a Russian somehow decoded the Mayan hieroglyphs during the period of the Cold War. In fact, Dr. Yuri V. Knorosov of Leningrad did play a key role in translating them, along with Tatiana Proskouriakoff, David Stuart, Linda Schele and others. His role and method were not as described in the story; however, the part about the bribe did happen and was too good to leave out of the story. See *Breaking the Maya Code* by Michael D. Coe for the full account of this accomplishment.

Port Canaveral. We don't know if it ever made it to the Kennedy Space Center."

"What do you think?" he asked.

"I'm an auditor, Dr. Shavinsky. I don't speculate."

"Indulge us, please," said Dr. Konosov unexpectedly.

"The records indicate it was to be turned over to a United Nations agency called the *Department des Illuminations Logistiques.* Ever hear of it?"

"No."

"No one else has either," she stated. "But the initials of the name are an acronym for LUNDI. A coincidence?"

"What is a loondie?" asked Dr. Shavinsky.

"*Lundi* is the French word for Monday," advised Dr. Konosov. "Probably not a coincidence. Please continue."

"It went to Port Canaveral. It hasn't been recorded any place else. It was small enough to fit in an Apollo spaceship. That's probably what happened to it."

"*Gracias,*" said Dr. Konosov, who appeared to have difficulty confining himself to a single language for very long.

"About the book...," reminded Rae.

"It is the key to the code of these transmissions we have received!" exclaimed Dr. Konosov. "Tomorrow morning at 8:30 A.M. we are riding horses to the remains of the original Mayan settlement, called *Chichen Viejo --- viejo* meaning 'old' in Spanish. It is South of *Chichen Itzá.* When we return to the hotel after dinner, I will arrange for a horse for you. We will discuss this matter fully at *Chichen Viejo.* It is necessary that this be discussed where no one could overhear us."

She reluctantly accepted his conditions. After all, she reasoned, he could refuse to tell her anything. And she realized that she had already told them what they wanted to know. "Scratch spy from the list of potential careers --- along with fan dancer," she said to herself.

The *pollo pibil* --- chicken covered in sauces, wrapped in a banana leaf and then baked --- restored her. She couldn't have found two more entertaining companions, she admitted. As they strolled back to the hotel, she was amazed at the number of stars and the blackness of the sky around them. She asked if the latitude made it possible to see more stars.

"No," answered Dr. Shavinsky. "It is the jungle. No pollution. No artificial lights. It is like this in Siberia, but not nearly so warm."

The mention of Siberia forcefully reminded her that she was sharing American secrets --- very possibly military secrets --- with two employees of the "Evil Empire." This thought undoubtedly contributed to the fact that she joined them in having a *Margarita Grande sin sal* (Large *Margarita* without salt) on the patio of the Mayaland Hotel. Dr. Konosov explained that the salt was superfluous when smooth tequila was used or it was mixed with *Triple Sec*, as in a *Margarita*. On another occasion, he promised, he would provide some excellent tequila for her to try *solo* --- by itself.

"Would that be the dark tequila?" she asked.

He sighed. "It is not so simple. In an attempt to introduce tequila to North Americans, caramel was added to some brands; so it would look more like whiskey. But --- aside from these impostors --- the best tequila has been actually aged in oak casks, which imparts a tan color to it. In addition, the best tequila is made from the Blue Weber variety of Maguay plant, found mostly in the State of Jalisco." He went on to explain that the tradition of putting *gusanos* --- little caterpillars, most assuredly not worms --- into bottles arose to combat counterfeiting. A beverage that resembled tequila could be made from grain, but the caterpillars could only be found living in the Maguay plant. "Primitive, but effective," he concluded.

"I'm impressed," admitted Rae.

"That he knows so much about tequila?" asked Dr. Shavinsky.

"No. That he knows the word for caterpillar in at least three languages. I drink to you, Dr. Konosov."

"*¡Salud!*" Dr. Konosov said, to no one's surprise.

"I have a tequila drink even you never heard of, Ivan," said Dr. Shavinsky. "If you can tell me the ingredients, I will pay for our drinks. If not, you must pay. Do you accept this challenge?"

"Of course. What is the name of this cocktail?"

"A Mayan Temple!" he announced triumphantly.

Dr. Konosov thought briefly, then conceded. "What is in it?"

"Tequila and limestone!"

"*Naturalmente.*"

They had missed the native dancing show, which was reported to have featured several generations of Mayans in native costume dancing with trays of beer bottles on their heads. She decided she would reserve judgment until she saw the show herself another night. For the present, the entertainment was a group of *mariachis* possessing the basic qualifications and a repertoire sufficient for foreigners. But it had rained that afternoon, which meant that every time they began to play, hundreds of frogs would commence croaking as if part of the troupe. When the music stopped; so would the frogs --- all at once. This delighted Dr. Shavinsky beyond comprehension.

By 9:00 P.M., the patio was nearly empty. Dr. Konosov explained to them. "Night life is a relative term in the Yucatán jungle. Everyone wants to get to the ruins early before the intense heat and the day-trippers from Cancún arrive together in a synchronized daily ritual. Only the French at the *Villa Arqueológica* --- just down the road past the *Hacienda Chichen* --- stay up later, eating *haute cuisine* and drinking wine; yet you can see them jogging up the road to the entrance at 8:00 A.M. Perhaps it's the wine," he speculated. "*Vive la France!*"

By way of farewell, Dr. Shavinsky said "Tomorrow my friend Ivan will tell you things that will knock off your nylons!"

"Socks," she said automatically before realizing she'd been had again.

"*Do svedanya.*"

"*Dos Equis.*"

Chapter Thirteen
Sunday, Mother's Day, May 9, 1993

The morning horseback ride through the jungle was hot and uncomfortable, yet somehow glorious. Rae knew she would never forget it. Conversation was limited by the narrow path which required single file. The fact that one was always ducking to avoid branches further discouraged discussion. It was nearly 9:30 when they all dismounted at the remains of the stone gateway into *Chichen Viejo*. A broad path went straight toward a large overgrown building. To the right and left were smaller ruins. The sky was clear blue, dotted with clouds that were bright white. The fern-like leaves of the giant *flamboyante* trees were ablaze with brilliant orange blossoms. It was peaceful and strangely welcoming. In Mayan, Dr. Konosov instructed the guide to stay with the horses in the shade, which the short brown man was clearly delighted to do. Enigmatically, Dr. Konosov produced a portable umbrella from a saddlebag, which he brought with him. The three of them then strode South along the main thorofare of *Chichen Viejo* toward *el Templo de los Falos*, which Dr. Konosov pointed out to be named for the numerous stone *falos* --- phalli --- that protruded from the walls. "These were fertility symbols," explained Dr. Konosov.

"Sure," muttered Rae, to the amusement of Dr. Shavinsky.

They went through the temple and emerged in a small courtyard populated by sunning iguanas which regarded their passage warily. They sat on a log facing two life-size limestone statues of Mayan warriors in full battle regalia, including --- Rae noted --- flaps to protect their *falos*. An hour before, she would have never guessed that she would learn how to say penis in Spanish. And the day was just getting started.

"I have decided not to engulf you with data," Dr. Konosov began. "I will give you an overview, like I gave Dr. Shavinsky."

"Sounds good to me. Please proceed." She would want all the data later, of course.

"We knew that the Americans had placed something in the South Lunar Pole region in 1970. We knew because it communicated.

We received the signals, but we couldn't decode them."

"We were extremely interested because the transmissions were not regular," interrupted Dr. Shavinsky.

"What do you mean?" Rae asked.

Dr. Konosov continued. "Machines in remote places tend to communicate either continuously or at precisely set intervals. When they do communicate, there is a continuous data stream, usually of compressed data. This saves batteries. Sometimes there is a prompt from Earth, but the communication is mostly to the Earth."

Unable to contain his enthusiasm, Dr. Shavinsky said "But these were more like telephone conversations between two persons!"

"Dmitri is right. The communication pattern --- which is something we examine first when we seek to decode messages --- was of ordinary human speech. I was certain these were communications between people. It was only when Dmitri told me one end of the conversation was on the Moon that I had any doubts."

"So you intercepted messages from the South Lunar Pole to NASA and believed them to be originated by humans?"

"Yes." They both answered.

"And now?"

"There is no doubt. They are human. We have read them."

"With the help of Dr. MacPherson's little communist propaganda book," added Dr. Shavinsky with a wry smile.

"Yes. The book was the key. Without telling you any state secrets, I can divulge that we have a computer program to assist in the identification of sources of code. It is the logical extension of the procedures established by the British code-breakers during World War II. But --- until very recently --- *La Fábula del Tiburón y las Sardinas* was not in the data base. Not only did Dr. MacPherson devise his own code, avoiding the advice of experts who all tend to think similarly, but his choice of the book to base it on was brilliant. I am sorry I can not meet him."

"So what did they say?" asked Rae, hoping to pick up the pace.

"I have written down four names. If you can tell me one of them, I will tell you all I can."

She stared straight into his eyes and said "Abby Lane."

Dr. Shavinsky looked troubled. Surely that was not one of the names. But Dr. Konosov was grinning at Rae. "She tests me back, Dmitri," he said approvingly. "Abby Lane was a singer with a mambo band 30 years ago. Do you remember the band leader?"

Dr. Shavinsky thought for a moment and then ventured "Catgut?"

His companions both began to laugh. They would never know if that mistake was intentional. Recovering first, Dr. Konosov said "Cugat! Xavier Cugat!"

"Ah, yes. Dr. Castro didn't like the mambo. Once this was known, you heard it everywhere in Cuba." He swayed slightly to indicate that he had once been a formidable mambo dancer.

"O.K. Miss Kirkland, you have passed my humble little test and given us amusement in the process. Kindly tell me what you know about Mr. Cugat."

"Nice try, my devious linguist."

Dr. Konosov shrugged. "One does what one can to protect the secrets of Mother Russia."

"Carlos Xavier was one of four United States Marines who left the Astronaut program on the same day in 1969. None was ever heard from again. The official story is that they were reassigned to the Marine Corps."

"Where were they sent?"

She looked at Dr. Shavinsky and said "I believe that to be an American military secret. Do you need to know?"

"We won't know until you answer, but neither of us cares about the war you Americans lost in Indochina."

She believed him. She didn't care much about it herself anymore. "They were supposedly all assigned to a secret base in Southeast Asia. I don't know the country."

They didn't say anything; so she continued.

"The name of the base was NOMAD/Y. Our contact at the Marines couldn't find it on any maps."

"He was looking at the wrong maps," said Dr. Konosov unexpectedly. "NOMAD/Y is an acronym for MONDAY."

"So?" asked Rae as calmly as she could, thankful that her pulse wasn't visible. She could get to like this guy.

"'THIS IS MONDAY' is the phrase used to identify

transmissions from the Lunar South Pole," explained Dr. Konosov.

She was trying to appear that this was no surprise and remember how to breathe at the same time. The combined effort proved too much for her. She slid backwards off the log.

Dr. Shavinsky looked down at her and said "Wait till you hear the good part!" Then the two men assisted her back upon the log. "Maybe you should not tell her all at once," he suggested to Dr. Konosov.

"Don't listen to him!" she protested. "He's a deranged person who's trying to commit assisted suicide."

"Very well. If you have secured yourself adequately upon this precarious perch, I shall continue."

"Secured. Perched. Whatever. Go! Speak!"

"I must inform you that Astronaut Xavier is dead. He died in a severe meteor shower near the South Lunar Pole on February 6, 1973." She reminded herself to concentrate on breathing and let him talk. "He was the communications officer. He was trying to retrieve the primary communications antenna before the meteors struck. There was little notice, not much time. He was unsuccessful. The antenna was damaged, but not destroyed. It was a devastating meteor shower, unprecedented in intensity. It appears that NASA was unable to communicate with the Moon Base after that. Of course, it was known that meteors had struck the facility."

Dr. Shavinsky interrupted with "They naturally assumed complete destruction of the base and its personnel. After a while, they closed the books."

"But you didn't," she observed.

"Ah yes. That's true. We had an advantage over NASA, didn't we Dmitri."

"Yes. You see, NASA had a secret to protect. The Moon Base was never authorized by your Congress. In fact, funding for it had been refused. We monitored these matters very closely. It was a covert operation."

To this Dr. Konosov added "Apparently this did not stop your President Nixon, who was rather zealous about it before the funding was turned down. He never spoke of it publicly after that, which was out of character for him."

"We suspected that he proceeded anyway, without the consent of Congress. The funding must have come from other operations...like the thermogenerator," added Dr. Shavinsky.

"You may have been correct about that," was all she gave him. "So what did you do after the meteor shower?"

"The same thing NASA should have done. Are you familiar with the project known as SETI, an acronym for Search for Extra-Terrestrial Intelligence?"

"Yes. Radio telescopes in various places --- real big one in Puerto Rico."

"We also have such a project. Dr. Shavinsky was able to appropriate time on it for intercepting signals from the Moon Base. After a delay of less than one week, we were able to pick up their signals once more. That is how we determined the fate of Astronaut Xavier."

"What about the others?"

"They survived the meteor shower."

"How many?"

"Three. Maybe your other three Marines. Their names are Fortney, Brown and Balocco."

"I can't confirm without checking," she said cautiously, "but I remember the first name of one was very Greek. Hercules or something."

"Demitrius Brown," said Dr. Konosov. "Were you testing me, Miss Kirkland?"

"No, I wasn't...and yes, that's it." She thought about the name, and how proud his parents must have been when he was born, only to die at the South Pole of the Moon. "And NASA doesn't know?"

"NASA doesn't know. Remember, until we received the book, we didn't know ourselves."

Her head was swimming. To keep the conversation going, she asked "What was the date of the last transmission from the Moon?"

"Yesterday."

Despite her best efforts, she slid backwards off the log. When she grabbed Dr. Konosov's arm for support, he too fell backward. He landed with his head on her chest.

"Distinguished colleagues!" exclaimed Dr. Shavinsky with mock disapproval. "This is no way to conduct a scientific inquiry."

/////

In deference to the recent manifestations of physical instability of Rae, they revised their seating arrangements. Bidding a respectful *hasta la vista* to the two stone warriors, they went around *el Templo de los Falos* to the shade of the large tree protruding from the center of a small ruin several meters away.

"This is all that remains of *el Templo de los Bujos*...Temple of the Owls," explained Dr. Konosov, as he motioned for them to sit on stone blocks. "Mind that hole over there. It's a *chaltún*, a Mayan well or cistern. It you fell in, you would have to wait until it rained to swim to the top."

"When does it rain?" she asked, looking at the clouds forming. She wanted to get back to the subject of the Moon.

"Despite the daily cloud cover and dense vegetation, the Yucatán is almost a desert."

"I hear the Moon is like that," she offered, hoping to refocus the conversation. Both men laughed at her obvious gambit.

"O.K., Miss Kirkland, you are right!" said Dr. Shavinsky unexpectedly. "Ivan, this lady is not here to discuss the local climate. Tell her about the transmissions before she falls into that hole."

He reflected a moment and then said "I have brought a sample transmission for you to read. These are disciplined men, but they are also disillusioned. Remember this as you read."

23 APRIL 1993. HELLO, UNIVERSE. THIS IS MONDAY. WE ARE HERE. WHERE IN HELL ARE YOU? IF YOU RECEIVE THIS TRANSMISSION, RESPOND BY SENDING UP SOME CHEESEBURGERS AND MILKSHAKES. ABOUT A HUNDRED. BROWN WANTS FRIES, TOO. DON'T FORGET THE KETCHUP. THIS DOES NOT---REPEAT, NOT---SUPERSEDE OUR REQUEST FOR WOMEN. WE DON'T CARE WHAT THEY LOOK LIKE. DEMITRIUS DOESN'T EVEN CARE IF THEY COME FROM EARTH. AS THE DATA TRANSMISSION WILL CONFIRM, THE EQUIPMENT IS STILL WORKING, BUT WE ARE USING THE REDUNDANT GAUGES AND CONTROLS FOR SOME

-119-

ACTIVITIES. WHAT HAPPENS WHEN THEY FAIL?
REPLACEMENT PERSONNEL WOULD BE
WELCOMED. COMPUTER DATA STREAM FOLLOWS.
HABITAT::I:17°/E:N172°/AP:0.85/G:0.39....

The data stream continued for two pages, all of it meaningless to Rae. "Can you read this?" she asked Dr. Shavinsky.

"Some, we can understand. Some, we have to guess. There are many unfamiliar symbols used. We don't know what they all mean. But, we work backways. We ask what we would want to know, calculate the likely number, and then we see if anything looks like that number."

"What can you tell me?"

"The first part is the habitat or environment. It is stable, although earlier readings indicate it has cooled. The second part reports on the equipment. It is obviously working, but we don't know how well. This is especially difficult for us because we are unfamiliar with the equipment." He shrugged his shoulders and continued. "We don't know what numbers to look for."

"And the Astronauts?"

"That is the third part. We think we understand all of it. The news is not good. Lt. Brown has had an elevated temperature for months. He sleeps most of the time. Since viruses and germs should not be present in their environment, this indicates the body is responding to a serious internal condition. In addition, these men are undergoing the normal aging process. One obvious problem is that they can't see well. Since Astronauts are required to have perfect vision, no one thought to provide them with even reading glasses. Despite their exercises, their muscles have been weakened by the low gravity. Their body mass is too low."

"So what we have is an Old Astronauts Home on the Moon, with its inmates weak and fragile, stumbling around because they need eyeglasses," she summarized.

"Almost," admitted Dr. Shavinsky, with sadness.

/////

"But I have a million more questions!" she protested when Dr. Konosov insisted they take a break.

"To answer a million questions, even if each question and its answer could be communicated in one minute, would take six years at eight hours per day and very few days off," said Dr. Shavinsky, who had obviously worked this out before.

"More to the point, you need time to digest this information. I know. I am still digesting it myself," added Dr. Konosov.

"There are more questions than answers," said Rae, reluctantly joining in the spirit of the moment.

"That's very good!" said Dr. Konosov. "Who said that?"

"I think it was Johnny Nash," Rae shrugged. "It's part of a reggae song from the 'seventies."[6]

"Imagine that!" said Dr. Shavinsky.

"Philosophy lurks everywhere."

As they walked back through the ruins of *Chichen Viejo*, the clouds parted to reveal the scorching tropical Sun. Dr. Konosov opened his umbrella and held it above Rae. "Chivalry isn't dead then?" she asked in jest.

"No, merely wounded."

"Did you bring this umbrella just for Miss Kirkland?" queried Dr. Shavinsky.

"No," he admitted. "I brought it for the *fer-de-lance*."

"You expected to find a French lady?" offered Dr. Shavinsky.

"A viper. Like a cobra, except its bite is always fatal."

"You could have told us!" said Rae, her eyes darting through the underbrush.

"I must agree, Ivan. And what do you do with the bumbershoot?"

"It's only a theory, but I plan to place it between us and the *fer-de-lance*; so that it strikes the umbrella while we escape."

"I hope you won't be disappointed if we don't have the opportunity to test your theory today," said Rae, eyes still watching

---

[6] *There Are More Questions Than Answers* is a song written by Johnny Nash, performed by him on his album *I Can See Clearly Now* (Epic Records).

the bush.

"I will only be disappointed if I don't see a *cerveza bien fría* when we get back to the hotel."

"Cold beer," explained Dr. Shavinsky. "You see, these words in Spanish are absolutely essential. I also know these words in many other languages."

"What are the most important words?" she asked.

"*Sin hielo* --- without ice," suggested Dr. Shavinsky. "Each evening you can watch the tourists discuss how they never drink the water, even while they're drinking *Margaritas* full of ice."

"Or *¿dónde está el baño?* --- where is the bathroom? This phrase would be especially helpful if you forgot the other. I hope you do not find this offensive, Miss Kirkland."

"Practical advice given courteously can never be offensive, gentlemen." Then she added. "I studied Spanish in high school. The first sentence we were taught was *¿dónde está la biblioteca?* --- where is the library? Not exactly practical."

"No, but extremely diabolical," said Dr. Shavinsky with obvious admiration.

/////

So they rode back to the hotel in silence. By the time they arrived, she had resolved the number of questions by a factor of ten thousand. She only had one hundred questions now. Give or take a thousand.

They had lunch and cold *cervezas* brought to her hut so they could resume their discussions in private on the porch. She had gone to get a towel to use as a table cloth, but discovered all the linens to be missing. Dr. Konosov explained that most Mexican hotels had only one set of linens, which were taken in the morning, washed and returned *insh'Allah* in the afternoon.

"Like in Russia," observed Dr. Shavinsky.

"*Insh'Allah?*"

"If Allah wills it."

"Not Spanish?"

"Arabic," he admitted. Rae rolled her eyes. "Many Spanish

words are in fact Arabic. A carriage is a *calesa* in Spanish. The Arabic word sounds nearly the same. And *alberca*, meaning pool, is pure Arabic."

"How do you stop him?" she asked.

"If I only knew," lamented Dr. Shavinsky. "Cover his lips?"

Whereupon, Rae abruptly seized Dr. Konosov's face with both hands and turned it toward hers. This startled him into silence. He thought she was going to kiss him. Instead, she put her mouth to his ear and softly whispered "*Alto.*" He smiled at her joke, but he couldn't speak.

"*Bravo!*" shouted Dr. Shavinsky.

She shot him a look.

"*Bravo!* It's English...isn't it?"

She didn't answer. They all worked on their food.

"We have a problem, *compadres*," announced Dr. Konosov.

"Pardon me, but you're doing it again."

"Comrades."

"Comrades," she repeated dully, the word reminding her of whom she was trading national secrets with. Just keeps getting better and better. "Proceed."

"The three of us have knowledge unique in the world. What we know could save the lives of the remaining American Astronauts. How do we proceed?"

"Remaining." The word stopped her cold. "How many remain?" she asked. She couldn't believe she hadn't asked before.

"Two," responded Dr. Konosov. "Lieutenant Balocco died several years ago. They believe it to have been a heart attack."

"These are no longer young men," added Dr. Shavinsky

"What are the options?" asked Rae, looking directly at Dr. Shavinsky.

"Contact the President. Contact NASA. Both. Neither. Only America has the craft needed to rescue them."

"Have you contacted the Astronauts?" asked Rae.

The two Russians looked at each other, then Dr. Shavinsky said "We attempted contact, but we couldn't get through to them. Perhaps they only activate their receiver at certain times. I left a simple message with my colleagues that we were to keep trying, saying only that we had received and understood their message and to tell us their physical condition in detail. I'm not optimistic that we will be able to contact them. Their equipment has been badly damaged. Contact may require a different frequency or a coded prefix, like your Strategic Air Command bombers. Without the prefix, no message gets through. If the decoding equipment was damaged, they may not be capable of receiving even messages which are properly coded. Perhaps the Americans have a way around this."

Dr. Konosov reminded them "We will have to tell our government very soon. The decision of what to do is not ours."

"What will your government do?"

Dr. Shavinsky said "That is not completely predictable. It may depend upon whom I can speak with."

"If your government announces this before mine does, it will be considered an act of hostility."

"To your President and NASA," agreed Dr. Konosov. "How will the Americans accept this?"

"Now is as good a time as any," Rae said, drawing a sip of beer. "There is a man watching Mrs. MacPherson now. He has rented the house next door. He nearly killed her daughter and he has done...other things. We believe he is trying to prevent any exposure of the MONDAY Project."

They looked at her like she had lost it; so she continued "Did you know that every man working on the MONDAY Project was killed?"

"Dr. MacPherson?" gasped Dmitri. "But he died in an automobile accident!"

"He drove his car into a canal along side a road miles from any place he had any reason to be. There were no witnesses. There was no investigation. Has this happened to any of your colleagues?"

"The others?" asked Dr. Konosov.

"All dead before they were fifty. Seven persons make a small statistical universe, I'll admit. Nevertheless, one or two out of a group can die that young, but not all seven."

"All unusual?"

"One had a heart attack. None of the rest was what you'd call bizarre. But they all died within a very short period after the communications were lost."

"So we have another factor to consider. The personal safety of ourselves and Mrs. MacPherson. There is an expression in...."

"Spare us, Ivan!" she ordered. It was the first time she had addressed him by his first name, which seemed to provide extra impact. He simply nodded at her in reply. "We may have to watch our backs, but we have to do something."

"The lady is right, Ivan."

"Of course she is. So, what do we do?"

"I need to talk to Mrs. MacPherson about this. She's the one in immediate danger. And Mr. Mason --- he's the one who found out about the four Marine Astronauts and started all this."

Dr. Shavinsky agreed, explaining to Dr. Konosov that Mr. Mason was to be trusted completely because he possessed extensive knowledge of edible crustaceans native to American coastal waters. This seemed to satisfy him.

"I can give you, at most, two weeks to notify the American authorities, before I notify my government," announced Dr. Shavinsky. "At the moment I have no more acceptable excuses for delay. I will have to tell them. You understand?"

"Of course. Since NASA doesn't know it has two Astronauts stranded on the Moon, I will need backup."

Dr. Konosov said "You shall have it. I will provide transcripts of all communications, including those that occurred before the accident, which hopefully can be verified. Do you have a computer at home?"

"Yes."

"Specifications?"

"Pentium 60, 686 megabyte hard drive, 16 megabytes of RAM, CD-ROM, 9600 bps fax modem...."

"Word processor?"

"WordPerfect 5.1. I haven't upgraded to Windows."

"Good. Windows was too cumbersome for the Russian scientific establishment. It is often said that Windows is the solution to a problem that doesn't exist. You'll get a CD-ROM to copy into WordPerfect," he promised.

"I ALT-3 WP51, as they say."

"The ALT-3 combination produces a heart shape?"
"Very good, Doctor."

Chapter Fourteen

Monday, May 10, 1993

At Cancún airport she changed her flight to go directly to Orlando. Four hours after leaving Cancún she pulled into the Satellite Motel and took a room. As she threw off the sticky clothes she had put on that morning in the Yucatán jungle, she called Laura on the cellular telephone. She instructed her to come with Ken to the Banana River Boat Rental on the Cocoa Beach Causeway, where they would rent the last power boat available and head South very fast. She would find them.

///////

Agent Koestler had taken to recording his memoirs on a portable cassette machine. Every time he got his story flowing, the miscreants he was watching would pull him away from it. He was getting fed up. This surveillance didn't seem to be leading anywhere. Maybe these two were falling in love, and the Secret Service was paying him to make sure they consummated. Another marvelous expenditure of taxpayer Dollars.

These thoughts shuffled through his cortex as he calmly went to his car to follow the widow MacPherson and her beau. He had placed transmitters on both of their cars; so he quickly sighted them. The yellow Mustang made it difficult to get too close, but it was no challenge to keep track of people on a narrow barrier island. Especially amateurs. So he was not happy when they took Route 520 toward the mainland.

When they turned off the causeway into the marina, his confidence faded. He parked down the street and walked back as they pulled away from the docks in a small speedboat. Since they had not had enough time to complete the normal paperwork, he understood that the boat must have been arranged earlier. This realization prepared him for the news that no other power boats would be available for several hours. "Damned if I'll follow them on a jet-ski!" he said to himself in disgust as Laura hit the throttle in the center of the channel.

/////

Laura drove. Ken was not a boat person. The most positive feeling he could muster on the water was wariness. The negative feelings ran from bored to seasick. Then there was his propensity to achieve a spectacular sunburn in less than one hour.

When they were underway, Ken inspected their craft. It was a 20-foot open bow with two seats with backs and the usual array of cushions right atop the fiberglass. "Useful only for kids, dogs and in-laws," he thought. There was a small cabin. Ever curious, Ken opened the door.

"Avast, ye swabbies!" shouted Rae, as she emerged through the hatch.

Ken fell backwards upon the deck in surprise, sending both women into gales of laughter. "Avast yourself!" he muttered.

"It's bad for you. Makes you deaf." She whispered the last part to Laura. Both tittered when Ken unsuspectingly fell for it.

"Huh?"

"You just fell for the oldest joke in the world," said Laura, by way of inadequate explanation.

"Old jokes, vintage wines, classic cars, aged whiskey, traditional values, that's me," he rejoined.

"Nice recovery!" said Rae. "Now don't ruin it by singing 'Gimme Dat Old Time Religion.'"

"You should be so lucky."

"Children, please!" The only parent among them took charge. She turned to Rae and asked, "Where are we going?"

"Nowhere. Just away from your snoopy neighbor. That's why I rented all the boats. He'll find it hard to follow us in a Mustang."

"Ken, I like the way this lady thinks."

"The intricate workings of the criminal mind."

/////

Secret Service Agent Terrance E. Koestler did not share in the appreciation of Miss Kirkland's mental processes. He decidedly did not like the way Rae thought. Not one bit. Now he was suspicious again, dammit!

He drove South fast, looking for another marina.

/////

"Bring her about! Maintain a heading of 3° Nor'East! Full power!" Rae bellowed these exaggerated instructions with gusto.

"Aye-Aye, Cap'n!" replied Laura, turning the boat around and increasing the speed.

"Belay the poop deck!" yelled Ken, clearly out of his element but determined to join in the sea banter. This did not produce the desired effect.

"Landlubber," observed Rae with mock derisiveness.

"Impersonating a sailor could land you in the brig," added Laura.

"Then poop your own deck," he grumbled.

It was going to be a weird day, he had already decided. As evidence of this, the two ladies began to recount among themselves their childhood nautical experiences. Ken had a premonition that the conversation would not soon offer an opportunity to discuss his accomplishments as a teenager at the Bowl-a-Rama in Parma, Ohio; so he simply watched the shoreline pass.

/////

Agent Koestler drove all the way South to Satellite Beach before he found another marina, where he rented a red Donzi speedboat, which he quickly pointed North up the Banana River.

It was not a bad plan. His car would have easily outrun the speedboat they had rented; so he would be South of them. Even if they had turned North, he would intercept them sooner or later.

/////

"Ninety degrees to port!" barked Rae. "Make a heading for that dock."

"Aye-Aye, Skipper!"

They docked at what seemed to be the 'Fresh Bait Cold Beer Gas Marina.' The ancient wooden facilities were barely adequate to support the sign. Ken wondered at the priorities involved in the selection of the name, particularly at the placement of the various nouns and adjectives. He wasn't in Kansas anymore. In fact, he realized, he would be in the water if he didn't watch his step on the decrepit wood dock.

Ken bought Dr. Peppers for all of them. They sat in some well used Adirondack chairs beneath a live oak tree.

"So, what's up?" asked Laura.

"I just got back from México, where I met with Dr. Shavinsky and another Russian."

"What?!" It was a brief duet performed spontaneously, after which their jaws remained in the lowered position.

"Yes. While you two have been gallivanting around --- or whatever it is you two have been doing --- I have been in México discussing the Monday Project with the only other people on Earth who admit it exists."

"What did you find out?" asked Ken.

"They've been monitoring transmissions from the Moon for decades, which they have now translated --- thanks to your little book, Laura. They've confirmed that there was a manned base established in the region of the Lunar South Pole in 1970. The four missing Marines were posted to it, as we suspected."

"Holy shit." It just slipped out of his mouth. Nobody took notice. Under the circumstances it was the appropriate comment.

"What happened to it?" asked Laura.

"That's where it gets interesting. It was hit by a huge meteor swarm in February, 1973. Your friend Xavier was killed. He was the communications officer, which was double bad luck, because the other three men survived but they couldn't communicate with NASA anymore."

"You mean they died up there?" asked Ken.

"Not all of them. Two are still alive. As of last week they were still transmitting. I have transcripts."

After a moment of stunned, utter silence, Ken asked "Who are they talking to?"

"The Russians...but they don't know it. They don't know if anyone is listening at all. They're just transmitting a brief message and data every day. They haven't heard anything back since 1973."

"Can the Russians communicate with them?"

"They've tried, but haven't been successful yet."

"What about the Astronauts?" asked Laura.

"Lt. Xavier was crushed in the meteor strike. Died instantly. Lt. Balocco died later; apparent heart attack. The other two are not what you'd call hearty, but still alive."

"Look, you've had a day or so to think about this. What do we do now?" Ken asked. Laura nodded in confirmation.

"Dr. Shavinsky has given us a deadline of sorts. He has not yet told the Russian leaders. But too many people there know. He can't keep a lid on it forever. He will prepare a report and submit it as early as next week. We don't have much time, but I can't blame him. We need to decide what we're going to do now, and keep your neighbor from interfering --- or worse. So think!"

They sat in silence for a moment, watching the red Donzi cruise by, carrying its lone passenger North.

"You didn't answer my question. What do you think we should do?" Ken reminded.

"Well, we have to notify someone, but whom?" she responded. "Laura, do you have any ideas?"

"I don't have any close friends at NASA, if that's what you mean. The Apollo people are mostly gone now. I don't know of anyone I could trust there. Nobody would know anything about the Monday Project anyway."

Ken suddenly thought of Will, the Archives Librarian. Will had said he did everything but snap the shutters on the Moon missions. He was still there. "Do you know Will?"

"Will?"

"The Archives Librarian."

"Is he still there? Why he must be close to seventy by now."

"That's the guy. Still there. What do you think?"

"That's a good question. I mean everyone knew Will, but he

wasn't part of the team. We didn't see him outside of work. I don't even know his last name. But Jonas certainly spent time with him going over the images and samples the missions brought back."

"Did he trust him?" asked Rae.

"He liked him. He was in a position of trust, but Jonas didn't put him there. I guess I really don't know the answer to that one."

"Ken, where are you going with this?"

"It's not completely baked," he replied defensively. "It's an idea from the clear blue, not a proposal. But maybe Will could be shown an old transcript and corroborate it. Then we could explain that the visiting Russian scientist gave it to us and we think someone should know that the Russians have this information."

"Not mentioning that the Astronauts are still alive?" asked Rae.

"No. We play dumb until we get to the right person. Then we can turn over a recent transcript...."

"Once we've established our credibility." finished Rae, growing enthusiastic.

"And reached the right person to reveal this to." said Ken.

"Laura?"

"Can this be done without us becoming targets?"

"Damn fine question, girl!" said Rae. "Ken?"

"If I use Will for the approach and make it clear that the Russian gave it directly to me --- presumably because I am in GAO --- it should keep Laura and Courtney out of the line of fire. But since there is no time, we should pursue an alternate plan. Is there someone at GAO you can approach with this?"

"Maybe, but even an agency that investigates the government doesn't like a scandal. Besides, you'll be implicated because of all the time you've spent here."

"I'm going to be in it no matter what happens, I guess."

"I'm already implicated; so don't exclude me from the action," Laura volunteered.

"Wouldn't think of it," Laura assured her, realizing herself that there was probably no way they could.

/////

The sun was setting as they approached the rental dock. Behind the homes along the West shore, the sky had turned orange, then red, then purple. Now horizon glowed and the few clouds were bright pink clumps on the darkening blue sky. There was a light breeze. They were enjoying the moment when Rae said "Oh, I nearly forgot." Both of them turned toward her. "You need to act like this was a romantic outing. That's the only cover that can work here."

"Uhm."

"Ken, take off your shirt. You look like a damn banker!"

He started to protest, but realized she was right. He self-consciously pulled off his short-sleeved shirt, with button-down collar.

"And they said the abominable snowman was a myth," quipped Rae, at the sight of Ken's furry back.

Ken winced, and countered, "Mister, if you please." He held the shirt out as if someone should take it. This gave Rae another idea.

"You put on his shirt," she said, holding it out for Laura to take. "How's that for intimacy?"

Laura looked briefly at the proffered garment, then turned her back to them and --- to their utter astonishment --- removed her top, letting it drop to the deck. Then she reached behind her and took the shirt, which she managed to acquire without revealing much. When she was attired, she tied it off at her midriff rather than use the buttons. She turned to them and asked rhetorically "How's that for intimacy?"

Rae looked at Ken, who merely explained that "Laura does not believe in halfway measures."

"I just meant for you to.... Oh, never mind. Mother of Pearl," Rae muttered as she assumed her hiding place in the cabin.

PART IV: DISCLOSURE

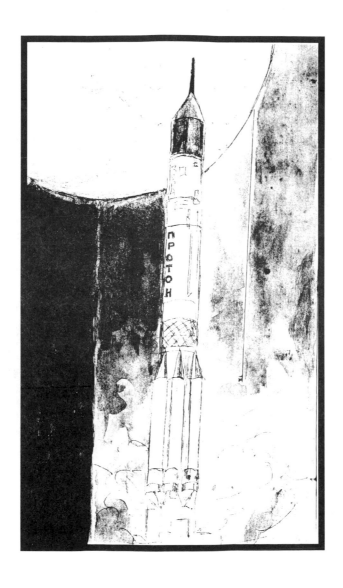

Chapter Fifteen

Tuesday, May 11, 1993

After some deliberation, it had been decided to show Will a copy of the transmission from the morning before the meteor shower. This would have been the last transmission received by NASA. Although the decision as to whether to deal with Will at all was to be made by Ken, there was no time to explore other options.

Ken arrived early --- before the tourists --- and walked right up to the Archives counter. Will was at his private desk in the back, drinking coffee. Ken came around the counter, through a sensing beam he hadn't noticed.

Beeeep!

Ken stopped short, assuming a sheepish grin. Will waved him back, asking "What'll it be, coffee or chess?"

"Too early for chess," Ken observed.

"Cream? Sugar?"

"Both."

"I was in Florence during the war and I drank my coffee black," he began cryptically as he prepared a cup for Ken. "I drank my coffee and the Italians drank theirs with milk --- when they had it --- and lots of brown sugar." He handed Ken his scalding cup, which Ken immediately set down on what he hoped were unimportant papers. "I drank with them, cup for cup, but a peculiar thing would happen every afternoon about 4:00." He looked straight into Ken's eyes, as if Ken should have guessed what occurred each afternoon in Tuscany decades ago.

"Uhm." Ken sipped at the liquid inferno to cover for his lack of inspiration. How did he get this so damned hot? NASA technology? Or did they just import it from the Sun?

"The Italians kept going and I just pooped out," he finished. "It was the sugar!"

"I guess so." He tried to sound interested.

"So you keep drinking your coffee that way. It helps even more when you get older, like me. So what are you doing back here?"

Just like that. It was now or never. "Well," Ken began slowly, "do you remember when that Russian space general was here awhile back?"

"Yes."

"Well, I was invited to the reception...."

"Visiting firemen are always invited to drink up the government's champagne," Will observed.

"Well, we were discussing stone crabs when the bomb threat happened; so a bunch of us ended up at the Spaceport Seafood...."

"Grill."

"Yeah, that's it."

"Water their drinks," Will grunted, unimpressed.

"Anyway, we all --- must have been seven or eight of us --- gorged ourselves on stone crab and lobster, and had a rollicking good time." Rollicking? C'mon, Ken, pull it together. "Saw him on the beach the next morning and shot the breeze a bit. Interesting guy. Turns out he was in Havana at the time of the Missile Crisis."

There was no reaction from Will --- or a deliberate non-reaction.

"Then I never saw him again --- or expected to," he added.

"So?" Will took a swig of coffee. Maybe it was cooling.

"The other day he sent me this printout. It looks like a copy of a transcript of some communication with NASA. But the date isn't right."

"What's wrong with it?" Will was definitely interested.

"Well," Ken said, pulling the document from his jacket pocket. "There were no missions at that time. It was after Apollo XVII."

"There are always missions." Will stared at the papers that Ken still held.

"But these seem to be human transmissions," added Ken, watching Will's curiosity increase. "It seems to have something to do with Monday. I thought that was the transmission date, but I checked and it wasn't."

Will snatched the papers from his hand and went rigid at what he saw.

"Bingo!" Ken said to himself, while trying to look confused and innocent.

"You say the Russian gave you this?"

"Yes. Dr. Shavinsky. He indicated that there were more. What are they?"

Will partially regained his composure. "If this is what I think it is, the Russians have no business knowing about it!"

"Not even with *glasnost?*"

"Are you tryin' to be funny?"

"It looked important. That's why I brought it to you."

"Do I look important to you?" Will asked with sarcasm.

"I didn't know what it was. Still don't, for that matter. I didn't want to make a big fuss over nothing. I figured you might set me straight."

"Have you shown this to anyone?"

They had anticipated this question. "No. I got it on Friday and flew down here Saturday. Nobody's seen it but me...and the Russians," he added for insurance purposes. "So, what is it?"

"Can I keep this?"

"Sure. I have another copy. It's on some kind of inferior East Block paper."

Will rose to the occasion. "Don't tell anybody about this until I see if it matches anything in our records...."

"Do it now."

"Beg pardon?"

"Do it now. You've got the date. You're not busy. I can wait. Check it now. If this is important, we probably need to do something soon. If not, I can go back to Washington."

"Ahh." Will thought a moment. "Right!" When Ken showed no sign of moving, Will turned the monitor away from Ken and began typing....

> C:\COMMUNICATIONS\MISC
> ENTER PASSWORD

Ken couldn't see the monitor; so he watched Will's fingers type NOMADY. "So Will knows...," he thought. Then Ken gazed about the office, hoping to appear nonchalant. He realized it probably wasn't good that he could hear his every heartbeat and that the sound was similar to a drum roll.

"It's classified," Will announced with what he hoped was finality.

"It's genuine then."

Will was exasperated. "See here, I'm not authorized to...."

Ken cut him off. "I'm not asking you to tell me what this is all about. I just needed to know if the Russians have classified NASA material. Apparently they do. And if they do, we need to tell someone. Now who do we tell?"

Will was sweating. He suddenly realized that he had badly underestimated this bean counter from GAO. He wasn't sure what to do about it.

"If we don't tell the right people, we might be helping spies. And that's treason," Ken prodded.

The thought of committing treason, even by inaction, took the starch out of Will. "I should have retired years ago."

"Who should be told about this?" Ken pressed.

"I need some time to think about this. This is old business. I'd like to find someone who has some knowledge of it, not one of the newcomers. Get back to me this afternoon."

"I'll call at 2:00."

"Don't discuss it with anyone. Don't even mention it on the telephone. In fact, why don't we just meet some place at, say 3:00?"

"Spaceport Seafood at 3:00."

"O.K. At the bar."

"Booth in the lounge."

"Yeah. Now get outta here; so I can think."

/////

It took less than a minute to think to dial 1-321-433-1561, the number he had memorized so long ago. As usual, a machine answered. It requested his identification code and that he leave a message.

"This is Will Peterson. The cable has gone out again. Handling this over the 'phone doesn't work. You're going to have to send someone out now. Call me at the office, extension 31, as soon as you can; so I can arrange to be there." In an emergency he had been instructed to leave an innocent message which nevertheless indicated a need for haste and a method of contact. Now he would have to wait and think. "To think, perhaps to stew. Ay, there's the rub," was his first coherent thought. Not at all promising.

/////

"This is Comtron Cablevision, what's the problem?" It was a man's voice. An older man.

"No cable on some channels and weirdness on others. You've got to see it to believe it."

"We'll have someone out there in ten minutes. Will that be O.K.?"

"Yes." No! He wasn't used to this intrigue. "Wait! It's kind of hard to find. Meet me at Hector's Market on South A-1-A and you can follow me there."

"O.K., just look for the van." It dawned on Will that there would not be a Comtron van for him to recognize. He would have to wing it.

/////

Ken had determined to get there first, but Will greeted him as he peered into the dark lounge. He had not yet become accustomed to sunglasses as a necessity; he had forgotten to remove them. Ken followed the voice to the booth, which he entered by touch.

"Assume you're a fellow beer drinker --- at least in the afternoon," said Will. There was a mug of beer on each side of the table.

The beer was ice cold. "How did you know when I'd get here?"

"Didn't. Thought I might have to drink it myself. The sacrifices one makes for one's country."

"So I didn't spoil your day completely?"

"No. I should do this more often."

"Did you come up with a name?"

"Oh yes, and then some," Will said smugly.

"Tell me."

"Let's wait till he gets here."

"He's coming here?"

Will shook his head in the affirmative.

"Now?"

"Might be a few minutes."

Ken raised his mug. "To a man of action!"

"Here's looking at you, kid!"

"To the four Marines!" offered Ken, just as Will took a drink.

Will choked. Beer dribbled from the side of his mouth. Tears came to his eyes as he tried to regain control. Ken waited.

Finally, Will said "You're just full of surprises today, aren't you?"

"I'm just passing them along. Before we go any further, I want to ask you two simple questions that I think you can answer without betraying any NASA secrets."

"You can ask," Will responded warily.

"Were Moon Suits ever made for one Astronaut then altered for another Astronaut?"

Will considered the question, decided the answer was available to the public and answered "No. The measurements are so precise that there wouldn't be much of a cost savings. It would be like making an Oldsmobile out of a similar model Chevrolet. It could be done, but why?"

"Makes sense. Now, was Carlos Xavier ever fitted for a Moon Suit?"

Will mulled the question and it's probable relation to the previous one. He shrugged. "I can't say for sure, mind you. But he probably was. All the Astronauts in the program were, up until Congress killed the last two missions. Can I ask why you want to know?"

By way of reply, Ken slid a piece of paper across the table. Will adjusted the *faux* hurricane lantern to maximize the utility of its 25-watt bulb and began reading.

"Uh-oh," said Will.

"Yep. Big time Uh-ho."

Will finished reading the page and removed his glasses. He took a moment to clean them before putting them back on. Then he looked directly into Ken's eyes, but said nothing.

"It's real," said Mason.

"Are there more?"

"One for every day of the year, I'm told."

"Holy shit!"

"Indeed. And a good measure of blessed dung, as well."

Will broke into a sweat. He looked confused. "I-uh...." He looked at the ceiling a moment, then tried again. "Look, Mr. Mason. I don't know what to make of this. It's incredible. You need to talk to someone else."

"You said he'll be here soon...."

"That may not be so good. You see, I thought this was just a security issue; but if this paper is legit, then it's a whole different ball game."

"So...."

"So, I called a security man."

"From NASA?"

"Hell! I don't even know what agency he works for. I think we should leave."

"Uhm."

"Now! Out the back door."

Agent Koestler parked his yellow Mustang in the disabled parking spot in front of the Spaceport Seafood Grill. He had a sticker.

/////

"I am definitely gettin' too old for this!" observed Will as they jogged down the beach behind the Spaceport Seafood Grill. Ken wasn't doing much better. Will's effort inspired him --- almost as much as Will's obvious fear did.

After about half a mile, Will executed an orderly collapse on the sand. He lay on his back, panting. Ken dropped to his knees several feet away. After a minute, Ken asked "Is it a good sign when you stop wheezing?"

"Only if you've got a pulse."

"I'll check when I have the strength." Then he added, "The security man you contacted, does he have a yellow Mustang?"

"He did this morning. You know him?"

"Saw one pull up in front of the restaurant as we left. That's all," he lied. "Guess we just missed him. What're you going to tell him?"

"Least of my worries. What do I do about you?"

"Uhm."

"I mean. There I was --- minding my own business --- and you drop the bombshell of the century on me. I still don't know how much you know...," he finished. letting the implicit question hang between them.

Ken sighed. It was time to show some cards. "I don't know what it is exactly that I know. But it looks like NASA established a Moon Base in 1970. This was done without the knowledge or consent of Congress. Before any announcement was made, something happened to cause NASA to believe that the Astronauts had died."

"Go on."

"Since the mission was unauthorized, the whole matter was then hushed up. Why announce a failure?"

"Not Nixon's style."

"Nor NASA's either, apparently."

"No. I guess not," Will admitted. "Anyway, nobody knew for all these years. I wasn't supposed to know, but I had too much access to remain in the dark forever. Nobody ever worried that the Russians might know. You know how they found out?"

"Guess you underestimated them," Ken responded without answering.

"Not the first time." Will looked at the horizon a while, then said, "This last transmission you showed me says Xavier was killed when the meteor swarm hit. I'm assuming it's genuine, for now. Do you know how the others died?"

"It looks like Lt. Balocco had a heart attack."

"And the others?"

Ken hesitated. He hadn't intended to reveal any more at this time, but he suddenly changed his mind. He trusted Will. "According to the Russians, they're still transmitting."

"You mean automatic transmissions?"

"No. Manual, too."

Will's eyes rolled back before he closed them tightly. When he opened them again, he asked "Those poor bastards! Do you know what this means?"

"The Russians are about to tell the world that America stranded Astronauts on the Moon and left them for dead," Ken said softly.

Will flinched as if stung by a scorpion. "How much time do we have?"

"Maybe a week. Nothing definite. Can you get to the Director of NASA?"

"I guess I have to."

"What about the security man?"

"I didn't tell him much, but I got him excited about you. Now he's wondering where I am. You should probably avoid him. He seems sort of ruthless. Kind of guy you imagine being in the murder-for-hire business."

Ken didn't know how to warn Will about Agent Koestler without bringing Laura into it; so he simply said "Trust your instincts."

They agreed that Will would contact the Director in the morning and that they would both be careful tonight.

/////

To avoid Agent Koestler, Ken spent the night at Kissimmee, in the midst of the Disney World crowds. He went to bed early; so he could be at Kennedy Space Center by 8:00 A.M., before the tourists began to arrive.

Will spent the night in his kitchen. When he arrived home, Agent Koestler was sitting at his kitchen table, drinking from a bottle of Squirt he had taken from Will's refrigerator.

"What the Sam Hill are you doing in my house!"

"Just trying to catch up with you. Don't know how I missed you earlier," he said with sarcasm. "Did he show up?"

"Yeah. But he didn't want to stay at the bar. Insisted we go for a walk on the beach. Y'know, I think he was afraid of being overheard, or taped. Real skittish." Will felt this sounded pretty convincing.

"So what did he say?" Agent Koestler was unmoved.

"Oh, he said that there were some suspicious occurrences toward the end of the Apollo program. Wanted to know if I knew anything about them."

"And did you?"

"I didn't know what he was talking about; so I kept it general. Told him that something fishy was going on all the time. I assumed it was the way government projects worked," Will improvised. "But he seemed disappointed; so I asked him point blank what specifically he was talking about."

"He's working with the Russians," Agent Koestler said softly.

"He is?"

"He's committing treason."

"How's that?"

Agent Koestler ignored the question. He stepped to within inches of Will and looked him straight in the eyes. "You're helping a traitor, old man."

Will's face turned beet red. He put out his left hand to maintain the short distance between them. His little finger was immediately seized and bent backward. There was a distinct snap. Will went down on his knees to lessen the pressure.

"I-ahh," he started to protest, but then a look of total surprise came over his face. The Secret Service man released him immediately. Will fell forward on the terrazzo floor, his heart no longer pumping. He rolled over and directed his final thoughts to the ceiling. His last words were "Still there." Agent Koestler heard them clearly, but he didn't have any idea what they meant.

Agent Koestler took Will's pulse to confirm his demise. He muttered "Damn you, old man." Then he started covering traces of his presence. When he was satisfied, he left.

Chapter Sixteen
Wednesday, May 12, 1993

Ken arrived at the Kennedy Space Center shortly after 8:00 A.M. When he discovered Will had not arrived, Ken checked out some Apollo films and pretended to watch them. At 10:48 A.M., he calmly received the word that Mr. Peterson had died of an apparent heart attack at home. He continued to feign work for twenty minutes more before leaving. On the way out, he told the receptionist "Sorry to hear about old Will. Seemed like a nice guy."

/////

METEOR TOTALS LUNAR ROVER screamed the headline. Rae was reading it when the telephone rang.

"Rae? It's Jake."

"You're up early."

"Been up all night."

"Gazing at the Moon?" she guessed. "I suppose that meteor shower I read about was exciting."

"That's not the half of it! You know you asked me to point my telescope toward the South Polar region?"

"I assume you would have called if you'd seen anything unusual."

"That's right, but...."

"But now you have?"

"Not at the South Pole. It's the rover!"

"From what I read, the warranty expired last night."

"No, it didn't! You see, it wasn't the rover! It was a mock-up, a fake. Couldn't detect it until it was smashed. But now it's obvious."

"To whom?" she asked, beginning to see the implications.

"To any scientist who really looks."

"So where is it?"

"That's the question, isn't it?" he responded.

"Could it be at the South Pole?"

"Wouldn't necessarily be able to see it."

"Could it have been driven that far?"

"Not with the original batteries, but...." He let it hang.

Her healthy paranoia returned. She decided to get off the telephone. "Weren't they Diehards?"

"I doubt it."

"Well thanks for calling me. I don't know what to make of this news."

"Nobody else here does either. Let me know if you have any useful ideas."

"I will, but don't wait by the 'phone." Then she added, "If you find out any more, give me a call, O.K.?"

"O.K. 'Bye."

To herself, she muttered "What next?"

The answer came four minutes later when Ken called her on her cellular telephone. He began without preamble. "I showed the old guy at the space center a couple of the transcripts and now he's dead."

"Whoa! I missed something here. Where are you calling from?"

"Pay 'phone in Kissimmee."

"Proceed."

"I met with this Will Peterson yesterday afternoon at a restaurant. We were going to meet someone he was going to ask to help. But before he came in I had showed Will a transcript and he became frightened. Insisted we leave by the back door. Hell, we ran down the beach. He said something about calling a security man because he didn't know what I was up to. Once he saw the transcript, he thought better of it."

"How did he die?" she asked evenly.

"Apparent heart attack. I really couldn't look too interested. I didn't find out any more."

"Could have been."

"Yeah," he conceded. "I know. Old Will was no Spring chicken. And he wasn't in great shape. The run down the beach might have done it."

"But you don't think so."

"Not with everything else that's happened."

"Like Laura's mysterious neighbor?"

"Definitely. Will said the man we were fleeing had a yellow Mustang. I mean, we know there's been a huge cover-up and someone's been watching us. It's not a stretch to assume violence might be used to silence us."

"Like Laura has been saying all along. Have you talked with her?"

"She's on her way here. It's about an hour and a half."

"Have you heard about the lunar rover?"

"No."

"It was smashed by a meteor shower --- at least, that's what the news is. But I have it on good authority that it was a replica that was hit."

"So where is....oh." And then for good measure "Uhm."

"Ken, we have to get to the President, soon. Any ideas how?"

Ken became analytical. "Who can get to see the President on short notice?"

"His family, his staff, some Congressmen, some Heads of State, some Ambassadors...."

"Like the Russian Ambassador?"

"Yessss." She rolled the idea around in her brain and liked it. "Looks like our best shot."

"So you'll call your boyfriends?"

"I'll send a fax from Mail Boxes."

"'Atta girl! I'll call you when Laura arrives."

/////

Agent Koestler was following Mrs. MacPherson in his repaired Oldsmobile. He could kill her now and make it look like an accident if there weren't so many other drivers. Although he had never intentionally killed a woman, he knew he could if he was convinced it was necessary. And that was a large part of the problem. Was it still necessary? Who needed protecting?

Agent Koestler only surmised that President Nixon and NASA had tried to establish a Moon Base and failed. He had no details. He had just been part of the cover-up: getting rid of the scientists. There had been a remarkably small team for such an ambitious project. Only seven people to silence. He assumed there must be many more with suspicions, but after two decades they weren't going to do anything.

And now this. Someone who wasn't around at the time --- this damned auditor --- stumbles onto something. Then he meets the widow of the project leader! On top of that, some Russian from the Soviet space program gets involved. God only knows what he's doing! The only person who might have shed some light on the situation went and died on him in his crummy kitchen.

It was a shit storm. No doubt about it.

It started to rain. "How appropriate," he muttered, as he reached to turn on the wipers.

/////

It was 7:30 P.M. in St. Petersburg. Dr. Ivan Konosov had taken advantage of the lengthening hours of daylight to walk along the canal on his way home from dinner. He had a good life here, but he longed for México. He loved the sun, the warmth, the vivid colors. He understood why Gauguin had hated Sweden.

He didn't notice the fax immediately. The plain-paper telecopiers didn't push the fax out in the manner of the old thermal machines, which he always thought looked like the machine was sticking its tongue out at you --- a rude gesture indeed in Russia.

He was sipping a glass of passable Hungarian Riesling when he noticed it. Although the large Cyrillic letters were just an advertisement which stated that 8 megabytes of random access memory could be purchased for only 90 *Rubles*, he smiled broadly. He tore off the top 15 millimeters and burned it in his ashtray, flushing the ashes down the toilet. The remainder he ripped up. He didn't need to read it. It was a copy of an advertisement he had received previously by fax, except for the simple change he had made to indicate it was the one he had given to Miss Kirkland. She needed to speak with him, urgently. They would use the intermediary she had selected.

He booted up his Compaq laptop and plugged in the modem. Then he faxed an order for a copy of a book to a fictitious bookseller that was really an accommodation facsimile number at a mailing and printing service in Tyson's Corners, Virginia. The book he selected was *Mayab* by M.S. Karl[7] --- an excellent book he knew to be out of print. This would alert Rae that he had received the fax.

The response came within minutes.

"MAYAB" OUT OF PRINT. ALTERNATE SELECTION OF
THE MONTH IS "AMBASSADOR FROM ST. BASIL'S" --- A
FICTIONAL ACCOUNT OF SHOCKING EVENTS BROUGHT
TO THE ATTENTION OF AN AMERICAN PRESIDENT.

"Mother Russia!" he exclaimed to his computer. "I'll need Dmitri for this." He typed:

NO THANKS. I SHALL OBTAIN IT MYSELF.

Thus he advised Rae that he would come to Washington to try to arrange for a meeting between the Russian Ambassador and the President of the United States.

"Just like that!" she marveled. "Oh yes. I could get to like this man."

/////

The rain was sliding across the land in near-horizontal sheets when Laura MacPherson arrived at the Residence Inn. She drove her Grand Am around the side of the building as she had been instructed, and parked her car. Leaving her luggage, she sprinted for the entrance. She looked as if she had swum instead.

Ken opened the door the moment she knocked. "Please make coffee," was all she said as she marched damply through the sitting room into the bedroom. Within a minute the coffee was perking and all her garments were arrayed on the shower curtain rod. She combed her hair, applied lipstick and selected one of his blue Oxford cloth

---

[7]

Mayab is an excellent mystery novel by M.S. Karl published by Leisure Books. The action takes place amid Mayan ruins.

shirts to wear. On a whim, she tied one of his neckties around her waist. She re-entered the sitting room rolling up her sleeves. "Sorry about the tie."

"Uhm." The effect was devastating. Ken stared a moment too long before recovering. "Sugar?"

"Yes, Sweetie?" she teased.

"Uhm. I meant did you want some?"

"Some what?"

"Sugar. For your coffee."

"That would be most agreeable, Mr. Mason."

He managed to figure out that this meant "yes" and added two packets of sugar to her cup. When he no longer held any scalding liquids in his hands, she said "Now I thank you for the use of this large shirt, but I don't really know if it will be adequate to the task when I sit down; so I'm asking you to look out the window while I arrange my garb."

"Arrange away," he said as he stood before the window, wondering at the intensity of the precipitation. Then he saw that the large gray car had someone in it --- who seemed to be looking at him. "Were you followed?" he said without turning.

She thought for a minute, then said "Hard to tell, with all that rain. Headlights all look pretty much alike." She sipped her coffee.

"Uhm. The man in the car could just be waiting for the rain to let up."

"What car?"

"Don't get up. If he followed you, I don't want him to know which room you're in."

"Maybe he recognized you?"

"And maybe not. I've seen better visibility 30 feet under water."

"How can we confuse him?"

He hadn't thought of it yet. She was ahead of him --- again. "We should have had you check into a room on the other side of the building, but now.... Well, it might be awkward for you to go to the front desk dressed like that."

"Not awkward. Scandalous, perhaps." She smiled innocently at him.

He was sure it just his imagination, but he thought he could feel the blood rushing from his brain into his genitals as he struggled to focus on the conversation. He sat down abruptly in case his zeal was beginning to show. The last thing in the world he wanted was for her to put on her clothes and leave, but that seemed to be the best plan. "You could put your wet clothes back on and rent a room."

"You're not kidding, are you?"

"I wish I were. I mean you look so dry and comfortable...."

"Yeah. I was." She sighed and skulked into the bedroom, closing the door with a tad more vigor than required for the task.

He studied the building chart on the back of the door to determine which rooms would be farthest from his room. He heard the shower come on briefly. He winced.

"How do I look?" She had evidently stood in the shower after dressing. She was soaked. Just like when she first arrived.

"Convincing," he replied with sincerity.

"I'll bet. You owe me dinner, Mr. Mason --- with wine. He'd better still be in his car."

Ken peeked through the curtain and indicated that he was. "Use your real name. Go to your room. Turn on some lights and make sure they'll show through the curtains."

"Television?"

"Uhm. No. Someone watching from outside would expect to see the flashes as you surfed the channels with the remote control."

"Never thought of that...."

"Men won't watch T-V without the blipper. Now off with you. Call me from your room. It's direct, not through the operator. I'll let you know if it's safe to come back."

"What makes you think I want to," she teased.

"I have *tortilla* chips and *salsa*."

"*Olé*, you smooth talker. *¡Hasta la vista!*" And she was gone, leaving only a puddle on the carpet.

/////

Agent Koestler listened to Wagner on his car stereo cassette and silently cursed the rain...and his job. Maybe he was getting too old for this lifestyle. He could retire at any time now. Maybe he should move --- to the desert, perhaps. He'd spent his entire life in humidity. And he reckoned the present situation to be about 150% humidity.

But what would he do?

Suddenly he said aloud "I could finish my memoirs, listen to classical music, cook Southwestern cuisine, learn Apache, charm rattle snakes and..." he strained for something even more outrageous and found it "...learn to line dance!" He was grinning. It was an epiphany. For the first time in his life he realized he could do whatever he wanted.

His enthusiasm waned when he looked over at Mrs. MacPherson's car. "First things first." He continued to watch the relentless downpour.

/////

"Drown Rat to *Tortilla* Chips. Drown Rat to *Tortilla* Chips. Come in *Tortilla* Chips. Do you read me?"

"Loud and clear, Drown Rat. You are cleared for landing."

"Roger, *Tortilla* Chips. ETA is 2 minutes." Click.

Ken went back to the curtain to watch the gray car.

When she arrived she was somewhat dryer than before, but she repeated her earlier routine. She entered the room wearing only his shirt and the necktie as a belt. She assumed a defiant stance --- feet slightly apart and arms folded --- and said "You don't get three strikes."

He stepped to her and took her damp head in both hands. She looked up at him and closed her eyes. Her arms fell to her sides as she went on tiptoes to kiss him. The light kiss became a serious one. Her arms embraced his neck.

It was the promising end of a beautiful friendship.

/////

The rain didn't stop. After an hour, Agent Koestler drove to the covered front entrance and asked if Mrs. MacPherson had checked in yet. He was told that she had. Incredibly, the receptionist gave him the room number without him having to ask.

While he was obtaining a room nearby, Laura and Ken drove out the side and went to the airport to turn in Ken's rental car. They would be in Georgia before nightfall despite the weather.

Rae had told them to come to Washington. They had agreed immediately. It seemed safer than Florida.

Chapter Seventeen
Friday, May 14, 1993

The black Lincoln limousine stopped at the massive iron gates. The stoic Russian soldier saluted. The gates were opened by unseen forces. Five and one-half tons of Detroit's handiwork edged into the traffic. Inside, Dr. Shavinsky was introducing Ken and Laura to Dr. Ivan Konosov and Alexi Rudikov, the Russian Ambassador to the United States. "Maybe someday when I want to meet with President Yeltsin, your American Ambassador can take me!" he roared. The irony of the situation was not lost on anyone present.

/////

At the White House, they were given the back door treatment. This was the routine whenever the Russian Ambassador insisted upon a meeting with the President and gave no reason. No less than twenty-seven aides and advisors had spent the previous night researching world and Russian events in a futile attempt to provide a reason for this meeting to the President. A report was written for the occasion. It specifically cited the absence of any known situations, concluding that the meeting must have something to do with "the incomprehensible realm of Russian politics."

"Byzantine, dammit!" he'd shouted. "It's the only known use of the word Byzantine in modern times. Don't they teach you anything at Yale?" The Chief Executive did not like being clueless.

"Will that be all, Mr. President?"

"Yes. Leave the report on my desk."

The telephone buzzed. He pressed a button and listened. "Entourage. Repeat: entourage. Two more Ivans and three Yanks with him." He released the button.

"Americans?" he said to himself. What had he done to piss off both the Americans and the Russians? He sat at his desk in the Oval

Office trying to look busy while he awaited his visitors. When the door opened, he waited until the group had all passed into the room before arising from his chair. "Alexi, my friend, how are you?" he greeted as he stepped from behind his desk slowly and motioned them to seat themselves. Still standing, he introduced himself needlessly and shook everyone's hand, finishing with the Ambassador whom he also patted on the shoulder. They did not appear threatening. His mood lightened a bit.

"I am fine, Mr. President. I trust that you too are healthy."

"Excellent. My doctors say I may live long enough to pay their bills."

"Then they must be excellent doctors," he beamed. "I have with me today a distinguished group of persons who have incredible news for you." He proceeded to introduce each one, giving offices held and credentials as appropriate. "I believe Mrs. MacPherson should begin."

"Mr. President, my late husband was Dr. Jonas MacPherson." She paused, but there was no hint that he recognized the name. "My husband was the project director for the NASA Moon Base program. That was the program which was going to establish a colony on the Moon in conjunction with the Apollo Missions. As you probably know, the Apollo program was cut short by Congress. Apollo XVIII docked with Soyuz instead of going to the Moon. Apollo XIX was cancelled completely, along with all subsequent Moon projects."

The President nodded.

"From the time Congress took this action, no one spoke of a Moon Base anymore. What Congress didn't know --- what the public didn't know --- was that the physical facility had already been constructed on the Moon by that time. It had begun before Apollo. Some of the Surveyor missions landed materials. This I knew. I could not have guessed the rest." She lowered her head. Ken gripped her hand for encouragement.

Dr. Shavinsky said "We can continue."

"No!" she shouted. "He needs to hear this." She looked straight into the President's eyes. "My husband and the other scientists working on the Moon Base program were all eliminated --- killed, Mr.

President. All traces of their work were hidden."

"Now that's a serious accusation, Mrs. MacPherson."

"Yes, it is. And it made no sense until now. The others can complete the story for you." She was done, drained. She had waited decades to say this. Her old life was finally ended.

Rae spoke up. "Mr. President. I don't have much to contribute, but this seems like a good time to ask you if you know what happened to the lunar rover."

"Does that have anything to do with this?"

"It may."

"I have requested a report. But as of now, I only know that the newspapers claim it's missing. Do you know where it is?"

"Probably at the Lunar South Pole."

"Parked in the garage, Miss Kirkland?"

"Well, I do believe we should move on. Ken?"

"Uhm. Mr. President, I'm a senior auditor with the GAO. Miss Kirkland is my superior. A Congressional request was made for a study on the Apollo program costs. To make a long story short, I went to the Kennedy Space Center to research this. One of the first matters that caught my attention was that four U.S. Marines who had completed Apollo training left the program on the same day in 1969. I should mention that this was years before Congress began talking about cutting the program. I checked with the Marines and was told that all four were sent to a place code-named NOMAD/Y. None of them was heard from again. The location of this NOMAD/Y was no longer known, but it was presumed to be a clandestine staging camp in Southeast Asia. When I told this to Miss Kirkland here, she pointed out that NOMAD/Y was an acronym for MONDAY, and that MONDAY is simply a contraction of Moon Day. I later found out that the Moon Base project had been officially called the MONDAY PROJECT."

"This is the official list of the Astronauts who completed Apollo training but left NASA during the Apollo program:"

Coughlin, Robert L.	reassigned Navy	13 May 1968
Thomas, Wilbur	reassigned USAF	24 Feb 1969

Balocco, David M.	reassigned USMC	17 Aug 1969
Brown, Demitrius F.	reassigned USMC	17 Aug 1969
Fortney, William T.	reassigned USMC	17 Aug 1969
Xavier, Carlos F.	reassigned USMC	17 Aug 1969
Coe, Henry J.	reassigned N/A	06 May 1972

The President took the list, glanced at it briefly, and said "Please continue."

"I made this photograph from a frame of the NASA archives films. This particular bit of film had been crudely edited to delete the remaining frames, but you can still see what someone was trying to cut out. May I?" Ken went to the President's side and pointed to the left sleeve of the Astronaut's Moon Suit. "This Astronaut was in the process of turning to his right, exposing the name patch on the left sleeve. That's why the film was cut. But if you look closely, you can see part of the first letter of his name."

The President squinted at the photograph. His head bobbed slightly as he mentally reviewed the alphabet. "X?"

"Yes Sir."

"As in Xavier?" It wasn't really a question. "I don't suppose there were...." Ken was shaking his head to indicate the negative. The President sighed. "Well, I assume there's more."

"Then I found a log of transmissions to and from the Moon, which continued after the Apollo program had ended. The log was not easy to find."

"It was hidden?"

"It wasn't properly named to be found easily. It also had a password."

"You got around the password?"

"No. I typed it in. NOMADY --- without the slash. It seems the computer won't allow a slash in the name."

"So, you're telling me that at least one Astronaut who had allegedly left the program was photographed on the Moon and you have circumstantial evidence that a Moon Base may have been established by NASA in secret. I assume you've already told our

Russian friends here," he said with irritation.

Dr. Shavinsky could contain himself no longer. "Mr. President, these brave citizens of your country have only given you a brief report. Both your government's records and ours establish beyond any doubt that your NASA did indeed establish a base on the Moon." Rae noted that he did not confuse any English words. "Now the story becomes interesting."

"Please explain." The President felt a headache coming on. He wasn't sure he was ready for "interesting." He recalled the ancient Chinese curse "May you live in interesting times." He turned to face Dr. Shavinsky.

"From the beginning, we have been monitoring the Moon Base transmissions. We believe it to be located in an ancient crater known as the Aitken Basin, where there are ample supplies of frozen water. Our expert regarding such matters --- Dr. Konosov here --- identified these as voice transmissions. Persons speaking with other persons. He could tell by the pattern. There were, of course, computer transmissions as well. Not surprisingly, they were in code. We suspected the code was based upon a book, but our data base did not have this book. Dr. MacPherson was most ingenious, you see. He selected a book that was not in English. But now we have the book!"

"So you can interpret the transmissions?"

"Please look at this one," he said, handing a report to the President. "Someone at NASA should be able to verify its accuracy. You will that the text contains the names of the four missing Marines."

"I see," he replied cautiously, as he thumbed through it.

"Also note that it begins with the words 'This is Monday' although it was sent on a Thursday. They all start in this fashion."

Feeling an acute need to act more presidential, he attempted to recap the situation. "So --- assuming NASA confirms what you've told me --- the United States established a Moon Base in the 1970's. What happened to it?"

There was a pause. Dr. Shavinsky nodded to Dr. Konosov, who proceeded with the explanation. "Mr. President, there was a terrible meteor event in February, 1973, which struck the base."

"Wait a minute. When was the last Apollo flight?"

"The last Apollo flight left the surface of the Moon on December 13, 1972. That was Apollo XVII," said Laura unexpectedly. "Apollo XVIII did not go to the Moon. Apollo XIX never flew."

"You mean we left these Marines on the Moon knowing there was no plan to return?"

"Yes sir. That's why silence had to be guaranteed," Laura explained.

"I promise you we'll deal with those accusations later," he said to her. "Right now I need to know what happened to the Moon Base."

Dr. Konosov continued. "The meteor strike badly damaged the antenna. NASA was unable to establish contact after that event."

"How do you know this?"

He handed the President another transcript. "This is a report sent by the Astronauts several days after the meteor strike. We presume that no one at NASA has ever seen it. It describes the damage and the death of Astronaut Xavier, who unfortunately was the radioman."

"So the base wasn't destroyed by the meteors?"

"No, it wasn't."

"How could you contact the base when we couldn't?"

"After the meteor strike, we were able to receive the transmissions by using a very large array of radio telescopes," explained Dr. Shavinsky. "It took several days to establish contact; so we are missing some transmissions. If we had not already known the frequency, it would have been impossible."

"So --- aside from a few days --- you were in continuous contact?"

"Contact implies mutual communication," said Dr. Konosov. "We have never succeeded in delivering a message to the Moon Base. We only received them. Perhaps there is some device that blocks unauthorized transmissions, similar to the coding devices on your Strategic Air Command bombers."

The President was not interested in pursuing this line of

inquiry. "But NASA was never able to contact them again?"

"No. Of course, NASA had to know about the meteor strike. They probably assumed the base had been destroyed."

Ken interrupted. "Mr. President, I found a computer log of transmissions which indicates that attempts were made to contact the Moon Base continuously until early in 1975."

"Couldn't you have found a way to tell us?" the President asked Dr. Shavinsky.

"That is what we are doing, Mr. President. Please understand that until we were able to understand the transmissions from the Moon, we were unaware of the unfortunate situation of your Astronauts," Dr. Shavinsky replied.

Ambassador Rudikov raised his hand slightly to indicate he wished to speak. Choosing his words carefully, the Ambassador asked "What could have been done about them, Mr. President?"

There was no hesitation. "We would have rescued them, brought them back home." He knew the instant he saw the Ambassador's thin smile that he had made a mistake.

"Then you should, Mr. President. I think we are all in agreement here."

"I...." The President crumpled into his chair. His face was ashen. "Do you mean to say...?"

Dr. Konosov handed him another transmission report. "From last week. Two of them are still alive."

His Excellency, the President of the United States of America, arguably the most powerful man in the world, gave every appearance of wanting to crawl into bed and pull the covers over his head. He winced at the words. He held the report at arm's length in the same manner as he might hold a venomous reptile.

"They that wait upon the Lord shall renew their strength. They shall mount up on wings as eagles. They shall run and not be weary, and they shall walk and not faint. *Isaiah 40:31*."

"Does that apply to the Moon, Mrs. MacPherson?"

"The Eagle has landed, Mr. President."

"Neatly done." The President brightened at Laura's remarks. "I

-161-

seem to be playing the straight man today."

"The part is not important as long as you play it convincingly, Mr. President."

"Thank you, Alexi. I shall try to remember that as we proceed. O.K. You all have had longer to think about this than me. Let me hear your thoughts while I try to assimilate this incredible news."

Dr. Shavinsky spoke. "The two remaining men are frail. They have low body masses. Because of this it may be possible to send two small Astronauts in an Apollo spacecraft and lunar module to retrieve them. Modifications would be needed to accommodate an extra person on each craft, but the weight should not be a problem. That is the only practical way to bring both back at once."

"What about an exchange of personnel?" asked the President.

"Only if one of these men can fly the lunar module without the pilot. And of course the pilot would have to be able to manage the Moon Base installation."

"You have no available...." He saw Dr. Shavinsky shaking his head.

"Nothing we have could be converted to such use in a reasonable time; however, we have the capacity to launch an Apollo spacecraft. We understand that NASA may not have this ability at the present time."

The Ambassador added "We do wish to assist and --- to the extent possible --- participate in this mission."

"Well, Alexi, it appears we will be needing your transmission reports and --- discretion."

"We understand that nothing should be disclosed to the public until the operation is ready."

"If then," added the President. He turned to Ken and asked "Who did you contact at NASA?"

"Uhm. The Archives Librarian --- a nice old guy named Will. Don't recall the last name, but it doesn't matter."

"You mean everyone there knows him?"

"No, sir. Will died unexpectedly a few hours after I told him."

The President groaned and shot a quick glance at Mrs.

MacPherson. "Natural causes?" he offered.

"We didn't stay to find out. Not that anyone would have told us anything anyway."

"I'll have someone look into it," he promised vaguely. "In the meantime, I'll telephone the Director of NASA and tell him you will be providing some vital information to him, Dr. Shavinsky."

"Yes. Thank you."

"Thank you all for coming in today."

After that the meeting dissolved into a thanking and hand-shaking routine, with the occasional simultaneous Presidential hand on the shoulder intended to convey deep sincerity.

He always marveled how women let him squeeze their shoulders. There was no telling what he might try if he was re-elected.

/////

Rae suggested lunch at *La Selva*, a nearby dining establishment whose culinary achievements were overshadowed by fruit-filled rum concoctions complete with tiny parasols. When they were seated next to an *ersatz* waterfall, she ordered *sopa de lima* for everyone. Ken and Laura were tentative in their reactions to the lime soup, but the two Russian scientists were delighted to find this Yucatán delight in this unlikely venue. (The Russian Ambassador had proceeded back to the embassy, where he was consuming red cabbage steamed in vodka.)

They all had *tres leches* for dessert. It's a Cuban dish, but no one had any problem eating the cake soaked in sweet cream with whipped cream on top.

/////

"Why did I get the feeling that you were going to put a lip-lock on Dr. Konosov before dessert?"

"Lawsy Me! Such language from a Virginia Belle!" responded Rae. "And what have you done to Ken? He's more confused than usual."

"But content."

"Like you taught him to heel!"

Laura shrugged. "I don't think he was ready for a...."

"Men are always ready for one," Rae interrupted.

"No, no! I meant a relationship!" The other women in the *Señoritas* lounge were eavesdropping by now.

"Oh. Then you're right. They're never ready. It's always a surprise to them. Is he resisting?"

"Not actively."

"Laura, after decades of exhaustive research, I have concluded that there are far more decent women than there are decent men. I think Ken is one of the decent ones --- a keeper. He may not be suave or ambitious, but...."

"I've already had my knight in shining armor, and --- in a small way --- I've helped put men on the Moon. Now I'd just like to fill the empty side of the bed with something furry, warm and compatible. I was thinking of something larger than a dog."

"Dogs don't have Corvettes," Rae observed.

"True. They have fleas though, which are only slightly smaller."

"Oh. So you weren't dazzled by the fiberglass whizbang."

"All the Astronauts had them. They're toys."

"Look. This is none of my business, but...."

"A lady doesn't tell."

"Congratulations," she said wryly. "Then you won't be needing a place to stay while you're in town?"

"I have already arranged suitable accommodations, thank you."

"Just a guess, but...near Ken?"

"Quite," Laura replied with understatement. "Do you think they miss us yet?"

"*Naturalmente!*"

"You're beginning to sound like Ivan, y'know."

"Is that good or bad?"

"Might impress some Eastern European types --- tall, intriguing Russians, for example."

"*¡Bueno!*" She smiled incorrigibly.

/////

Back at the table, Dr. Shavinsky was explaining that the V-1 rocket had made a sound like *kaput!* when it was launched. Hitler had reportedly found this hilarious.

When that morsel was digested, Dr. Konosov announced "I have received some good news. I shall be returning to México to study Mayan glyphs. When I have a residence, you are all invited to visit."

"You will miss these capitalists?" cried Dr. Shavinsky with mock alarm.

"I will miss their crazy language --- so reminiscent of another tongue...."

"English?" ventured Ken.

"Perish the thought, old chap," he said, affecting an Eton accent. "I was referring to Australian."

"Throw some shrimps on the Barbie dolls!" Dr. Shavinsky added with great satisfaction.

/////

It was late afternoon. He had been invited to "a sweet sixteen party," which meant that he was to report immediately to 1600 Pennsylvania Avenue. Who came up with these ridiculous codewords?

Agent Terrance Koestler had not been in the Oval Office since Nixon had been the President. It appeared to be the same, although the upholstery seemed new.

"Agent Koestler?" The President looked over the top of a report to address him.

"Yes, sir."

"Please come over to my desk and sit in front of me."

"Yes, sir."

"I began my legal career working in the county prosecutor's office. Spent quite a bit of time there, in fact. After a while, you develop an ability to sense when something isn't quite right --- not what it purports to be. If you're there long enough, you take nothing at face value."

Since the President had paused to look at him, he said "Yes, sir" again.

"You know what I have here in my hand, Agent Koestler?"

"No, sir."

"It's an autopsy report from Brevard County, Florida. Know where that is?"

"Melbourne, I believe."

"Melbourne, Titusville, Cocoa Beach, Patrick Air Force Base and the Kennedy Space Center. Big county, stretches along the East coast of Florida. You know it?"

"Yes. sir."

"This is the autopsy report of Will Peterson, the Archives Librarian at the Cape. He shuffled off his mortal coil in a surprising fashion earlier this week."

"Surprising, sir?"

"Seems like he died of a massive heart attack. Not so unusual for an old man."

Agent Koestler did not like being toyed with, but could say nothing. He stared politely at the President and waited.

"But the little finger of his left hand was broken when he fell. Broken backward. You know what the odds are of that happening?"

"No, sir. I have no idea."

"Zero." The President stared at him. Neither moved for a minute. Then the President continued. "This other document is the form used to elect retirement. You certainly qualify. I would suggest that now would be an excellent time to complete it and submit it. You've worked hard and deserve some quality time." He handed Agent Koestler the form. "Complete this and give it to the receptionist by the elevator." It was a command.

"Thank you, Mr. President." He started to leave, but realized the President wasn't finished with him.

"State secrets are like water. Put water in a storage tank for a long time and it loses its taste. Eventually, it will leak out. No one is to blame. It is simply the nature of things."

"Sir?"

"Embrace retirement, Agent Koestler! Forget about your work in the Service. It is over. That is the healthy approach. 'Our life is what our thoughts make it.' Marcus Aurelius said that."

"'O' grinning damned villain,' Shakespeare said that," he thought. But he said "Yes, sir." This time he was permitted to leave. The President stared at the back of the Secret Service agent with contempt. A large man in a plain gray suit met Terrance Koestler at the door and escorted him down the hall to a small desk in an antechamber --- to help him fill out his retirement election forms. Nothing was left to chance.

Ex-Agent Koestler left the White House without badge or official identification. At the door, he was given a paper bag he was told contained the personal belongings from his former government vehicle. It didn't. He ambled down Pennsylvania Avenue clutching it, squinting at the setting sun. His Foster-Grants had not been in the bag.

He didn't feel like learning Apache. Maybe that would come later.

Chapter Eighteen
Saturday, May 15, 1993

They were awakened by the sirens, which seemed to be just outside. Ken looked at red numbers on the clock by his bed. It was 4:33 A.M. He struggled to the window. Firemen had the hoses on a small but intense blaze in the parking lot. Others were hosing down the adjacent cars to prevent their ignition. He put on his trousers and a tee shirt and ran out the door barefoot with his keys, ignoring Laura's queries.

When he arrived, firemen were directing the removal of vehicles. He offered his keys.

"What kind of car?"

"Corvette!"

The fireman took the proffered keys, but simply pocketed them.

"Aren't you going to move it?"

"Too late!" he yelled back. Just then the gas tank exploded, blasting the T-tops high into the air.

"Uhm."

Civilian Terrance Koestler was now miles away from the scene. He could enjoy it via the media. He didn't have to watch. He'd seen cars burn before. He felt better, not going quietly. He was damned if he was going to spend his retirement at some casino owned by the Bingo Indian Nation. And line dancing was still out of the question.

/////

Dr. Konosov arrived at the Russian Embassy at 5:18 A.M. He was awake, but not --- he admitted to himself --- alert. After receiving the call, it had taken him about one-half hour to groom and dress. The limousine had been waiting at the curb, or kerb. No, it was curb in the United States; kerb in the United Kingdom. He had no idea which it might be in Canada. It was just too early.

He was taken to a windowless room in the center of the building. It seemed to be fortified. It had the feel of a bank safe, a soundproofed one. Radio transmitting and receiving apparatus covered desks along the walls. There was a large square table in the center. Spread out on it were more than a dozen sheets of letter-size bond paper. He was amused to see that it had been faxed, by-passing all the Embassy security systems. The reason was obvious: it was gibberish.

He asked for black coffee and sat down at the table. He retrieved his copy of *La Fábula del Tiburón y las Sardinas* and sighed. After a minute, he had determined that it was indeed a Moon Base transmission.

Then it hit him. The pattern!

There were breaks in the transmission! It was not a soliloquy! It looked like half of a conversation!

But who were they talking with?

Forty-five minutes later, when the translation was done, it was apparent that NASA must have managed to contact the Astronauts. So it was with great relief that he contacted Dr. Shavinsky with this news.

"Why didn't we monitor the ground transmissions?" he asked.

"I'm asking you," replied Dr. Konosov.

"I will investigate and call you."

"*Do svedanya.*"

///////

"I know it's Saturday. That's why I'm still in bed."

"Uhm." Poor start. "Here's Laura."

"Didn't mean to bother you so early, but it's such a great day for a picnic. Do you want to come with us? Go out to the Shenandoah forest? Maybe we could persuade an ex-Bolshevik to join our troupe," she suggested. "After all, this is the day the Lord hath made. Let us rejoice and be glad in it. *Psalms 118:24.*"

Rae was awake now. "And let us make merry whilst the sun doth shine. O.K. I'm in. I'll call Dr. Konosov. Give me a few minutes."

"We'll take your car."

"Yeah, yeah. We don't know each other well enough to ride four in a Corvette."

"That too," Laura said cryptically. "'Bye!"

Laura's Grand Am had escaped with only a broken windshield.

/////

Even with a heavy load in the trunk, the blue Lincoln Continental seemed to fly along I-95. Terrance Koestler had a new form of transport. Only 19,000 miles on the odometer. At $24,000.00, he'd felt it was a good investment.

Retirement was beginning to agree with him.

And he was already in South Carolina.

/////

"You kids be good in the back. This isn't a drive-in movie," Rae admonished, embarrassing Ken. Taking a cue, Laura said "Watch those hands, buddy!"

"Uhm."

The ladies chuckled, but Dr. Konosov asked "Why 'buddy'? Why not 'bubba' or 'buster'? These are the things that make languages baffling at times."

Rae sighed and rose to the occasion. "Only Humphrey Bogart could say 'buster' convincingly, so it's now *passé*. 'Buddy' is Irish and is still used in the movies to mean friend, although sometimes used in a threatening manner by implying an intimacy that doesn't exist. 'Bubba' is Appalachian for brother, but it sometimes has the connotation of a country bumpkin or hick."

"She works crossword puzzles," explained Ken. "She can't help herself."

"A fascinating explanation. Is it true?"

"It could be, Doctor."

"Wait! No more 'Doctor' please. My name is Ivan."

"No offense, Ivan, but in America 'Ivan' is synonymous with 'Russian.' We might as well call you 'comrade' and have done with it," Laura commented.

"How about 'Yvon' then? It's the French version," he offered in good humor.

"Wrong gender," said Rae. "Yvonne is a silent screen starlet with a questionable past. Do you have a middle name?"

"Yes. It's Lenin." He was grinning. "I'd hoped you might ask."

Ken and Laura were laughing, but Rae was determined. She announced "O.K. Comrade Lenin. Let's see. 'Lenin' is the Russian word for 'lion;' so we could call you 'Leon' or just 'Leo.'"

Laura made a face at this suggestion.

"Unless there's a Mayan word for 'lion'" Rae offered.

"No lions; therefore no word. They had jaguars, though. Still do."

"Now we're getting somewhere. What are they called?"

"*Balam*."

"Can't do it, comrade," Rae choked. "Can't call you 'Ball 'em.' Just no way." Laura was doubled over with silent laughter.

Sensing victory, he asked "You see how 'Ivan' grows on you?"

"Sure do, Tiger." She winked at him. He thought he liked his new nickname. He knew he liked the wink.

/////

After the picnic, Rae pulled the Cougar off the highway, following Laura's instructions. Minutes later they were on the lane in the cemetery, among the departed members of the MacPherson clan. Both Ken and Laura went straight to the same spot, then began walking around.

"What's wrong?" asked Rae.

"It isn't where I remembered," Laura responded. Rae and Ivan joined the search.

"I sat right there just a few weeks ago, and I was in front of it," said Ken, pointing.

"I've found something!" Ivan approached them with a bent piece of brass plate. He straightened it out and wiped it with his sleeve. The letters could still be clearly seen.

IN RECOGNITION OF HIS SERVICE TO HIS COUNTRY
National Aeronautics and Space Administration

"Oh my God!" said Ken.

"When my anxious thoughts multiply within me, Thy consolations delight my soul. *Psalms 94:19.*" This was recited at approximately the speed of light.

Rae and Ivan understood from this that the tombstone was missing.

/////

After dropping off Ken and Laura, Rae insisted Ivan return to her apartment to finish off the remaining fried chicken and have a glass of wine. The trip back had been silent. They both needed to put the incident in perspective.

Upon arriving, Ivan phoned Dr. Shavinsky. "Yes, that is most perplexing. I agree. If I have any suggestions, I shall call you." Then he added dryly "It will not be necessary for you to wait by the telephone."

She handed him a flute of sparkling white wine. "*¡Salud,* Comrade Tiger!"

He smiled back at her. "*¡Salud, compadre!* Now that we are comrades again, it is time to share state secrets once more."

They sat on opposite ends of the couch, facing each other. Close but not intimate. "Now what?"

"Just this morning --- about 6:00 A.M., in fact --- I discovered that the Astronauts at the Moon Base were communicating with someone. We only received the transmissions from the Moon Base; so I only had half of the conversation. I naturally concluded that NASA had managed to re-establish contact. I so advised Dr. Shavinsky immediately."

"That's wonderful news."

"But Dr. Shavinsky has just told me that NASA is not yet ready to attempt transmission."

"What do you think that means?"

"Someone is not telling me the truth."

"Would Dr. Shavinsky lie to you?"

"If he was ordered to, yes. On the other hand, he may simply be passing on incorrect information he has received."

"If you want to spread a convincing lie, have an honest man tell it for you."

"This situation doesn't equate."

"Try thinking in Russian," she suggested. "I assume that is your mother tongue. Would vodka help?"

"Vodka never helps the thought process; but it is good that you tease me. It cheers me."

"Then my Comrade Tiger, prepare to be teased."

Despite this promising start, the evening ended early because the day had begun so. Dr. Konosov was asleep in his hotel room by 9:30 P.M.

Rae remained awake in her apartment puzzling over the days events and revelations. She even called up Laura and offered to go to church with her in the morning. She had declined. Apparently, she wanted to convert Ken first.

Chapter Nineteen
Sunday, May 16, 1993

After church services, the foursome visited Monticello. None of them had ever actually been inside. After a leisurely lunch at a country inn, they all went to Dulles International, where Dr. Konosov caught the Finnair flight to St. Petersburg via Helsinki. He explained that it had the best connections because no one ever just went to Helsinki.

He bade them all "*Do svedanya.*" To Rae he added, "*Hasta la vista.*"

"*Hasta la vista, compadre.*"

Rae became so quiet after the plane left that Ken suggested "Can we drop you somewhere?"

"It's my car, you cretin!"

"Details."

"Come by for a glass of wine," invited Laura. "We bought a huge wheel of brie. I put almonds on top."

"Well, we should discuss recent events. I accept your kind invitation to dine at your place."

The implication that Laura had taken over was not lost on Ken; so he responded as profoundly as he could. "Uhm."

/////

"I guess we should feel relieved," ventured Laura. "Our burden has been lifted."

"More like dropped on the unsuspecting President. Isn't he a piece of work? We drop this basket of snakes on him and he smiles and thanks us."

"Is it over for us?" Ken asked.

"It doesn't seem possible."

"There is a new wrinkle," said Rae; who proceeded to tell them of the one-sided conversations now coming from the Moon Base, as well as the theories as to the identity of the other party. "Any other explanations?"

"Secret pal," said Laura unexpectedly.

"Could you expand upon that concept?" asked Rae.

"Perhaps they are not communicating with anyone. They're just pretending to."

"They're delusional?"

"Maybe, but not necessarily." She hesitated.

Ken picked up on it. "It's a possibility. After all, they've been sending one-way messages for twenty years. They obviously think no one is receiving them. Why not make a game out of it?"

"Probably sick of gin rummy, by now. You may have something. And congratulations to each of you for each finding someone as demented as yourself."

"Thank you," they said in unison. Then they shook hands. "We'll still find time to drive you crazy," Ken promised.

"What are friends for?" added Laura.

"Enough!"

"I believe she means *bastante*, don't you Ken?"

"Oh, yes. Indeed. *Claro*, as we used to say in Cleveland."

"And what's that toast in Russian? Sounds like 'dis-robe ya.' Now there's a phrase to conjure with."

"Thank you for a lovely evening. I've got to leave here before I acquire any more wisdom. I seem to have bagged my limit."

/////

Courtney had to return to the house to feed the frogs. She was picking up some more clothes and necessities. Ultimately, she decided to take a shower and lighten her hair, as well. The result to the outside world was that she spent several hours running about the house in various states of undress --- towel around her waist one minute, around her head the next.

The outside world specifically included Terrance Koestler, who was in the back yard watching the spectacle with nary a scintilla of titillation, hoping she would finish soon. He was tired from his long drive. His legs were wobbly. He needed sleep.

When Courtney finally left, he pulled the Lincoln into the carport of the house he had rented next door. He intended to remove all his belongings remaining in the house. First he would have to remove the headstone from the trunk. It had broken into two pieces when he had uprooted it. This had proved a blessing; for the weight of each piece was nearly all he could carry.

He was a big man, still in good shape. Nevertheless, he staggered under the weight of the top chunk of marble headstone, lurching across the back yards to the Florida room screen door. It was there that he trod upon something unseen in the darkness.

Rrrrraagh!

Just as the sound entered his ears, the claws ripped into his trousers and socks --- and the flesh of his right leg. He instinctively pulled backward. Off balance, he fell clumsily, his head resting awkwardly against the side of the house. The weight of the headstone on his chest snapped his neck.

By this time, the raccoon called Snooks had already limped through three neighbors' yards. And she was still moving at a respectable clip.

Chapter Twenty
Monday, May 17, 1993

A neighbor had investigated the blue Lincoln with the trunk standing open. By 11:30 A.M. the body had been found and been identified as the owner of the car. The house did not appear to have been broken into. The headstone pieces and the scratches on the leg were still mysteries. No one seemed to know how to contact the owner of the house, who had the same last name as the headstone. The investigator had no theories that would apply this far from Halloween. He did have a headache.

/////

Ken had gone to work, leaving her alone in the apartment. While she did her laundry, she perused his magazines. Bored, she turned on the television and found CNN Headline News. The commentator said "A bizarre death in Florida has authorities baffled. This morning a native of Washington, D.C. was found dead behind this house in Cocoa Beach. Part of a marble grave marker was on his chest." Laura stared at her home on the screen. "There were slashes of an undetermined origin on his ankle, but the cause of death appears to have been a broken neck. Authorities have refused to speculate as to whether the dead man had been attacked or was involved in some ritual. Concerned neighbors have been assured that there is no cult activity in the neighborhood."

Laura sat speechless through the business news, sports and several commercials before reacting. She bowed her head and recited the *23rd Psalm* very slowly. It calmed her enough that she could curl up on the couch and cry softly. She knew this was a halfway measure, but she was too exhausted to scream.

/////

Twenty minutes later, she telephoned the Cocoa Beach Police, who assured her that her home was secure. It appeared that the "deceased had not attempted entry."

"Any idea who he was?" she asked.

Detective Sergeant Lopez replied "His name was Terrance Koestler of Arlington, Virginia. One of your neighbors identified him as the man who was staying in the house next door to yours. You didn't know him?"

"The place was vacant until about a month ago. We didn't see him move in. He never seemed to be at home. I went over with a pie once, but no one answered the door. So we ate the pie ourselves."

"Would you recognize him?"

"Never saw him."

"Do you know what kind of car he had?"

"There was a new yellow Mustang in the drive. Kind of hard to miss."

"I guess it would be," he commented, wondering why the man now had a Lincoln. "Anything else?"

"Nothing I can recall. If I remember anything else, I'll let you know. I should be home in a few days."

"Thanks. Oh, by the way, this guy had a lot of surveillance equipment. Any idea what he might have been doing with that?"

"Surveillance equipment? You mean like on a stake-out?"

"Exactly. Sophisticated stuff."

"Unless he was writing a book about the dullest neighborhood in Florida, I can't imagine what he could have used it for."

"You weren't aware of any such activities, then?"

"Of course not."

"The reason I asked is that all your blinds and curtains on that side of your house are closed."

Her mind raced. Her tongue idled.

"Mrs. MacPherson?"

"I'm sorry. Was that a question?"

"I guess the question was implied. Could you explain?"

"Privacy, Detective. I have a young daughter who walks around the house half dressed. I don't worry about the spinster on the other side."

"That makes sense," he admitted. She understood that this did not mean he believed her. "When you get back, give me a call. We'll tell you what we've found out in the meantime." But he wasn't finished. "We have your husband's grave marker at the station. Officially, it's evidence, but we should be able to return it to you soon. You know that it's broken?"

"That's what the news report said."

"Too bad about that. Where was your husband buried?"

"In Maryland."

"In Maryland," he repeated dully. "Did you know the marker was missing?"

"I was at the cemetery last Saturday. That was when I first knew it was gone. I never thought it would show up in Cocoa Beach."

"Did you report it?"

"No. It's a small rural cemetery. I have the number to call at home." Then she added, "Guess I don't have to call now."

"Any idea what the deceased was doing with it?"

"None whatsoever."

/////

Amazingly, the windshield had been replaced right in the parking lot by a man sent by her insurance company. In Cocoa Beach, the adjuster would still being trying to figure out if the damage was covered. Life was, indeed, different in the big city.

At lunch, she related these latest events to Rae, who responded by ordering two glasses of kir for them. Eating *crepes* at an outside table in the sunshine lifted Laura's spirits enough for Rae to embark upon the real purpose of their meeting.

"So what are you going to do about Ken?"

"It's sort of up to him."

"You don't get it. Ken is on total overload. He's smitten! You've bewitched him. Having his 'Vette burn up didn't help much either." Her expression changed suddenly. "You didn't...."

Laura laughed. "No, I didn't do it."

"Too bad. It would have been brilliant."

"Why do say that?"

"Because it represented his former life. Post-Cindi and Pre-Laura. The destruction of his toy could be an explosive segue into his new life."

"Explosive segue could be an oxymoron," Laura observed dryly.

"We're in Washington. This is the place that gave us 'Peacekeeper Missiles' and 'Military Intelligence.' The oxymoron is not an endangered species here." Rae shrugged her shoulders to indicate it didn't matter to her. Picturesque speech had its price. Then she leaned forward over the table in a conspiratorial fashion and advised Laura to "Take charge of the situation."

"Jonas was more than ten years older than I was. Ken is...."

"Younger, but not by much."

"It's so different. With Jonas, making love was a comfortable ritual, and...it's different with Ken."

"It's more intense?"

"If that term encompasses the bed collapsing," she said with a blush.

"Oh my!" Rae observed. "Were you thrown clear?"

"No one was maimed. But the timing was cruel," she added wistfully.

"We've all been there. At least it wasn't Ken's fault. I assume the mood was broken."

"Shattered. Obliterated. Scattered at sea."

"You had a good laugh at least?"

"I never knew I could moan and laugh simultaneously," she admitted with a grin.

"Then it wasn't all bad."

"But this is new to me. I don't know if it will continue."

"That's up to you. When a couple co-habit, sex becomes more of a ritual than the seismic encounter you described. It's inevitable. But the woman should control the ritual. Otherwise, it becomes one-sided."

"That's a new one."

"Think about it. The time required for male arousal is measured in nanoseconds, whereas...well, you know. The trick is to have sex when you want to. That way the woman has time to put herself in the mood. This does not harm your partner, since a man is always ready. In fact it may make it more exciting for him. Let's face it. If his partner isn't enjoying sex anymore, a sensitive man will eventually detect it. This may make him feel guilty about it. This could diminish his pleasure."

"The French say the wives are responsible for mistresses, not the husbands."

"The French are an amusing people."

"So how does one put herself in the mood?"

"Whatever works. I had a friend in college who only wanted sex when she was completely stoned. Unfortunately, she would get her dates so stoned they often simply passed out; so that's not a good example. I knew another who would practice what she euphemistically called self-arousal techniques before going out. She claimed it worked, although she once had an orgasm at Pizza Hut."

Laura choked on her cappuccino, but managed to ask "What did she do?"

"She said it was the best pizza she'd ever had. Probably was, all things considered."

"So I'm to take charge?"

"We wouldn't be having this conversation if you hadn't already. Admit it. How did you do it the first time?"

"If you must know, I removed all my clothes and put on one of his shirts. My own clothes were soaked by a downpour."

"How handy that was."

"I had to dally."

"Like Gene Kelly?"

"Without the hat and umbrella."

"You know, I don't think the difference is between Jonas and Ken so much. It's possible that you've changed."

She thought for a moment. "I have become more mature about these matters."

"Bordering on craven?"

"Never."

"Never?"

"Seldom? Occasionally? When the Moon is full?"

"Confession is good for the soul."

Chapter Twenty-One
Tuesday, May 18, 1993

It was nearly 3:00 A.M. Laura had been awake for several hours. She sat in a chair, wearing socks and one of Ken's robes. Actually, it was a 'happy coat' --- a cotton Japanese version of the smoking jacket. It had Oriental writing on it which could have been advertising a wok shop for all she knew. "Where do bachelors find these things?" she asked herself.

She had decided to return home soon, now that it was safe. Not tomorrow, but in a few days. She had told Courtney.

She watched as Ken moved in bed, oblivious to her absence therefrom. Men understand --- on a genetic level --- that sleep is beneficial. It renews the body and the spirit. The mind awakes refreshed. A good night's sleep is one of life's great blessings.

On the other hand, women see sleep as a forced interruption to their lives. It is a form of sloth. When they awaken during the night, they believe that they should stay awake. Then they are frustrated that they can't accomplish anything without disturbing their mates' slumbers. So they just worry. The following afternoon they are tired and grouchy from lack of sleep. This is their system.

She arose and padded out to the refrigerator, looking for a glass of milk.

/////

After Ken left, Laura took a taxi to "Glamour Shotz --- the *boudoir* photograph salon." She didn't want to leave her Grand Am in an unfamiliar neighborhood for any length of time. She got out only after she had checked out the neighborhood. She had one of Ken's long-sleeved blue shirts on a hanger. She also had three of his neckties. She meant business.

She emerged about two hours later, clutching a manilla envelope containing negatives --- and what she devoutly hoped were all the prints from her session. She was smiling.

Rae seized the initiative. In this case, it took the form of her MCI calling card. She placed the call to St. Petersburg as easily as if it had been the city in Florida. She knew that modern communications were supposed to work this way, but she still marveled when they actually did.

"*Ya slusha vam.*"

"*Buenas noches* from the capital of capitalism, Ivan."

"Rae!" he exclaimed. "What are you doing in London?"

"*Touché*, my witty *compadre*. I'm in Washington. Have you any news about our friends who carry on conversations with themselves?"

"Only that they continue to do so."

"Our friend from the South hypothesizes that it could be a game for them. Conversations with an imaginary friend to pass the time."

"If that is so, then they have excellent imaginations. Their discussions are quite detailed."

"Are they consistent with each other?"

"An excellent question. The answer is in the affirmative. These appear to be genuine communications with --- with someone."

"Oh well. It was just a thought."

"I will review the transmissions again with this explanation in my mind, to see if we have missed something. In a few days we will release the transcripts to NASA. We would like to provide an explanation at that time. This may be helpful."

"Will you be coming back to America then?"

"Probably. I shall call you when I do."

"I will meet your plane. You can even bring along Dr. Shavinsky if you wish."

"I think you have eyes for him," he teased.

"I'm merely overcome with *glasnost*," she demurred.

"This is a treatable condition. Don't worry. You should see a doctor. A Russian doctor, of course."

"Then let me know when I can have an appointment, Doctor," she said brazenly.

"I shall call you soon for a *cita*."

"Then, *Ciao.*"

On the hunch that *cita* was Spanish, she sought out Maria in the secretarial pool, who advised her that the word meant 'appointment' or 'date.' Rae liked the implication. After all, he had intentionally switched languages to use this word which had two meanings, both of which could apply neatly. The sly devil.

/////

She immediately told this to Laura, when they met for a late lunch. Laura nodded and agreed that it appeared Dr. Konosov wished to see Rae again. Then she slid a matte photographic print across the table, face down. Rae gave her a curious look before she turned it over.

"Mother of Pearl! When did you do this?"

"This morning," Laura replied casually. "You said I should take the initiative."

"Ken was right. You do not believe in halfway measures. Was this the outfit you had on when...."

"Pretty much the same."

"What are you going to do with this?"

"I have to go home. I thought I'd give it to Ken to remind him of me."

"If this doesn't do it, he's a eunuch."

"I have it from reliable sources that he's not a eunuch."

Rae scanned the photograph again. "This should have a warning. Like do not attempt to drive or use heavy machinery after viewing."

"First time I've heard one called that."

"What?"

"Heavy machinery."

"Oh." Then she added "What have you done with the real Laura MacPherson?"

"This is the new Laura MacPherson. The old one has been terminated."

"Put to bed?"

Laura smiled innocently and batted her eyelashes.

New Yorkers didn't want the capital to remain in Philadelphia. Residents of the City of Brotherly Love had little love to spare for the Dutch merchants of the former New Amsterdam. (They referred to them as "Yankees" --- a minor corruption of the prominent Dutch name "Janke.") Boston was too far North and the other contenders were too far South. So the States of Maryland and Virginia donated a square tract of swampland along the Potomac River. When the new capital was being laid out on the Maryland side, Virginia reneged on the deal.

Despite its marshy location, Washington has a magnificent Springtime, lasting up to a week. Then Summer grips the former swampland with hot, humid days. Ken returned to his apartment sweaty and tired. The air conditioning in his rental car had proven inadequate to the task.

Laura met him at the door with a glass of champagne which she insisted he drink immediately. As he did so, she removed all his clothing and led him to the bath tub. She followed him in and massaged his shoulders as he washed. The chilled bottle of *Perrier-Jouet* was next to the tub. "I bought it because I liked the painting on the bottle," she admitted after their second glass.

"You may have spoiled me. Makes the other stuff taste like ginger ale."

"Oh, the spoiling is just beginning," she said, rubbing her breasts against his back. "You soak a few more minutes. I have more surprises."

The dining room table was laden with stone crab claws. There was nothing else, save lemons, bowls of warmed butter and another bottle of champagne. For dessert there was Key Lime pie and Cuban coffee. She wanted him alert.

In the morning, she would tell him she had to go home. She would hide the photograph in his apartment. She didn't need it right now.

There is such a thing as overkill.

Chapter Twenty-Two
Friday, May 21, 1993

"Ken's going to drive back with me, then fly home," Laura announced at lunch.

"You showed him the photograph?"

"No. I'm saving it."

"Then he's hooked," declared Rae.

"I hope so."

"I'm going to miss you. There's a shortage of interesting people."

"You should live in Cocoa Beach!"

"We'll stay in touch then?"

"Of course! You'll be my eyes in Washington."

"I get to watch Ken for you?"

"Think of it as a spectator sport."

"Can I have a tail-gate party?"

"Where would you have it?"

"Behind the car."

"Of course. What a foolish question. Just don't get rowdy."

/////

Detective Sergeant Lopez wrote in the file. "Initial determination: accidental death. No witnesses. Deceased was alone. There are no indications of foul play." That gave him pause. He still couldn't account for the scratches. The Medical Examiner had said they might have been inflicted by an animal, but so what. He didn't die of them. He couldn't very well round up the neighborhood dogs and cats for questioning. If he'd wanted this kind of crap, he'd have stayed in Miami and shot it out with the Colombian drug gangs. He'd keep the file open for a few weeks, in case something materialized from out of the blue. Then he'd quietly close it. He didn't need an open homicide on the books.

They had barely closed the books on that NASA geezer who'd had a heart attack in his kitchen. Sergeant Lopez had thought the kitchen was too clean --- no prints on the faucets or refrigerator door. Then the medical examiner had discovered the broken finger. If that death smelled, then this latest one positively reeked. Prowling around someone's house carrying a piece of tombstone stolen from a grave over 1,000 miles away! Nobody seemed to care that the guy was dead anyway.

"Not completely accurate," he reminded himself. Someone was coming down from Washington to claim the body. Washington couldn't be good news. "Deceased was probably a Pentagon bureaucrat," he thought. Curious, he shuffled through the file for a note identifying the person who had called. "*¡Mierda!*" Expletives still tended to find voice in his native tongue. He was, after all, born in Miami.

As he stared at the fax on the letterhead of the United States Secret Service, he began to wonder if one file folder would be enough. Would one file cabinet?

/////

21 MAY 1993. THIS IS MONDAY. WE ARE STILL HERE. LOOKING FORWARD TO SOME COMPANY AND A RIDE HOME. DEMITRIUS SENDS REGARDS TO COLONEL SAUNDERS. AIR LOCK NOT OPERATING WITHIN NORMAL PARAMETERS. HAVE CURTAILED USE TO ONCE EVERY TWO DAYS. WILL WE BE REPLACED OR WILL PROJECT TERMINATE? COMPUTER DATA STREAM FOLLOWS. HABITAT::I:16°/E:N175°/AP:0.79/G:0.39....

"Aha!" exclaimed Dr. Shavinsky. "Contact the American Liaison Department at once. I wish to know all about a Colonel Saunders of NASA. Then we can determine what the Americans are doing." To his chagrin, NASA was accepting his data, but not sharing any information. They still insisted they hadn't re-established communications, when it was obvious that they had. It was insulting.

Nevertheless, he had to help. And wait for NASA to pull together one more, unscheduled Apollo Mission. "They must still have a spacecraft from the cancelled Apollo XIX mission. It would have to be refitted --- and reconfigured to accommodate four persons on the return voyage from the Lunar orbit. But that was the easy part. How much of the original spacecraft would they use?" he wondered. He could picture the manufacturers' scientists arguing with their NASA counterparts over which components might still be sound after twenty years. But were the scientists themselves still sound?

"All considered, it may be better to be part of the audience instead of a performer in this production," he reasoned.

PART V: ACTION

Chapter Twenty-Three
Tuesday, June 1, 1993

The intercom came to life at 8:02 A.M. "Major Sanders? I have someone on the telephone who wants to speak with a Colonel Saunders."

He sighed. People were always confusing his rank and his name. "Tell them we're out of Extra Greasy," he responded automatically, then thought better of it. "Wait! Who is it?" He believed that the first call set the tone for the entire day. It was superstition of the worst sort; *i.e.*, accurate superstition.

"He says he's calling from the American Liaison Department of the Russian Aerospace Bureau." It was going to be an interesting day. He picked up the telephone receiver.

"Buck Saunders here," He said, conceding the name and ignoring the question of rank. It saved time.

Within an hour he had personally contacted Dr. Shavinsky and discussed the situation in depth. When they disconnected, each thought he had accomplished a great deal.

/////

Ken had taken some of his accumulated vacation time; so he and Laura could drive to Florida via the Skyline Drive and Blue Ridge Parkway. "It's the time of year for the rhododendron to bloom," he had offered by way of explanation.

"Sounds better than I-95 any day," she had responded truthfully. Smashing your hand in a car door sounded better than I-95, when you came right down to it.

"We'll miss South of the Border." He referred to the famous gas station *cum* souvenir stand that had become a monument to Americans taking things beyond their logical extreme. The secret to its success? Some said it was the fireworks. Others pointed out the fifty million gaudy signs along I-95. In truth, the facility had been enterprisingly located at a point on the highway where bladders tended to be full and clean rest rooms were rare.

"Not much."

The trip had been bliss, but he had been back in the office for a week. To say he had been back at work would have been a stretch. He was going through the motions.

"Close the door," Rae commanded. Ken did so and seated himself. "You talking to her?"

"Every night."

"You know you have to do something soon, or you'll lose her."

He adjusted his posture without any perceived effect. "I suspected I might."

"Why is it so damned hard for men to commit?" She almost shouted it.

"Well..."

"It was rhetorical!"

"Uhm."

She tried another approach. "I have a rush assignment for you. Has to be on my desk by Friday Noon. Written report. Original and one copy."

He began taking notes.

"You've been with GAO more than twenty years. That gives you half pay for retirement. Figure what half pay would be after all withholding. Then add up your savings, excluding retirement accounts."

"About $31,000.00."

"More than I thought," she said with a smirk. "Then figure the equity in your condominium, net of costs of sale, and compute a Five Percent return on that amount. Lastly, estimate what you'll have in your retirement accounts and compute a Three Percent payout on that amount, starting when you're sixty. Lay it out by years, showing each category as a separate source of income."

"May one inquire as to the purpose of this exercise?"

"I think the results will demonstrate that you could retire comfortably at any time now, especially if you found the right woman with her own means."

"You referring to Laura?"

-191-

"Yes. Think about it. Her husband was a top NASA scientist. She obviously gets his pension. He probably had insurance too. They bought the house in the 1960's when mortgages only ran 20 years; so it's probably free and clear. In other words, you two could have it made!"

"I do believe all this romantic talk is makin' me lightheaded, Miz Kirkland."

"You know, some people could have more money than brains and still qualify for food stamps."

"Flattery will get you no where." After he'd opened her office door to leave, he turned to ask "Is this your idea?"

"Entirely. Believe me. This conversation is strictly *entre nous.*"

"Laura was right. Dr. Ivan has affected your speech."

"You ain't seen *nada* yet, *amigo.*"

Ken shrugged and left. He would start the report now. Rae might just be right. She also might be the best friend he had ever had. It was strange that he hadn't realized it before.

/////

Tiffany Reed, M.D. looked at herself in the mirror. Her skin was taut, her eyes were green, her hair was light brown. "Waif," she said without thinking. She was barely five feet tall and only weighed 100 pounds after a big dinner and fully dressed. At the moment she was 96 pounds in her undies. She struck a weightlifter's pose, flexing as many muscles as she could at once without inducing cramps. "96 pounds of fury."

Her inspection was interrupted by the telephone. It was the director of Astronaut training, her boss, former Apollo Astronaut Buck Sanders. He told her she had been selected to receive special training and to report to his office ASAP.

"Am I being bumped from the Shuttle?"

"For now."

"But why?"

"We need you elsewhere."

"But I want to be in space."

"Patience. Just report as soon as you can." Then he added, "You may need to lose some weight."

"Are you sure you have the right telephone number?"

"Affirmative, Dr. Reed."

/////

The office of former Navy test pilot Buck Sanders was standard NASA cubicle, albeit a large cubicle. (He referred to it as "spacious " when he was being witty.) On the wall behind his desk was an enlarged photograph of him standing on the surface of the Moon displaying a sign that said

THE BUCK STOPS HERE.

It was not only a unique memento. It served to remind all who entered his office that he was one of the very few who had actually done it. The photograph and its implicit message were impossible to ignore.

On another wall was a small brass plaque on which was engraved:

ODE TO THE CENTER OF THE UNIVERSE

Blow the trumpets in your Honor!
Ope' wide the gates to see you through!
This has surely been your hour.
Tomorrow I hope you're dead, you Bastard!

--- C.W. Mummert

Visitors to his office invariably found this message perplexing, which was its sole reason for being there. He personally had no idea what it meant, had never heard of the author. He'd found this quaint example of twisted philosophy in an antique shop on Rue Royale in New Orleans' French Quarter some fifteen years ago. It was the best $4.00 he'd ever invested.

Dr. Reed appeared in this office within the hour. She closed the door behind her and stood before his desk in a quasi-military manner that some of the civilian Astronauts affected by way of fitting in. He had no intention of letting her control the conversation; so he immediately said "You're to be fitted for a space suit."

"I already have one."

"Not like this. Do you like the retro look?"

"Major Sanders, what in the world are you talking about?"

"That style," he said nonchalantly, pointing to the photograph. "Not exactly the height of fashion today, but a comfortable garment in hostile conditions. I'd lend you mine, but it's not a junior petite. I think fit is so important, don't you, Doctor."

"I thought you could only find those in the boys' department."

"That's true. However, you'll be pleased to know that the decision was made to alter the suit to fit the gender rather than the other way around. It was close. I cast the deciding vote."

"It goes without saying then that you have my undying gratitude. I'd have had to let out my unmentionables to accommodate all that extra paraphernalia," she remarked casually. "But where am I to wear this antique article of apparel?"

"The Aitken Basin --- near the South Pole."

"The South Pole," she repeated dully. "Is the hole in the ozone layer that bad?"

"I hope not, Doctor. I was referring to the Lunar South Pole. It is, after all, a Moon Suit."

She sat down abruptly, without grace. He shuffled papers a for nearly a minute to allow her time to recover. "When?" she asked.

"That was the right question. As soon as possible."

"But the shuttle wasn't designed for that."

"If you listen very carefully you will hear the sound of thousands of workers preparing Apollo XIX for its belated maiden flight."

Unexpectedly, she reached inside her blouse. "Ouch!" Then she withdrew her hand. "I pinched myself to insure I was awake," she explained. "The nipple is one of the most sensitive parts of any mammal."

"I learn something new every day," he said dryly. "Now, after you're fitted, you have to learn how to fly the LEM. The simulator is set up. Rockwell is going over the LEM they built for Apollo XIX, which was never delivered. They hope to have it ready in a month."

"Who's going to fly the command vehicle?"

"Not my decision." Someone knew, but not him. "I'll let you know. Of course, you'll both have back-ups."

"The LEM co-pilot?"

"None. You're on your own once you leave the command module."

"No dancing partner? I always thought it would be great to waltz in low gravity."

"Maybe you'll meet someone."

She ignored his remark. "What experiments will I be doing?"

"Still being determined. As you might expect, there's a long list of candidates. You won't have time to read a paperback."

"Why me?"

"What do you weigh?"

"96 pounds."

"That's one reason. Try to drop a few more pounds. We have a weight limitation."

"What's the other reason?"

"You're single with no family. It's easier for you to disappear. You see, this is classified. One leak --- even to a fellow Astronaut --- and the project will be scrubbed. This comes directly from the President. So you are going to disappear. Can you handle all this?"

"It is a bit much to assimilate before breakfast, but I can handle it. As my father used to point out when I complained about my name, Tiffany is associated with diamonds, the hardest mineral found in Nature."

"Then I'm glad your name isn't Faberge."

"As in eggs?" She added "It seems to me I have the easy part."

"Oh? And what would be the tough part?"

"Launching an Apollo Mission without anyone knowing."

"We're still working on it."

"Good luck."

"The same to you Doctor. A driver is at the front door to drive you to the Orlando airport where someone who could be your twin will board a plane with your ticket and disappear. You will be disguised in a closed rest room for your return trip to the base. Take all your identification with you. Your new identity kit will be provided there. The Secret Service is assisting us with this. I will be one of the few people with whom you will continue to have contact. Hopefully I can help with any problems that arise for you."

"Thank you."

"Hey, I threw you into this quicksand. The least I can do to is watch you thrash around and offer encouragement."

"Most reassuring."

"It's nothing."

"True."

/////

As the President had instructed, the call from the Director of NASA was put through immediately. "Good morning, Mr. President! I have Major Buck Sanders on the line. You may remember Buck from his corny antics on the Moon."

"I was too young," he bantered.

"How could I forget? Anyway, Buck has come up with a proposal that might just take the pressure off of us. I'd like him to explain it to you, but I must warn you to clear your mind of all other matters first."

"Should I take aspirin now?"

"It wouldn't hurt. O.K. Buck, you're on."

"If this line is not secure, stop me now, Mr. President," Major Sanders began. "As I understand the situation, the Russians can blow

-196-

the lid off the rescue operation at any time by revealing the existence of the Moon Base. They have implied that this may happen if they don't participate. On the other hand, we have been told to launch an Apollo Mission without anyone finding out about it, which simply can't be done from the Cape."

"I was afraid of that."

"What if the mission originates in the Turan Lowlands instead?"

"And that would be...?"

"Just East of the Aral Sea. Beyond the Steppes."

"We're talking about Russia?"

"Kazakhstan, actually, but the site is tightly controlled by Russia."

"That's comforting. I'm reaching for the aspirin. Please continue."

"It can be done. The Russians have the lifting power to put our Apollo into the proper trajectory. We don't have any Saturns ready. It can all be monitored by Kennedy and Houston, either of which could shut down the launch if necessary. We get secrecy and the Russians get to participate."

"After the launch, it would be our show?"

"We would be in control, although the command module pilot would be a Cosmonaut."

"Did I hear that right?"

The Director broke in. "We can train him in time. And he would remain on the command vehicle while our Astronaut actually carries out the rescue operation."

"I suppose the Russians insisted on this."

"Yes sir. Major Sanders spoke with Dr. Shavinsky himself."

"If I may Mr. President," Buck broke in.

"Go ahead, Major."

"This way the operation can remain a secret. We don't have to deal with the press over the Moon Base debacle until we have corrected the problem. Since you weren't involved when it was established, you'll be the hero. You'll have to share some of the glory with the Russians, but isn't that what *glasnost* is all about?"

"And the Russians still won't have walked on the Moon." The President was thinking out loud. "*Glasnost* has its political limits. O.K. gentlemen, tell me what happens if the mission fails?"

"A mission such as this can fail in several ways, Mr. President, but basically it comes down to two categories. Partial failure would be that neither Moon Base Astronaut returns alive. Complete failure would be that no one returns. The second scenario would be the easier to deal with. The public would never be told. The first one would be stickier, but again we could show that we had made the attempt at rescue."

"Can you keep it quiet?"

"We believe so, sir."

"What would we be giving away in technology?"

"Soyuz docked with Apollo XVIII. Cosmonauts have seen and photographed it. Anything else they wanted could be found in a ten-year old encyclopedia."

"O.K. gentlemen. Proceed along these lines, but let everyone know that I reserve the right to pull the plug after I've had a few days to think it over."

"Yes sir, Mr. President. One more item. Should there be a leak, the cover story is that we are assisting the Russians with their space program. Our Astronaut is listed on the manifest as Cosmonaut Natasha Russoff. Her code name is Georgia, which she still thinks refers to her state of birth instead of her country of birth. We have deniability."

"You're enjoying this, aren't you?"

"As we used to say back in Tennessee, I haven't had so much fun since granny caught her nose in the meat grinder, sir."

"What are we calling this operation?"

"We wanted the name to be obscure, to avoid giving any clues. It's being called Operation KFC."

"KFC refers to?"

There was a pause, then Buck Sanders said "Kentucky Fried Chicken, Mr. President."

"I'm sure you have a fascinating explanation which you'll reveal at the appropriate moment, Major Sanders. But for the time being, does it involve your last name?"

"Yes sir!"

"Doesn't anyone say 'Roger' anymore?"

"Roger that, Mr. President," snapped Buck Sanders.

Chapter Twenty-Four
Wednesday, June 30, 1993

Nearly a month had passed since Rae made Ken realize he could afford to retire. Yet he hadn't been able to discuss these matters over the telephone. "You can't talk to a woman without watching her eyes," he'd explained to Rae. "The words they say aren't always in synch with the eyes."

"You're learning," she had replied. Another critique!

So he found himself aboard a flight to Orlando again, wishing there were a real commercial airport close to Cocoa Beach. They would spend the Independence Day weekend together and --- with luck --- establish some sort of more permanent relationship.

Upon hearing he could come down, Laura had told him to dispense with the rental car and hotel room. The house had an extra bedroom; so appearances could be kept up. She found this concept amusing after her erstwhile efforts to convince the former neighbor that they were lovers. She sent Courtney to stay with a friend for the first night.

"You going to fool around, mom?"

"A lady never tells."

"Mom! It's the '90's. Ladies are extinct!"

"An endangered species, maybe. But not extinct."

"Well then, you two have my permission to dance the minuet all night if you want to."

They didn't take advantage of this generous offer.

/////

Dr. Tiffany Reed had short black hair when she left the Orlando airport. Her eyes were runny and brown, thanks to contact lenses. Her new name was Natasha Russoff. She even had a nickname: Georgia. She found it all rather strange at first, but to be the first woman to walk on the Moon she would have tolerated far more.

Far more arrived sooner than expected. In addition to the gross insult to her privacy that was part and parcel of being fitted for her Moon Suit, she was measured with the same degree of accuracy for her seats on the command vehicle and on the LEM. When they were finished there would be full-scale models of her vagina and her rectum. Someday they might be in the Apollo museum they were planning, next to a smiling photograph of her taken prior to this indignity. She tried to push the thought from her mind; yet she now knew with certainty what her last mortal thought would be.

When they thought she could operate the LEM by herself, she was given a course in the operation of the command vehicle --- "just in case." Then it was back to the LEM simulator again for a refresher course. In the meantime the physical training was intensified. She was operating near her limits.

She emerged from the simulator that afternoon in flight gear, looking forward to a shower. Instead she was told to don her Moon Suit for practice. She entered an adjoining cavernous building, where a lunar rover was waiting for a test drive across a facsimile Moon surface. Unlike the one she would use on the Moon, this one had a reinforced frame and rubber tires. Actual rovers have wire mesh wheels and frames that are too frail for use in full gravity. They had her drive in large circles for a measured amount of time, after which she was told to stop in front of a type of door or hatch.

"What in blazes is this?"

"It's one hatch of an airlock, Georgia. You need to enter the lock, pressurize and then open the other hatch." The voice was that of Buck Sanders. He quickly continued, "You have to know how to work an airlock in case you're ever diverted to the MIR Space Station." He hoped she'd never have to open an airlock on MIR, since they were not remotely the same. "I understand you did well in your conversational Russian classes."

"*Dah.*" She could converse with the best of them, provided the conversation didn't stray too far from spaceflight, food and bodily functions.

She finished this task shortly before her air supply ran out. She was instructed to switch on the other air tank so she could retrace her steps, including the long circular ride in the lunar rover.

She confronted Major Sanders when she was finished. "What was that all about?"

"Besides the needed practice on the rover, it was about air consumption."

"The airlock, Major?"

"We don't have much time. We will be combining exercises."

"Diverting to MIR?"

"If we'd had that option when Apollo XIII ran into trouble, we'd have considered it."

"Does anyone ever call you Bull Sanders?"

"No, Georgia. You can be the first. Just don't use my real name."

"Oh, real names are so *passé* anymore. Positively no one is using them. But tempt me. What is it?"

"Mary Lou," he said with a grin.

"You should come with a warning label. Why do I talk to you at all?"

"Because I'm your link to reality?" he suggested.

"Then I'm in serious trouble."

"I do have news from the outside world."

"Speak. Talk to me. Is Carter still President?"

"The rover is ready. The LEM has been shipped. The command module is nearing completion. The pilot is in training. How's that?"

"Overwhelming. I guess I'm not the only one working overtime. Who's the pilot?"

"You don't know him."

"How could I not know him?"

"Maybe he has a new name," he suggested.

"Lot of that going around lately. Do we have a date?"

"My wife frowns on that sort of thing."

"You know what date I mean!"

"The mathematical geniuses are calculating the optimum time. Nobody's done this for a while. They'd like to get it right the first time. They've recalled some of the old team --- whom they refer to as the Fossil Nerds when they're out of hearing distance. Which is all the time for some of them. Any more questions?"

"You got any more answers, Major?"

"Nope."

"Then why ask more questions?"

They actually managed to avoid the Spaceport Seafood Grill. It was only because Laura was driving. She had collected him at the airport. They dined at the Satellite Steak House, sometimes known simply as the Other Place because of the paucity of good restaurants. (Actually there were several excellent Italian restaurants, but she wanted to avoid garlic on the first night of their reunion.) They split a Chateaubriand --- if split is the proper word to use when one person eats most of it. A bottle of Pinot Noir complemented the experience. Laura suggested they have dessert at home. She had found *tres leches* at the local Publix Supermarket.

In the morning they would talk. It was understood.

Chapter Twenty-Five
Thursday, July 1, 1993

Ken found Laura at the door leading to the back yard from the Florida room. She seemed to be conversing with a Cossack hat. He rubbed his eyes and approached. It was an animal.

"Ken, meet Snooks." The raccoon rose in preparation for flight.

Ken stepped back quietly and went into the kitchen. He returned with a egg. "Do you mind?" he asked.

She shook her head to indicate the negative. He gently rolled the egg out the door past animal's nose. Snooks cast a look at both humans and decided they posed no immediate threat. Then she addressed the egg, putting both front paws on it and bearing down. "She knows what to do with it," Ken announced. When the shell cracked, she gently separated it just far enough to lick out the egg without spilling much on the grass.

"Well, if it isn't Mr. Nature," Laura commented.

"Raccoons were very big in Ohio. One became Governor."

"Was it re-elected?"

"No. The sleeping all day didn't seem appropriate behavior for a Governor. So now it's in Congress, where such conduct is acceptable."

/////

Over breakfast, she commented "I like the fact that you like animals, you know."

"Always liked them better than most people. They're more predictable. And they're not malicious. Even a snake won't strike you unless it feels threatened."

"Of course, there is the occasional poisonous frog," she reminded him.

"Maybe where they live they're in constant danger."

"Could be. You certainly give them the benefit of the doubt."

"They probably can't control the secretion of the toxins either."

"Apparently not. Do we have anymore to discuss on the topic of frogs?"

"I hope not."

"Ken, do you have any vices you're hiding from me?"

"No. My vices are on permanent display," he asserted cheerfully.

"Let's check off the list together."

"The list?"

"From the Book of *Exodus*. The Ten Commandments. They had these back in Cleveland?"

"Actually, there was an Eleventh: Thou shalt not drink from the Cuyahoga River. If you violated that one, the others became moot."

"That sounds like a good one. Now from the top, do you worship any other deities?"

"No."

"Do you worship graven images?"

"Idols and such? No --- unless Porsches count. This is easy."

"Don't get cocky. Do you take the name of the Lord in vain?"

"That's Number Three? Are they in order?"

"A lot of people think so."

"Well, I don't swear often. It's become so common, it has no impact on other people. But as Mark Twain said, it can provide relief denied even unto prayer on occasion."

"I'll count that as a negative response."

"Do you observe the Sabbath?"

"If it's Sunday, although I've never understood why it's not Saturday."

"These are not essay questions."

"Sorry."

"Do you honor your parents?"

"Sure."

"Have you killed anyone?"

"No."

"Do you steal?"

"Never! I'm the type that would get caught," he explained. "How am I doing?"

"We're coming to the Home Stretch. Have you committed adultery?"

"Not knowingly." She shot him a look. "I didn't fool around when I was married, but I might not know if someone else was lying about being married."

She sighed. "Have you borne false witness against your neighbors?"

"The Carmichaels?"

Despite herself she began to laugh. "One more! Hang in there. Just one more!"

"O.K."

"Do you covet your neighbor's wife or chattels?"

"You haven't seen Mrs. Carmichael."

"I'll take that as a negative. You passed."

"Now it's your turn."

"I pass that test too."

He ignored this comment. "This is my test. It's shorter. Only three questions. Do you like liver and onions?"

"Not really."

"Do you ever watch Jerry Lewis movies?"

"With Dean Martin?"

"Either way."

"I can truthfully say that I've never watched a Jerry Lewis movie with Dean Martin."

"Well, the important questions are over. You'll be relieved to know you're batting one thousand."

"Ask me the last one then."

"Do you think you could live with me?"

"Yes."

/////

1 JULY 1993. THIS IS MONDAY. EXPECTING YOU SOON. AIR LOCK SITUATION WORSE, BUT NO APPARENT EFFECT INSIDE. COMPUTER DATA STREAM FOLLOWS.
HABITAT::I:16°/E:N173°/AP:0.78/G:0.39....

"I hope they get there in time," Dr. Shavinsky said to himself.

Chapter Twenty-Six
Saturday, July 24, 1993

The primitive tribesmen of New Guinea had seen the cargo planes landing and unloading their wondrous contents. They had come to the reasonable conclusion that the airport was a device contrived by the Europeans to divert the gifts sent by the gods. Making up for in resourcefulness what they lacked in education, they constructed crude airfields, complete with bamboo control towers, on the tops of mountains to lure these gifts to their intended recipients. This anthropological wonder was referred to as the Cult of the Cargo Plane.

The Mexican government had taken a similar approach in Mérida, but with more success --- possibly due to the lack of an alternative place to land. The airport terminal was in the shape of a giant "U." The bottom of the "U" contained the ticket counters, the Rent-o-Matic Itzá car rental agency ("We have Volkswagens & VW's" the sign proclaimed enigmatically), the baggage claim area and the tiny glass kiosks which offered that last irresistible opportunity to purchase a bottle of tequila with a miniature *serape* around its neck. The tops of the "U" contained the boarding gates. Between the bottom and each top was a useless mile of empty corridor, just like a real airport.

The Mexicans, adding their own twist, had paved the corridors with small glazed tiles, set unevenly. Surveillance cameras mounted along the walls recorded the misadventures of the *turistas* as they stumbled down the corridors. The best falls fell into two distinct categories which were saved and stored separately: those involving breakage of bodies or property and those involving loss of dignity.

After negotiating the corridor successfully, Rae presented her passport, which was then passed around for the amusement of the immigration officers. She accepted it back without asking. It had been a long day.

"Blame your parents for giving you the middle name Darla," Ivan explained. "In Spanish it can mean 'give it.' Not exactly what an attractive woman traveling alone wants to be called. Nice photograph, though."

"You did say 'attractive', Tiger?"

"*Sin duda*. Without doubt."

"*Entonces, yo pagaré para la cena*." She had switched to Spanish to tell him she would pay for dinner. They talked for several more minutes before he realized they were not speaking English. She hoped this indicated that the Berlitz intensive course had indeed done the job. He seemed impressed.

/////

He was staying at a downtown hotel called the *Casa de Balam*, which had been a mansion when locally produced sisal rope had made Mérida one of the wealthiest cities in the world. He had one of the mansion suites. To inhabit these spacious historical quarters required that one overlook the obvious decay. Rae was pleased to have a room in the modern building that had been joined to the mansion to form the hotel. After she had showered, they dined looking over the *Paseo de Montejo* --- the local version of the *Champs Elysées*. They took a *calesa* (carriage) back to the hotel.

She began to calculate whether she could retire, too.

Chapter Twenty-Seven
Sunday, July 25, 1993

Ivan and Rae had breakfasted on *huevos motuleños* (fried eggs on a *tortilla* with ham, peas, cheese and mild *salsa*) at the hotel café. Afterward they had strolled the quiet avenue, detouring through the little parks which appeared every few blocks.

In the afternoon, they would drive North to *Dzibichaltún* to see the immense expanse of that ruined Mayan city. "There will be many people because it is Sunday, when admission is free to all archaeological sites, but they will be swimming in the *cenote* mostly. Sadly, the Spanish pulled down most of the stone buildings to construct the very road we will take to see it. The *Conquistadores* had a different agenda," he'd explained. Then they would have a delightful seafood dinner by the Gulf of México in the old port of Progreso. That was the plan. Tomorrow he would take her to *Uxmal* to see what many architects considered to be the most beautiful building ever constructed by man, *el Palacio de los Gobernadores* (the Palace of the Governors).

"*Doctor, había una llamada.*" There had been a telephone call. It was from Dr. Shavinsky. Ivan was to call a number which began with 95-800 using the modem of his laptop computer. He knew from these numbers that this would be a toll-free call to the United States or Canada. This method allowed the caller to get a line immediately, instead of dealing with the ineffective *Teléfonos de México* long distance operators who still used manual switchboards and went home at 6:00 P.M. each night --- effectively isolating 130 million people from the rest of the world until they returned to work twelve hours later.

Since hotel rooms in Mérida did not have telephones, he retrieved his laptop and placed the call through his modem in the hotel office. When the assorted chirps and beeps indicated that the transmission had occurred, he and Rae went to his suite to access the message. He activated a de-coding program and the text appeared on the screen.

22 JULY 1993. THIS IS MONDAY. WE ARE FULLY PREPARED FOR EXTRACTION. BROWN NOT WELL. AIR LOCK DOES NOT PRESSURIZE. INTERIOR HOLDING. COMPUTER DATA STREAM FOLLOWS. HABITAT::I:14°/E:N176°/AP:0.77/G:0.39....

A message from Dr. Shavinsky followed.

"This is the last message we received. We have scanned all frequencies. No transmissions have been detected from the region. Our caped friends assure me they have had no contact. Preparations are continuing. Transmit any ideas by same means. Dmitri."

"Was I supposed to see that?"

He sighed. "Probably not. Of course, Dmitri doesn't know you're here. I don't think he'd mind. He considers you to be one of the...."

"Comrades?"

"Yes."

"What do we do now?"

"It isn't really up to us. It sounds like the mission is going ahead."

"They have to find out if only the transmitter is dead, or the Astronauts."

They went forward with their plan for the afternoon, but it was only hours later that the sight of several dozen flamingos wading in the lagoon South of Telchac Puerto displaced the message in their minds.

"They're the same color as the lawn flamingos!" Rae gasped. "And they look like dancers, the way they all move together."

"Flamenco dancers?" he suggested.

"Yes. That's it. How did you know?"

"Flamenco is the Spanish word for flamingo, comrade."

"Oh. I guess I'm not the first to notice the similarity then."

"I fear not. Now tell me, what are lawn flamingos?"

"Capitalist secret, comrade."

"I have ways of making you talk."

"Promises."

/////

The Air Force C-147 lifted off from Patrick Air Force Base just before 4:00 P.M. and headed North along the East coast of Florida. It was configured for cargo, but had well appointed passenger accommodations on the upper level, just behind the flight deck. There was cargo as well.

Dr. Tiffany Reed, now known exclusively as Natasha Russoff or simply as Georgia, sat in the second of seven rows of what appeared to be first class seats, two on each side of the aisle. Most of the seats were empty. Others were occupied by crew members. The only person she recognized sat in front of her across the aisle. He turned to her and asked her to come forward.

"How are you today, Georgia?"

"As we say in Georgia, I'm fine as frog hair, Major."

"I'd like you to meet Major-General Piotr Gregorovich."

"What the Hell is this emaciated Russian doing on board?" she wondered to herself. "It is my honor," she proclaimed in perfect Russian.

"You do the mother tongue tribute," he responded in Russian, then continued in English "but it will be more polite to speak English in the presence of Major Sanders."

"Quite right," she agreed with some relief.

"Kindly excuse my appearance. My recent travels have weakened me, Doctor."

"Exotic locales frequently have that unfortunate effect. What was the cause? Virus, bacteria or deficiency?"

"Deficiency."

"Do you know what was deficient?"

"Oh yes. Beyond question."

"And...?"

"It was gravity."

"Gravity?"

Major Sanders could no longer suppress his laughter. "Piotr has a Russian sense of humor. Call it mirth."

"Mirth?" she said.

"With a capital M I R," he added.

It took a moment, but she got it. "You've been on MIR?"

"Yes, three months ago I was vacationing in the space *dacha*.

When I returned, I spent the first month eating and swimming, but then Major Sanders put me back to work --- and on a diet!"

"Georgia, meet your pilot," said Buck with a grin.

"Move," she ordered. "I need to sit here."

"Exactly. Get to know each other," conceded Major Sanders. "Now play pretty and don't fight."

She ignored him. "Where are we going now?" she asked Major-General Gregorovich.

"The space flight center."

"We just passed it."

"The other one. The Baikonur Cosmodrome. Take the road South from Orsk, hang a left at Leninsk, and you're there."

"Lord help us."

"Congratulations, you are now Cosmonaut Georgia. Is exciting, no?"

"Is exciting, yes."

"You worry about Russian rockets? I have flown them many times. They are safe as American rockets."

"Actually, they may be safer," she admitted quickly to avoid any question on this critical issue. "No. But let me ask you this. Are they putting an Apollo capsule on top of a Russian rocket?"

"Yes. That is the plan."

"And you plan to be in that Apollo spacecraft?"

"With you."

"So you think this will work?"

"Probably."

"Probably!" she almost shouted.

"You two keep it down or I'll have to separate you!" yelled Major Sanders.

"The Proton rocket is capable of lifting three of your Apollo spacecraft into orbit at the same time. Furthermore, it was not constructed by the lowest bidder. After it has done its work, your NASA space agency will control the Apollo flight and its return. They have done this before. Our only worry is that Apollo falls off the rocket during launch. That is the only new thing happening here."

"That would be embarrassing."

"I am confident the velcro will hold," he stated with fatalism.

"Wonderful stuff." She wisely decided not to mention that she knew about the Russian attempts to send men to the Moon. The Russians had finally abandoned their efforts only in 1991. Before that there had been four failed missions. "You are familiar then with American rockets?"

"Enough that I won't fly over Afghanistan again."

"You have an interesting point of view, Major-General. You've obviously been told much more than I have."

"I have to fly it."

"If you get on board, so will I. Can I call you Piotr?"

"If I can call you Georgia."

"Agreed. By the way, did anyone happen to mention what our mission is?"

"I thought you would know. After all, I will be in lunar orbit."

"I'm sure they'll tell me when they think it's time," she sighed.

"Perhaps we can figure it out. My body mass is now about 60 kilos. Yours must be about 46. Together we do not weigh much more than a single Cosmonaut. That could be one of our qualifications."

"I'm sure it is. It was mentioned that there was a weight limitation. Obviously the lift-off rocket does not impose this limitation; so it must be due to cargo."

"To, from or both ways?" he mused. "What type of doctor are you?"

"Medical. My specialty is pathology. For the past few years I've been studying the effects of extra-terrestrial activities on the vital organs and immune system."

"And where do you obtain the data to study?"

"From the Moon flights, the shuttle and the odd scraps that your scientists release. There's plenty of data. It's well accepted that lower gravity causes loss of muscle and bone mass over time. This does not appear to have any permanent consequences. MIR Cosmonauts have all returned to normal within six months; so there's hope for you yet," she teased. "The complex muscle system known as the heart may not recover completely, but the Olympic gold medalists in track events may do more damage to their hearts."

"That is reassuring."

"Have no doubt. The human body was designed with gravity in

mind. It was meant to function in an upright position with a constant external force pulling downward. But it is flexible and adaptable up to a point. The big problem in space is radiation exposure, which can take decades to manifest symptoms. I'm sorry, is this troubling?"

"I'm used to it. For your information, the living units on MIR are shielded. You are receiving more radiation right now at 8,000 meters."

"Now there's a cheerful thought."

"Georgia, what is it about your work that would cause the National Aeronautics and Space Administration to suddenly --- and secretly --- decide to send you to the Moon in a 20-year old capsule launched by a Russian rocket?"

"I don't have a clue, Piotr," she admitted. "I am aware of no dramatic event or breakthrough that would require experimentation on the Moon or even the retrieval of additional samples from the Moon."

"Then the event must have occurred on the Moon," he concluded.

"But what...?"

"Something recent."

"Perhaps it has some connection to the meteor shower last Spring," she suggested. "The timing would be right."

"But why the urgency? Why would it matter how soon we investigated?"

"Why not send a robot?"

"Exactly. And why send a pathologist to investigate minerals?"

"A life form," she said quietly. "They've detected a life form."

"And they want us to bring it back."

"Is it alive?" she wondered. She'd had enough. "Major Sanders! We need to speak with you! Now!"

/////

It was as singer/comedian Jim Stafford had once said. "There's a fine line between lonely and horny." Until he'd met Laura, Ken could assume he was merely horny. Now he could no longer pretend he wasn't lonely. Ken had plenty of practice handling non-specific loneliness. But now he was lonely for one person. And it was unnecessary. He could be with her.

All he had to do was give up his career and leave his home. These were things he would do soon enough anyway. Why not now --- while he had someplace to go?

"Would you mind having a roommate?" he had asked her.

Men are not particularly adept at these matters. Fortunately, mature women recognize this flaw and work around it.

"Temporary or permanent?"

"Depends on you. It's your house."

"What would you do --- besides eat me out of house and home?"

"Take a nice long trip, then I could find an accounting job in Cocoa; so we could afford to keep Snooks in eggs."

"I could use a nice long trip; provided it's outside the U.S."

"Old Will told me that Tuscany was the most beautiful place in the world. Maybe we ought to see it."

"Tell me more."

"Uhm. That's as far as I've gotten so far." he admitted.

"Then we can plan it together," she promised. "Do you miss me?"

"Uhm. After work. I'm not allowed to miss you at work. Rae says it has something to do with productivity rules."

"Ah, the plight of the non-union employee," she sympathized with sarcasm. "Well, when you go home tonight, look in your World Atlas under Florida."

/////

At 5:52 P.M. that afternoon, Ken opened his World Atlas. By 5:53 P.M., the fine line between lonely and horny had been erased.

Chapter Twenty-Eight
Tuesday, July 27, 1993

The Proton rocket was huge, much larger than the Saturn V rockets used in the original Apollo Missions. If size translated into power, it could hurl them right out of the Solar System. In the first rays of dawn, the shadow was a mile long. Perched atop it was a tiny conical gray object --- the Apollo spacecraft command module. The words and flag that usually adorned such vehicles had been removed. The spacecraft was anonymous. Without the markings, it could have been mistaken for an Apollo capsule from Paraguay or Sri Lanka. Such were the depths of deception plumbed by Operation KFC.

The Apollo spacecraft itself consisted of the command module with the controls and seating, and the service module with the propulsion and support systems. Together they were less than 9 meters high and barely 2½ meters across.

The morning air felt nippy as they rode an open elevator to the gantry to inspect their quarters. There were four seats instead of the usual three. "Sardines in a tin," Piotr commented.

"What if they're dead?"

"That's what the bags are for."

"How will we get them in?"

"I see that we have reserved seating. Their seats are not next to the hatch. That won't help."

"Let's hope they can walk."

"When they see you, Doctor, they'll be dancing." She smiled faintly as she recollected Major Sanders comment about meeting someone to dance with. "The devious bastard," she thought.

/////

Despite being less than two hours out of Mérida, Ivan and Rae had stayed overnight at *Uxmal* to see the excellent sound and light show. Ivan said that it was the best one anywhere because the magnificent temples and unique pyramid were close enough to all be included in the show. As for the sound portion of the show, he explained that "There is a theory that only one script exists for all sound and light shows throughout the world, which is translated with varying degrees of accuracy. Only the names are changed to fit the location."

"If you've heard one, you've heard them all?"

"Yes. Fortunately, no one attends them to hear the story. I personally would prefer appropriate music."

"Rimsky-Korsokov?"

"Wonderful, but too oriental. Something occidental."

They had continued their discussion of appropriate music for the sound and light show right to the poolside bar of the *Hotel Hacienda Uxmal*, a splendid hotel with wide tile verandas. After rejecting the Grateful Dead and the Beach Boys, they decided to spend the night. When advised that there was only a large room with two double beds available, Rae had said "We'll take it," before he had the opportunity to respond. "I like it here, Tiger" she'd explained coyly.

They had slept in separate beds, but she had kissed his cheek before retiring, opening his mind to possibility that he might not spend the rest of his life alone.

Typical of the accommodations she had so far visited in rural Yucatán, the hotel could have been converted into a plumbing museum by merely changing the sign out front. *El Museo del Plomo*. It had a nice ring to it, she thought. As they drove through the countryside, she noted that the curious oval stick and thatch dwellings of the local Mayans appeared to be one-room affairs. That room did not appear to be a bathroom. For all the talk of infrastructure, it was simply plumbing which set apart the third world. Everything else could be leap-frogged. Lack of telephone lines could be overcome with cellular telephones. But there was no substitute for pipes and sewers.

They were approaching a town. "*Oxkutzcab?* I thought they spoke Spanish here," she complained.

"At school they do. At home, it's strictly Mayan. By the way, all the spellings are phonetic Spanish. There is no written Mayan language. That's why the hieroglyphs are so important to understanding their past."

"So what does *Oxkutzcab* mean?"

"This land is abundant with turkeys."

"Oh. In the United States it would be called The District."

A little while later they stopped in Ticul for lunch, selecting the local specialty. Sitting by the window, they watched a young boy chase down and apprehend a turkey. They immediately turned away in unison and looked at each other sheepishly. "I guess it will be fresh," she said.

/////

When they returned to Mérida shortly after 4:00 P.M., they were greeted with "*Había una llamada, Doctor.*" The previous routine was repeated and the message from Dr. Shavinsky received.

"No new transmissions. Team leaves nine hundred local 28 July. Conditions BRG. I will advise you only if any change."

"That's tomorrow!" Rae gasped.

"That's 11:00 P.M. tonight here."

"What is BRG? Some technical term I wouldn't understand?"

He smiled broadly. "Perfect conditions for a launch are dictated by many factors, but most important for a launch of this type is the relative position of the planets. The trajectories have to be computed accordingly. For reasons we don't need to understand, some times are more favorable than others. Condition Green indicates perfect. BRG indicates favorable conditions which are not quite perfect."

"BRG stands for...?"

"British Racing Green, of course. It's not true green, but close."

"Of course. Have you always been mad?"

"I find it helps when dealing with Dmitri."

"It's probably essential. You know, I like that old bear though."

"He absolutely adores you. Especially since you helped put him back in the game."

"The game?"

"A Russian rocket sending a spacecraft to the Moon. He's delighted. He says it's like the old days."

"I'm glad to hear it."

"When I get settled here, I'm going to have a little *dacha* for him to stay in. He is getting too old for the Russian winters."

"Can I visit too?"

"Yes, but I'd like you to stay in the main house."

"I love it when you talk dirty, comrade," she teased.

This confused him. He blushed.

She kissed him softly and said "The main house it is, Tiger."

/////

The nerve center of the Johnson Manned Space Flight Center in Houston is a long room with the typical drop ceiling found in modern office buildings. One wall contains the Mercator Projection map of the world on which the location and tracks of the Astronauts are displayed electronically across a black background. Facing this are rows of control panels and monitors attached to each other, interrupted only by three narrow aisles. Toward the rear of the room, the rows elevate in theater fashion to provide visibility. In front of each control panel is a continuous expanse of desk or work space, about 40 centimeters deep. Atop the built-in monitors and in other available areas additional monitors have been set up. Rarely does the number of persons in the room exceed the number of monitors. When a launch is underway in summertime, the air conditioning requirements of this one room exceed that of the entire White House. Everyone sweats anyway.

Tonight was no exception. Dawn had already come to the Baikonur Cosmodrome. All of NASA seemed to be here, dripping with perspiration. The President of the United States was present virtually through closed circuit television. They were all engaged in the same silent prayer: "God, don't let us screw this up."

No one else in the United States had any idea what was happening.

Chapter Twenty-Nine
Wednesday, July 28, 1993

"*Dobray yutro*, Cosmonaut Georgia."
"Good morning to you too, Cosmonaut Piotr."

/////

While Houston watched on 32-inch Sony television sets brought in for that purpose, the giant rocket came to life half a world away. When the countdown reached six, the main engine ignited. Four seconds later all six engines were burning. The Earth shuddered. Gantries dropped away. There were the familiar seconds of hesitation, seemingly designed to allow a brief contemplation of mankind's audacity.

Then the rocket shot forward at an incredible rate, delivering G-forces sufficient to black out the Astronaut briefly. Within thirty seconds, there were 1.9 million pounds of thrust --- equal to 150 Boeing 747 engines at full power. The first stage burned for two minutes and six seconds. The second stage kicked in. Mouths gaped in Houston as escape velocity was rapidly achieved, but no one spoke. The stunned silence in Houston was broken by the amplified voice of Major Buck Sanders via closed circuit from the Cosmodrome. "I've been telling you guys we should remove the catalytic converters!"

/////

"You O.K., Doctor?" asked Cosmonaut Gregorovich.
"I feel like I've been blown up."
"Look!"
She looked out the tiny window. "Oh my God! We're in space."
"First time is exciting, no?"
"Breathtaking, in more ways than one."
"Apollo, This is Baikonur Cosmodrome. Second stage separation is complete. You have attained escape velocity. Trajectory

appears on target. Houston will assume primary control now. We will monitor. *Do svedanya.*"

"Apollo, do you copy? This is Houston."

"Hello, Yankees! This is Cosmonaut Gregorovich. Thank you for letting me borrow the car. All stages have fired successfully and separated. All readings are within normal parameters. Advise if course correction needed."

"None indicated at this time, Apollo."

"Good. Cosmonaut Russoff has a report."

"Aside from a temporary excess of adrenalin, we are A-OK up here, Houston. Are we go?"

"We're go down here, Cosmonaut Russoff. Major Sanders asked me to pass along a message. He says you're looking fine as frog hair up there. We're still trying to decipher that one, Apollo."

"Keep us advised, Houston."

/////

Dr. Shavinsky was confused. "I thought it was Colonel Saunders," he said to his aide, who simply shrugged by way of reply.

"And what is frog hair?"

/////

Driving East along the Bee-Line Highway, Laura suggested to Ken they should go to Italy before making any permanent arrangements. "What's the rush?"

"Wasn't Valentino from there?"

"You question my motives, sir?"

"Uhm. Not really." He was as relieved as she knew he would be. She didn't want him to feel pressured. Not in that way.

/////

The distance between the Earth and the Moon varies with their relative positions. The usual figure given is 240,000 miles. However, this straight-line measurement does not apply to actual

Moon flights, which are aimed at a point in space where the Moon is calculated to be when they arrive. Then the Apollo capsule goes into lunar orbit instead of landing on the surface. Only when a stable lunar orbit has been achieved about sixty miles above the Moon does the LEM descend to the surface. The name of the lunar excursion module had been shortened to lunar module because someone thought excursion sounded too frivolous, like going on a picnic. But no one could pronounce LM; so it was usually referred to by the original initials.

If they kept to the schedule, Cosmonaut Russoff would arrive at the Aitken Basin in four days.

/////

Huddled in her shawl against the dry cold of Southwest Colorado, the old woman stared at the pre-dawn Moon. "*No te olvido, mi hijo. Te amo Carlos.*" (I don't forget you, my son. I love you Carlos.)

/////

"I've never worked with the Secret Service before," Detective Sergeant Lopez began. "You got any special procedures or do you just want to review the file?"

"Did someone kill him?"

"Doesn't look like it."

"Simple accidental death?"

"If you can stretch simple to cover bizarre."

The agent smiled for the first time. "That sounds right. Terry never did anything normal in his life. Let me ask you this, Detective. Do you collect unsolvable homicide cases?"

"Try to avoid that if we can."

"Then close it."

"You speaking for the Service now?"

"Absolutely. They have no interest."

"This file will be closed by the end of the month unless new evidence comes up to change that decision. And no one here's looking for any."

"*Hasta la vista*, Detective."

"Same to you, Agent."

It was undeniable that it would be a relief to close this file, but it would be a triumph of restraint over suspicion.

Chapter Thirty
Sunday, August 1, 1993

As she stepped onto the gray surface, Aerosmith's words flashed through her mind and she smiled. She wanted to sing "Doo-da-da, Doo-da-da, Astronaut looks like a lady!"[8] to celebrate her achievement. Maybe if she could carry a tune. Maybe if she wasn't a Cosmonaut. Maybe if she hadn't been told exactly what to say.

"With this step, the people of the United States and of the Russian Republic --- on behalf of all the people of Earth --- affirm their dedication to the exploration of the solar system." Without a pause she repeated this in Russian. Not a word about women. Not a clue about any rescue. There wasn't even a camera to speak into. She was glad that was over.

She began to retrieve and assemble the lunar rover. If she worked fast, she would have time to test drive it before she was required to return to the LEM for mandated rest.

Before she had left the command vehicle, Piotr had reminded her to change the oil every 2,000 miles.

///////

The flight was late arriving at National Airport. Rae was pleased to see that Ken had come to meet her. Perhaps he was lonely too.

"How was México?"

"*¡Magnífico!* I'm ready to move tomorrow."

"Lot of that going around lately," he observed.

"Yes! Tell me! Will the lady have you?"

"Incredible as it may seem, yes."

8

Dude Looks Like a Lady written and performed by Aerosmith on the album *Permanent Vacation* (Geffen Records).

"You two may just have been made for each other."

"Like you and Ivan?"

"No one else would have us. It's not quite the same."

"Does he know this?"

"He wants me to come back...often."

"Close enough."

"So when do you and Laura tie the knot?"

"When we come back from Italy. I guess I'm going to be taking some time off."

"Let me see if I can promote you first. Increase the pension if you can wait a week."

"You have my attention. We're not that prepared yet anyway."

Chapter Thirty-One
Monday A.M., August 2, 1993

She was barely doing ten kph across the uneven terrain. Without the weight of a real atmosphere to hold it down, the dust formed an unseen plume that followed the lunar rover across the crater. The halogen headlamps of the rover were on. Her positioning device was backlit. It was darker than a basement closet at midnight in winter.

On command from Houston, she stopped and shut off the lights. Less than three kilometers ahead of her was a flashing white light. Just below it and to the left was a steady red one. "I see them!"

The familiar voice of Major Sanders took over. "Maintain your present course heading until the white one is directly above the red one. When it is, turn and drive directly toward them. That way you won't run into any of the expensive equipment on the ground."

"Clever! Who thought it up?"

"The Phoenicians."

"Thank them the next time you see them."

"Roger. By the way, there may be another lunar rover out there; so watch out for it. If you hit it, your insurance won't cover the damage."

"Blasted insurance loopholes," she muttered. She knew they were trying to keep the spirits high for the impending.... The impending whatever.

"Changing course for final approach, Houston."

"Keep speed under 5 kph. Approach cautiously, Doctor."

The headlamps caught the structure. It had once been white, but now was mostly dull metal. The drifting particles of the Moon's surface had nearly covered parts of it. She fancied it looked much as MIR would have, had it crashed here twenty years ago. The only sign of life was the lights.

"I've arrived, Houston. No activity to report yet."

"Do you see another rover?"

"Negative. I'm going to the airlock."

"Be careful. It wasn't functioning properly. Talk as much as your exertions will permit. We want continuous contact now."

"Legs get stiff when you ride, just like home, despite the lower gravity."

"Shepherd said that too."

"I never said I was original. I'm at the outer hatch of the airlock. I see nothing unusual. No activity. The indicator shows the inner hatch to be sealed. Request permission to open the outer hatch."

"Permission granted. Proceed."

"Power assist not working. Request permission to try manual."

"Hold while we check other options."

"Just how much air do you think I've got?"

"Proceed with manual operation of outer hatch."

"Hatch is opening. Nothing appears unusual. Request permission to enter."

"Enter with caution and investigate. Before closing the outer hatch, use the viewing port of the inner hatch and report."

"I'm inside. Outer hatch still open. Airlock status lights are on and appear to be functioning. Approaching viewing port. You should have sent along some Windex. It's more translucent than transparent."

"Can you see light inside?"

"Affirmative. Ample light inside. Does not look like auxiliary lighting."

"Any movement inside?"

"Negative, Houston. Request permission to close outer hatch and attempt pressurization."

"Attempt to initiate pressurization before closing outer hatch. Understood?"

"Affirmative. Initiating pressurization." *Wank! Wank! Wank! Wank! Wa....* "Well, the alarm still works."

"Apparently."

"You could have warned me. Scared the living daylights out of me!"

"Sorry. We forgot about it. Proceed to close the outer hatch, but keep talking as you do. If we lose contact, proceed with your mission and contact us at first opportunity. Understood?"

"Understood, Houston. Closing outer hatch. Closed. Still

there?"

"Reading you clearly."

"Pressurizing." *Sssssssssssssssssss.* "No whoosh. This could take a while. The gauge is hardly moving."

"Give it a minute. We don't have a lot of options here."

"Understood. I'll make sure the outer hatch sealed."

/////

"Telephone for you Dr. Shavinsky." As a slight growl began, the messenger hastily added "It's the Prime Minister."

Cursing silently, he picked up the receiver. "*Dobray Yutro*, Mr. Prime Minister!"

"Has the Cosmonaut arrived at the facility?"

"Just now, Mr. President. She is in the airlock. No contact yet."

"If the mission succeeds, will she be a Cosmonaut or an Astronaut?"

"God save us from the political mind!" he thought. He replied "She will be an Astronaut who was taken to the Moon on a Russian rocket by a Cosmonaut. It will be a glorious moment for both nations."

"And if the mission fails?"

"She remains a Cosmonaut until she returns to Earth," he said flatly. He preferred not to think about that. He hoped she would be an Astronaut again.

"I see. Give me a report later. *Do svedanya.*"

/////

"It's the seal, Houston. When I pulled the outer hatch tight, the pressurization gauge jumped. I'll check it on the way out if I have time. Pressurization nearly complete. Turning to inner hatch. Request permission to activate inner hatch."

"Activate your video camera, then proceed."

"Camera activated. Hatch mechanism functioning. Request permission to enter."

"Can you see anyone?"

"Negative, Houston. Hatch fully opened now."

-229-

"Step inside, but do not close inner hatch yet."

"Understood. Entering now."

"If someone is there, you should be able to see them from where you are standing."

"There is no one here but me, Houston. Request permission to close inner hatch."

"Permission granted, but re-open immediately if contact lost."

"Inner hatch closed. Proceeding to control panel. Everything appears normal. Maybe they went to the Little Bandit. You still with me, Houston?"

"Affirmative. What was that about bandits?"

"Oh. Little Bandit is slang for convenience store."

"Thank you for sharing that with us."

"According to the gauges, I don't need this helmet in here. Request permission to remove it." When there was no immediate response, she added "I won't have time to check everything with it on."

"It's your call. Make sure you keep it close by."

"Removing helmet. Air is a trifle musty, but not bad. Should I be noticing an ozone smell?"

"Yes, but it should be slight. If it's strong, replace your helmet now. You will grow accustomed to it and be unable to detect it later. You may get a headache."

"It's slight. Helmet stays off for now. I'm in the center of the facility turning slowly so the camera will get a panorama."

"Don't forget the floor and ceiling."

"I'll do my best, but I'm going to have to ditch this suit to conduct a search."

"Avoid direct contact with your skin. Can you do that without the suit?"

"Affirmative. I have surgical gloves on."

"What about your feet?"

"Garbage bags over knee socks, Houston."

"Why didn't we think of that?"

"I won't speculate."

"Could you step in front of the camera?"

"Modesty forbids, Houston."

"You do have something else on?"

"Indeed I do, Major. I'd love to say it's a black lace teddy from Victoria's Secret, but it's an Atlanta Braves tee shirt."

"Did Ted Turner pay you to wear it?"

"Let's just say that I have box seats for all home games for the next 100 years."

"Anything else we should know about?"

"No. It's a long tee shirt."

"Are you searching while we talk?"

"Affirmative."

"Good. How are you feeling?"

"Extremely well, but a bit lonely. Where are the locals?"

"Go to the communications desk and play back the last transmission. Maybe they left a message."

She did as instructed. The playback was a written document that slowly chattered into existence on an ancient dot matrix printer. The last message was

23 JULY 1993. THIS IS MONDAY. BROWN SLEEPING MOST OF THE TIME. NOT WELL. ADVISE YOUR TEAM THAT WE WITNESSED THEIR LANDING. WE COULDN'T SEE MUCH, BUT THE SPACECRAFT SURE IS A LOT BIGGER THAN THE OLD APOLLO. WE AWAIT EXTRACTION. COMPUTER DATA STREAM FOLLOWS.
HABITAT::I:14°/E:N176°/AP:0.77/G:0.39....

The data stream was incomplete. Unable to cope with the message itself, she addressed the transmission.

"Houston, are these transmissions sent in bursts?"

"When the communication was complete, the message would be compressed and sent, if that's what you mean."

"So if the data stream was incomplete, the message wouldn't have been sent?"

"Affirmative. What have you found?"

"The last message, which wasn't sent. It's dated 23 July 1993."

"That's the day after the final transmission!"

"It's the day they left," she said as calmly as she could.

"What do you mean?"

"I'll read it to you. Maybe you can tell me what it means." She read the message. "Did you get that, Houston?"

Major Sanders became the first person to broadcast the words "Holy shit!" to two continents and the Moon simultaneously.

"I was hoping for more depth in your analysis, Houston --- although I share the sentiment. I'm going to continue examining the facility while you work on it."

"Do that," was the best they could muster. The buzzing in the control room of the Manned Space Flight Center had gone way past beehive. It was more like a dozen food processors working on marbles. And it was hotter than the hinges of the very Gates of Hell in that room. "Any ideas from Baikonur, Major?"

"So far, they've been grilling their translators in the hope they misunderstood the message."

"I'm going to search the living area now." One side of each bunk was attached to the wall by hinges so it could be folded out of the way, a trick learned from the yachting industry. While she was inspecting the lower bunk, she felt a light blow to the back of her head. She lost consciousness immediately.

"Did you say something, Georgia? Georgia?" Major Sanders shouted across Space. "Check her microphone. Is there anything being received?"

"Negative, Major. It could be a mechanical problem with the microphone."

"Isn't it redundant?" he asked, referring to the use of double microphones.

"Could have come loose as she walked around. Let's give her some time to notice it and take corrective action," suggested the unseen engineer.

"How long has it been?"

"Coming up on sixty seconds. Still no sound from the microphone," replied the same unidentified voice.

"Georgia, can you hear me? Are we sure it's a mechanical problem?"

"High probability, sir."

"Is the receiver working?"

"Affirmative. All Earthbound components functioning within normal parameters. It's a transmitting problem, sir."

"Is it interference?"

"Negative. Complete loss of signal."

"Time elapsed since loss?"

"Just past ninety seconds, sir."

"Georgia, please respond!"

"Still here, Houston." The signal was clear. She sounded groggy.

"We've been unable to read you. What happened?"

She looked up at the bunk above her and came up with an explanation. "Upper bunk came down unexpectedly and coshed me. Must have knocked the microphone off too."

"You were off the air for nearly two minutes. Are you O.K.?"

"All parts accounted for, Major." She was lying in the lower cot. There was a tingling sensation at the base of her skull which tended to corroborate her explanation. She looked down and found that her tee shirt had managed to work its way up to her neck, exposing every inch of skin down to her ankles. The Law of the Perversity of Inanimate Objects apparently operated on the Moon too. Then she made sure that the camera was indeed still pointed away from her. "Continuing search, Houston."

"Be careful."

"Closet's bare," reported Cosmonaut Russoff. "They took their gear. All of it. They're not coming back."

"Could it be a prank?" someone in the Control Room asked too loudly.

"Impossible! How would they have known on July 23rd that we were coming?" another anonymous voice responded.

"Pardon me," said Dr. Shavinsky from Baikonur, "but the final transmissions we received discuss extraction. They have been preparing to leave the Moon."

"Houston, I'm retrieving data tapes. Do you need any other souvenirs. It looks like I'll have plenty of room."

"Go to the communications desk and try sending a message. We want to see if it works. Type it in and press SEND. The computer data stream will attach automatically before transmission." A few minutes later radio-telescopes of the Siberian very large array received the following message:

2 AUGUST 1993. THIS IS MONDAY. GREETINGS. THIS

LIFE IS A TEST. REPEAT, IT IS ONLY A TEST. HAD IT BEEN A REAL LIFE, YOU WOULD HAVE RECEIVED INSTRUCTIONS ABOUT WHAT TO DO AND WHERE TO GO. COMPUTER DATA STREAM FOLLOWS. HABITAT::I:14°/E:N178°/AP:0.77/G:0.39....

This was the first uncoded message sent from the Moon. It was passed through Baikonur onto Houston, where it raised eyebrows as she had hoped.

"Glad to see you still have your sense of humor. Now, de-activate the discriminator. We want to see if the facility can receive. Kennedy, proceed now. Keep it under two minutes. Baikonur, please attempt after a two-minute delay to avoid interference."

After de-activating the discriminator, she took a moment to take a small capsule from her tee shirt pocket. She opened it and poured two drops of *Sauza Hornitos Reposado* onto her tongue. It was symbolic, barely enough to even taste. But enough to make her a celebrity or a spokesperson for a distillery during retirement. "First person to shoot tequila on the Moon," she thought with satisfaction. "The good stuff, too. No sense spending a billion Dollars to come here just to drink rotgut."

"Receiving something, Houston. How do I retrieve it?"

"Wait until the panel indicates it's finished. Then wait for a message from Baikonur. In the meantime, finish your search."

"Not much left. Just some lockers."

When she had reported that the lockers were completely empty, she was asked to "Set the computer to automatic data transmission and minimum power usage."

"Auto data transmission activated. Powering down to minimum. Is it O.K. to leave a note?"

"Affirmative. We'd have probably thought of that later ourselves."

"Of course you would have. Messages received. Let's see what you said."

MOON, THIS IS KENNEDY. CONGRATULATIONS ON YOUR ACHIEVEMENT. THE FOLLOWING IS A 60-SECOND COMPUTER TRANSMISSION DESIGNED TO

TEST THE SYSTEM.

"There is a break, followed by some gibberish. After that is another message."

COSMONAUT RUSSOFF, THIS IS BAIKONUR COSMODROME. ALL THE WORLD SALUTES THIS IS MONDAY. HAPPY TO SEE YOU APOLLO. PROCEED WITH EXTRACTION. REGARDS TO COLONEL SAUNDERS. PON YOUR SAFE RETURN TO EARTH.

"Apollo, could you repeat that last part?"
"Try and stop me, Houston!" she replied.
"Baikonur, did you copy that?"
"*Dah*. Something interrupted our message."

COSMONAUT RUSSOFF, THIS IS BAIKONUR COSMODROME. ALL THE WORLD SALUTES THIS IS MONDAY. HAPPY TO SEE YOU APOLLO. PROCEED WITH EXTRACTION. REGARDS TO COLONEL SAUNDERS. PON YOUR SAFE RETURN TO EARTH.

"Is there anything else on the printout, Apollo?"
"Negative, Houston."
"We have made copies."
She began to write a note.

2 August 1993. Astronaut Dr. Tiffany Reed dropped by for tea. I'm staying at the LEM in the Aitken Basin, if you care to visit. I repaired your radio. Do not reconnect the discriminator. It is faulty. You may communicate with Russians now. The Soviet empire is gone. Everyone's a capitalist now. Sorry I missed you.

She left the Moon Base humming away to itself. She figured that she would be the last person to set foot in it while it was operational. She made sure the outer hatch sealed tightly.

Chapter Thirty-Two
Monday P.M., August 2, 1993

The lunar rover bounced across the dark landscape. She could see the beacon atop the LEM, about a kilometer away. "Well that certainly was anti-climactic, Houston."

"We'll make sure you get an extra packet of honey-roasted peanuts on the flight home."

"Promises, promises, Major Sanders."

"Do you think the airlock will hold?"

"Once I removed the sand, it closed tightly. Ready for the next occupants. Any idea when that will be?"

"There are no plans. Studios are a tough sale. Everyone wants two bedrooms now."

"Location, location, location," she reminded him, "but then again, the commute is.... Shit!"

"What is it?"

"Traffic! I almost hit something!"

"What?"

"I'm turning around to check." Houston waited. The Control Room was silent but for the hum of machinery. "It's a rover! Unoccupied."

"Does it appear to be operational?"

"Let me put it this way, Houston," she said with deliberation. "It wasn't here this morning."

"Are you positive?"

"Positive. I've been following the tracks I made this morning. It's sitting across them."

"Are you saying that you think it was put there intentionally for you to find?"

"Either that or someone wanted to cause the first traffic accident on the Moon."

"Can you follow the tracks to see where it came from?"

"Negative for now, Houston. Insufficient air. Must return to the LEM. Maybe later. The tracks will last for days."

"Are there any signs of exit from the vehicle?"

"You mean footprints?"

"Affirmative. Footprints, hand prints, any type of trail."

"Negative."

"Exercise caution."

"I appreciate your concern, gentlemen, but I am unarmed and driving the brightest object on the Moon. I'm not sure how to fit caution into this scenario."

"I suggest you circle the LEM twice before leaving the rover."

"Is that a military tactic?"

"It works for my dog."

"Great. Maybe you should think about installing alarm systems on future LEM's. O.K., I'm starting a large circle from this point. Driving very slowly." She guided the electric vehicle through a quadrant. "Hold on, Houston. I am crossing tracks of the other rover. They appear to head toward the LEM."

"Proceed with circling."

In two minutes she reported "I'm back at the other rover. Request permission to proceed directly toward LEM, with a small circle before stopping. I'd like to come out later for a look at this other rover."

"Proceed to the LEM and circle once."

"Am proceeding. When within 100 meters or so, I will circle. Approaching LEM. No signs of activity. Beginning circle. Nothing to report. Intersected tracks again as anticipated. Proceeding.... Wait, Houston. Request permission to stop and examine tracks."

"Do have sufficient air?"

"I need to do this, Houston."

"Then proceed." How could they stop her?

"Houston, I'm no scout, but these tracks are obviously deeper than mine and I've got an identical vehicle riding over the same surface."

"How much deeper?"

"On average, about four centimeters."

"Well, your vehicle is a bit lighter. Different alloy in the frame and a compact battery. The battery is the most up-to-date equipment on this mission."

"Does that account for the difference in depth?"

"Not entirely. We knew the weight of the two Astronauts last month. We're computing that now to see if that would make up the difference."

"You'll let me know?"

"Before you leave the rover. Now continue circling."

She completed her circle and stopped. "I'm waiting for your analysis before closing on the LEM."

"The preliminary estimate is that the additional weight of the two Astronauts and their Moon Suits would not, repeat not, account for the difference. Even all their gear would not account for it. It looks like there would be another 65 to 75 kilos. Could be cargo."

"I hope it's not passengers. I'd hate to have to bump someone," she muttered. "Proceeding with caution to the LEM. The other rover tracks parallel mine. It came from the LEM."

"Keep talking. Tell us what you see."

"No tracks."

"Repeat."

"The tracks have disappeared. All of them. The area around the LEM is undisturbed. Even where I assembled the rover. Does Welcome Wagon do that?"

"Stop now. Where are you?"

"About twelve meters from the LEM."

"What do you see?"

"The LEM. Nothing else."

"What don't you see?"

That required a mind shift that took longer than she would have liked. "O.K. No tracks. No disturbance of the surface. No footprints." She closed her eyes to picture the scene earlier today. "Ah! And none of the packing for the lunar rover!"

"You're sure it's the same site?"

"That's an interesting question. Wouldn't you know if the LEM had been moved?"

"We like to think so. But if it was moved gently for a short distance, we might not detect it. Look under it."

"You may have something, Houston. There's no sign of the rocket blast from the landing."

"Is it your LEM?"

"Who thinks up these questions?" she asked rhetorically. "Sure looks like it."

"Then proceed to the LEM before you run out of air. Maintain constant contact. Leave the rover lights on."

She positioned the rover so that the lamps lighted the LEM as bright as the *Arc de Triomph* on Bastille Day. "Leaving rover, Houston." She trudged to the steps of the LEM slowly, her eyes searching to all sides to the extent possible in the Moon Suit. "Why would anyone move the LEM?" she asked. It had taken her this long to come to grips with the probability that it had been moved.

"We've come up with three possible explanations. Number One, it was unsafe for some reason to leave it where it landed."

"Unsafe for whom?"

"Good question. No answer. Number Two, it was moved to a more convenient location."

"Convenient for whom? Not much of an improvement on Number One," she observed. "I'm almost there. What's Number Three?"

"To demonstrate that it could be done."

"Lovely. What psychopath came up with that one?"

There was a brief silence, then "Dr. Shavinsky."

"Ooops. Sorry Doctor. No disrespect intended. It's a little tense here."

"As Dr. Shavinsky reminded us, that's why we first went to the Moon --- to show we could do it."

"O.K. I get it. But what about the tracks I followed back here?"

"Would you have noticed if they'd been altered somewhere along the way?"

"Probably not," she admitted. "I've reached the steps. It still looks like the LEM I came in. Certainly the same make and model. I can't believe we're discussing this! It's not like I'm in a LEM parking lot, you know."

"Remain calm to conserve oxygen."

"This is calm, Houston. You'll be the first to know when I lose it."

"You said when, not if."

"Let that be a warning then. Request permission to enter."

"Can you see inside?"

"Negative. Window's too high. Send someone taller next time."

"Permission granted. Proceed."

"Opening the hatch."

"Is everything all right?"

"Oh, my God! We've got company!"

"Repeat, please."

"There are two men in the seats!"

"Are they alive?"

"Don't know yet. They're not moving."

"What are they wearing?"

"What?!"

"Are they wearing Moon Suits?"

"Oh. They seem to have on Apollo Suits. The names on the suits are Fortney and Brown."

"Do not remove your Moon Suit! Acknowledge!"

"Acknowledged!"

"Are they plugged in?"

"Yes, both of them. They are in the correct seats, by the way."

"Then power up and we'll check them out."

"You know, there is a doctor 240,000 miles closer," she reminded them.

"Let's find out what we can first, Doctor. We don't know what's wrong with them yet."

"O.K., but I need to get out of this suit soon." She closed the hatch and went to full power. The LEM came to life.

"They're alive!" came the cry from Houston. "Vital signs acceptable. No indications of contamination, but suggest you avoid direct contact as a precaution. As long as they're doing O.K., leave them sealed up."

"What about the lunar rover? The lights are still on."

"Let 'em burn."

"I was hoping you'd say that."

"Remove your Moon Suit and prepare to go. The next window is in about six hours. Try to rest. We'll wake you up in time."

"Roger, Houston."

Something had changed while she napped. The light had gone out. But what light? To wake up faster, she pinched her earlobe until it hurt. She blinked and forced her eyes to focus. She turned on the dome lamp. It worked. Had she turned it out? "Think!" she urged herself. "It wasn't on," she remembered.

"Ah, Houston."

"Time to rise and shine, Doctor," advised the cheerful disembodied voice.

"About that shine part, Houston. How long should the rover batteries last?"

"Minimum 96 hours at full usage, why?"

"Next time pay the extra 20 bucks for the Diehard, Houston. The lamps are out. I figured they didn't all burn out at once."

"The lamps should last for decades, even with power surges. It must be the battery or an electrical fault."

"Good thing it didn't happen earlier," she observed.

"You're sure the rover's still there?"

"I don't even want to think about that possibility, Houston. I'll turn on the front stoop light and check, though. Yes, it's still where I left it. Just far enough away so the liftoff won't damage it."

"O.K., Doctor, make sure your passengers are wearing their seat belts and let's bring you all home."

"No argument here, Houston. Tell Piotr to fold out the sofa bed. I'm bringing company."

Chapter Thirty-Three
Tuesday, August 3, 1993

"How are your passengers?"

"Still sleeping. You're sure they're alive?"

"Affirmative, Apollo. Major Sanders has a question."

"*Dobray yutro*, Colonel. Your fame has preceded you."

"Just a thought. Did you monitor the incoming transmissions?"

"Negative."

"Why not?"

"I was busy. If you must know, I was shooting tequila."

"Of course, you were. And may one ask why?"

"I didn't have time to chill the champagne properly."

"Sounds like our plan had a flaw."

"What's the problem? It was just a garbled transmission, wasn't it?"

"That's the working hypothesis."

"Good. I've had enough weirdness in the past twelve hours to last a lifetime."

"You and Piotr just bring home your passengers and let us sort things out down here as best we can."

"Roger, Major."

/////

"Ivan, can you come here?"

"Where are you, Dmitri?"

"Baikonur."

"Not as easily as you can come here. It is difficult to get there. And you forget I have to use my own funds to travel now."

"Our Mother will pay for your ticket. What if we meet in the middle?"

"London and New York have the most flights."

"I like London better."

"Miss Kirkland could meet us in New York."

"In that case we go to *la manzana grande* (the Big Apple). I'll see you on Thursday. Fax me your travel plans."

"*Hasta luego.*"

"*Do svedanya.*"

PART VI: CONTACT

Chapter Thirty-Four
Thursday, August 5, 1993

"Georgia, I would like to tell you something before we re-enter the atmosphere."

"If you're going to tell me I look good in a space suit, you've been away too long, cowboy."

Piotr grinned. "*Nyet, comrade.* You have been most excellent company, but there is something about having a pipe on my dingdong that discourages my libido --- is that the word?"

"Dingdong or libido?"

"Either."

"They are both proper usage of the language. Maybe not the Queen's English...."

"I am not a queen."

"Glad to hear it. Now what did you want to tell me?"

"I believe we will be allowed to live."

"Well, that's certainly good news. Why do you say allowed?"

"I was thinking when I circled the Moon. If the mission had failed, they would never have told anyone about it. Does this make sense?"

"Yes. I'm afraid it does."

"Then what would they have done with us?"

"I see where you're going with this. But so many other people know about this mission?"

"What do they know, compared to us?"

She thought about that for a while. "How would you kill us?"

"There are two easy ways to make it look like an accident. A slight deviation in the re-entry angle and we burn."

She shuddered. "Or they could let us sink in the ocean."

"Exactly. So I thank you for finding these Astronauts and bringing them back alive."

"Finding them wasn't hard," she admitted. "Looking for them was an absolute bitch, though."

Fortunately both planes arrived at about the same time in the late afternoon. Unfortunately, they arrived at different terminals at JFK International, which was evidently designed on the premise that passengers can fly under their own power for short distances. One can cross Luxembourg on foot in less time than it takes to move between most terminals. The only terminals that are really adjacent in a meaningful sense of the word are the sprawling TWA terminal and the terminal for obscure foreign carriers, which makes it handy for the passengers whose deranged travel agent has booked them from Casablanca to Rome via New York. Such hapless passengers probably need all the handy they can get.

Nevertheless, a determined Rae managed to collect her two Russians without serious incident and get them to their hotel. While waiting with Dr. Shavinsky on Ivan's flight, she had confessed that she found Dr. Konosov to be charming, with "just the right amount of gray in the temples."

"He is also gray in the churches," had been the response.

/////

Even the jolting splashdown had failed to rouse the Marines. The four of them bobbed in the Pacific for at least ten minutes before the Navy Seal team arrived. The Seals remained with the capsule until it was on the deck of the ship. The day was gray. The air was heavy. The two Cosmonauts were the only ones who thought it was glorious.

The Captain greeted them warmly but briefly. They were allowed to change into sweat suits, then they boarded three waiting helicopters. Each slumbering Astronaut had his own chopper. If one went down, NASA would still have the other. Piotr and Georgia were obviously less valuable.

"We're not out of the woods yet, Piotr."

"Few ships. Small ships. No reporters. No NASA officials." He had noticed.

"They want to inspect the merchandise."
"*Dah.*"

/////

They had three adjoining rooms on the tenth floor, overlooking Central Park. Dr. Shavinsky couldn't wait to get down to business. Uncertain how long this would take, Rae ordered a snack from the fast-food restaurant in the lobby.

"Join us, Miss Kirkland, I need all the help I can get." She brought the desk chair over to join them at the table. "When the radio was restored, NASA sent a message to the Moon Base. After NASA finished, we sent one as well. This is the message that was sent from Baikonur to the Moon Base when the Cosmonaut was there.

COSMONAUT RUSSOFF, THIS IS BAIKONUR COSMODROME. ALL THE WORLD SALUTES YOUR COURAGE. YOU HAVE THE GRATITUDE OF MANKIND. THIS REMARKABLE ACHIEVEMENT WILL BE THE CAUSE FOR CELEBRATION UPON YOUR SAFE RETURN TO EARTH.

"Stop right there, please," said Rae. "Who wrote this?"
Surprised, Dr. Shavinsky responded "I did. Why?"
"You went over the top. Did you write this in advance?"
"Before the LEM landed on the Moon," he admitted.
"That explains why it's so vague. Tell me about Cosmonaut Russoff. Who is she?"
"She is.... How did you know it was a woman?"
"The words you used. You would not have mentioned courage if the Cosmonaut had been a man. I fear you may be a latent male chauvinist, Doctor. Nothing to worry about. It's curable. Is there more?"
"Yes. Cosmonaut Russoff is an American Astronaut. Russoff is not her real name."
"That's why you started the message by clearly identifying her as a Russian."
"This is a remarkable woman," he said to Dr. Konosov.
"So I am learning."

"This is the message that was received at the Moon Base."

COSMONAUT RUSSOFF, THIS IS BAIKONUR COSMODROME. ALL THE WORLD SALUTES THIS IS MONDAY. HAPPY TO SEE YOU APOLLO. PROCEED WITH EXTRACTION. REGARDS TO COLONEL SAUNDERS. PON YOUR SAFE RETURN TO EARTH.

The two versions were typed on a single piece of paper, which he handed to them.

"The Americans were not transmitting?"

"No."

"The Cosmonaut was not...."

"She claims she was not near the radio receiver or the printer at the time."

"Then where did this other message come from?" Rae asked.

"That is what I want to know."

"It didn't come from the Americans," Dr. Konosov stated. They both looked at him. "These are Astronaut words, but they are not arranged as the Astronauts would have done."

"Vocabulary!" Rae exclaimed.

"Limited vocabulary," he added. Their eyes locked in confirmation.

"*Sin duda.*"

"Would someone please be so kind as to tell an aging rocket scientist what you are talking about?"

"Can you get a list of all the words used by the Astronauts in their transmissions?" asked Dr. Konosov.

"In alphabetical order, if you wish."

"Yes, that would be most helpful. Make the call now. Have them fax it directly to your room without any names, description or identification. Do it now, Dmitri, please. This is very important. Then, while we're waiting for a reply, you should tell us what else occurred up there."

Within minutes, the computer center at the Baikonur Cosmodrome was the scene of frantic manipulation of computer bytes. It was after midnight. Dr. Shavinsky inspired loyalty.

The fried chicken arrived while Dr. Shavinsky related the events that had taken place on the Moon. Rae and Ivan were too absorbed in the story to eat. By the time he had recounted all events, Dmitri was finishing the last drumstick. "By this time, they will have returned to Earth."

"Mother of Pearl!" Rae said. Ivan nodded by way of adopting this curious expression to convey his sentiments as well.

Dr. Shavinsky examined the fried chicken container as if it were a treasure map. "Who is the gentleman with the beard?"

"Colonel Saunders," they answered in unison.

A thoughtful look crossed his face, then he beamed with understanding. They noticed, and their expressions queried him.

"Operation KFC," he said to himself. Then, for the first time in days, he laughed. It was a great booming laugh that went on and on until tears formed in his eyes. As they watched in astonishment, he struggled to regain control of himself. Pointing to the picture of the elderly man with the goatee, he announced incredibly "This man is a hero in the exploration of the Moon!"

"He sold fried chicken," Rae said cautiously. Someone had once advised her to speak gently to the insane.

"Do you know what this mission to the Moon was called?"

"No."

"Operation KFC! I have just now discovered why. I fear I'm responsible. Would you like to hear about it?"

Rae shrugged casually and said "I don't know about you, Ivan, but I'm going to throw him out the window if he doesn't start telling us in ten seconds."

Ivan opened the window.

/////

It came as a total surprise to her, but her heart leapt when she saw Major Sanders waiting to greet them at Pearl Harbor. It was relief. Then he said "Welcome to America" in Russian. He was including both of them. Was the charade to continue?

He showed them into a comfortable room. In the center was a round table with linen tablecloth and what appeared to be real silverware. A modest buffet had been set up to one side of the room. Major Sanders walked over to it and began preparing a swiss and ham sandwich on rye. "Great spicy mustard. Chinese." He said this in English.

"Cut the crap, Major. Am I a Cosmonaut or an Astronaut now?"

"Damned if I know. Let's just call you two Georgia and Piotr until we find out. Speak any language you want except Arabic --- it makes them jumpy for some reason. C'mon, get something to eat. Then we'll sit down and chat."

Piotr approached the long table and began selecting various meats. "Anyone want shrimp cocktail" Georgia asked. When no one indicated they did, she took the entire bowl over to the table and placed it in front of her.

"I admire your style," commented Major Sanders. "I'll make sure to mention that in my autobiography."

"I thought Bram Stoker already wrote your biography."

"Cute, Georgia. Did she give you any trouble, Piotr?"

"Constantly. Always wanting to stop to use the rest room. You know how women are on trips."

"Don't forget the Stuckey's," she said.

"I can tell you Major, I don't care if I never see another praline again."

"Nice to know you two are *simpático*."

"That's more than he said during the entire mission," she observed.

"If we argue now, one of us can leave the room," Piotr explained.

She looked at him with new appreciation. "And I thought you were the dumb, silent type." She turned to the Major and asked "What's next for us?"

"As you've already guessed, there's still a great deal of uncertainty about this mission."

"No parade, Piotr."

"I wanted to ride behind Bullwinkle."

"Maybe you can ride behind Major Sanders. Personally, I wanted to be on the Ed Sullivan Show. Before the dog that farts the Star Spangled Banner. Tough act to follow --- for a couple reasons."

Piotr smiled broadly.

The Major tried the direct approach. To insure their undivided attention, he threw his sandwich against the wall --- hard. "I'm here to save your ungrateful skins, you assholes! I don't expect thanks, but I need cooperation if I'm going to succeed!"

Piotr was startled to witness such conduct on the part of a fellow officer. Georgia stared at the Major and said "That deep, huh?"

"And still descending. Oh, it's not your fault. You both know that. But this mission is a political nightmare. We don't know if the Marines --- that's what we are calling them for now --- are going to recover. We thought they'd be dead or alive. Either way, we had a plan. But they seem to be in between right now, with the outcome uncertain."

"So the mission is still a secret."

"We can't go that far, but the nature of the mission is a secret."

"So if the Marines die soon, we're toast?"

"Croutons."

"Ouch!" remarked Piotr, who evidently believed croutons to be much worse off than toast. No one inquired as to his thoughts on this matter. Maybe it was a Russian thing.

"But," she brightened "if the Marines wake up, then we're heros?"

"Could be."

"Major, I don't like to play games, especially games where the outcome possibilities are limited to croutons and could be. What's the problem if the Marines are O.K.?"

"While it may be that NASA has an open mind about these matters, the quite considerable remainder of the United States government has publicly taken the position that there is no extra-terrestrial life, at least in our neighborhood."

"I didn't see any. Did you Piotr?"

"*Nyet.*"

"Nevertheless, you have seen and heard too much if the authorities decide to put the lid on this. You and the Marines could be headed for Nevada."

"Area 51 exists?"

"I am not going to speculate on that one. But there certainly seems to be a black hole for E-T information somewhere out there. That's my personal take on it, totally unsupported by anything resembling evidence. And I'll deny having said it."

"Charming. First woman to walk on the Moon and I have to keep it a secret. Where's the National Organization for Women when you need them?"

"What about my government?"

"Good question, Piotr. The details haven't been worked out, but the general agreement is that we can do what we want with you as long as your government has access. I assume that means you would be alive."

"What happens now?"

"I'm going to try to get you both back to Florida, where I can watch you --- and hopefully protect you. In the meantime, don't say a word about the mission. Don't even look at the Moon. Tell them you're under orders from me to maintain silence. Give me some time to help you."

"There's something about bamboo splints that leads me to believe I'll become quite the chatterbox if they approach my fingernails. What do I do in that case?" she asked.

"By all means, scream," he advised cheerfully. "But that won't happen. I can guarantee it. I'm going to stay here for a while, ostensibly to de-brief you. During that time you'll be safe."

"Thank you, Major. I realize you had no idea what you were getting me into. And I did get to be the first woman on the Moon."

"And the first Cosmonaut," Piotr added.

"And proud of both," she conceded. "I'm suddenly overcome with fatigue, gentlemen. Have you drugged me?"

"No, but I can arrange it."

"Thanks, but I don't think I'll need it. When's breakfast?"

"Whenever you want. Excellent Egg Foo Yong, I hear."

"Not for breakfast, Major," Piotr demurred. "I want a pan-san."

"Sounds Chinese, too," she said.

The Major explained. "It's a fried egg between two pancakes, covered with syrup." Piotr nodded. "Since it's only found in the Western United States, I must conclude that you are a spy, Piotr."

"Don't you have enough excuses to shoot me already?"

"That's tellin' him, comrade."

Chapter Thirty-Five
Friday, August 6, 1993

The fax came in at 12:47 A.M. It woke Dr. Shavinsky, who promptly put on his robe and strode into the adjoining room of Dr. Konosov, who was just taking off his socks.

"We should get Rae," he suggested.

"Yes. Wake her."

Ivan knocked on the door and it opened. The lamp from his room threw light across her eyes, waking her. She sat up and said "What is it?"

When he failed to respond, she realized she was naked down to her waist. She made no attempt to cover herself. "They must have these in Russia, Tiger. Did the fax come?"

"Yes, that's it," he suddenly remembered.

"Then close the door and I'll be right in," she instructed. He did as told. "Couldn't have planned it better," she thought.

They were already examining the list that had been faxed to them. So far, every word in the message had been transmitted by the Moon Base previously. This pattern continued for the remainder of the brief message.

"Just as we thought," Dr. Konosov said, including Rae, she noticed.

"Whoever sent this message used only those words on the list. Why do you think this is so?" asked Dr. Shavinsky. "It could be coincidence, of course."

"But that's no fun," Rae candidly observed.

"She's right, Ivan. Let's have fun!"

"It could be that these are the only words they know. Words they learned from the Moon Base transmissions," ventured Dr. Konosov.

"That would mean they haven't monitored any other transmissions, which would be most curious," Rae concluded.

"But perhaps comforting," Ivan added.

"Comforting yes, but hard to swallow," she said.

"It could be a clumsy attempt to imitate the Moon Base --- to trick us," Dr. Shavinsky hypothesized.

"At last!" she said. "The heralded Byzantine Russian thought process manifests itself. *Bravo*, Doctor!"

"That's a most interesting idea, Dmitri. But why would they tell us to proceed with the extraction. It reveals that they knew the Cosmonaut was there at the time."

"If we were at the Moon Base, then we would know that the message was not originating from there. So they must have known we wouldn't be misled. Yes. That is a good point, Ivan."

"Wait," she said. "Don't let that idea go. Let's take it another step. You said they would have known it would confuse us, right?"

"Something like that."

"Maybe that was the idea...."

"You make this old Russian dizzy, Miss Kirkland."

"The issue then would be the sincerity of the message, would it not?" Dr. Konosov speculated aloud.

"Cuts straight to the bone, doesn't he Doctor?"

Dr. Shavinsky tried to sum it up. "If the message was sincere, then they have a vocabulary limited to this list which they obtained exclusively from Moon Base transmissions. If it was not sincere, then...?"

"Then they are messing with our minds, Doctor."

"That doesn't augur well," observed Dr. Konosov.

"I hope to kiss a duck!" They both looked at her in astonishment. "Don't look at me. That's a quote from Marx." She could mess minds with the best of them.

"This is true?"

"You bet your life."

"Amazing."

Dr. Konosov picked up the conversation again. "Thus far we have two possible explanations, neither of which is satisfactory. Let us assume for the moment that the message was genuine. Is there another explanation for the limited vocabulary?"

"Perhaps they don't want to reveal how much they know," Rae ventured tentatively.

"Why?"

She continued "Because it might alarm us even more?"

"It fits."

"It also makes them considerate, which is compatible with them assisting the Astronauts to the LEM," Rae added. "Hey, I could get to like these guys!"

"I'm not sure they are guys," Dr. Shavinsky interjected. "They don't leave footprints."

"You have a point, Doctor," she conceded.

He continued "I have been considering the significance of the message being received during the transmission from Russia. Was this intentional? Was it necessary? Does the fact that it does not overlap the transmission from Baikonur tell us something about their transmitting capabilities?"

"Like did they have to piggyback it?" Rae asked. "Oops, strange Yankee slang. Sorry. I meant did they have to attach it to another transmission for it to reach the Moon Base?"

"Exactly. And if they did, why was it necessary?"

"They lacked the ability to transmit it to the Moon Base themselves," said Dr. Konosov. "Again, why?"

"Maybe they didn't know how. Maybe they were too far away," suggested Rae.

"And maybe they were too close," Dr. Shavinsky offered cryptically. They just looked at him. He smiled slyly and asked "In all the universe, what is the one place that cannot transmit to the Moon Base?"

"Dmitri, you're a genius!" shouted Dr. Konosov.

"Just doing my job for Mother Russia."

"I missed the punch line, gentlemen. What is the one place that cannot transmit to the Moon Base?"

"The Moon Base."

"Oh my granny's fanny! Can I kiss him, Tiger?"

"If one of you is going to kiss me, it should be Miss Kirkland!" So she did. On the forehead, near his brain.

"Let's recapitulate." suggested Dr. Konosov. "We already have ample evidence that these aliens were near the Moon Base. They seem to have delivered the Astronauts to the LEM. Then they sent our Cosmonaut a message to proceed with the extraction. To do this, they used the Moon Base transmitter to send the message, which required that it be attached to an incoming message since the Moon Base can't transmit to itself. Does it fit?"

"It's incomplete. It doesn't explain the limited vocabulary, for example," she said, "But I only see one problem with it. How did they transmit from the Moon Base when the Cosmonaut was there, without her detecting it?"

"With messages coming in and her inspecting the facility, she would not have noticed that an outward transmission was occurring," Dr. Shavinsky explained.

"I was referring to the six-eyed Smurf at the console. She would have noticed that."

"What a vivid image!" Dr. Shavinsky feigned to marvel. "Indeed, she would have."

"The transmission was in the queue. It had been placed there earlier, waiting for an incoming transmission," hypothesized Dr. Konosov. "It was not essential that it happen. It was simply a chance to communicate."

"Conceding that for the moment, why would it be programmed to skip the first transmission?"

Ivan and Rae simply looked at each other, knowing there was no satisfactory explanation. Dr. Shavinsky said "Since there would be no reason to program it to skip the first transmission, we must assume that it wasn't programmed to do that. Maybe it was an accident. Maybe it was programmed to commence after a set interval. You are picking at grits."

"Nits," she said without thinking. She was tired. "The adrenalin's wearing off. Do we get caffeine or sleep on it?"

"Let's restore ourselves with some rest," Dr. Shavinsky advised. "Maybe we will awaken with the answers."

/////

She awakened with questions. At 6:00 A.M. she woke them both. "Breakfast will be here in fifteen minutes. Get yourselves presentable. The topic for discussion will be why did the Astronauts stop transmitting if they still could?"

"And *buenos días* to you too. You certainly know how to wake someone up."

"I'll bet you say that to all the *gringas*, Tiger."

"Tiger?" said Dr. Shavinsky.

When they had assembled around the table and begun nibbling at the fare, she asked "Dmitri, did the transmitter operate?"

"Yes. Cosmonaut Russoff sent a message without any difficulty. It was received in the usual manner."

"Then why did the Astronauts stop transmitting?" She turned to Ivan and asked "And why are you just sitting there eating?"

"I remember what happened to the fried chicken last night." He grinned sheepishly. She quickly put toast and bacon on her plate. "I see you do also."

"I forgot something yesterday. There was a final message which was never sent. I have a copy."

23 JULY 1993. THIS IS MONDAY. BROWN SLEEPING MOST OF THE TIME. NOT WELL. ADVISE YOUR TEAM THAT WE WITNESSED THEIR LANDING. WE COULDN'T SEE MUCH, BUT THE SPACECRAFT SURE IS A LOT BIGGER THAN THE OLD APOLLO. WE AWAIT EXTRACTION. COMPUTER DATA STREAM FOLLOWS.
HABITAT::I:14°/E:N176°/AP:0.77/G:0.39....

"The data stream was incomplete. NASA advised that this would have prevented transmission of any portion of the message under normal conditions. Perhaps there was a malfunction in the data portion."

"But there was no malfunction when the Cosmonaut transmitted, correct?"

"Correct."

"So the Astronauts may not have realized that this message wasn't transmitted."

"Yes. That's probably true unless they interrupted the transmission themselves."

Ivan joined it. "That's the point, isn't it? The transmission must have been interrupted intentionally --- but by whom?"

"Why would the Astronauts interrupt their own message?" Rae

asked. "And look at the message. It says they saw a spacecraft land on the Moon before the Apollo even left Earth!"

"It would be easy to believe that they saw no further reason to transmit after they thought a rescue team had arrived," Ivan postulated. "But it makes no sense for the Astronauts to stop the transmission of their message reporting the landing."

"So they didn't stop it," concluded Dr. Shavinsky. "Which means someone else did."

"Intentionally? Have we decided that?" asked Rae.

"I think we have," Ivan said.

"Then we are left with why." she said. "And that seems obvious to me. Whoever landed did not want Earth to know about it."

"If so, they succeeded," Dr. Shavinsky observed.

Ivan said nothing. He was staring at the message. "Maybe there's another reason. What if it was something in the data stream that they objected to? Dmitri, does the data stream contain a report on the condition of the Astronauts themselves?"

"I understand that it does."

"Perhaps there was something wrong with Astronaut Brown which they did not want detected."

"Like a plague?" Rae offered.

"Perhaps."

"That doesn't square with the friendly image we had last night," she observed.

"No," agreed Dr. Shavinsky, "but last night we were assuming that the apparent concern with getting the Astronauts home was motivated by good will. The facts would still fit if the motive were hostile, as you have just suggested is possible."

"Two hundred years ago American soldiers gave blankets to the native American Indians. These blankets had been taken from persons who had died of smallpox; so there is precedent for such treachery."

"What happened?"

"Not much. The vector for transmission of smallpox was not blankets," she explained.

Ivan said, "Dmitri, I think you should warn the Americans that we have this suspicion and explain our reasons. I will assist if you wish, but I think it should be done now."

"I agree. I will call Major Saunders."

///////

The two Marine Astronauts lay in separate isolation chambers because of the reported illness of Astronaut Brown. Neither had stirred from his coma, but there were no apparent health problems except those associated with living with one-sixth gravity for twenty years. Both men were receiving intravenous nutrition. There had been no attempt to awaken them. Heal the body, then the mind.

Georgia looked at them through the double glass. It was the first time she had seen them outside their gear. Between the feeding tubes, catheters and monitors, the scene reminded her of the time her slinky became completely tangled. It had never functioned properly afterwards.

Last night Major Sanders had separately de-briefed each one of them. Her session had lasted nearly four hours. When it was over, she was exhausted. After only two hours of sleep she had been awakened and asked the same questions under hypnosis. When that was finished she felt refreshed and hungry. She assumed that was the result of post-hypnotic suggestion.

Now she was waiting for Major Sanders to tell her what was next. She hoped it was breakfast. "You promised pan-sans, Major," she reminded him when he came through the door.

"That I did. And that's the next stop, but I have a question."

"Why doesn't that surprise me?"

"This may be important; so I want you to think about it before answering."

"O.K., Major. No smartass answer."

"Have you ever experienced anything that was undetectable by the five senses? Something that others didn't detect?"

"Like paranormal? I don't think so. Certainly not in adulthood. If I were psychic, I probably would have refused this assignment."

"I doubt it."

"What happened when I was under? Did I regress to a previous life?"

-261-

"No. Nothing so quite colorful, but it is nonetheless thought-provoking." She gave him a tell-me-now-or-die look. "Under hypnosis you completely ignored the presence of Captain Brown. Someone who listens to your statement will conclude you brought back one Marine, not two."

"Shit, Major. That's downright spooky."

"Yes. Isn't it? There's more. When I asked you how many persons were aboard the LEM with you, you replied 'Two' without hesitation. When I asked you their names, you named Colonel Fortney and just stopped. I asked if the other person had a name and you said 'no.' Can you think of any reason?"

"No. I sure can't. What about Piotr?"

"One purpose of de-briefing you separately is to avoid collaboration, even unconscious collaboration."

"But...?"

"I think it's safe to tell you that his account was more... predictable."

"Interesting choice of word, Major."

"Thank you. Don't mention this to anyone. Shall we dine?"

"As soon as possible, please."

"Demitrius! Demitrius!" It was a whisper, amplified by the speaker above their heads. "Oh my God! He's dead! They didn't make it in time! He's dead!" With these utterances did Colonel Fortney briefly foray into the conscious world. Medical pandemonium ensued, as it always seems to when doctors and staff are suddenly confronted by the anticipated event at an inconvenient moment. Buck and Georgia were politely shoved into the hall.

"He'll be relieved to know his partner made it," she said.

"Unless you're psychic."

"Are you kidding me?"

"I wish I knew."

"Has anyone told you lately that you're one exasperating S.O.B.?"

"My wife --- over the telephone yet! She delights in forgetting its five hours earlier out here. Calls in the middle of the night, then tells me I'm surly."

"Men have to kept on a short leash."

"We're talking choke chain here," he said with a smile as they arrived at the small canteen. From the degree of protest, it was obvious he had a good marriage.

"Pardon me, Major, There's a Dr. Shavinsky on the telephone from New York," announced the Seaman First Class at the door. He told her to go ahead while he took the call.

When he joined her at the table, he announced "Dr. Shavinsky sends his greetings." He grabbed a blueberry muffin from her plate and chewed on it thoughtfully. "Your de-briefing is essentially over. I'd like to breach protocol and involve you in analysis right now. Are you game?"

"Sure! I'd love to know what the Hell happened up there."

"I want you to understand that what I am about to tell you is even more secret that what you already know."

"Major, we have already discussed the possibility of my permanent disappearance, which I now understand started with my complete cooperation in your office several months ago. I can't be disappeared twice. So tell me what's going on. Who knows? I might just be psychic."

"Without the distractions of live bodies to deal with, it seems the Russians have been reviewing the actual data --- and coming to some interesting conclusions. Let me run them by you and then we can discuss them, O.K.?"

"Fine."

He referred to a note he had taken. "One, the Marines thought they saw a spacecraft land nearby, which they assumed was ours although it did not look like any they had seen before." He put two fingers out. "Two, Captain Brown had become seriously ill. Three, they attempted to send a message advising us of these two events, but the message was not received. Four, that message was intentionally interrupted, but not by the Marines. Five, after that, something happened to the Marines that prevented them from sending any more messages." He began counting on the fingers of his left hand. "Six, the message that overrode part of the Russian message was sent from the Moon Base while you were there." She shuddered involuntarily. "Seven, every single word used in that message was a word that the Marines themselves had previously transmitted. Eight, it was intended that you would receive the message while you were at the Moon Base. Nine, the placement of the lunar rover across your tracks was another message. Ten, these two messages were intended to prepare you for the shock of finding the Marines aboard the LEM. Eleven, the Marines were passengers in the other rover that day. Twelve and most importantly, every single one of these events was calculated to assure that the Marines returned to Earth."

"Hard to believe they lost the Cold War."

"Dr. Shavinsky advised that we examine these events to verify that there is no conflict with the conclusion that the intended result was to return the Marines. He also said we shouldn't speculate as to alternative ways to accomplish this, since we already know what has been done."

"And if we conclude that his assertions are correct?"

"We are to ask ourselves why it was so important that the Marines return to Earth."

"That was the purpose of the mission, wasn't it?"

"That's exactly why we never questioned it before."

"I see. Be careful what you wish for; you may get it."

"Let's check back on Colonel Fortney before we start. He may be able to tell us something by now."

"Good idea. Let's go!"

/////

She had seen Major Sanders commit calculated violence, but his uncontrolled fury at hearing Colonel Fortney had just been sedated was incredible. At one point he had the doctor backed up against the wall on tiptoes. She had grabbed his arm and tugged him out of the room. It had taken all her strength until she had whispered "Maybe they want you to do this."

/////

Rae entered Dr. Shavinsky's room to inquire if he had reached Major Sanders yet. He was studying the room service menu, an indication that he was hungry. "Looking for anything special?"

"I am saddened by the lack of variety these days in room service." He shook his head to demonstrate the intensity of his feelings on this matter. "No longer can you have a *soufflé* or even *crepes*," he lamented.

"Nonsense! Most chefs can prepare those if they're not too busy."

"Then why aren't they on the menu?"

"Probably not enough demand."

Ivan had entered the room and jokingly said "Maybe they can't spell *soufflé*."

"That's it!" Rae shouted. "*Eureka!*"

"What does a vacuum cleaner have to do with the menu?" asked Dr. Shavinsky, who was now beyond confusion. They ignored him.

"What's it, Rae?" asked Ivan.

"They can't spell! They're illiterate! The Moon Base transmissions are the only written ones they've monitored! Yes! Yes! Yes!" she shouted as she ran from the room.

Ivan sat down gracelessly in the nearest chair to consider this proposition. "It could be," he admitted.

"The young lady is right again, it seems. I'm glad she's here to assist two feeble scientists figure things out."

"Do you know what this means?" He answered his own question. "We are not limited to the vocabulary. All we have to do is send them new words to increase it."

"We could transmit a CD-ROM dictionary," Rae suggested. "For that matter, we could send the encyclopedia and an atlas."

"You are assuming they are still at the Moon Base," Ivan said. "Besides, it is one thing to enhance our ability to communicate with them. It is quite another to educate them about Earth."

"How much do we want them to know?" asked Dr. Shavinsky.

"You've convinced me. Maybe we should send them a children's dictionary to start. By the way, I came in to ask if you had reached Major Sanders."

"Yes, he is in Hawaii with the Cosmonauts. The Marines have not been able to speak yet."

"Should we tell him about this?"

"When he calls back. Let him consider the previous message

first."

/////

The sun had recently set over Siberia, where the days are long in summer. The very large array was set to receive weak signals from distant galaxies. When the radio telescopes moved to scan closer, no one thought to reset the audio control.

> 6 AUGUST 1993. THIS IS MONDAY. REGARDS TO
> FORTNEY AND BROWN. COMPUTER DATA STREAM
> FOLLOWS.
> HABITAT::I:14°/E:N174°/AP:0.76/G:0.39....

The duty officer monitoring at the time ripped off his earphones in pain. The encoded message was automatically recorded as a series of unintelligible beeps and squawks.

/////

Major Sanders called back. He told them he had new information and that he would be returning to the Cape with the Cosmonauts the following day. He asked them to meet him there Sunday morning at 8:00 A.M. to confer.

Nothing could have stopped them from attending.

Chapter Thirty-Six
Sunday, August 8, 1993

The red pullover shirt featured parrots, macaws and tropical flowers. Jimmy Buffett would have been embarrassed to wear it. "I decided to let my shirt make an entrance for me," the President explained. "I understand everyone here speaks English, but NASA has its own spin on the language; so if anyone needs a translation, speak up. Major, will you bring us up to date?"

"Yes sir. Colonel Fortney came out of his coma, or whatever it was, on Friday. He was disoriented at first and had to be sedated. Since then he has adjusted to the fact that he has been rescued and is in Hawaii. This was no easy matter, since he is still isolated in a room with no windows to the outside. Cosmonaut Russoff refused to put on a hula skirt; so we had to bring him a pineapple to convince him. The medical staff has examined and tested him as thoroughly as they can while wearing their bio-hazard outfits. The consensus is that he is underweight and slightly malnourished. Of course, his body needs to adapt to full gravity again as well. Complete physical recovery will take months, but they think he is going to be all right."

"What about mentally?"

"When the mission first got underway, Mr. President, we had a history professor from the University of Florida prepare a series of VCR tapes showing what happened in the world each year since 1957. That was the year of Sputnik-1, launched by a rocket simply called Old Number Seven. Going back to 1957 was intended to avoid suspicion as to their real purpose, but the psychologists decided to show Colonel Fortney the entire series to remind him of what occurred before he left and provide a smooth transition into the period he missed."

"Is he watching them?"

"He loves them! The poor guy is starved for information."

"How far has he gotten?"

"The last time I checked he was marveling over the Mid-East Peace Accords. No one had the heart to tell him how the implementation was proceeding."

"Lucky bastard."

"Roger that, Mr. President. Anyway, at the rate he's going, he should be caught up in a few days. I'm told that there will be a period before this new knowledge sinks in. There will always be references he won't get. He won't know what disco was."

"Did I already say lucky bastard?"

"Yes, I believe you did, sir."

"Anything so far that has provoked a strong reaction?"

"Yes sir. He was beside himself when he saw President Nixon's resignation speech. It seems he feels Nixon was responsible for them being stuck on the Moon."

"Now tell us the bad news, Major."

"As you all know, when Colonel Fortney regained consciousness, his first words were that Captain Brown had died. He was extremely upset. Since then we have taken measures to assure that Colonel Fortney does not see or hear about Captain Brown. We have tried to de-brief Colonel Fortney gently --- without upsetting him. He distinctly remembers that Captain Brown was seriously ill when a large spacecraft landed. He still thinks it was ours, by the way. He recalls sending a message reporting the landing. Shortly thereafter, Captain Brown died in his sleep. Colonel Fortney not only tried taking his pulse and placing a mirror at his mouth, he then connected Captain Brown to the computer device with which they monitored their temperature, heart rate and blood pressure. This device confirmed that Captain Brown had no heartbeat and no blood pressure."

"What happened next?"

"The inner airlock hatch suddenly opened without warning. He says there was a problem with the airlock, but that the hatch had never popped open before. Apparently, the air became too thin to support brain function and he blacked out. If the outer hatch was not sealing properly, this could occur in a matter of seconds."

"Did he see anything unusual in the airlock?"

"No sir. When it opened, he knew what caused the sound. He turned the other direction to get his helmet, but didn't make it. He remembers nothing else until last Friday. We tried hypnosis. Nothing new emerged."

"Have they found out what put him to sleep for two weeks?"

"Whatever it was had pretty well worn off by the time we got him, sir. There are no indications as to how it was administered, which most likely means we missed it or it was introduced through the lungs. We have been unable to find out any more from Captain Brown, who's still under."

"Let's talk about Captain Brown then."

"Captain Brown is still unconscious. His vital signs are fine. They expect him to awaken normally sometime soon. No attempt has been made to awaken him, because they don't know why he is unconscious. There are the non-medical reasons as well. We know that Captain Brown was seriously ill and that Colonel Fortney attempted to send a message that he had died. Upon awakening, Colonel Fortney told us that again. He still believes Captain Brown is dead. We do not intend to tell him otherwise at this time."

"Is there any evidence that he is being sustained artificially?"

"None, Mr. President. They tell me his brain has a normal level of activity for a comatose condition. His heart is pumping without assistance."

"So either he didn't die or he died and...recovered?"

"There is a third possibility, sir."

"Let's hear it. It can't be any stranger that the others."

Major Sanders thought for a moment about how to preface his response and decided there was no way to ease it into the discussion. "That Captain Brown died and something else is using his body, sir. This is not a working hypothesis at this time, merely a possibility."

"Aside from Colonel Fortney's beliefs on the subject, is there any evidence to indicate this might be the case?"

"I don't know if it qualifies as evidence, but under hypnosis Cosmonaut Russoff referred only to Colonel Fortney, as though Captain Brown was not on the return flight." Everyone looked at her.

"I have no idea why that happened. In fact, I didn't know it had until Major Sanders told me afterward. I can assure you that I never had any question that both Marines were coming back with us."

Rae spoke up. "Pardon me, Major, but would it have been possible for the Moon Base monitoring devices to have been switched;

so that the medical reports for Captain Brown were actually those of Colonel Fortney?"

"No. We thought of that ourselves, but one piece of data was the blood type, which is different."

She continued, "So we are quite certain that the Marine who was seriously ill was indeed Captain Brown?"

"Yes. There is no doubt. That, of course, simplifies matters greatly." When he saw some confused expressions, he added "We know Colonel Fortney was healthy; therefore, we assume that he did not die."

"If we are willing to discuss the possession of dead bodies by aliens, how can we eliminate the possibility that live bodies could be similarly possessed?" asked Dr. Konosov casually.

"We haven't eliminated that possibility, Doctor. We are concentrating our efforts on the enigma of Captain Brown for now, but we continue to monitor Colonel Fortney closely."

"I apologize for what I am about to say, but it must be said. Cosmonaut Russoff was also on the Moon when the aliens were there."

"I'll bet it only takes 25¢ for you to call all your friends from a payphone," she said.

Ivan shrugged.

The President said "This isn't about you. It's about the safety of the world. I don't want anyone holding back to spare someone's feelings. What he said is true. It has to be considered. On the other hand, you are not in quarantine and have passed your post-flight physical. While we might frown on you going on retreat to the Himalayas at this time, no one intends to lock you in a room."

"Actually, I have explained to both of them that they will be restricted to base until we figure out what has happened."

"We understand that, Mr. President. We'd like to know ourselves."

"Good. Now what new developments have we?"

"We have received a transmission from the Moon Base. Here is a printout."

6 AUGUST 1993. THIS IS MONDAY. REGARDS TO FORTNEY AND BROWN. COMPUTER DATA STREAM FOLLOWS.

"All the words are in the vocabulary consisting of the transmissions the Marines made from the Moon Base."

The President turned to Rae and her Russians. "That was an excellent deduction you made. Does it mean these are the only words they know?"

Rae responded. "No sir, I'm afraid it doesn't. We threw quite a few ideas against the wall. Only one stuck. We believe those are the only words they know how to spell." No one said anything, at first.

Then Dr. Konosov explained "Mr. President, English can be a treacherous language for someone learning it. If we had been transmitting in Spanish, they might be tempted to attempt phonetic spelling. It appears that they have grasped the inconsistencies of English and opted to avoid a misunderstanding. We have discussed sending them a dictionary."

"Why not just talk to them?"

"That assumes they can speak," he responded.

"Oh. Yes. I guess we can't take that for granted."

"As a lawyer, you know they may prefer written expression to avoid faulty recall of what was said, but we are all hoping they're not lawyers," said Rae, eliciting a Presidential chuckle.

"So, do we send them a dictionary?" he asked.

Ivan said "If we believe they have monitored our voice transmissions, there is probably nothing to lose. If they have to construct a dictionary themselves, it could take them decades. What if they have an urgent message for us?"

Major Sanders said "If they don't know much about us, though, a dictionary would reveal quite a bit. For example, their present vocabulary does not include words like gun, war and murder. Do we want them to know about these?"

"We had thought about sending a children's dictionary to avoid the problem raised by the Major," Rae said. "Then we could see if we wanted proceed further after we analyze the results."

"I have no conceptual problem with that, Mr. President."

"Then let's implement it. Major, I want you to work on this with the NASA Liaison Office. Nothing happens without you and the

Director agreeing on every detail in writing, then you still need verbal approval from me. No copies to anyone."

"Pardon me, sir. I don't know who that is."

"It's Miss Kirkland here. I assume she'll take the job."

"I'm honored, Mr. President, but I could use some details."

"You're the auditor. Figure out what GAO would approve for such a position and that's what it pays. Your office could be in Washington, Houston or right here. Whatever you think will work best."

"Right here. What about staff?"

"Tricky because of the secrecy."

"I was thinking of Ken Mason, whom you met at the White House. He's the one who started all this."

"Perfect. Bump his pay a notch at GAO before you bring him over. Let them take the heat."

"Major, as of now, Miss Kirkland is my direct representative as to all matters concerning the Moon Base, the Marines, the Cosmonauts and...ah, anyone else involved."

"While we are at it," added Rae, "I want you to know that Cosmonaut Russoff will be working with me on this matter."

"Excellent. And Cosmonaut Gregorovich?"

"Major-General Gregorovich will remain with us for a while for observation, but aside from mission secrecy there is no reason to keep him here after that," said Major Sanders.

"Hopefully he will be permitted to return home soon," said Dr. Shavinsky.

"As soon as we get our story straight, Doctor." To Major Sanders he said, "Tell them to become proactive regarding Captain Brown if he hasn't awakened yet."

"Yes, sir."

"Miss Kirkland, find a suitable dictionary. If you and Major Sanders approve it, send it."

"Yes, sir."

"I've got a plane to catch. Thank you all for coming." A few handshakes and squeezes later, he was gone, marveling at the firmness of Cosmonaut Russoff's bicep.

"Congratulations on your battlefield promotion, Miss

Kirkland."

"Thank you, Major. Can you find me space near your office?"

"You're lucky it's Sunday. Easy to clear space when no one's around to object."

"We call it 'Midnight Expansion' at GAO."

"How much space do you need?"

"Two adjoining cubicles near yours. Four desks with chairs. Four PC's. Four telephones. Two faxes. Ballpoint pen or two. View of the Atlantic."

"Ouch!"

"O.K., I'll bring my own pens."

/////

It was a unique situation; yet the action taken was ordinary. After much discussion, a vial of ammonia was opened beneath the nose of Captain Brown. He reacted within seconds. That was the simple part.

His eyes popped open and all Hell broke loose. He grabbed the doctor standing over him by the arm of the bio-hazard suit and flung him against the monitoring equipment. The technician assisting the doctor threw himself across the Marine to prevent him from rising. Captain Brown twisted his helmet off, breaking his neck. The stunned staff outside called for security. The doctor managed to shoot several milligrams of sodium pentothal into the I-V line before it was ripped out. Captain Brown was approaching the doctor with hostile intentions when it took him. He collapsed on top of the doctor.

They quickly restrained Captain Brown and reattached the tubes and monitors. The printouts from the monitors did not indicate any increase in cerebral activity after he had awakened. Although the significance of this was debated, all agreed it was ominous.

When the videotape was reviewed, Cosmonaut Russoff remarked that he hadn't spoken. They cautiously examined his throat while he was still unconscious. His trachea was abraded as though a tube had been forced down it. His vocal chords were crushed. Captain Brown was a mute.

"Haul your lazy ass out of bed, I've found you a job."

"As a preacher?" he asked. "It is Sunday, you know."

"You're impossible! Let me speak to Laura."

"O.K., but we're getting ready for church."

"Are you converted?"

"I'm not sure. The deal is I give up my heathen ways, but we go to the late services. Is that conversion?"

"Hallelujah and a-men, brother. You have been converted."

"I was afraid of that. Where are you?"

"Near your new office at the Kennedy Space Center at lovely Merritt Island, Florida. You and Laura meet us for brunch at the Cocoa Beach Pier at 11:30. We'll talk then."

"Us?"

"Rooskies!" she said in a stage whisper. He heard laughter in the background.

"Uhm." The line went dead.

/////

This time Captain Brown was awakened gradually by withdrawing the drugs. He was completely docile until the doctor moved. The movement triggered an attempt to break free of his restraints, which continued until he was exhausted. There was no acknowledgment of the doctor's words, spoken in a soothing tone. His eyes showed primitive fear. He lacked understanding of all around him.

/////

Amid the cracking of crustaceans, they held their reunion and resolved to hold more. Ivan made them all promise to visit at Christmas. Dmitri threatened to stay until the upper Volga thawed. Rae told Ken he could commute to his new job in flip-flops. Laura told them about the forthcoming vacation to Florence. The Russians were told about the mystery of the tombstone.

The Moon Base was discussed only briefly. It was a nice change.

Chapter Thirty-Seven
Tuesday, August 10, 1993

Colonel Fortney couldn't believe the Berlin Wall fell in 1988. He replayed that portion of the tape several times. He cheered every time it showed a section falling. The collapse of the Soviet Union was the icing on the cake. "I've got to know," he asked. "Have they turned the Pentagon into a roller rink?"

"Disney bought it for a theme park."

"Who's going to play Goofy?"

"Everyone."

He felt fine until he exerted himself. Gravity was murder.

/////

NASA had transmitted a children's dictionary to the Moon Base that morning. The response came within the hour.

10 AUGUST 1993. THIS IS MONDAY. THANK YOU FOR THE DICTIONARY. DO YOU HAVE BIGGER DICTIONARY. IS FORTNEY WELL. DOES BROWN STILL LIVE AGAIN.

When a copy finally reached Major Sanders, he showed it to Rae.

She said "See Martian run. Run Martian, run. We've got to get them a real dictionary!"

"Did you catch the part about Brown live again?"

"Yes! How can we find out what happened if they don't know the words to tell us?"

"Let's call the President."

The President was staring at the British tabloid on his desk. "Secret Russian Moon Mission?" the headline blared. It was time for an announcement. The call from the Cape came as he made the decision.

"I understand the problem. Let me think about it," he told Rae and Major Sanders. "In the meantime, draft a press release for me about the joint U.S.-Soviet mission to the Moon."

"Do I mention the Moon Base?"

"No, but you can say that an American Astronaut landed on the Moon to retrieve experiments left there during the original Apollo Missions. Be sure to play up the Russian cooperation angle, but make it clear the Cosmonaut did not set foot on the Moon. Clear it with Dr. Shavinsky."

"What about Colonel Fortney?"

"No mention for now. We'll deal with him later. After all, he's officially listed as dead by the Marines. It may take some time to sort his status out."

"Yes, sir."

"We have to have an announcement by tonight; so the morning papers can run it."

Georgia and Piotr received new leases on their lives.

/////

"I will not be able to take any questions," he told they press corps with all the considerable charm he could muster, "because I hate not knowing the answers. This was a scientific endeavor. I won't tell you what my grades were in high school science, but I didn't go to M.I.T. afterwards." He gave them time to chuckle before continuing. The Washington press corps knew when they were supposed to chuckle. "On July 28th, a Russian Proton rocket launched an Apollo space vehicle from the Baikonur Cosmodrome. Aboard was the pilot, Major-General Piotr Gregorovich, who is an experienced MIR Cosmonaut, and Astronaut Dr. Tiffany Reed. On August 1st, Astronaut Reed landed the LEM on the surface of the Moon, becoming the first woman in history to do so. She then assembled the lunar rover and tested it before taking a scheduled rest. Cosmonaut Gregorovich remained with the Apollo vehicle in lunar orbit. Later, Astronaut Reed used the lunar rover to collect experiments left behind by previous Moon missions. This is the reason she flew the LEM alone, to provide space for the experiments. It is also the reason there were only two persons on the mission. The mission was successful. The crew of Apollo XIX is healthy and resting. The experiments will require years of scientific analysis; so don't expect another news conference tomorrow about this." Chuckle Time. "I would like to take this opportunity to thank the Russian people and their government for their cooperation with this mission. The part they played was critical to its success. We believe this joint effort will be of great assistance as we go forward with the international space station project. Thank you for coming out tonight."

Smiling and waving --- or was he trying to bat the questions out of the air? --- he strolled briskly from the podium.

Major Sanders' portable telephone rang the instant it was over. "Does this mean I don't have to stay in the attic anymore?" Dr. Reed asked.

/////

Over a celebratory pizza dinner at Laura's house, there were *Carlsberg* toasts to the Astronauts, Cosmonauts, the NASA Liaison Office and "all the little people who made it all possible."

The final toast was delivered by Dr. Shavinsky. "Here's to the Russian General who leaked the story to the press!" He refused to elaborate.

Chapter Thirty-Eight

Wednesday, August 11, 1993

The story did not make the headlines. The San Andreas fault had become restive that night with devastating results. Photographs of crushed apartment buildings and broken freeways dominated the front page of every U.S. newspaper. The attention of the public would be diverted for days. The mission became a footnote in history, much to the President's relief.

On the advice of scientists and with the consent of the Russian President, CD-ROM dictionaries, encyclopedias, atlases and great works of literature were transmitted to the Moon Base that day. Rae was in charge of selecting them. It was only Laura's insistence that caused the Bible to be included, however.

///

It was midnight in Siberia when the transmission came through.

11 AUGUST 1993. THIS IS MONDAY. THANK YOU FOR THE LITERATURE. IT WILL TAKE MANY OF YOUR YEARS TO ASSIMILATE. WE HAVE ESTABLISHED A TRANSMISSION FACILITY AT THE BASE ON YOUR MOON. IT WILL NOT PREVENT THE USE OF THE BASE BY YOU, SHOULD YOU RETURN. THIS WILL PERMIT US TO COMMUNICATE IN THE FUTURE. RESPONSES WILL NOT OCCUR FOR DAYS OR WEEKS. WE DO NOT SEEK TO COLONIZE. THAT IS NOT OUR WAY. EXPERIENCE HAS SHOWN THAT DIRECT CONTACT BETWEEN SPECIES CAN HAVE DISASTROUS RESULTS. WE LEAVE SOON. CHERISH THOSE WHO RETURNED. PLEASE ADVISE IF THE RE-ANIMATION OF ASTRONAUT BROWN WAS SUCCESSFUL. SOME SPECIES DO NOT RE-ANIMATE. MAY YOU DWELL BENEATH THE BENEVOLENT SHADE OF THE FIRST TREE OF THE WORLD PERPETUALLY REFRESHED WITH

CHOCOLATE. GOOD-BYE FOR NOW.

"What do you make of it, Rae?" asked Major Sanders.

"That last part is something. Where did they get that?"

"It could have been in the literature, I guess. We sent them a library."

"I guess we did.

"It sounds like the Songs of Solomon. 'Thy hair is like a flock of goats descending from Mount Gilead.' It has that kind of feel."

"I agree, as long as you weren't talking about my hair. But, there's a problem with that. Chocolate came from the New World. It can't be in the Bible." Then she dropped it. "I wonder where they're going...."

"Maybe they'll tell us some day. In the meantime we're supposed to cherish Dr. Reed. That should be a trick."

"She must have made quite an impression on them. You know this could be the first inter-planetary Valentine," she mused.

"You don't know Dr. Reed well, do you?"

/////

That evening the decision was made to send Demitrius Brown to a secret government medical facility in the Nevada desert for further recuperation and study. It was generally understood that this would be a one-way trip.

Colonel Fortney was given a new identity with accompanying documentation furnished by the F.B.I. As Daniel T. Smith, he was made part of the NASA Liaison Office at very respectable pay. Both he and Dr. Reed signed Official Secrets Act documents in Major Sanders' elaborate cubicle that afternoon. Dr. Reed was given a NASA desk job too. Each was promised a future shuttle flight, subject to passing the standard physical exam. It was assumed that Colonel Fortney would not.

Major Sanders felt that his end of the situation was under control.

Chapter Thirty-Nine
Friday, November 26, 1993

"You were right again, Tiger. *Oxkutzcab.* The land is abundant with turkeys. That was a great Thanksgiving dinner yesterday. I wonder if they'll have turkey sandwiches today."

"You like leftovers?"

"I must. I like ruins."

"I hadn't thought of the great fallen cities of Meso-America as leftovers."

"That's what I'm here for --- to straighten you out."

"And I thought you were here to tempt me from my academic life of study."

"Maybe I can get around to that too. You know, one of the advantages of eating so much that you pass out is that you wake up early. Let's visit the ruins before they heat up!"

"We have but to stroll down the road," he motioned. They were staying in a room at the Mayaland. So far they had used both beds.

"Let's go back to *Chichen Viejo.* I didn't get the full tour the last time."

/////

"What do you mean, I flunked the physical, Major?"

Buck Sanders sighed. Cherishing Dr. Reed was a real challenge. "Which word didn't you understand, Doctor."

"Damn you! Why am I being bumped?"

"Because you're with child," he said as calmly as he could. "Please tell me it's not Piotr's."

"No, it's not Piotr's. I know whose it is, too!"

He observed her. She was obviously shocked by the news. "I didn't get this job because I was a warm and caring person. I apologize for being gruff and insensitive. Would you like to talk to someone more qualified in those areas?"

"No. I'm O.K. I'd better take home some smelling salts for my roommate, though."

"Poppa?"

"Poppa. Roger, that. Well, I guess I can stop worrying about the old biological clock now."

"The only thing I distinctly remember about raising a baby is sleep deprivation."

"Thanks for the advice and the apology, Major. I know I've been a bitch, but nothing in my life ever prepared me for the past four months."

"I've tried to put myself in your shoes, and I just can't. It was simpler for me. I went up there, did what I was told most of the time and came back to pick up my hero badge. Compared to your experiences, it was a walk on the beach. You are one tough cookie, Dr. Reed. And you'll need to be to have a baby."

"Call me Georgia. I got used to it. It's a reminder of my clandestine Cosmonaut days, too."

"Did you figure out the *double entendre?*"

"No. Piotr told me. It had never occurred to me that Georgia could refer to anything but the Peach State."

"Nice guy, Piotr."

"Yeh. But he's not the father."

"His loss."

"Careful, Major, your humanity is showing through."

"Good morning, Georgia."

"*Dobray yutro*, Buck."

/////

The site was maintained only to the extent that the grass was cut periodically with a scythe. Otherwise, *Chichen Viejo* stood unattended in the bright sun, as it had for ten centuries. The local farmers walked past it daily. Occasionally, one would plant a field of *maíz* nearby. Some nights there would be copal incense burning at *el Templo de las Fechas* in celebration of a Mayan religious ritual. This was not part of the tourist México. Nor was it connected with the official México. *Chichen Viejo* was still part of the Mayan realm.

"It's different!" she observed.

"It's dry. There won't be a significant rain until next April. By then the grass will be yellow and crunchy."

He described the various buildings as they walked. Both wore long pants to protect against the insects. Because it was hot, his shirt was open; she wore a silk scarf across her chest, having removed her covering shirt as soon as they entered the jungle. His finger was poised on the umbrella's button like it was a trigger. After passing through *el Templo de los Falos* they tip-toed past the sunning iguanas to the two stone warriors.

Standing between them she said "Take our picture," which he did. Afterward, she observed "Something's wrong here. We aren't dressed the same."

He couldn't imagine what she was talking about. After all, these were statues of warriors. Before he could comment, she said "They don't have tops on. That's it. I can fix that! Close your eyes."

His mind went numb in a way he wasn't familiar with, but he managed to close his eyes. After what seemed like hours, she told him to open his eyes. "Take the picture."

But he couldn't. He was laughing too hard. Brightly colored silk scarves were tied around the chests of the stone warriors, too. When he finally regained his composure, he snapped the picture. "Now take those scarves off before we get arrested for vandalizing an archeological site."

She removed all three scarves and struck the pose between the statues again. Wordlessly, he took the picture.

Normally, the exposure operation of a Minolta Maxxum 35 millimeter camera is a quick sliding sound with an abrupt click at the end. This time it was the screech of a Defining Moment Formula One accelerating on dry pavement. He knew his life was changed forever.

So did she, of course.

/////

Captain Demitrius F. Brown no longer received the respect accorded an Astronaut. This is a predicament those who have lost their higher brain functions should expect --- if they could expect anything at all. He suffered from apparent hypoxemia, lack of sufficient oxygen supply to the brain. In such situations, what oxygen that is available is utilized to keep the heart and lungs functioning. It is not a bad system, since brain cells can live without oxygen for at least five minutes under normal conditions. Put simply, you don't need to recite Shakespeare in order to flee a smoke-filled room --- although it would be a classy thing to do.

As a living experiment; however, he was a star. That would have to suffice. The good news was that the doctors were starting on the outside, with the skin. In preparation for a microscopic examination of his epidermis, he was stripped. All his hair was removed and placed in plastic bags. He did not appear to enjoy this procedure.

Captain Brown growled at the team of doctors as they surrounded him. It was not long before the doctor examining his scalp noticed a mark just above the base of his skull. It was a darkened circle having a diameter of nearly three millimeters. A single line formed a concentric circle outside it. The diameter of the outer circle was six millimeters. The circles appeared to be precise, as if made by a machine or an instrument. It was agreed that they were burned into the flesh, most likely by heat or chemicals. After detailed photographs were taken, a sample was removed for testing.

There was general agreement that the instrument which made the mark had penetrated the scant soft tissue at that spot. Just how far it went would remain a question for now.

/////

The new sign on the wall announced

**WHAT ALL THE WISE MEN PROMISED
HAS NOT HAPPENED,
AND WHAT ALL THE DAMNED FOOLS PREDICTED
HAS COME TO PASS.**

--- Lord Melbourne, Prime Minister

It seemed appropriate.

Daniel T. Smith, formerly known as Colonel Fortney, was at his desk in the NASA Liaison Office, recording his recollections of twenty years on the Moon into a transcriber for posterity. He adjusted his new eyeglasses. It was great to see well again, but he wasn't comfortable with them yet. He was bored. His face lit up when Buck Sanders entered the room.

"Major!"

"Mr. Smith."

"Is this business or pleasure?"

Major Sanders displayed a pair of scissors.

"Doesn't look like pleasure."

"The doctors found a mark on Captain Brown that they can't explain. Sooner or later, they'll think to send out a scalping party to visit you."

"Ouch!"

"With your permission, I'd like to see if you have a similar mark without inflicting too much damage to your hair."

"Why don't I hold onto the scissors while you take a peek?"

Major Sanders laughed as he handed over the scissors. "I've faced men with deadly weapons who weren't as intimidated as you are by these scissors."

"Maybe they were too busy firing back."

"Come to think of it, they were. Bend your neck forward, please." The concentric circles were there, just as described. He didn't want to alarm Mr. Smith; so he simply said "Well, what do you know? There's a tiny scratch or burn. I don't know whether that's what they're talking about or not. Sure doesn't look important."

"So now what?"

"They're analyzing a microscopic sample from Captain Brown. I'm sure they'll want one from you. Come on, let's go to the medical lab and volunteer. That always confuses them."

"Let's go, then!"

As they walked down the hallway, Major Sanders asked as casually as he could, "Colonel, do you remember dying?"

/////

Georgia set the chilled bottle of champagne down on the kitchen table with a flourish. "Time to celebrate another miracle of life."

Her roommate came in and observed the label. "It's barely afternoon....*Bollinger*! Must be some miracle! I'll dust off the champagne vessels."

When the cork was popped and the glasses filled, Georgia proposed a toast. "To family!"

"To family!" They drained the glasses and poured refills. "Whose family?"

"Ours, damn it! I'm pregnant."

"Not by me!"

"How can you be so sure?"

"In case you haven't noticed, I'm a woman."

"Technicalities. Nobody accepts responsibility anymore. Let's drink to responsibility!"

"Now I know why you bought the good stuff. If this was *Andre*, I'd be gone. You want to tell me about it?"

"Not sober."

"Don't worry. But, remember, you're drinking for two now."

"Meg, I've got to find a husband fast. NASA hasn't entered the era of unwed mothers yet."

"At the risk of being *gauche*, how about the father?"

Georgia gazed thoughtfully into her glass without responding.

Meg whistled the first bar of "I'm Just a Girl Who Can't Say No" from Oklahoma, then asked "You do have some idea who the father is, right?"

She sighed. "I could probably track him down, but what's the point?" She refilled their glasses. "When I thought about sitting in that ancient capsule, balanced on top of that gigantic rocket, I decided to have a last fling."

"So it's some local cowboy?"

"*Nyet.*"

"Astronaut Reed, you tramp, you certainly have an interesting life. We may need more champers."

"I put it in the fridge already. It's a shame Marie Antoinette had such tiny tits. If Sophia Loren had been the model for champagne glasses...."

"Is he married?"

"It didn't come up."

"Something must have," she giggled.

"The Phantom, as I recall."

"He called it that?"

"In broken English he said 'It comes in night time, then disappears' like the Phantom." Her attempt to sound like a drunken Russian baritone combined with the alcohol to send the conversation into hysterical laughter for the next few minutes.

/////

The *fer-de-lance* popped up in the uncut grass next to the path, about seven feet in front of them. It stood facing them, motionless, soundless. Without warning, Ivan hit the switch on the umbrella, dropped it and turned around, running. She followed on his heels. Neither uttered a word. They ran down the path back to the ruins and scrambled up atop *el Templo de las Fechas*. It would be difficult for the viper to follow them up there because of the sheer stone walls. The same walls they would willingly jump from if it did.

"Do you see it?" he asked.

"No, but let's keep looking!"

"They're very tenacious," he said as he peered over the edge of the stone platform.

"That makes me feel a whole lot better."

"Maybe the umbrella confused it."

"I don't know what startled me more, the snake or the umbrella. Got to hand it to you, Tiger. You've got some quick draw."

"John Wayne films," he explained, continuing his searching.

"Can you whistle and make your horse come over here?"

"That was Bob Steele."

"Oh. Well then how do we get back to the horses?"

"We wait here a respectable interval, then I bring them here. In the meantime, we work on our tans --- unless you want to retrieve the umbrella."

"I've got sunblock in my bag, thank you."

"It is my inebriated opinion that you don't need a husband. You need a father."

"Keep talking. You may be on to something."

"Everyone wants to know who the father is, right?"

"Major Sanders has already suggested that it might be Cosmonaut Gregorovich. He thinks I don't have a boyfriend, the bastard!"

"That's a rumor of the worst kind! A true rumor!" Meg declared.

"He thinks a man and a woman can't be in the same space ship for six days without having sex."

"How typical! Men are pigs. So did you?"

"It's not really conducive. In fact it would be dangerous, Floating around bumping into instruments. And Houston could probably know what you were doing from the monitors."

"I guess you didn't, then."

"No, we didn't. Tell me about not needing a husband."

"If you could identify someone suitable as the father, who was not in a position to get married...."

"He's already married?"

"Too complicated. Maybe he's away --- or dead."

"Dead men get no tail," Georgia said with mock seriousness.

"I'll even love you when you're dead --- and the wind is right. Do you get the feeling we're digressing?"

"That's how it all starts. Undressing!"

"What a good idea!"

It was suddenly nap time.

Ivan announced with mock solemnity, "It's time to meet my fate."

"Go forth, young Lancelot, and retrieve yon steeds. Your fate awaits you elsewhere."

"Forsooth, my Lady. Soon we will dwell beneath the benevolent shade of the first tree of the world perpetually refreshed with chocolate."

"What was that?"

"That's from the *Popol Vuh*, the Mayan Book of Creation. It's their vision of the heavenly afterlife."

"I know we didn't send that!"

"What are you talking about?"

"The Moon Base transmitted that message you just said. Where did they get it?"

"Maybe the horses will know," he said as he descended the crumbling stairs. He had to concentrate on what he would do if the viper reappeared.

/////

They were lying next to each other on top of the bed.

"Why does my mouth taste like rotted flesh?"

"Whatever you do, don't open your eyes!" Meg warned.

"Now I remember why people aren't supposed to drink in the afternoon. What time is it?"

"You're awfully damned pushy for an unwed mother." She turned her head gingerly to see the clock face. "It's 6:30. Time for the news."

"I already know the news, thanks. It's in my uterus. I don't seem to recall reaching any solution. Did we?"

"Oh yes. It was brilliant, absolutely perfect. It's a shame neither of us can remember it."

"Bitch! I'd slap your ass if I could find it."

"Be happy if you can just locate your own."

"I don't have the strength to even look, but it's always been there in the past --- like a faithful companion."

"You may want to re-think that faithful part."

With supreme effort, Georgia turned ninety degrees to face the ceiling. "Meg, would you stay with me?"

"Through the birth, sure."

"Do you want to raise this child with me?"

"I honestly don't know. If you've got a husband, it would be awkward, to say the least."

"Don't I know it. I need what you suggested, a father I can explain away...."

"Or an absentee husband you wouldn't mind being seen with occasionally."

"That may be possible. What about sex?"

"If he's your husband, you're going to have to have sex with him. Men consider it one of the percs of marriage --- that and laundry service pretty much sum it up for men."

"How would you feel about it?"

"Occasional sex with your husband I could take, as long as you don't tell me how great it is."

"If it's great, maybe you could jump him too."

"Let's not get into that right now. The problem would be how to explain my presence."

"We could get a place with an attached cottage or suite...."

"The term is mother-in-law suite. Let's not gild the lily."

"Well, some arrangement where you, my old friend, live with us. It would make sense since he's not around much."

"Great. From lover to nanny in five minutes."

"Look! It can work. We'll have to figure out the minutiae, but the concept is sound, Meg."

"Unless I come up with a better plan, I'm willing to try it. And I promise not to split before the baby comes, no matter how uncomfortable it gets."

"Thanks."

"I didn't promise I'd refrain from murder and mayhem."

"Naturally. Those are inalienable rights."

"So who's the lucky victim to be?"

"Shit! I knew we overlooked some detail."

/////

The three generations of identical Mayan women dancing with trays of empty *cerveza Bohemia* bottles on their heads proved to be unexpectedly charming. "Another event that must be seen to be appreciated," thought Rae. Like countless curious *gringos* before her, she inspected the bottles and trays afterward. No adhesives were found. The performers encouraged this partially because it proved their ability, but mainly because it placed the *turistas* in close proximity to the beautiful dark-eyed little girls of the troupe. Tips became inevitable under these circumstances.

Mama and grandma circulated among the less curious, each with a basket, a smile and a *muchas gracias.*

They finished their *Margaritas* on the moonlit terrace as the *mariachis* played *Quizás, Quizás, Quizás* softly. Rae had heard the song before, but now understood it to describe a courtship in which the *señorita* always responds to her suitor's entreaties with "Perhaps, perhaps, perhaps." When it was finished, she turned to Ivan and said "*Por cierto, por cierto, por cierto.*" (For sure, for sure, for sure.) Just in case there were any doubts.

As they strolled through the gardens, he explained that the term *mariachi* was a corruption of the French word *marriage.* It was used to describe the small musical groups who played for the guests at weddings of the court of Maximilian, which ingratiated itself upon its conquered hosts by speaking French whenever possible. This inevitably led to the Battle of Puebla, which freed México until the *Yanqui* invasion.

"What am I going to do when you run out of these wonderful stories?" she teased.

"*Imposible.* I will never run out."

Chapter Forty
Saturday, November 27, 1993

It was the day Major-General Gregorovich submitted to the weekly examination to measure his progress in recovering from the effects of prolonged weightlessness on MIR. The procedures had been provided by the Russian doctors and the results were sent to them. Being her specialty, Dr. Reed administered the tests personally and maintained her own set of notes. After all, no Astronaut had ever approached his time in orbit.

His weight was coming back rapidly, mostly as muscle so far as she could determine. He wore only shorts and athletic shoes. His body was tough. His face was hard, but not chiseled. As the weight returned his prominent cheekbones would fit his face better. If he let his hair grow, he'd be almost handsome. Of course, he was barely an inch taller than her, but that only seemed to matter for slow dancing and the jitterbug. A woman could suffer a broken windpipe jitterbugging with a short man.

"Do you dance?" she asked as though it were one of the questions on her chart.

"Just like Nureyev."

"What I meant was, do you take your girlfriend dancing?"

"Modern women --- even Russian women --- don't wait for Cosmonauts to come back. They don't want an idiot who sits on top of rockets, either."

"Do you plan to quit and settle down then?"

"No. This is my life. I can't trade it for a house and a family. By the time I'm too old to fly, probably no one will want me. Of course, this breaks my mother's heart. She wants grandchildren and I'm the only child."

"Maybe we can help each other...."

/////

It was brisk and clear. They were inside the *Kaffe Haus*, a whimsical structure shaped like a stubby lighthouse. It was at a high point in the Boboli Gardens. Ken and Laura sat next to a large window in silence. To the left was the Pitti Palace, which they had just toured. Below them was the *Ponte Vecchia*, the only Arno bridge the retreating Nazi commander could not bring himself to destroy. Slightly to the right was the *Piazza della Signoria*, the center of ancient Florence. Inevitably, their eyes came to rest on the *Duomo*, the magnificent dome of *Santa Maria del Fiore*.

They dipped their *biscotti* in their cappuccinos --- with plenty of brown sugar, per Will's advice --- and tried to memorize the panorama of Florence. "I'm ready to come back." she said.

"Uhm. Do you suppose we should leave first?"

"That would be the traditional approach. Besides, you should get back to your new job before events outrun you."

"That," he admitted, "is a definite possibility. I may have to take a language course just to speak to Rae."

"Which language? She answers the telephone in several --- including Russian."

"That could drive the folks at NASA around the bend. Then there's this situation with Captain Brown."

"Which one? His condition or his non-existence in the subconscious mind of Dr. Reed?"

"I was referring to his condition, but the other is a puzzle too. As I recall, she had the number of persons right, but she said he had no name. Why would she say that?"

"Maybe she sensed that he was no longer...himself. He was a body, but not the individual recognizable as Captain Brown."

"But how would she have known what he was like before?"

Laura sighed. "She wouldn't. There is no way it fits."

"Then she wasn't talking about Captain Brown."

"Who else could she have been talking about?"

"I'm only saying that we appear to have eliminated Captain Brown. What if Dr. Reed subconsciously deemed him to be dead?"

"Then who were the other two persons in the LEM with her?"

"Colonel Fortney and someone with no name," he offered.

"Who has no name?"

"How do people acquire names?"

"Except for some nicknames, they are given."

"When?" He was smiling. The fog was lifting.

"At birth," she said slowly. "Oh my. It fits."

"Only if she was pregnant...."

"I think we should call Rae."

"Do you think you can use an Italian pay phone?"

"We have an 800 number."

"From Italy?"

"*Per certo!*"

/////

"So when are you going to get your *hacienda?*" They were lying in bed together.

"For now, I'm just looking for a place to rent. Something with two bedrooms, garage, garden and staff."

"Staff?"

"Yes, when you rent a house in México, you get the cook, maid and gardener as part of the package provided by the landlord. Sometimes they live there. Of course, you have to pay them yourself if you expect them to work."

"One-stop shopping," she marveled. "A bachelor's dream, too."

"But when you examine the property, you also need to interview the staff."

"Sounds complicated."

"That's why I want you to come with me."

"Is this a sign that I may be visiting?"

"Often, I hope."

/////

Major Sanders took the call from Italy. Without preamble, Ken asked him "Is Dr. Reed pregnant?"

"Word certainly does travel fast. Please tell me how you found out."

"We — Laura and I — were drinking cappuccinos and discussing the answers she gave under hypnosis. They didn't seem to apply to Captain Brown; so we tried to figure out who she might have been talking about. She could not come up with a name. Everyone who has been born has been given a name. That left the unborn."

"Maybe we should serve cappuccino around here," he suggested. "In any event, you're right. Dr. Reed didn't know she was pregnant until she returned."

"Then she wouldn't have even been thinking of a name for the baby."

"But what about Captain Brown?"

"We think she may have written him off."

"She may have company on that call," he observed.

"It's none of my business, but I don't recall that Dr. Reed was married...."

"You're right. She isn't. But you're dead wrong about it not being any of your business."

"I'll be back in a few days."

Chapter Forty-One

"You told me it wasn't Piotr!"

"I lied, Major. You'll get over it. I wasn't going to tell you Piotr was the father until I told Piotr. Is that so hard to understand?"

"I guess not," he conceded. "Are you going to be married?"

"What does NASA want?" she asked.

"NASA wants you to be chaste, probably."

"Someone should have told me sooner. And yes, we plan to get married, a quiet civil ceremony. Just you, Dr. Shavinsky and the President."

"The President!"

"He gives good shoulder."

"You are out of your damn mind, you know that?"

"Left hand like a masseuse. You should try it sometime."

"You can invite him. He'll come if he wants."

"Fair enough."

"Why me?"

"Because I need someone to give me away, and that is supposed to be done by someone who cherishes me. I believe that's part of your job description now."

His manner changed. "I'm not very good at it, am I?"

"You do need reminding."

"O.K., Georgia, when is this going to happen?"

"ASAP. The blood tests are being done this afternoon."

"That's crazy! We can do that here."

"The State of Florida does not recognize this as a facility having the competence to perform such precise scientific evaluations is more or less what I was told by the fat lady in charge at the Brevard County license department. I could have gotten a fishing license without it, but that didn't seem sufficient."

"Invite Rae Kirkland too. She's due back sometime today. She's the only one around here who can get through to the President."

"Roger."

"Is it too soon to inquire about the honeymoon?"

"I get to go to Novosibirsk to meet his family."

"Something you've always wanted to do, no doubt."

"Well, we did go to the Moon together. How many couples can say that?"

"But he didn't go all the way."

"You'll never know, Major." She winked at him and left the room.

"Cherish. Cherish. Cherish." He was muttering.

/////

"You, sir," announced Major Sanders, "are in the clear. The sample the lab took from your scalp is benign."

"They don't intend to carve me up any further?"

"No plans for now."

"Why did you ask me if I remembered dying?"

"It was just a thought."

"Well, it's a Hell of a question to be asked. It sort of shook me."

Rae entered the conversation. "You asked him if he remembered dying?"

"I apologize. It was a thoughtless remark."

"No, it's O.K. I mean, it made me think about those last few days. I know I was supposed to be thinking about them before, during the de-briefing, but there was so much going on...."

"Have you thought of something else?" Rae asked.

"I don't like the way you two are looking at me; so let me make it clear. After reviewing all the facts, I'm positive that I didn't die. I was feeling good. I was doing push-ups and squats and leg lifts. I was prime when the space ship landed. Poor Demitrius was another matter. He was dying."

"O.K., we believe you or you wouldn't be here. Zombies are one minority even the government won't hire," she quipped to lighten his mood.

He smiled briefly to acknowledge her attempt, then continued "I was so happy to see that ship. It was huge! Where do you keep those things?"

"I'm afraid that's a secret, even from you, for now. In fact, it's existence is a national secret. In fact, you're a national secret."

"I'm betting it only operates in space. Never comes to Earth. Built at a space station."

"Bingo," replied Major Sanders. "Unofficially, bingo."

"I knew it."

"What puzzles us is that you don't remember the Astronaut coming to the Moon Base," Rae said.

"Maybe it had something to do with Demitrius dying. I was pretty upset. All I can remember is that I was kneeling by Demitrius and the inner hatch blew open. That meant the outer hatch wasn't sealed. I went for my helmet. After that, I'm a blank."

"You were sedated for the trip home; so you didn't miss much. If you think of anything, let us know."

"What does the Astronaut say?"

"Well, if we tell you that, we'll never hear your version of the story. NASA always likes to hear at least two versions, even if they agree."

"No wonder Georgia calls him Bull Sanders," thought Rae.

/////

"Thank you for coming right over, Major."

"What have you got, Captain?" Major Sanders looked around the Audio/Video Lab and realized he'd been left behind by the computer age. Not an oscilloscope in sight.

"As you know, we had faint audio on the Astronaut's videotape, probably attributable to the fact that she was wearing a separate communicating device. These tend to make people speak softly or mumble; so the microphone on the VCR couldn't pick much up when she wasn't holding it."

"So?"

"We tried to enhance it, but didn't really get anything new. Just made it easier to hear what we'd already heard. This morning we synchronized the audio conversation with the videotape. Let me show you."

They sat before a 15-inch computer monitor. An expensive

video tape player was connected to a Compaq 486 computer by a tangle of cables that defied his comprehension. Captain Evans started the black and white tape replay. "We used black and white for two reasons. First, aside from the Moon Suit, there isn't much color up there. Second, black and white can be enhanced and digitized much better than color. As a trade-off, it was a no-brainer."

"I'll give you a third reason for the future. Camouflage is usually in color. It doesn't fool a color-blind soldier. It shouldn't fool black and white tape."

"This may be a digression, sir, but do color-blind soldiers get sent out ahead of the other troops to look for camouflage?"

"Yes. The worst part is these poor bastards think they're going to flunk the physical if they make it clear they're color-blind. It's like volunteering for hazardous duty."

"Jeez," said the Captain as he started the tape.

Major Sanders had seen the tape before and had participated in the conversation; however, the combination added a dimension of reality which surprised him. His voice could be heard in the Moon Base. It brought home his participation in the event.

Captain Evans began explaining. "As we watch the tape, we are listening to three synchronized audio sources: Houston, the VCR microphone and the Astronaut's personal microphone. Now she sets the VCR down. Look for shadows."

"There are none."

"Right. That's because we have low-level, multi-source lighting. Like this lab, soft light comes from all sides, to prevent shadows. When you want to examine something, you turn a specific light on it. But there are faint shadows. We'll enhance them in a minute. Now listen carefully...."

Whumm.

Captain Evans paused the tape, and said "We thought that was the upper bunk coming down on the Astronaut. The VCR mike was not picking up her voice at that time." He hit the pause button and the tape continued.

"She's still talking!"

"Right!" He pushed pause again. "The noise you just heard was not recorded by her communications microphone, only by the VCR mike."

He re-started the tape. A loud bang was heard. Then there was no sound except the humming of the machinery.

"Why doesn't the sound occur at the same time on both devices? It has to be a synchronization problem," asserted Major Sanders, still in denial.

"Synchronization is perfect before and after this brief period. And remember, she's still talking after the first sound."

"Shit! Is there more?"

"I'm afraid there is. The two sounds have distinctively different wave patterns. I checked. It gets better. I'm silencing the VCR mike now, as well as the transmission from Houston."

There was no sound at all, not even background noise.

Since the Major was too confused to speak, the Captain continued. "The only explanation for complete silence is that her communications mike was disconnected --- or turned off."

"Could that have been caused by her being struck in the head by the bunk?"

"It's possible...."

"But improbable."

"Highly, although we can't rule it out. Did you hear two noises when you were communicating with the Astronaut, Major?"

"No. I'm certain."

"Good. Then it's likely that she didn't hear the first one either. Which means it was closer to the VCR than it was to her. What's over there, Major?"

He thought for a moment, then said "Storage lockers."

"Is the first noise similar to the sound a storage locker door makes?"

"When opened maybe."

"Later on she went over there and opened them all. The opening sound we picked up on her microphone matches that first noise exactly. So we know what made that sound, Major. Let's get back to the shadows." He re-wound the tape and typed some commands on the keyboard. This time the shadows became darker, easier to see.

"I still can't tell what's making these shadows," the Major said.

"Some we have identified as permanent, because they never move. I'll have the computer delete those now." After a few more keystrokes, about half the shadows disappeared. The remaining five shadows were indistinguishable shapes, but they moved in unison.

"Ladies and gentlemen, the June Taylor Dancing Shadow Blobs," thought Major Sanders.

Whumm.

"Holy shit!"

A second set of shadows appeared and quickly joined the first set. The two shadows stayed together for nearly two minutes. One was stationary most of the time. The other seemed to move all about it. They replayed it twice. Then Major Sanders said "Captain, as of now this lab is restricted. Only you are to be admitted. The exceptions are the President of the United States, Rae Kirkland, Ken Mason, me and whoever we bring with us. Under no circumstances are any Astronauts or Cosmonauts to know about this. Got that?"

"Yes, sir."

"Fix this so no one else can use it, but be prepared to go through it again on ten minutes notice. Can that be done?"

"Yes, sir."

"Damn fine work, Captain Evans."

"Thank you, sir. There is one more thing I've thought of. Whatever it was can fit into a storage locker."

/////

Rae came to his office as soon as he called. "What's up?"

"We need the President down here now."

"But the wedding...."

"This isn't about the wedding, although it might prevent it. Can you get him to come down the afternoon before so we can show him something?"

"It had better be good."

"Oh, it is! I've just sealed the Audio/Video Lab. Access only to the President, you, Ken and me --- and Captain Evans because he knows how to work the equipment and he's already seen it. They synchronized the communications tape with the VCR tape and came up with a second noise that occurred just before Georgia was hit on the head --- one her communications mike didn't pick up. It may have come from storage locker across the room."

"You mean something opened it?"

"Yes, indeed! It gets better. It's complicated, but right after that sound she is still talking and a new set of shadows appears on the screen."

"Major, you are giving me the willies!"

"No, I'm just sharing them. Want to see the tape?"

"*¡Espero que besar un pato!*"

"You hope to kiss a what?"

"A duck. Been away too long. That means affirmative, Major."

"Don't tell anyone, especially Georgia and Piotr."

Chapter Forty-Two
Wednesday, December 1, 1993

"If you summoned me to discuss the birds and bees, I should tell you I've flown and tasted honey."

"Cute. Isn't she something, Miss Kirkland?"

She ignored him. "The Major has a problem dealing with delicate matters, Georgia."

"No kidding? Is this recent?" she said with mock concern.

"Before you take off on your honeymoon, I want to take a look at the spot where the bunk banged your head. Just to make sure it's healed."

"Are you a doctor?"

"No. If I see something I don't understand, it's off to the medical team with you. On the other hand, if your bruise has gone, so can you."

"Do you have to cut my hair?"

"I hope not. Major Sanders only has a guillotine available."

"Feel free to gang up on me," he said.

"Go ahead and look then."

After less than one minute, Rae pronounced her healed and sent her off. Then she drew what she had seen and handed the picture to Major Sanders. "This what you're looking for?"

"Exactly."

Rae asked "Major, if you were going to knock someone out, would you use a bunk bed?"

"It wouldn't be my first choice of weapon. Too risky. No, I'd follow standard operating procedure."

"Which would be?"

"Apply the old concentric circle zapper-doo to the base of the skull. Why?"

"She'll figure it out someday, you know."

"Yes. She's a bright girl. I hope Piotr has a sense of humor."

"That would be helpful."

The President was obviously shaken by Captain Evans' presentation. He simply stared at the blank computer screen almost a full minute before turning to his companions. "Could you wait outside please, Captain."

"Yes sir."

The President smiled weakly and said "Miss Kirkland, have you made it your personal crusade to complicate my life?"

"Are you asking me to vote for the other candidate?"

"*Touché!* I don't need my life simplified quite that much, thank you. Major, what do we know about these aliens?"

"For security reasons, we're calling them visitors, sir. Intellectually, we know they can communicate intelligently and put words together in a manner that demonstrates reasoning. We believe that they have taken space travel to a level considerably above ours, from which we conclude that they are technologically advanced beyond us."

"Re-animation?"

"A good example, although it didn't work well on Captain Brown. We also know they are capable of stealth and are not particularly afraid of humans, one on one."

"If I may interrupt, Major," said Rae, "I think this may be a key point. Their messages indicate a reluctance to have direct contact, citing disastrous results. They fear contamination."

"Ours or theirs?" asked the President.

"My guess is both."

"Then why did they initiate contact?"

Rae responded. "There are two obvious reasons for contacting the Marines. The first is rescue, which I would like to believe was the motive. It is noble. The second is that they wanted the mission to succeed, which makes me uncomfortable."

"Why?"

"It is not a simple response to an emergency situation. It indicates they have an agenda. It demonstrates advance knowledge of the nature of the mission, which had not yet begun when the Marines reported their landing. It's a little too calculated."

"Which reason do you think is correct?"

"I have grappled with that question. Mr. Mason came up with the best answer. He said if we take care of calculated, we've got noble covered."

"Then that's the approach we shall take. I may have underestimated Mr. Mason."

"It's easy to do. He prefers it that way."

"Major, what do we know about their physical characteristics?"

"Starting with the basics, they need to open doors. They cast shadows which indicate a density similar to humans."

"They're opaque," the President said.

"From the analysis of the videotape, we know they can move quickly and stealthily. They left no footprints at all on the Moon. Our examination of the tape reveals more of a gliding motion than humans make, but that could be attributed to the footwear or the need for silence. It may not be the normal gait."

"Just one quick question, please. Was the word slither used at all?"

"No, Miss Kirkland." Major Sanders continued "Isolating one shadow on the computer and running it through an experimental program, it has been concluded that the one in the facility was slightly taller than the Astronaut. Again this could be attributable to footwear. The neck area is thick, like a linebacker's and the face is elongated."

"Like a dog's snout?"

"Like this." He showed them an enhanced printout. It was just a darkened outline.

"That's an iguana," suggested Rae. "Could that be a breathing apparatus?"

"They think so. They also hope so. We aren't too comfortable with the idea that they can breathe our atmosphere."

"Amen," said the President. "Now why did it attack the Astronaut?"

"Attack may be too strong a word, but it fits technically. One theory is that the visitor was trying to avoid detection. If it had been hiding in a storage locker, observing her through the slits, it could have concluded that she would soon be searching there. It may have transferred to the wardrobe, which she had already searched. To make such a move undetected would have been impossible; so the visitor had to put her out."

"If that's what was intended, it worked. Until now, the loss of contact was blamed on the bunk hitting her head," Rae added. "What if it wanted to examine her? After all, they hadn't seen a human woman before."

"She was out of contact for about two minutes. That's enough time for a cursory examination and to take some pictures. It would be normal to at least look her over."

"Wasn't she in a Moon Suit?"

"No sir. She found it too confining to conduct a search. She removed it off camera. She reported that she was wearing garbage bags on her feet, surgical gloves on her hands and a long tee shirt at the time."

"Now that's a vivid image," remarked the President. "So she was exposed. There is no indication of any testing?"

"Her skin was unmarked, except for the concentric circles, which we now believe induced the unconsciousness. The visitor could have taken hair, part of a toenail, a tongue scraping, navel lint or any number of other samples without detection. The Astronaut reported no symptoms of such activity. That's all we know."

"Visitors 3; Home Team zip," said Rae.

"Well, what are we doing about our precocious Astronaut?"

"I'm giving her away tomorrow," Major Sanders offered lamely.

"Won't work, Buck. She'll come back. Let's look at the choices. If we let her get married, we don't have an unwed Astronaut on our hands. We have a public relations field day because she's marrying a Cosmonaut. It's all warm and fuzzy. The press eats it up. The public eats it up. And most importantly, she continues to cooperate with us. The sky is blue. The grass is green."

"So long as the baby isn't," said Rae. Buck almost choked.

"While I share your sentiment, for this decision it's irrelevant," continued the President. "Now, what do we get if we attempt to stop --- or even postpone --- the wedding?" He opened his hands to encourage participation.

Rae said "Well, for starters, she hates us, the Russians hate us, the press hates us and the public hates us. Did I leave anyone out?"

"Only the Iraqis, and they already hate us," the President observed.

"And that's if we're successful in stopping it. We might not be able to," added Major Sanders.

"The only thing worse than being hated for your actions is when they fail to achieve their goal as well."

"That's very profound, sir. I may just vote for you this time," said Rae.

"Thank you. As they used to say in Chicago, don't let bad weather or death prevent you from voting."

"She and Piotr do make a handsome couple. The magazines will love this."

The President stared at them a moment. "You don't know, do you?"

"Don't know what?" Rae asked.

"She's bi-sexual. She's been living with a lesbian for two years. That's another reason I want her to get married!"

Major Sanders recovered first. "Sir, if you'd like, I'll run her down the aisle!"

"Now that's the spirit!"

"Shit storm brewing," was all Rae could say.

"Now I expect you to do all you can to foster the image of two love struck space pioneers, embarking on a new and wonderful journey together."

"He's going to be in Russia most of the time!" Rae protested.

"If it were easy, you wouldn't be earning the big bucks. You are aware that your salary is right up there with mine."

Buck looked at her with new appreciation.

The President shook hands with them and went down the hall whistling "I'm Gettin' Married in the Morning."

"She's right!" marveled the Major. "He does give good shoulder!"

"Morty Simonson," she said cryptically.

"Who's that?"

"Pimply neighbor. Could have married him and been a doctor's wife in Philadelphia now. Avoided this whole mess." She walked out the door toward her office, still mumbling. "Three point two kids, lousy sex life, Lexus...mother-in-law from Hell." She brightened at this last recollection.

/////

"This is probably the most hypocritical thing I've ever done, you know."

"And I get to be part of it. How can I thank you, Meg?"

"You could bring me his dick in a jar of formaldehyde."

"Oh what a witty maid of honor you are, my dear. Shall we celebrate my impending nuptials with several hours of raucous sex --- or is it bad luck?"

"Only several hours?"

"I have to compose myself to look virginal in the morning."

"Then you should have started last week, you tart!"

Chapter Forty-Three
Thursday, December 2, 1993

The ceremony itself was held in the Rocket Garden at the Visitors Center in chamber of commerce weather. A platform had been erected in front of the Saturn/Apollo configuration on display there. Dr. Shavinsky, impressive in his general's uniform, was best man. Major Sanders walked Georgia down the aisle and gave her a sincere hug. Then he shook hands with Piotr and Dr. Shavinsky before sitting down. A Brevard County Circuit Court Judge performed the brief civil ceremony. Outranked, he yielded to the President as soon as he was finished. The President raised his arms as if in blessing and declared "Cosmonaut, you may kiss the Astronaut."

It was a sound bite heard 'round the world. As instructed, they held the kiss long enough to allow the exposure of plenty of film and videotape. The ceremony was seen live everywhere there was television.

Reactions were varied, but overwhelmingly positive. An old dear in London tearfully declared that Dr. Reed "looked just like Princess Diana." In New York people blew horns --- even more than usual. All over Russia, where it was already night, copious amounts of vodka were consumed in celebration. (After all, a Cosmonaut was going to dock with an Astronaut. What better way to end the space race, comrade?)

/////

The reception was held in Room 2001, next to the Rocket Garden, to keep the press from the good food. (The Fifth Estate had to content itself with an outdoor buffet.) Meg stood alone with two empty champagne glasses on the table beside her.

"Hello, I'm Rae Kirkland. You must be Meg."

"I've heard a lot about you, Miss Kirkland."

"Well, only the scary parts are true."

"That's refreshingly candid. I can see why Tiff likes you."

"Yes, old Tiffany is not much taken with bullshit, is she?"

"No. Except her own, of course."

"Well, I'm afraid we're all going to have to get used to it, aren't you."

"I confess to having that nightmare."

"Oh, it's reality. Don't doubt it for a minute. It is my unhappy lot to have the job of shoveling it for her."

"How unfortunate for you."

"At least I'm getting paid cash. Your payment is less tangible."

"My payment?"

"You see that man over there?" She indicated a man in a gray suit near the door. He was one of the Secret Service Agents sent to guard the President. "At my signal, he would walk you out the nearest exit and you would never be seen again. But I don't intend to do that as long as you behave."

"Are you trying to scare me?"

"I am warning you, Meg. So when it happens, you'll at least know why. I may not be present at the time."

"Why is it going to happen?"

"Because you are a dyke with an attitude. Sooner or later, you're going to do something stupid. Are you terminally stupid, Meg?"

"I hope not," she admitted.

"I don't care what you do, as long as the world thinks you are just Tiffany's good friend. If you make any remarks or take any action which even threatens to reveal the truth, it's out the nearest exit with you. Same result if you tell Tiffany or Piotr about this. Take a good look at that man. There are thousands who look just like him, waiting to take you out with no hesitation when the order is given." She pulled Meg closer and whispered in her ear. "Actually, the order was given yesterday, but I got the execution itself put on hold. All other phases are complete. That is how close you are to extinction. Do you understand?"

"Yes."

"Don't even think about running away. If you and Tiffany break up, contact me immediately. We may be able to work out a solution. As it stands, the order is to be executed if you leave."

"That's not fair!"

"We're not playing gin rummy here. This is life. This is how it is. Life is not fair. But it's better than death. So smile at the people and be a good girl. With a little patience, you'll survive this." She waved to the agent. "On the other hand, it wouldn't hurt to make your peace with God."

"What are you doing?"

"Most people only stare death in the face once. I'm giving you a preview, Meg." The agent joined them. He was nearly seven feet tall. "I'd like you to meet Tiffany's best friend Meg." The agent's name was not offered.

"Pleased to meet you, Meg." He didn't look pleased. He held out a tiny wafer that appeared to be silicon. "Swallow this. Now!"

"What is it?"

"A tracking device. Swallow it!"

"I don't think I want to...."

"You can put it in your mouth or I can."

She took the wafer and swallowed it with some difficulty. Rae and the agent immediately walked away from her together.

"Great job! What was that you made her swallow?" Rae asked.

"Sen-Sen. Want one?"

"I may never touch one again."

/////

Rae joined Ken, Laura and Dr. Shavinsky at the buffet table dedicated to seafood. Predictably, they stood before the platters of stone crabs. "Who wants to play good cop in about one minute?" Rae asked.

The question was directed at Ken, but Dr. Shavinsky volunteered. "I will charm the young lady," he predicted, unaware of her proclivities. "As proof, I will deliver her to our table. Mr. Mason, would you be so kind as to carry my plate to the table?" Ken cast a wary eye at the overloaded dish and nodded his assent.

"How do you do, young lady. I am the man who shot your friend."

"You what?"

"Georgia, your friend. I shot her to the Moon. On a rocket. I am Dr. Shavinsky, but you may call me Dmitri."

"Oh," she said with obvious relief. She had never thought of a wedding reception as being a heart-stopping event before.

He indicated the buffet and said grandly "And now I will give you crabs."

"How can I resist?"

When they arrived at the table, he made the introductions. She winced slightly when introduced to Rae. Meg was seated between Laura and Dmitri. After breaking open a claw for her, Dr. Shavinsky became occupied with his own crustaceans.

"This must be a difficult day for you, Meg," said Laura. "But as I hear it, you're going to stay with Tiffany and help her. With all her duties at NASA, she'll need it. She doesn't know it yet, of course. My late husband worked on the Apollo Program, and he needed all the help he could get. And he never had a baby."

"I have found today to be a bit unsettling. I thought I was ready for it, but I guess I wasn't."

"We're counting on you to help our little hero," boomed the recognizable voice from behind her. She felt strong hands on her shoulders. She wondered what his view must be and silently cursed Tiffany for making her wear a low-cut dress. She turned to face him.

"How do you do, Mr. President."

"It's an honor to meet you, Ms. Chandler. I'm sure Miss Kirkland has told you how much we appreciate your assistance."

"Oh yes. She made that very clear, sir."

The President then turned his attentions to the others at the table. Laura introduced her daughter by saying, "This my daughter Courtney, who brought Mr. Mason home one night. I've decided to keep him."

"You're a lucky man, Ken. And, Courtney, I don't know how to thank you for being the catalyst in this matter. But I am pleased to meet you."

"I'd like to ride the shuttle," she replied, surprising everyone.

"We'll see if that can be arranged then."

Detective-Sergeant Lopez, who was providing extra security, watched in wonder as his only possible suspects in the Koestler homicide spoke with the President on a first-name basis. He vowed to bury the file deep.

Meg thought "I'm truly in deep shit if the President authorized this."

/////

A subdued Meg Chandler drove the happy couple to the Orlando airport to begin the series of flights which would take them to Novosibirsk in about the same time it takes to achieve lunar orbit.

/////

Dr. Shavinsky was persuaded to stay in town for the wedding of Ken and Laura. Afterward, he was going to check out his "dachita" in México. Rae said she would join Ivan and Dmitri in Mérida for Christmas. Ken and Laura were invited.

The four of them stood in the parking area and watched the Moon rise over the Kennedy Space Center. A soft breeze blew from the ocean. Ken said, "It's hard to believe it was less than eight months ago that this all began."

"It began twenty years ago," said Laura. "We just finished it." Ken put his arm around her. She tilted her head onto his shoulder.

"It has been an incredible adventure, all right," Rae added. "Just when you think your life is never going to change, it does — at warp speed."

"Yes. Key Lime pie and *tres leches* both in the same year. It is almost too much." Dr. Shavinsky turned to face them. "Does it trouble anyone else that we began by revealing a large secret, but now we conspire to hide that same secret?"

"Not to mention the new secret," answered Ken. "Yes, it troubles me, Dmitri."

"The truth we uncovered brought the Astronauts home. I doubt that Colonel Fortney would be so critical," suggested Laura. "Then you will know the truth, and the truth will set you free. *John 8:32*."

"You are quite right. And Dr. MacPherson's project has finally been completed. Men have lived on the Moon continuously for twenty years."

"I still wonder why the visitors were so determined that the rescue mission be completed successfully," Rae said.

"We will learn that some day. Have patience. Enjoy what we have accomplished. Be grateful that we no longer have to meet sneakretly," recommended Dr. Shavinsky.

"I'm going to let that one pass, Dmitri. You may have invented a new word."

"*Do svedanya,*" he said with a wink.

"*Dos Equis,* comrade," Rae returned the wink.

EPILOGUE

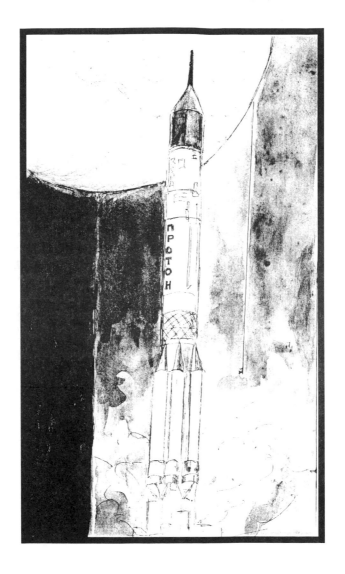

Labor Day, Monday, September 4, 1995

Cosmonaut Gregorovich and Astronaut Reed were back in space together, aboard the shuttle. They had become fast friends since their marriage. To say that he had accepted Meg's role would be an understatement. Piotr was a pragmatist. He could pursue his career without guilt. He knew his wife wouldn't be lonely. Nor would she be chasing other men. Life was good for Cosmonaut Gregorovich. This Christmas, his mother and father were coming to visit. They wanted to see their grandson Sergei, who had been named in honor of Dr. Sergei Korolev --- the father of the Russian space program --- as part of the marriage contract.

Being Labor Day, the media was gathered at the Kennedy Space Center to hear the Astronauts to say a few words of greeting to their families down on Earth. The proceedings were broadcast live on CNN. Rae and Ivan watched from their home in Mérida.

Ken Mason, the current Director of the NASA Liaison Office, was there with his wife Laura. It had nothing to do with his job. Astronaut Courtney MacPherson spoke to them from orbit, saying "I feel like I was born to do this." All her mother could say was "You were. Your father would be so proud of you." With tears in her eyes, she relinquished the microphone to Major Sanders. Ken gave her a hug.

Buck Sanders smiled at the camera and said "Meg Chandler is here with us in Mission Control with little Sergei. She has some news for our man-and-wife team up there. Can you hear us, Piotr and Tiffany?"

"We read you loud and clear, Major. Put her on."

"We miss you two. We'll have a celebration when you return. Sergei said his first words today."

"And what profound statement did our son utter as his first words?" Georgia asked with enthusiasm.

"He must have gotten it from the television. I wasn't sure I heard him right the first time; so I had him repeat it for me. I'll let him tell you himself."

"Drum roll, please!" Major Sanders quipped. Then he held the microphone in front of the child's mouth. Little Sergei had been watching. He knew what to do with it. After a moment of hesitation, he clearly announced to the world and beyond...

"THIS IS MONDAY."

Notes

The only character in this story who is real is Snooks, the raccoon. The President of the United States as portrayed herein is a generic figure, not intended to be the actual person holding the office at the time of the story.

The spellings of the Mayan, Arabic and Russian words are phonetic since they do not exist in our alphabet.

The quotes from the Scriptures tend to be from the New International Version of the Bible published by Zondervan Bible Publishers. Whenever this translation seemed too modern for the passage, the author hath yielded to the temptation to use more traditional language.

Most of the opinions expressed in this book are those of the characters who expressed them, not of the author.

This book began as a movie concept. The novel was written to obtain copyright protection not available for movie concepts. The author intends to write a sequel. He can't wait to see the movie.